STEVENSON · ELLIS · WATTERS · ALLEN · LAIHO

# LUMBERJANES™

## FRIENDSHIP TO THE MAX

BOOM!
BOX™

# BOOM! BOX™

**LUMBERJANES Volume Two, October 2016.** Published by BOOM! Box, a division of Boom Entertainment, Inc. Lumberjanes is ™ & © 2016 Shannon Watters, Grace Ellis, Noelle Stevenson & Brooke Allen. Originally published in single magazine form as LUMBERJANES No. 5-8. ™ & © 2014 Shannon Watters, Grace Ellis, Noelle Stevenson & Brooke Allen. All rights reserved. BOOM! Box™ and the BOOM! Box logo are trademarks of Boom Entertainment, Inc., registered in various countries and categories. All characters, events, and institutions depicted herein are fictional. Any similarity between any of the names, characters, persons, events, and/or institutions in this publication to actual names, characters, and persons, whether living or dead, events, and/or institutions is unintended and purely coincidental. BOOM! Box does not read or accept unsolicited submissions of ideas, stories, or artwork.

A catalog record of this book is available from OCLC and from the BOOM! Studios website, www.boom-studios.com, on the Librarians Page.

BOOM! Studios, 5670 Wilshire Boulevard, Suite 450, Los Angeles, CA 90036-5679. Printed in China. Third Printing.

ISBN: 978-1-60886-737-0, eISBN: 978-1-61398-408-6

## THIS LUMBERJANES FIELD MANUAL BELONGS TO:

NAME:_____

TROOP:_____

DATE INVESTED:_____

## FIELD MANUAL TABLE OF CONTENTS

# LUMBERJANES FIELD MANUAL

*For the Intermediate Program*

*Tenth Edition • February 1984*

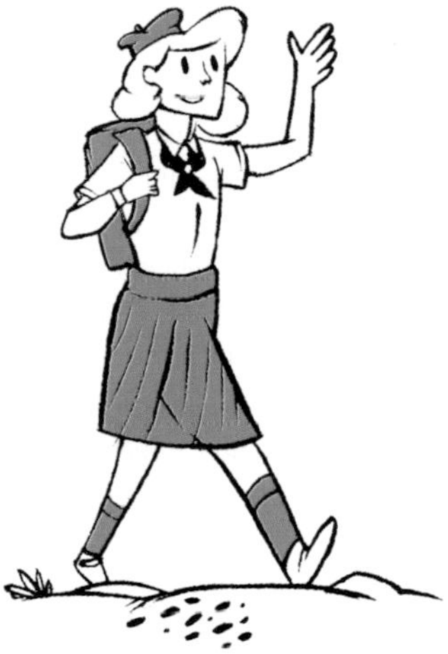

*Prepared for the*

**Miss Qiunzella Thiskwin Penniquiqul Thistle Crumpet's**

**CAMP FOR** [redacted] HARDCORE LADY-TYPES

*"Friendship to the Max!"*

## A MESSAGE FROM THE LUMBERJANES HIGH COUNCIL

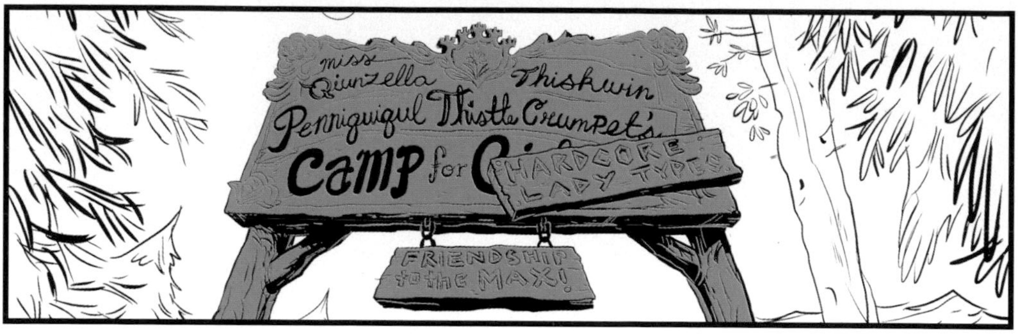
Miss Quinzella Thiskwin
Penniquiqul Thistle Crumpet's
Camp for
HARDCORE LADY TYPES
FRIENDSHIP to the MAX!

Time is a constant teacher as we continue our journey through the wilderness. When we were young women walking through the woods, learning with every step we took and every mistake we made, it was our passion that drove us further hungry for the next problem to solve, thirsty for the secrets of the world that we would learn to hold in our hearts. There is so much the world has to offer and so much more the world does not yet know it has for us, just like us at the beginning of our journey, the world is new and it learns with us.

It was at Lumberjanes camp that we learned to grow with the world instead of around it and it is our privilege and honor to welcome the new class of young adventurers to this camp. We hope that you enter this next stage of your development as a refined young lady with open eyes as we not only prepare you for a better future but as you prepare yourself. It was at Lumberjanes camp that we learned our love for carvings, the joys of building with your own two hands and the peace that comes from molding something into life. It is with those fond memories that we still put a hand over our hearts and recite the pledge of a Lumberjane scout for we swear to give you the tools to do your best every day.

Never think less yourself, believe in your natural talents and do not be ashamed if you have your doubts. Instead, if you can't believe in yourself then believe in your friends. Your friends will be with you as you explore the unknown even after leaving this camp. Being a Lumberjane is more than just something you did one summer, it is a choice that will follow you for the rest of your lives. Go out and enjoy the mysteries that life has to offer and do not leave one stone unturned. As always, this handbook is meant to guide you on your path as a Lumberjane, as a friend, and as a human being. We hope it will show you different sides of life that will help guide you on your future journeys.

## THE LUMBERJANES PLEDGE

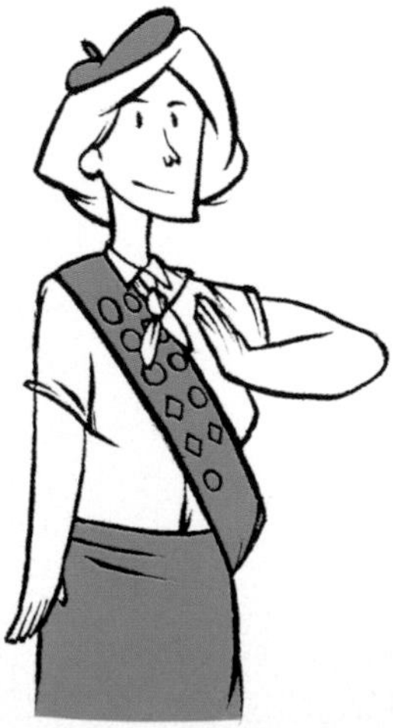

*I solemnly swear to do my best*
*Every day, and in all that I do,*
*To be brave and strong,*
*To be truthful and compassionate,*
*To be interesting and interested,*
*To pay attention and question*
*The world around me,*
*To think of others first,*
*To always help and protect my friends,*
[redacted]
*And to make the world a better place*
*For Lumberjane scouts*
*And for everyone else.*

THEN THERE'S A LINE ABOUT GOD, OR WHATEVER

## FRIENDSHIP TO THE MAX

**Written by**
# Noelle Stevenson
# & Grace Ellis

**Illustrated by**
# Brooke Allen

**Colors by**
# Maarta Laiho

**Letters by**
# Aubrey Aiese

**Cover by**
# Noelle Stevenson

Character Designs......**Noelle Stevenson & Brooke Allen**
Badge Designs...............................................**Kate Leth**
Designer..........................................**Scott Newman**
Associate Editor...................................**Whitney Leopard**
Editor..........................................**Dafna Pleban**

*Special thanks to **Kelsey Pate** for giving the Lumberjanes their name.*

**Created by Shannon Watters, Grace Ellis & Noelle Stevenson**

LUMBERJANES FIELD MANUAL

# CHAPTER FIVE

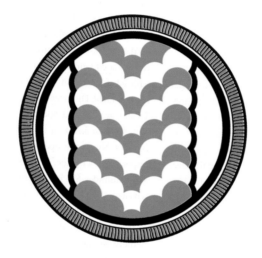

*Lumberjanes "Arts and Crafts" Program Field*

## FRIENDSHIP TO THE CRAFT

*"I get by with a little help from my yarn."*

Being a scout requires more than what most might think. While Lumberjanes do the typical nature hikes and wood cutting competitions that are essential to every scout's growth, she will also do more. Every Lumberjane should leave camp with the basic understanding of problem solving, as she will encounter many problems through life. One of the many goals of the Lumberjanes is to make sure every young lady leaves with the tools to succeed. As a Lumberjane, it is vital to have a deep focus on friendship in every one of the courses offered. It should come as no surprise that both friendship and problem solving are combined in the *Friendship to the Craft* badge.

Crafting is a fine art that contains a multitude of mediums ranging from fibers to sculpting. It is the tendency for a Lumberjane to want to work with her hands and her mind that makes this badge one of the camp favorites. Each scout will be divided into groups

and then given a task to complete within a limited amount of time. Some of these tasks will be easy to complete individually and will be an opportunity for the more advanced scouts to help out the less experienced. Other tasks will be so advanced that they will most likely never be completed. As every scout eventually learns, some things are bigger than us.

To obtain the *Friendship to the Craft* badge a Lumberjane must have already mastered the art of glue, and shown great promise in her creative thinking skills. She must enjoy color theory as well as be able to explain how the theory of colors works in nature and in the modern world. She must have shown that not only is she a natural leader, but is able to take a step back and allow others to guide on their journey as well. The importance of this badge is the lesson of teamwork and to learn how to make a friendship bracelet.

huff huff huff huff
JO! WHERE ARE YOU?
I'm over here! Where are you?
Jo, HURRY!
I'm coming! Hold on!!
Ripley! What's going on?
There you are.
We've been waiting for you.
AHHHHHHH!

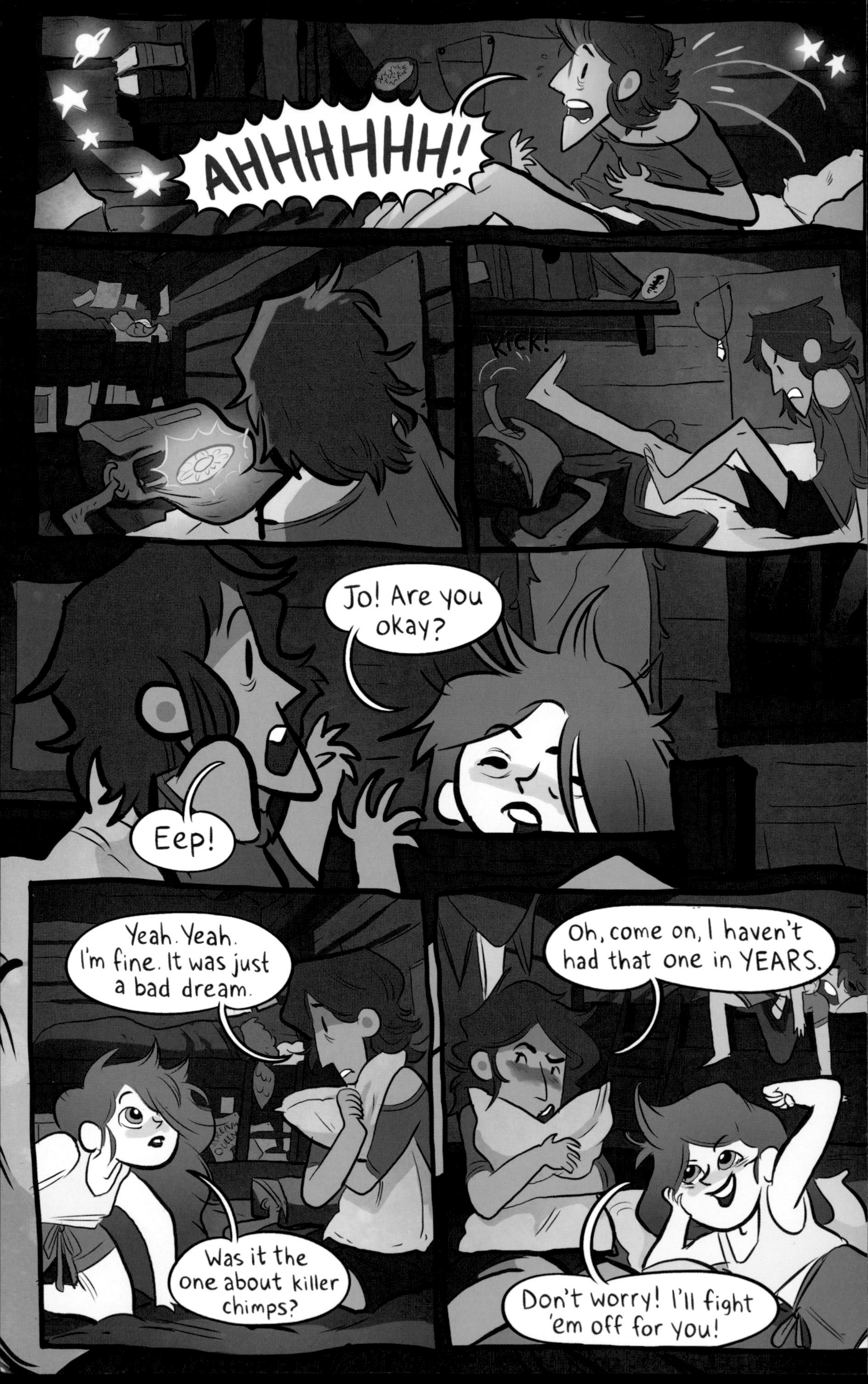
AHHHHHH!
KICK!
Jo! Are you okay?
Eep!
Yeah. Yeah. I'm fine. It was just a bad dream.
Was it the one about killer chimps?
Oh, come on, I haven't had that one in YEARS.
Don't worry! I'll fight 'em off for you!

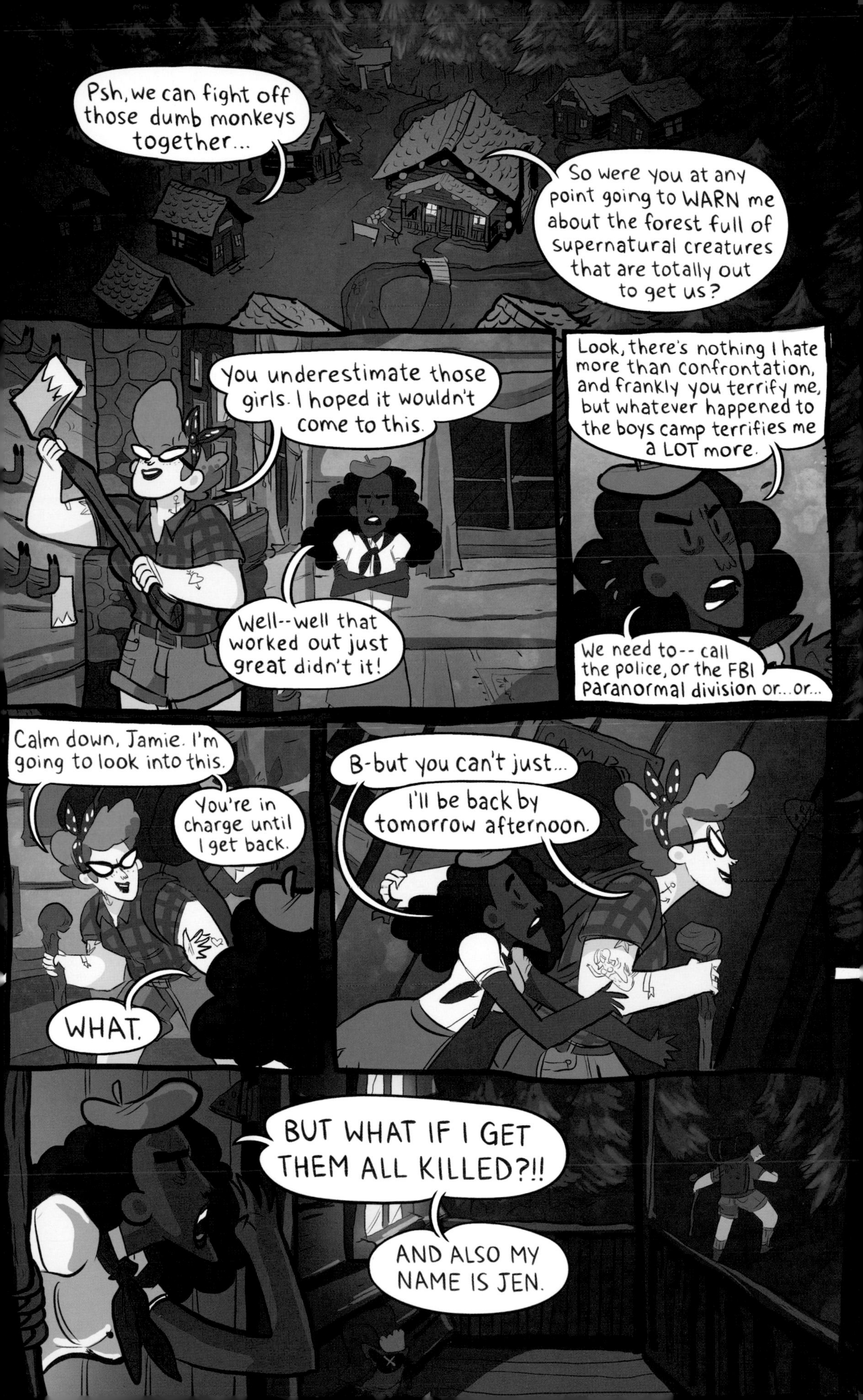
Psh, we can fight off those dumb monkeys together...
So were you at any point going to WARN me about the forest full of supernatural creatures that are totally out to get us?
You underestimate those girls. I hoped it wouldn't come to this.
Well--well that worked out just great didn't it!
Look, there's nothing I hate more than confrontation, and frankly you terrify me, but whatever happened to the boys camp terrifies me a LOT more.
We need to-- call the police, or the FBI paranormal division or...or...
Calm down, Jamie. I'm going to look into this.
You're in charge until I get back.
WHAT.
B-but you can't just...
I'll be back by tomorrow afternoon.
BUT WHAT IF I GET THEM ALL KILLED?!!
AND ALSO MY NAME IS JEN.

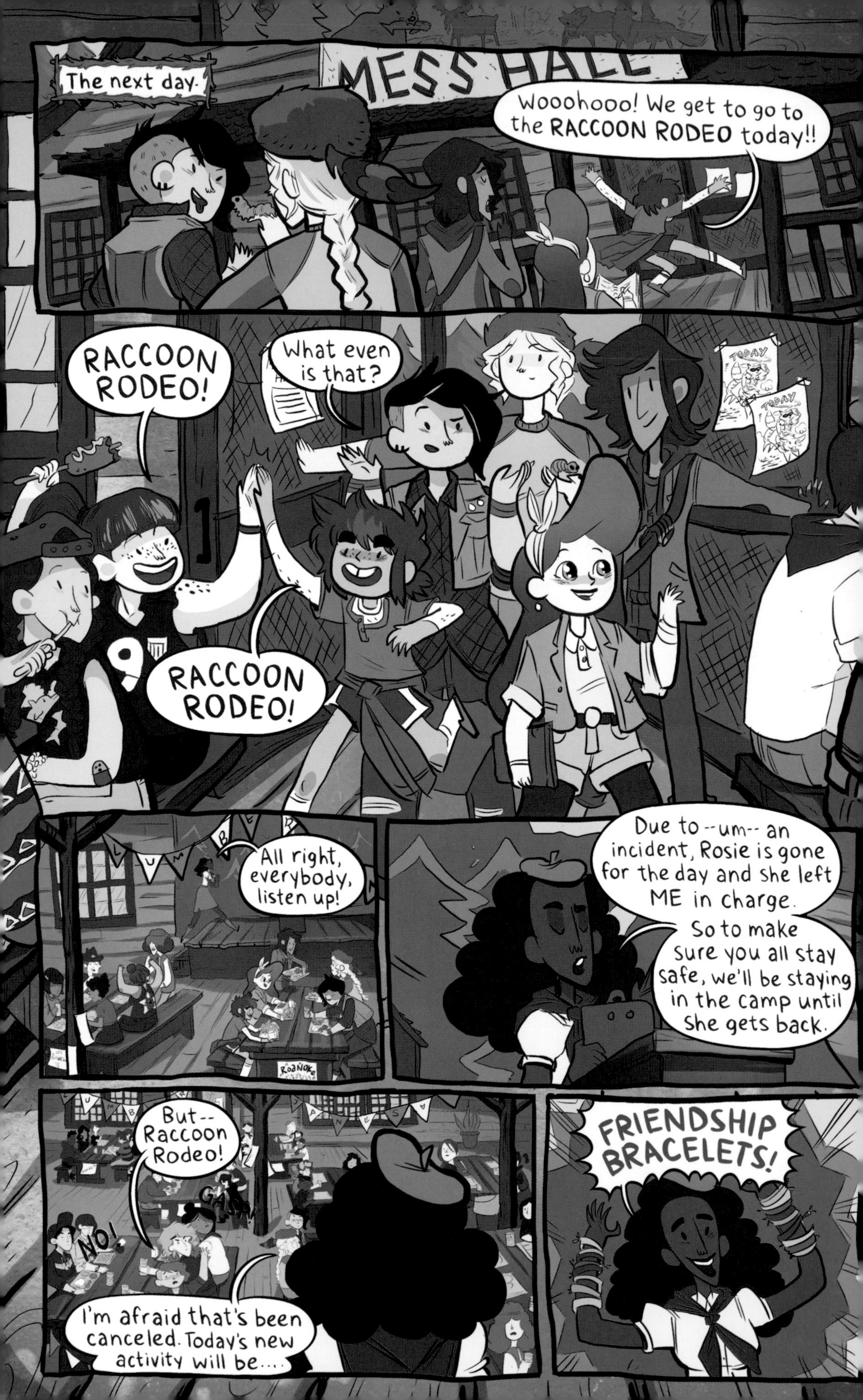
MESS HALL
The next day.
Wooohooo! We get to go to the RACCOON RODEO today!!
RACCOON RODEO!
What even is that?
RACCOON RODEO!
TODAY
TODAY
All right, everybody, listen up!
Due to --um-- an incident, Rosie is gone for the day and she left ME in charge.
So to make sure you all stay safe, we'll be staying in the camp until she gets back.
But-- Raccoon Rodeo!
NO!
GASP
I'm afraid that's been canceled. Today's new activity will be...
FRIENDSHIP BRACELETS!

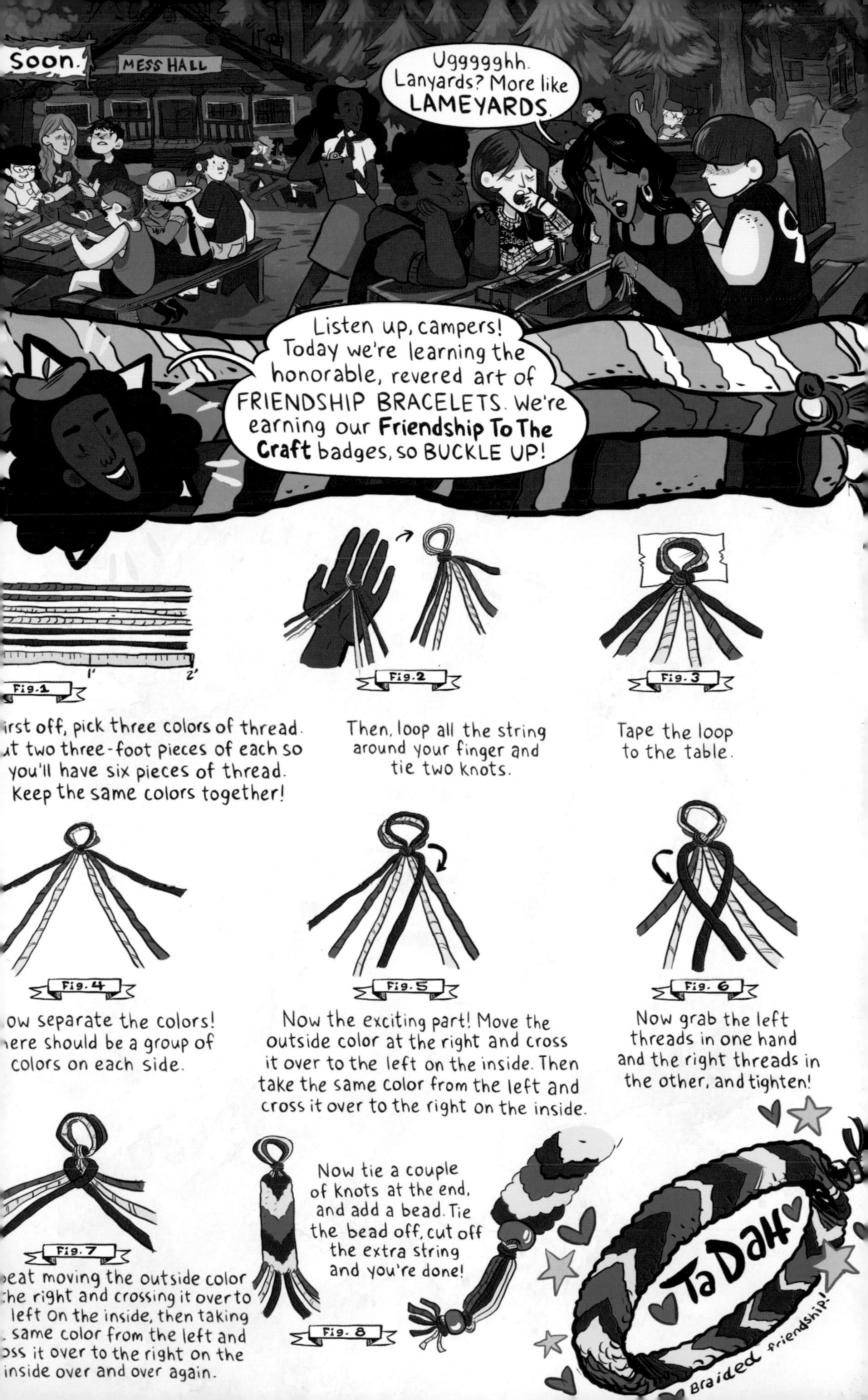
Soon.
MESS HALL
Uggggghh. Lanyards? More like LAMEYARDS.
The Saddest
Listen up, campers! Today we're learning the honorable, revered art of FRIENDSHIP BRACELETS. We're earning our **Friendship To The Craft** badges, so BUCKLE UP!
1'
2'
Fig.1
irst off, pick three colors of thread. ut two three-foot pieces of each so you'll have six pieces of thread. Keep the same colors together!
Fig.2
Then, loop all the string around your finger and tie two knots.
Fig.3
Tape the loop to the table.
Fig.4
ow separate the colors! here should be a group of colors on each side.
Fig.5
Now the exciting part! Move the outside color at the right and cross it over to the left on the inside. Then take the same color from the left and cross it over to the right on the inside.
Fig.6
Now grab the left threads in one hand and the right threads in the other, and tighten!
Fig.7
eat moving the outside color he right and crossing it over to left on the inside, then taking . same color from the left and oss it over to the right on the inside over and over again.
Fig.8
Now tie a couple of knots at the end, and add a bead. Tie the bead off, cut off the extra string and you're done!
Ta DaH
Braided friendship!

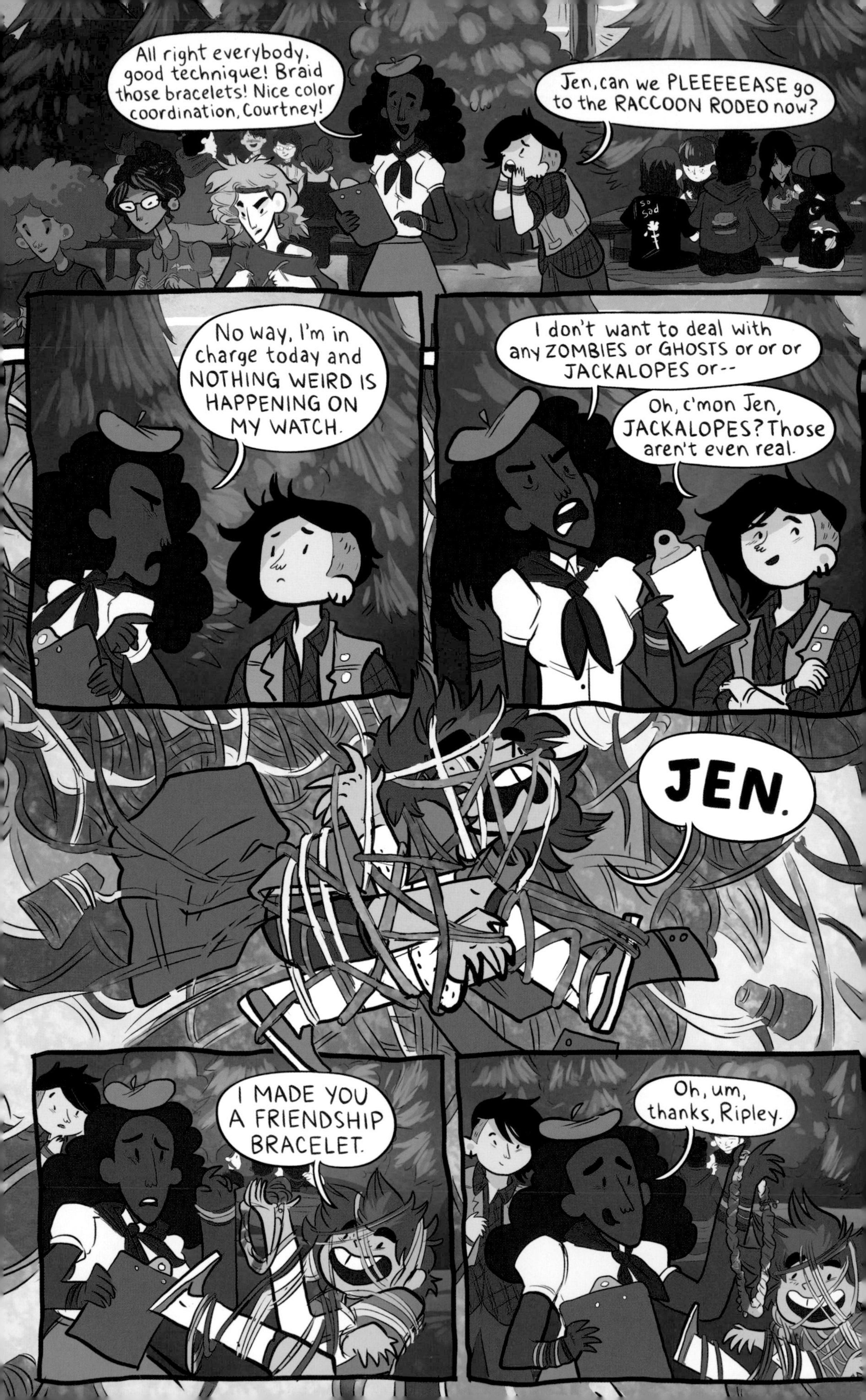
All right everybody, good technique! Braid those bracelets! Nice color coordination, Courtney!
Jen, can we PLEEEEEASE go to the RACCOON RODEO now?
No way, I'm in charge today and NOTHING WEIRD IS HAPPENING ON MY WATCH.
I don't want to deal with any ZOMBIES or GHOSTS or or or JACKALOPES or--
Oh, c'mon Jen, JACKALOPES? Those aren't even real.
JEN.
I MADE YOU A FRIENDSHIP BRACELET.
Oh, um, thanks, Ripley.

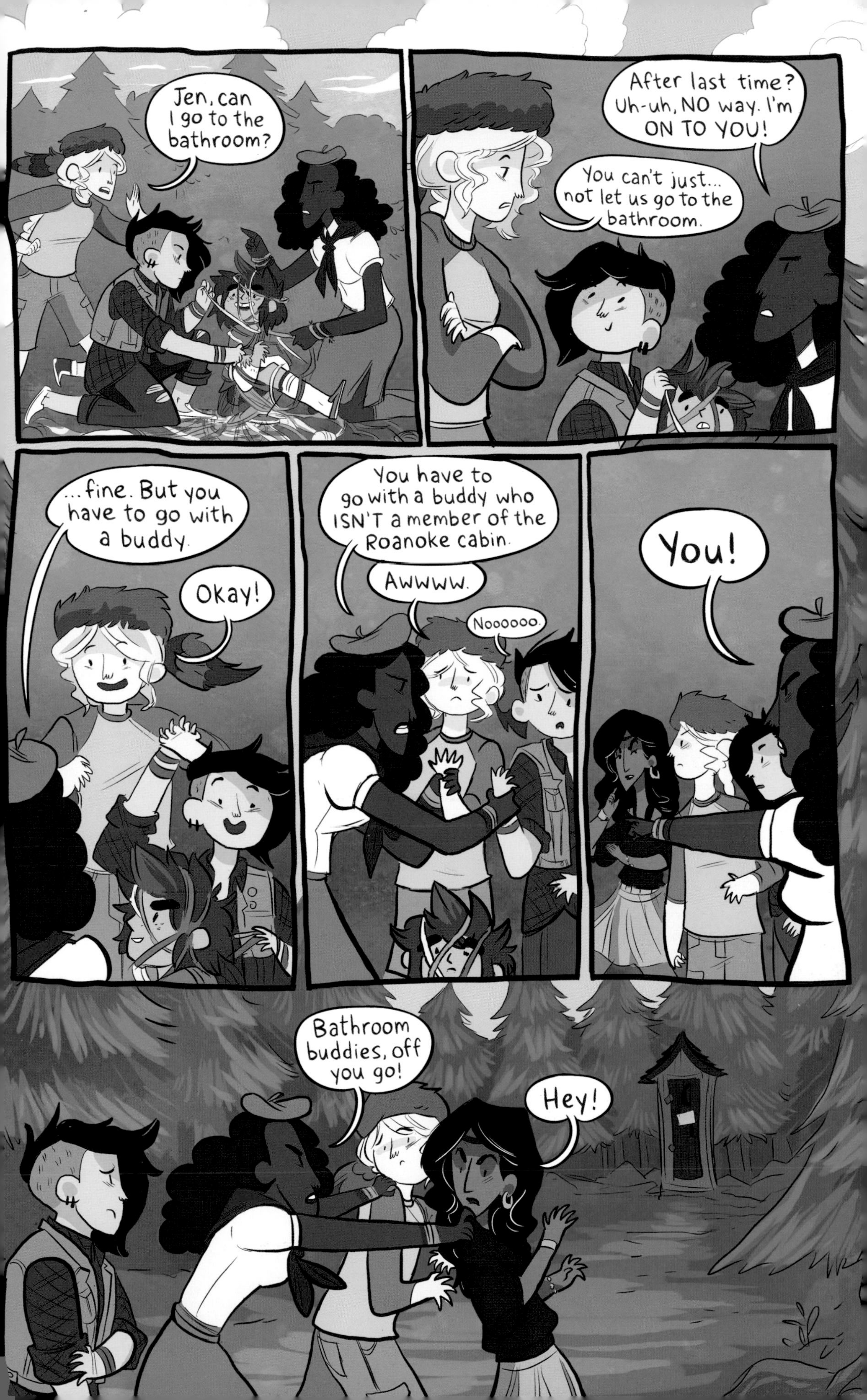
Jen, can I go to the bathroom?
After last time? Uh-uh, NO way. I'm ON TO YOU!
You can't just... not let us go to the bathroom.
...fine. But you have to go with a buddy.
Okay!
You have to go with a buddy who ISN'T a member of the Roanoke cabin.
Awwww.
Noooooo.
You!
Bathroom buddies, off you go!
Hey!

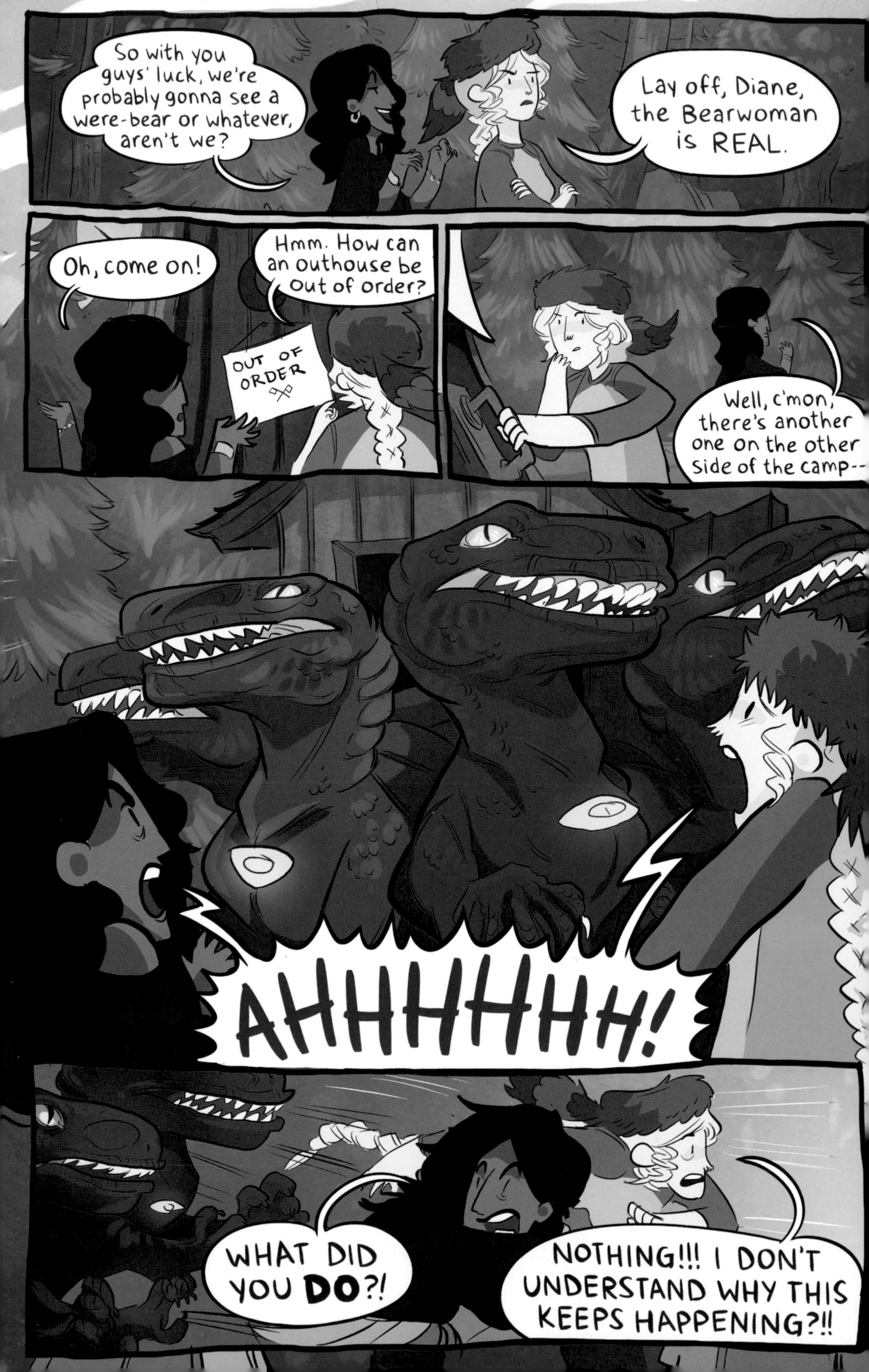
So with you guys' luck, we're probably gonna see a were-bear or whatever, aren't we?
Lay off, Diane, the Bearwoman is REAL.
Oh, come on!
Hmm. How can an outhouse be out of order?
OUT OF ORDER
Well, c'mon, there's another one on the other side of the camp--
AHHHHHH!
WHAT DID YOU **DO**?!
NOTHING!!! I DON'T UNDERSTAND WHY THIS KEEPS HAPPENING?!!

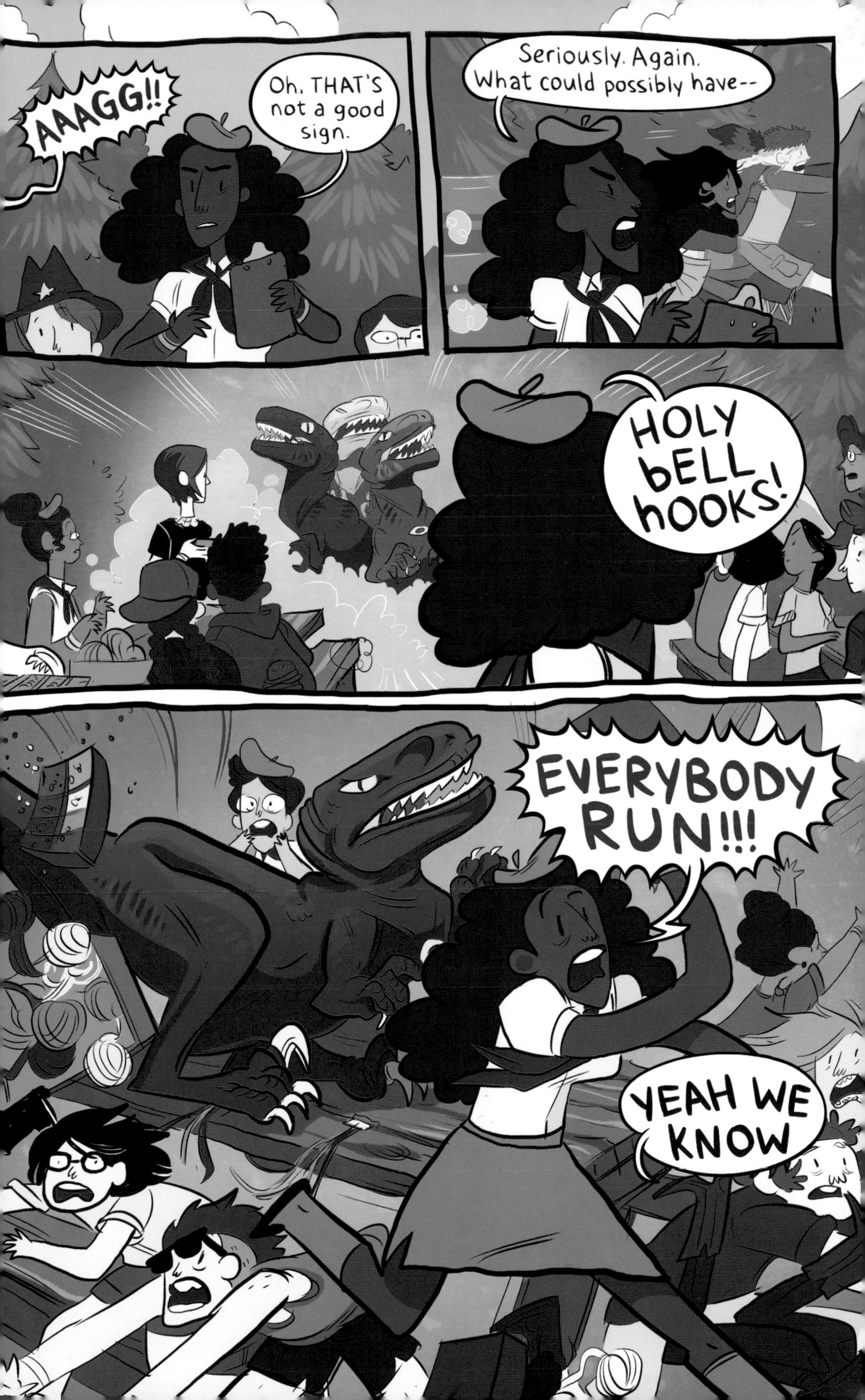
AAAGG!!
Oh, THAT'S not a good sign.
Seriously. Again. What could possibly have--
HOLY bELL hOOKS!
EVERYBODY RUN!!!
YEAH WE KNOW

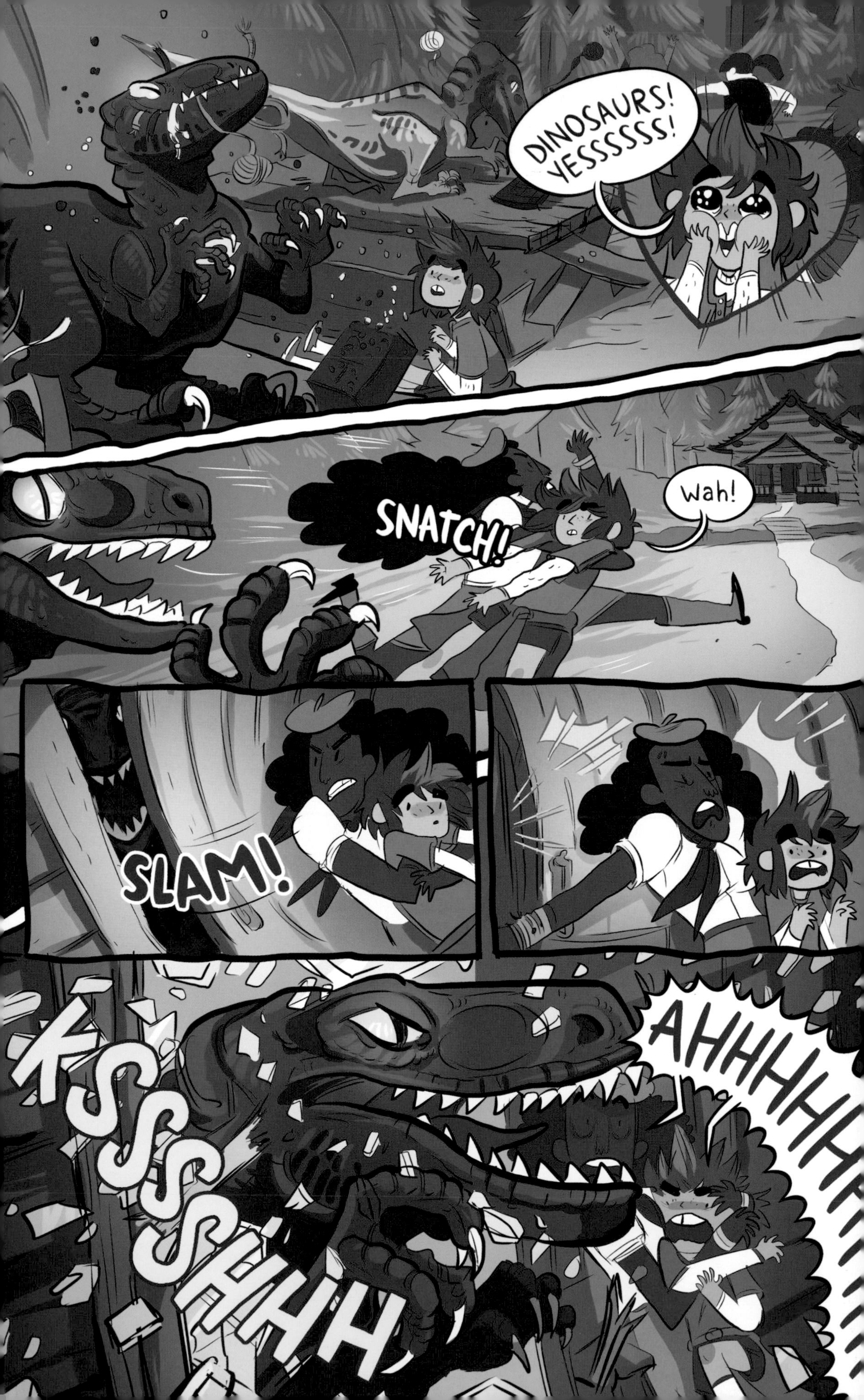
DINOSAURS! YESSSSSS!
SNATCH!
Wah!
SLAM!
KSSSSHHH
AHHHHH!

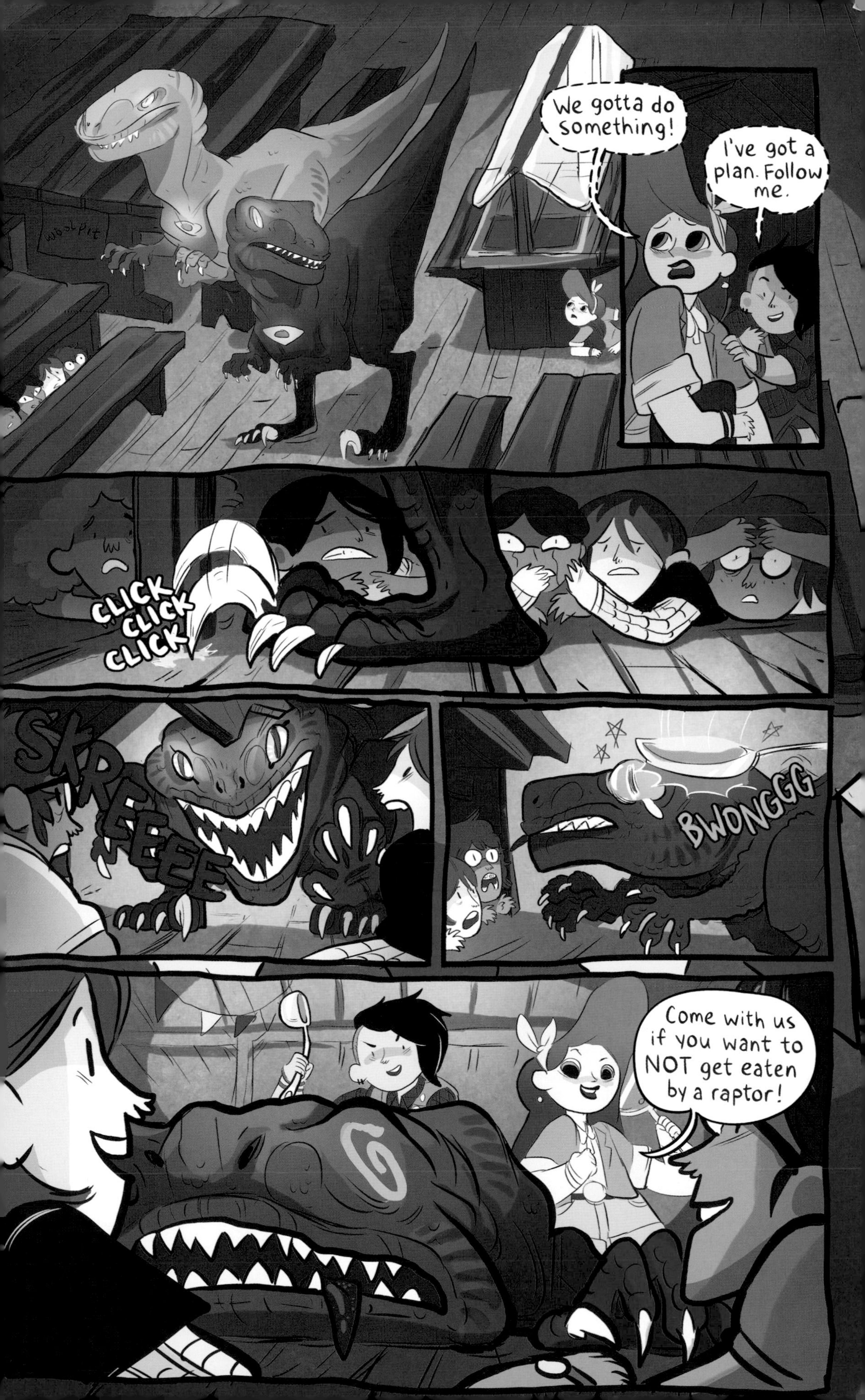
Woolpit
We gotta do something!
I've got a plan. Follow me.
CLICK CLICK CLICK
SKREEEEE
BWONGGG
Come with us if you want to NOT get eaten by a raptor!

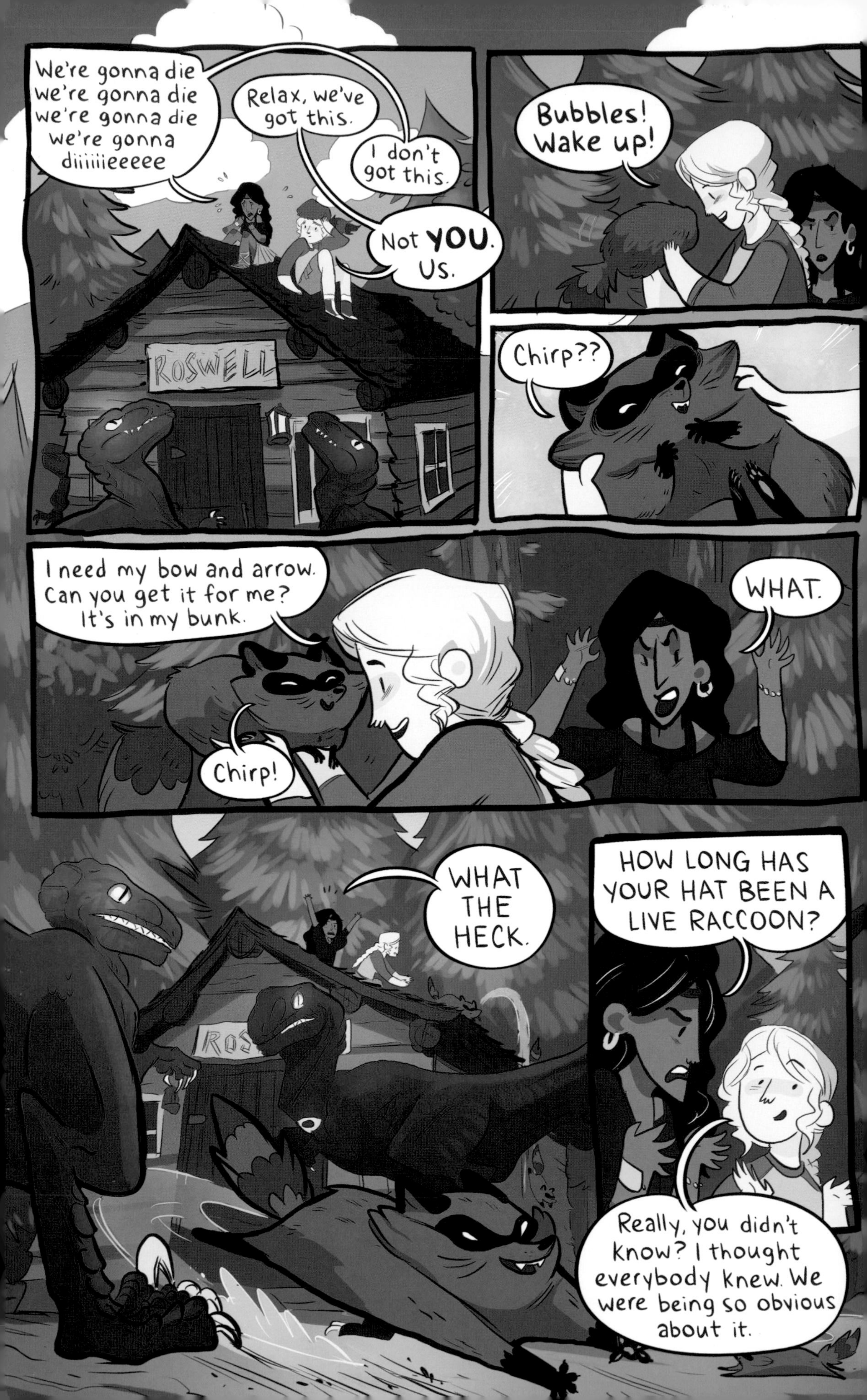
We're gonna die we're gonna die we're gonna die we're gonna diiiiiieeeee
Relax, we've got this.
I don't got this.
Not YOU. Us.
ROSWELL
Bubbles! Wake up!
Chirp??
I need my bow and arrow. Can you get it for me? It's in my bunk.
WHAT.
Chirp!
WHAT THE HECK.
ROS
HOW LONG HAS YOUR HAT BEEN A LIVE RACCOON?
Really, you didn't know? I thought everybody knew. We were being so obvious about it.

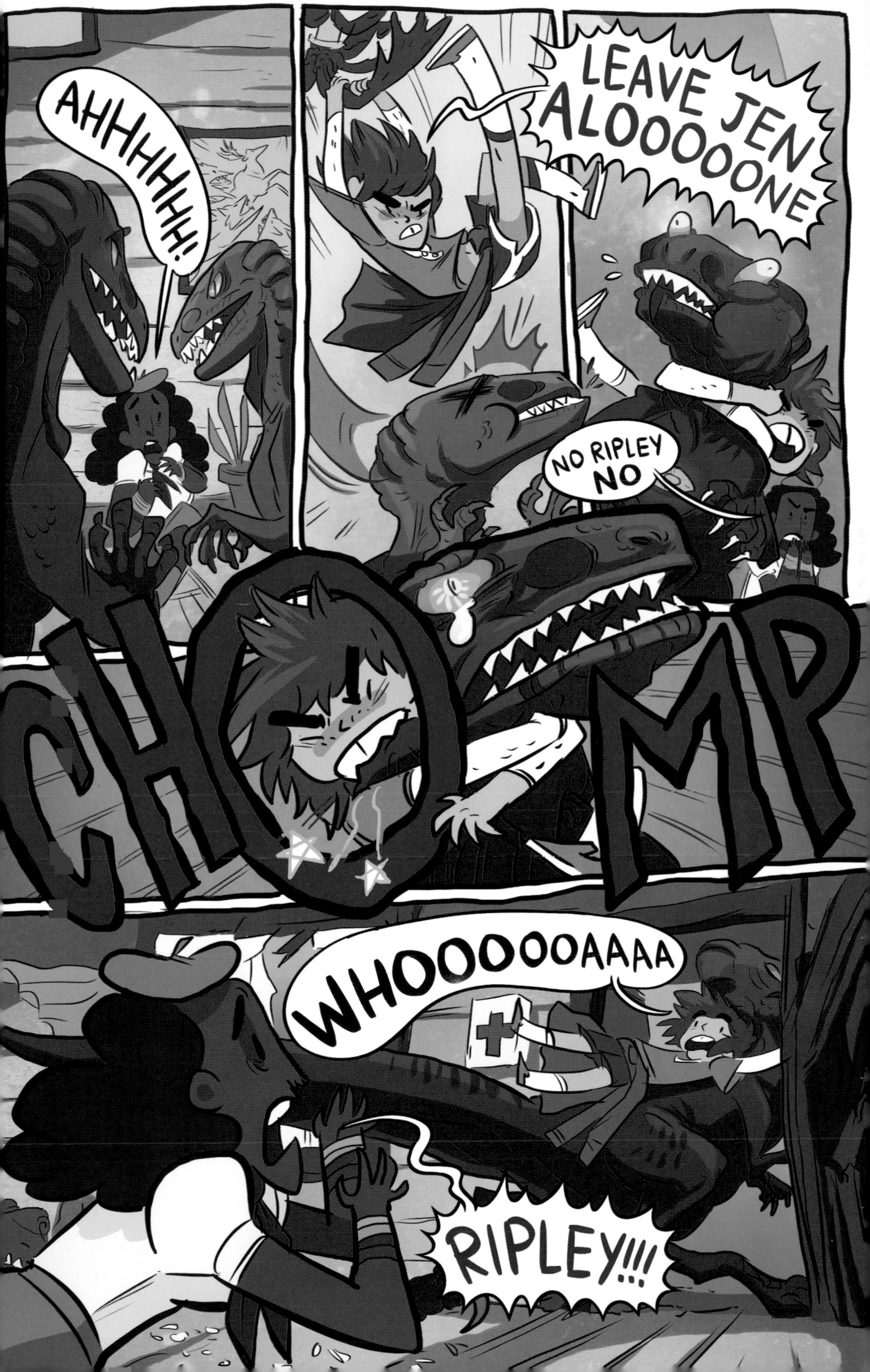
AHHHHHH!
LEAVE JEN ALOOOOOONE
NO RIPLEY NO
CHOMP
WHOOOOOAAAA
RIPLEY!!!

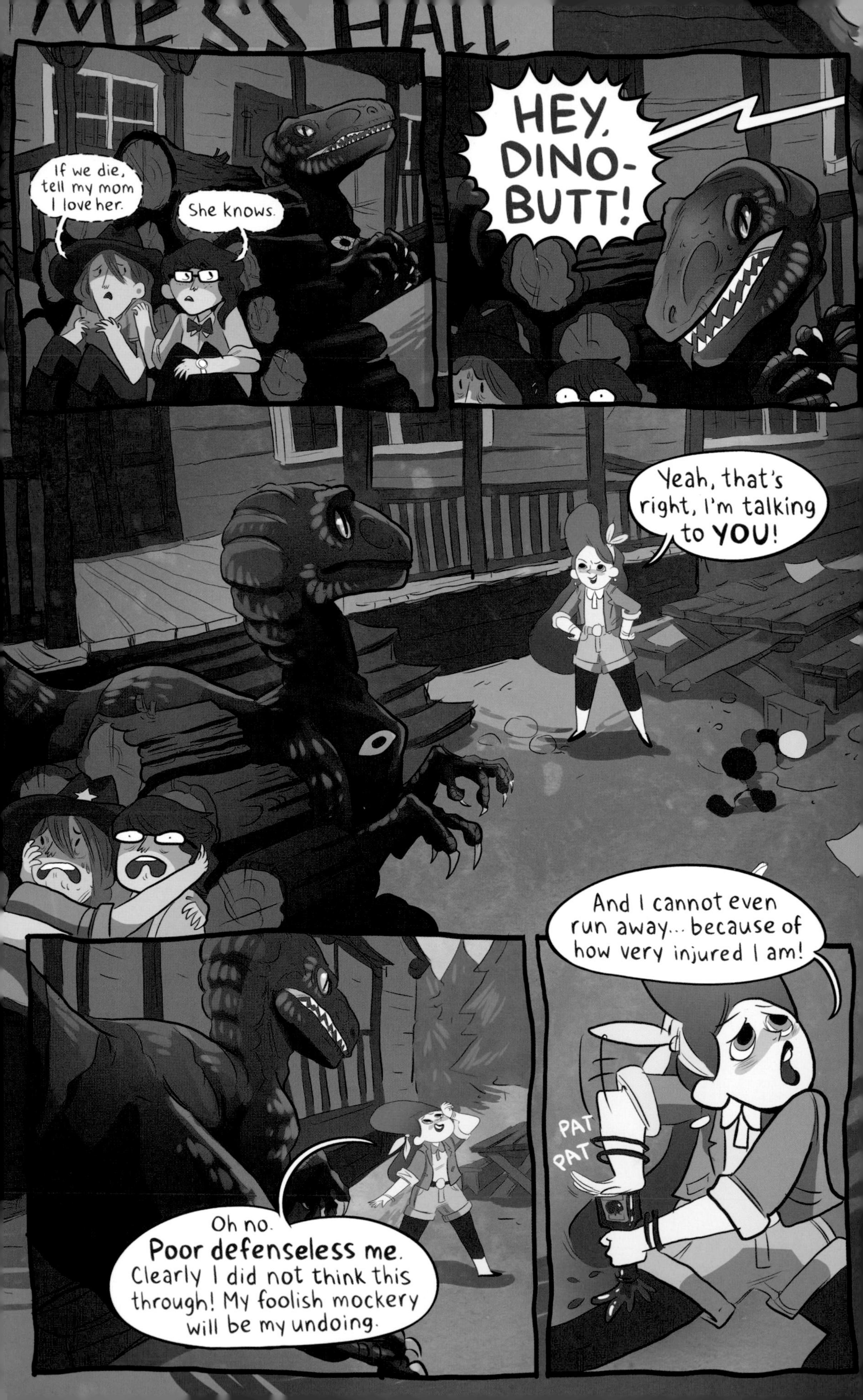
MESS HALL
If we die, tell my mom I love her.
She knows.
HEY, DINO-BUTT!
Yeah, that's right, I'm talking to YOU!
Oh no. Poor defenseless me. Clearly I did not think this through! My foolish mockery will be my undoing.
And I cannot even run away... because of how very injured I am!
PAT PAT

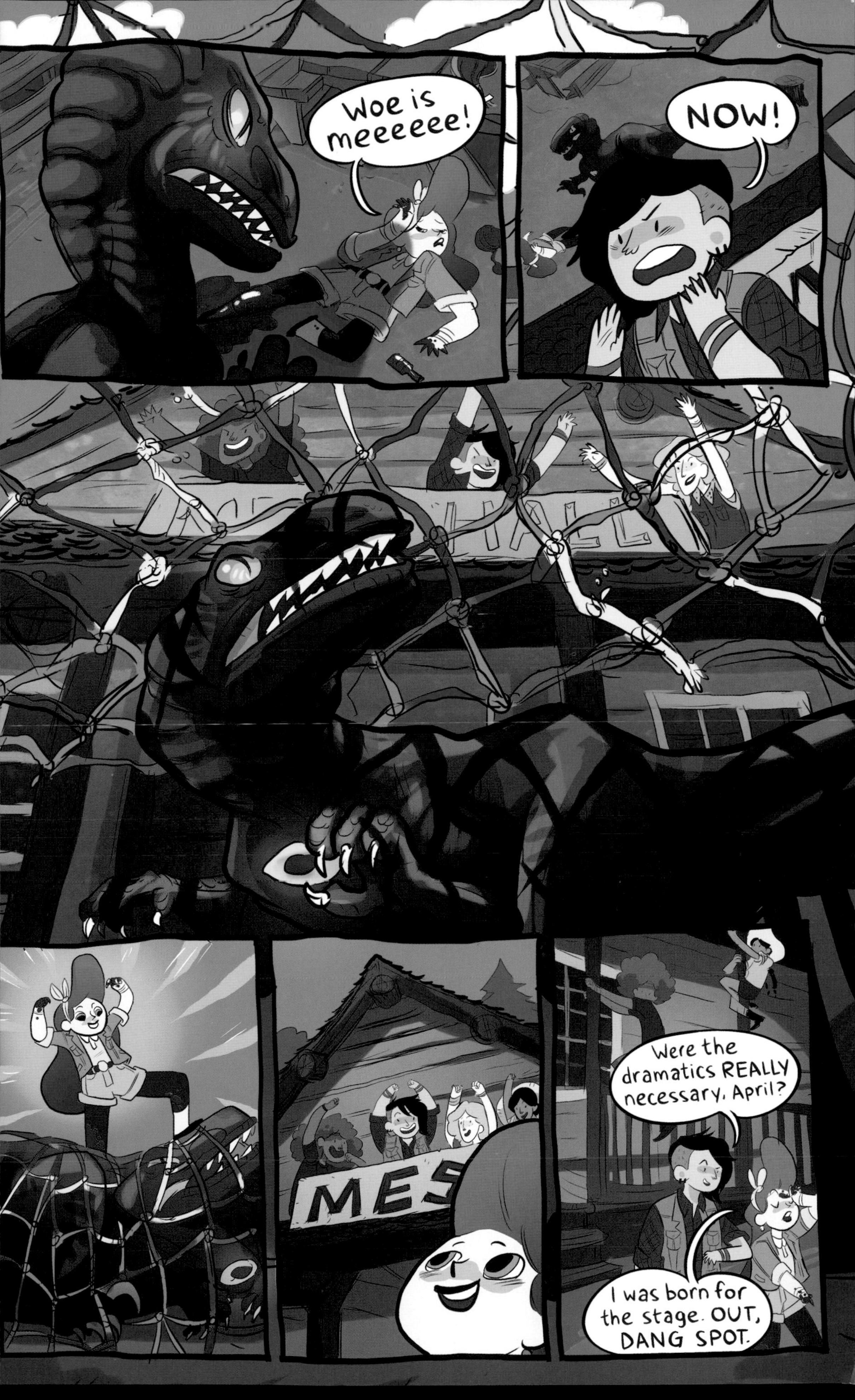
Woe is meeeeee!
NOW!
Were the dramatics REALLY necessary, April?
I was born for the stage. OUT, DANG SPOT.

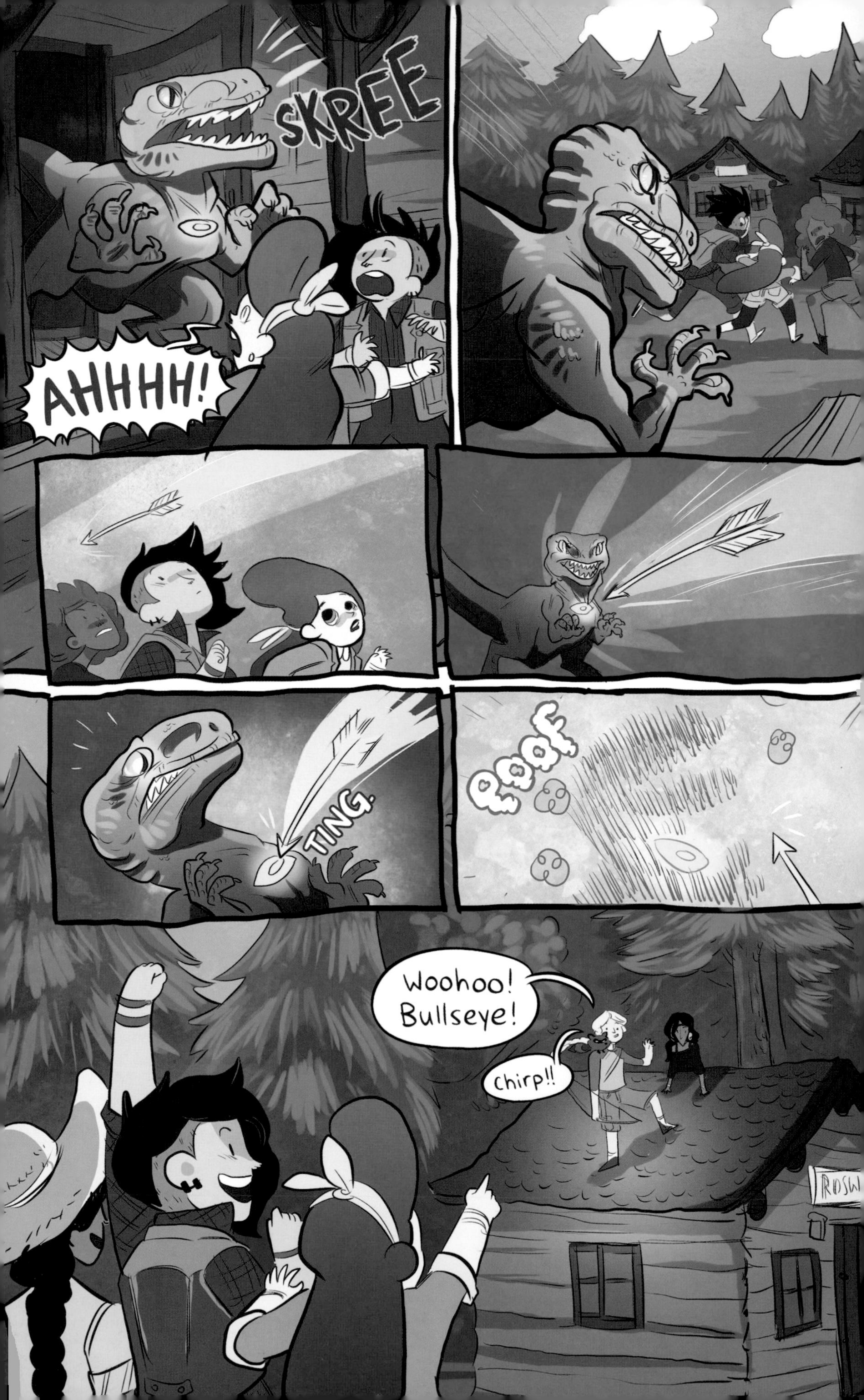
SKREE
AHHHH!
TING.
POOF
Woohoo! Bullseye!
Chirp!!

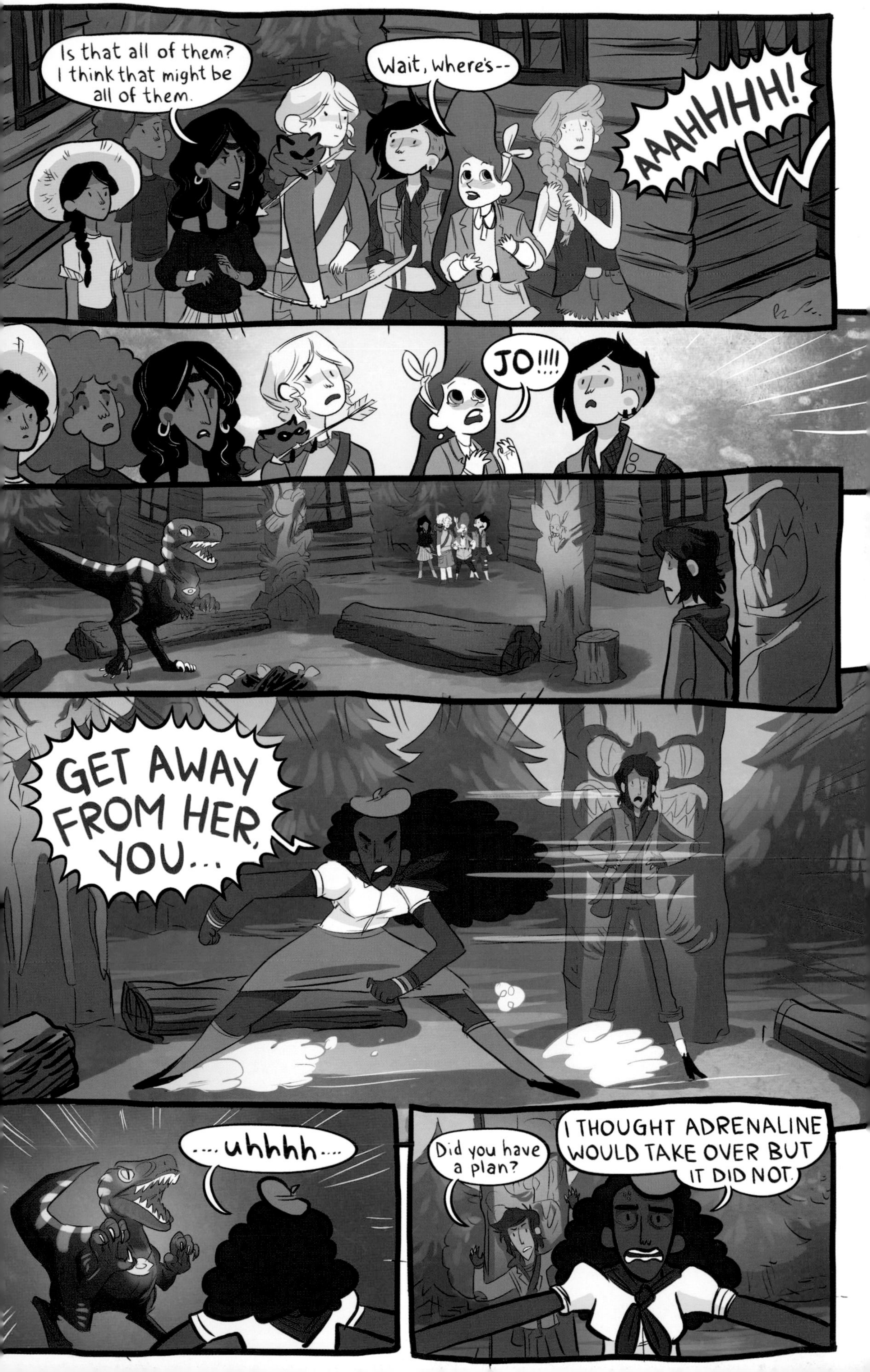
Is that all of them? I think that might be all of them.
Wait, where's--
AAAHHHH!
JO!!!!
GET AWAY FROM HER, YOU...
....uhhhh....
Did you have a plan?
I THOUGHT ADRENALINE WOULD TAKE OVER BUT IT DID NOT.

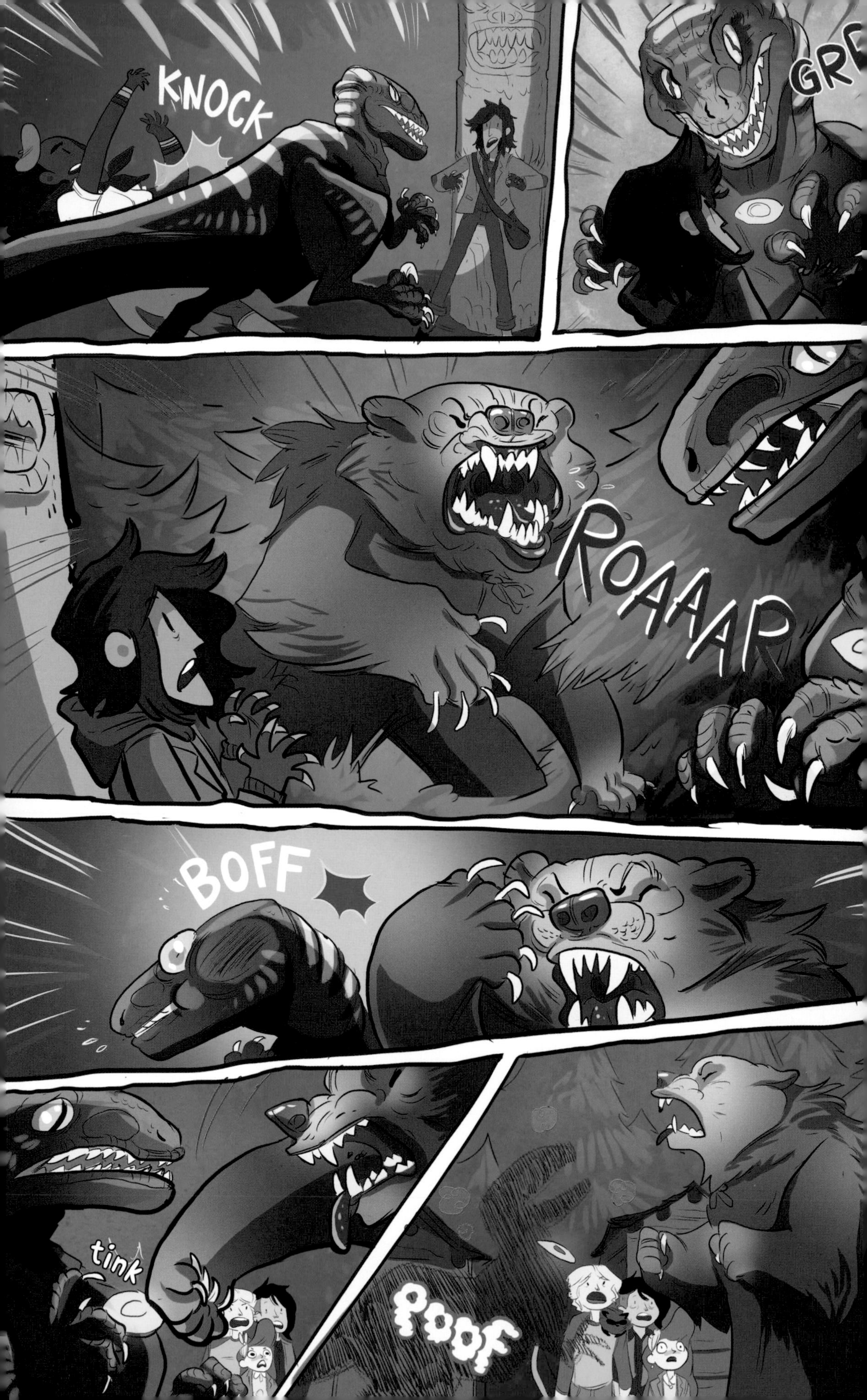
KNOCK
GRR
ROAAAR
BOFF
tink
POOF

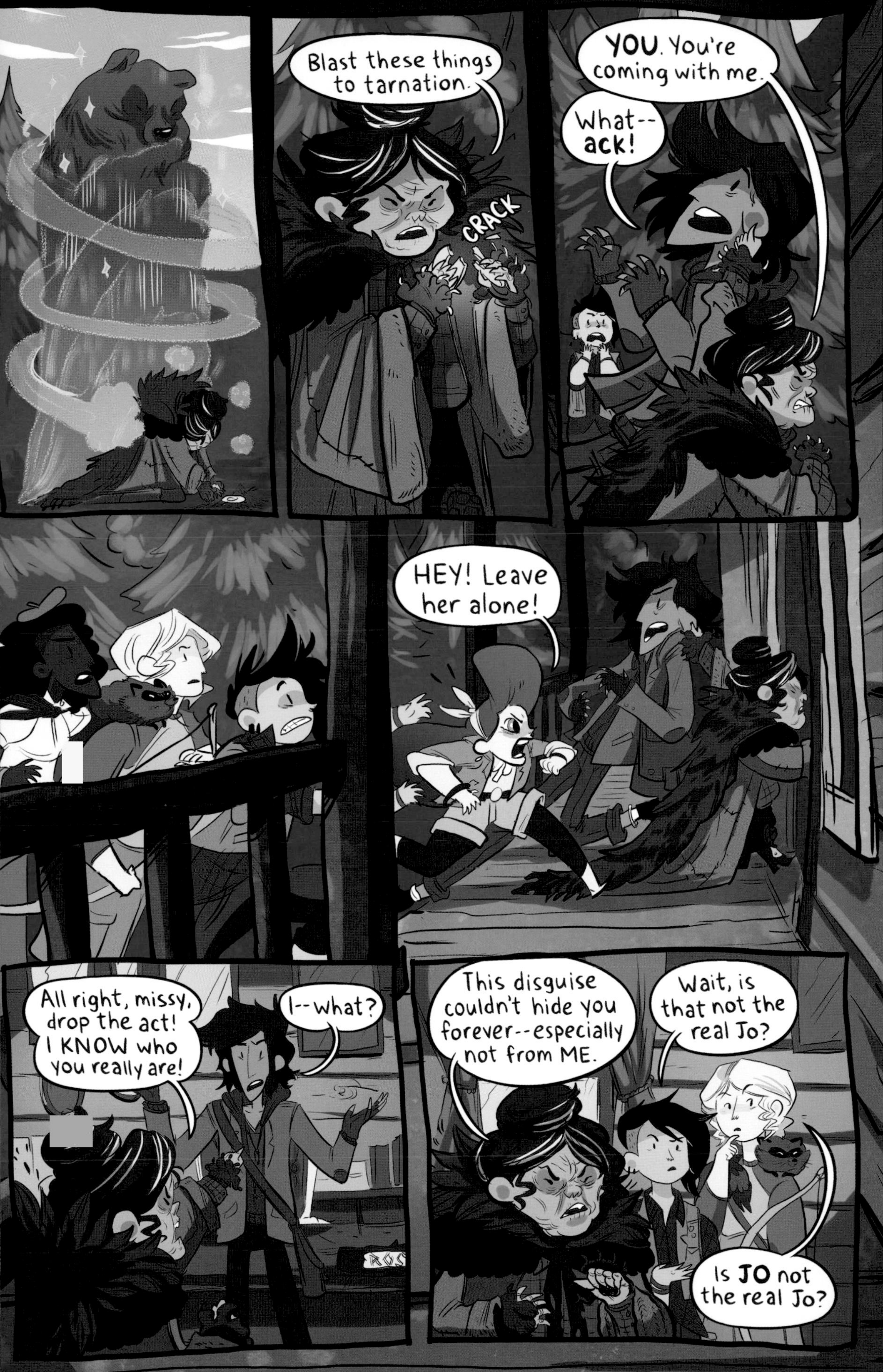
Blast these things to tarnation.
CRACK
YOU. You're coming with me.
What-- ack!
HEY! Leave her alone!
All right, missy, drop the act! I KNOW who you really are!
I--what?
This disguise couldn't hide you forever--especially not from ME.
Wait, is that not the real Jo?
Is JO not the real Jo?

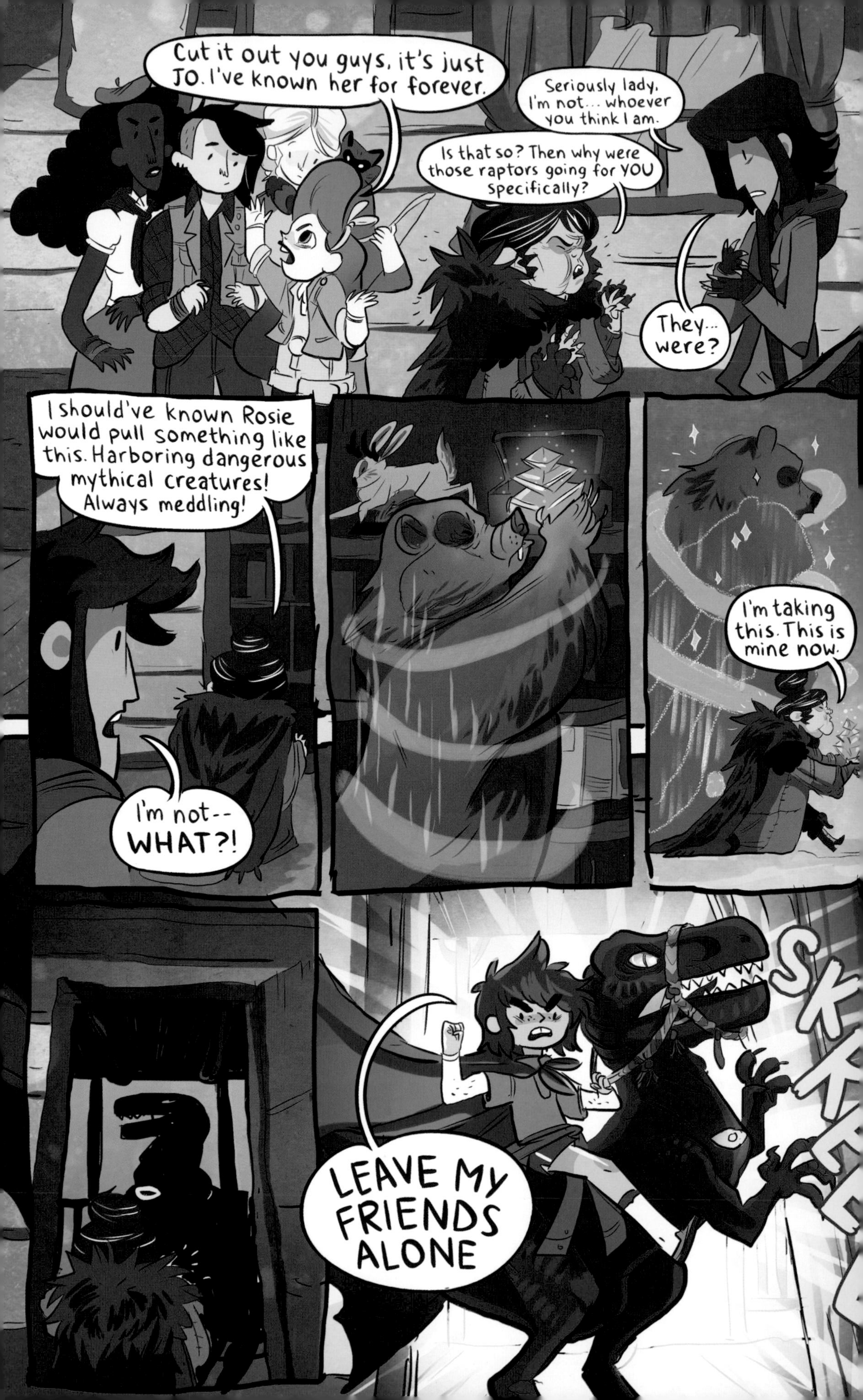

Cut it out you guys, it's just JO. I've known her for forever.
Seriously lady, I'm not... whoever you think I am.
Is that so? Then why were those raptors going for YOU specifically?
They... were?
I should've known Rosie would pull something like this. Harboring dangerous mythical creatures! Always meddling!
I'm not-- WHAT?!
I'm taking this. This is mine now.
LEAVE MY FRIENDS ALONE

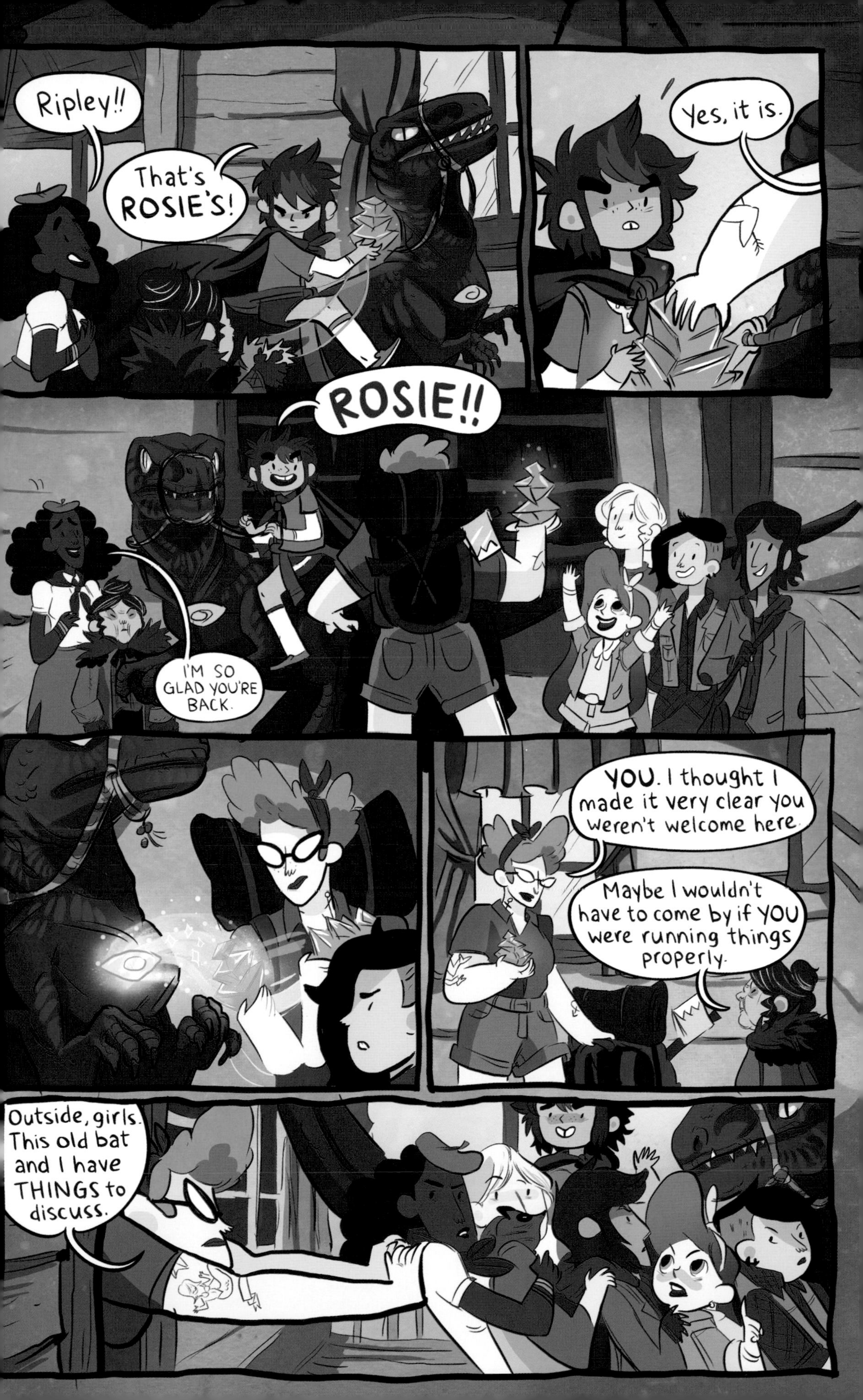
Ripley!!
That's ROSIE'S!
Yes, it is.
ROSIE!!
I'M SO GLAD YOU'RE BACK.
YOU. I thought I made it very clear you weren't welcome here.
Maybe I wouldn't have to come by if YOU were running things properly.
Outside, girls. This old bat and I have THINGS to discuss.

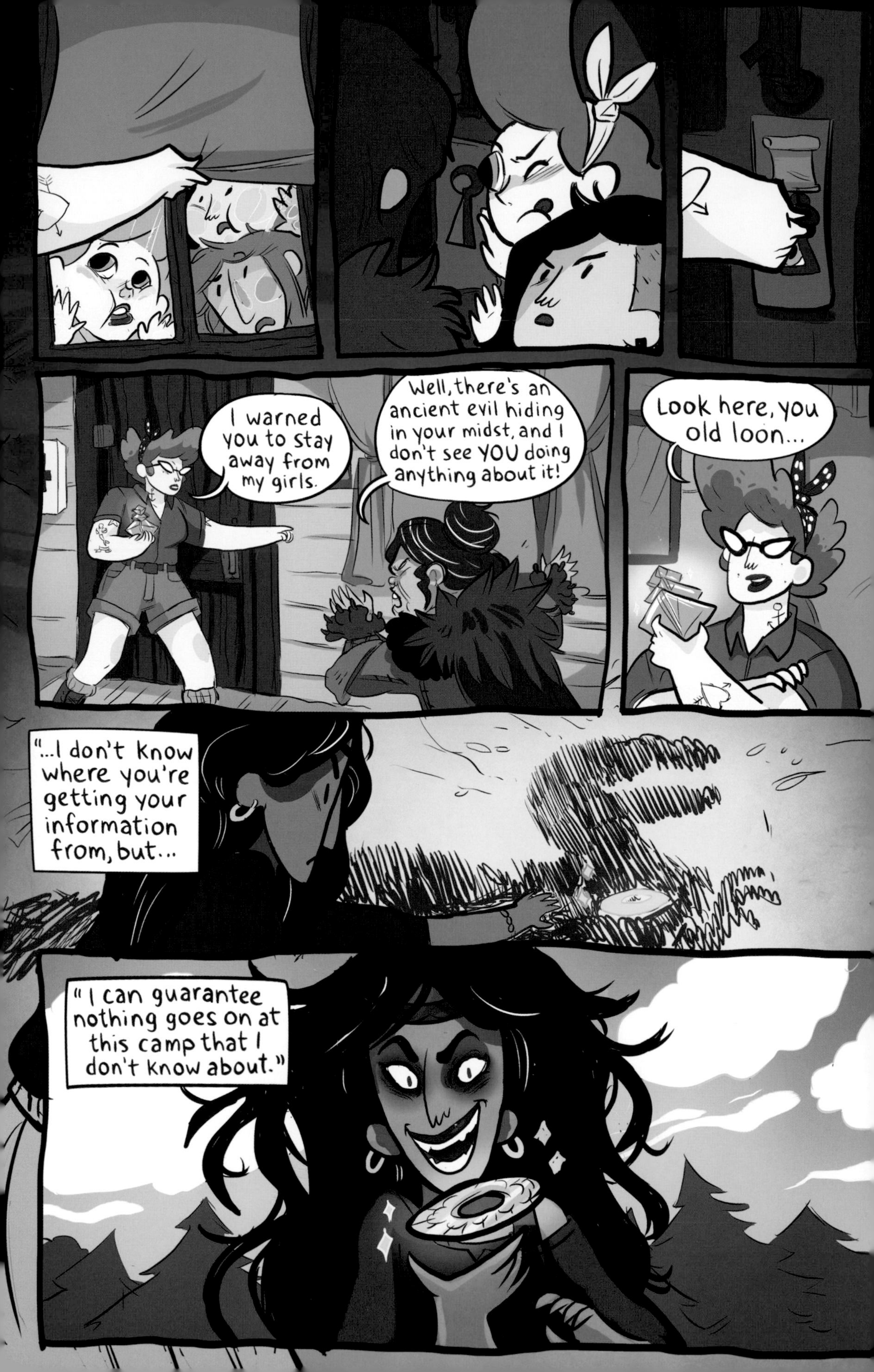
I warned you to stay away from my girls.
Well, there's an ancient evil hiding in your midst, and I don't see YOU doing anything about it!
Look here, you old loon...
"...I don't know where you're getting your information from, but...
"I can guarantee nothing goes on at this camp that I don't know about."

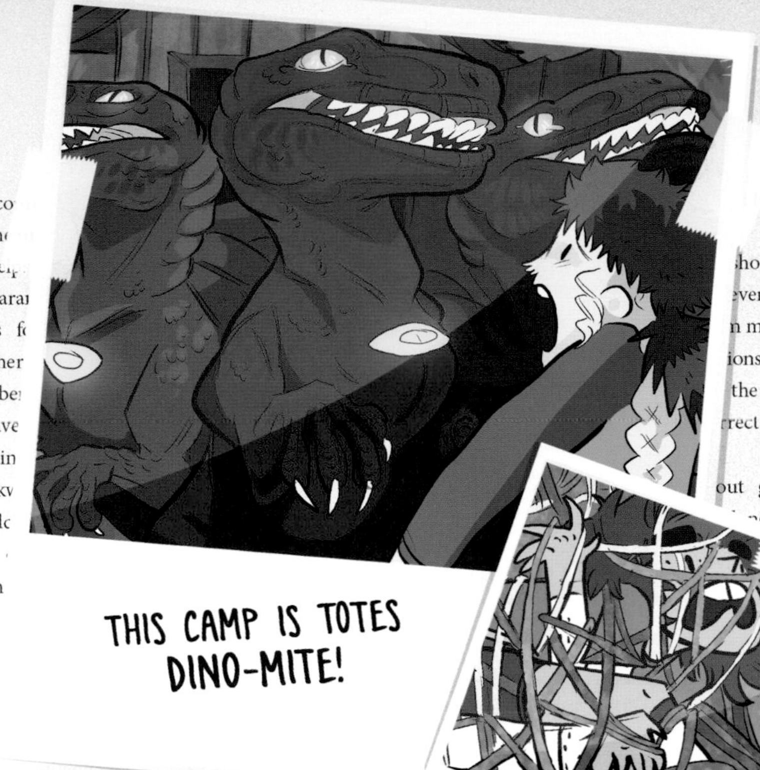
THIS CAMP IS TOTES
DINO-MITE!

will co
Th
It he
appeara
dress f
Further
Lumbe
to have
part in
Thiskv
Hardc
have
them

...E UNIFORM

...should be worn at camp ...events when Lumberjanes ...n may also be worn at other ...ions. It should be worn as a ... the uniform dress with ...rrect shoes, and stocking or

...out grows her uniform or ...ter Lumberjane. ...a she has ... her ... her

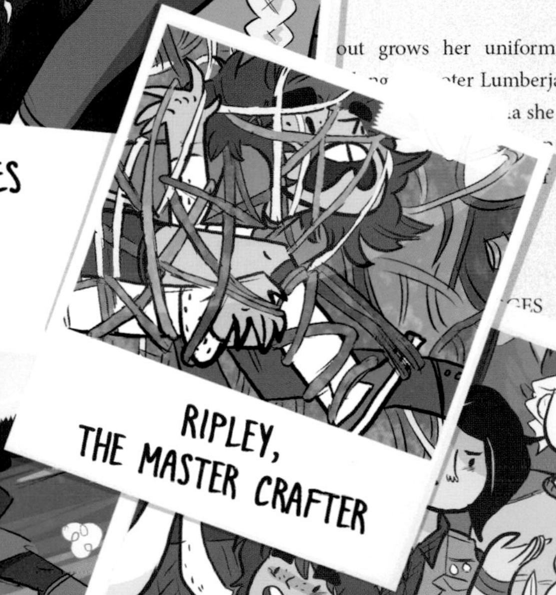
RIPLEY,
THE MASTER CRAFTER

...GES

The
yellow, short sl...
emb...
the w
choose
slacks,
made o
out-of-dc
green bere
the colla
Shoes ma
heels, rou ... ...ings or
socks shou ... with the shoes or wi...
the uniform. Ne..., bracelets, or other jewelry ...
belong with a Lumberjane uniform.

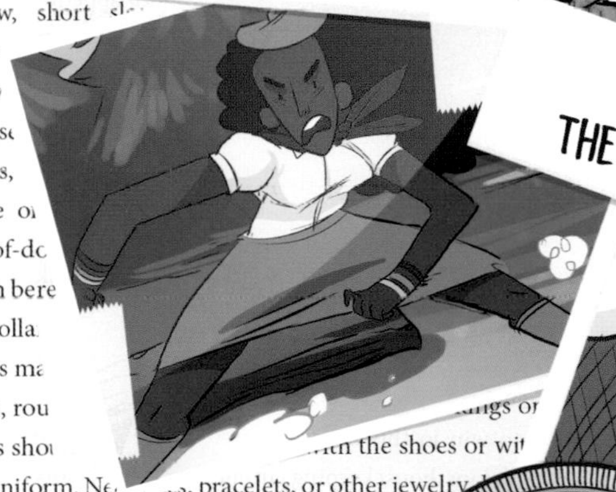

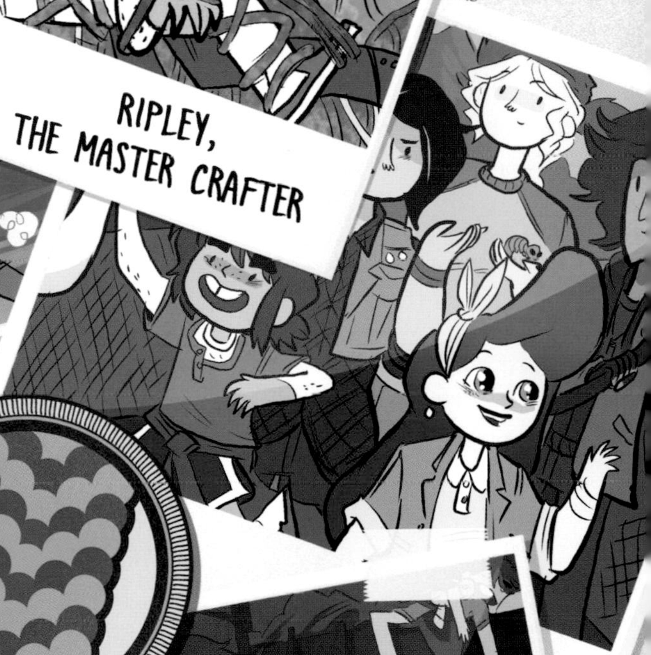

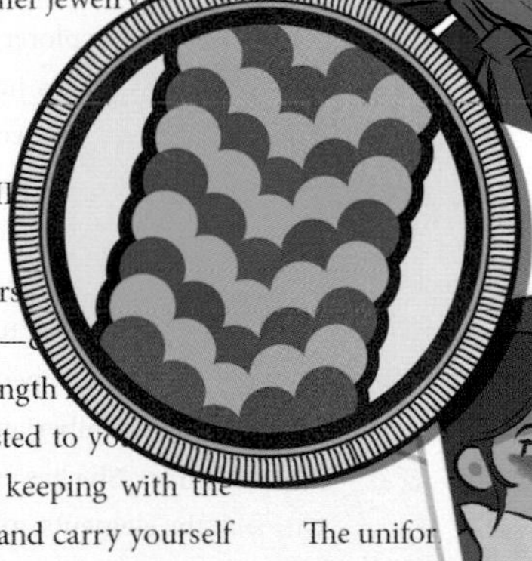

HOW TO WEAR THE UNI...

To look well in a uniform demans firs... uniform be kept in good condition—... pressed. See that the skirt is the right length ... height and build, that the belt is adjusted to yo... that your shoes and stockings are in keeping with the uniform, that you watch your posture and carry yourself with dignity and grace. If the beret is removed indoors, be sure that your hair is neat and kept in place with an insonspicuous clip or ribbon. When you wear a Lumberjane uniform you are identified as a member of this organization and you should be doubly careful to conduct yourself in a way that will show everyone that courtesy and thoughtfullness are part of being a Lumberjane. People are likely to judge a whole nation by the selfishness of a few individuals, to criticize a whole family because of the misconduct of one member, and to feel unkindly toward and organization because of the

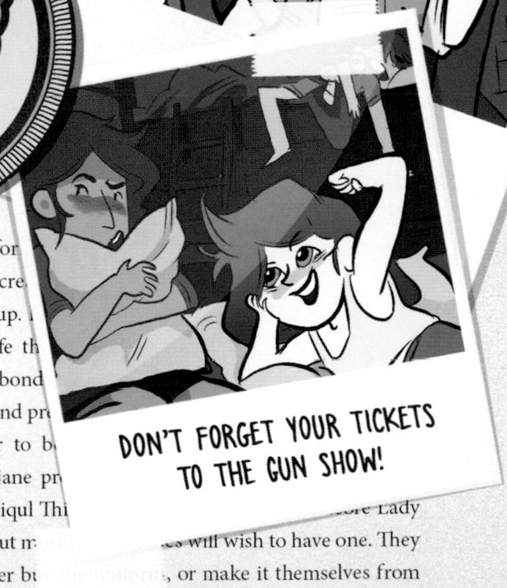
DON'T FORGET YOUR TICKETS
TO THE GUN SHOW!

The unifor...
helps to cre...
in a group. ...
active life th...
another bond...
future, and pr...
in order to b...
Lumberjane pr...
Penniquiqul Thi... ...ore Lady
Types, but m... ...s will wish to have one. They
can either bu... ...uniform, or make it themselves from
materials available at the trading post.

## LUMBERJANES FIELD MANUAL
# CHAPTER SIX

*Lumberjanes "Sports and Games" Program Field*

## JAIL BREAK

*"Run as fast as you can."*

Everyone experiences troubles, it is not something that is unique to one individual and it is something everyone must acknowledge. Some things can be planned for, some things require much luck, and some things require a bit of both and a lot of chaos. Incarceration will happen in some form or another, whether it's because she finds herself at a party that is terribly dull with only the window as a valid escape or she wasn't fast enough to escape the authorities after a good street race. Lumberjanes are considered to be girls who can find their way into and out of any situation.

The *Jail Break* badge is a badge that is only earned on the battlefield. It is something that every scout will get a chance to earn whether they are taken by their captors against their will or because they let it happen. One of the many fun opportunities with this badge is the chance to get the better of her enemies while freeing her fellow soldiers so that they can return to their base and start again. Capture the flag is and will always be the biggest battle of the summer, but the real challenge to the game actually isn't getting the flag. It's breaking out of your enemies' prison.

To obtain the *Jail Break* badge a Lumberjane must be participating in one of the battle royales that summer. She will have to find herself captured by her enemy and taken into their holding cells. A Lumberjane must be able to adapt to her surroundings, she must be able to predict the movement of the other team and above all else, she must save as many fellow prisoners as possible. She will know the importance of teamwork, she will be able to step down if she doubts in her abilities to free everyone safely just as she will be able to stand up to help a fellow scout in this challenge. She will never doubt her enemy, never underestimate their knowledge

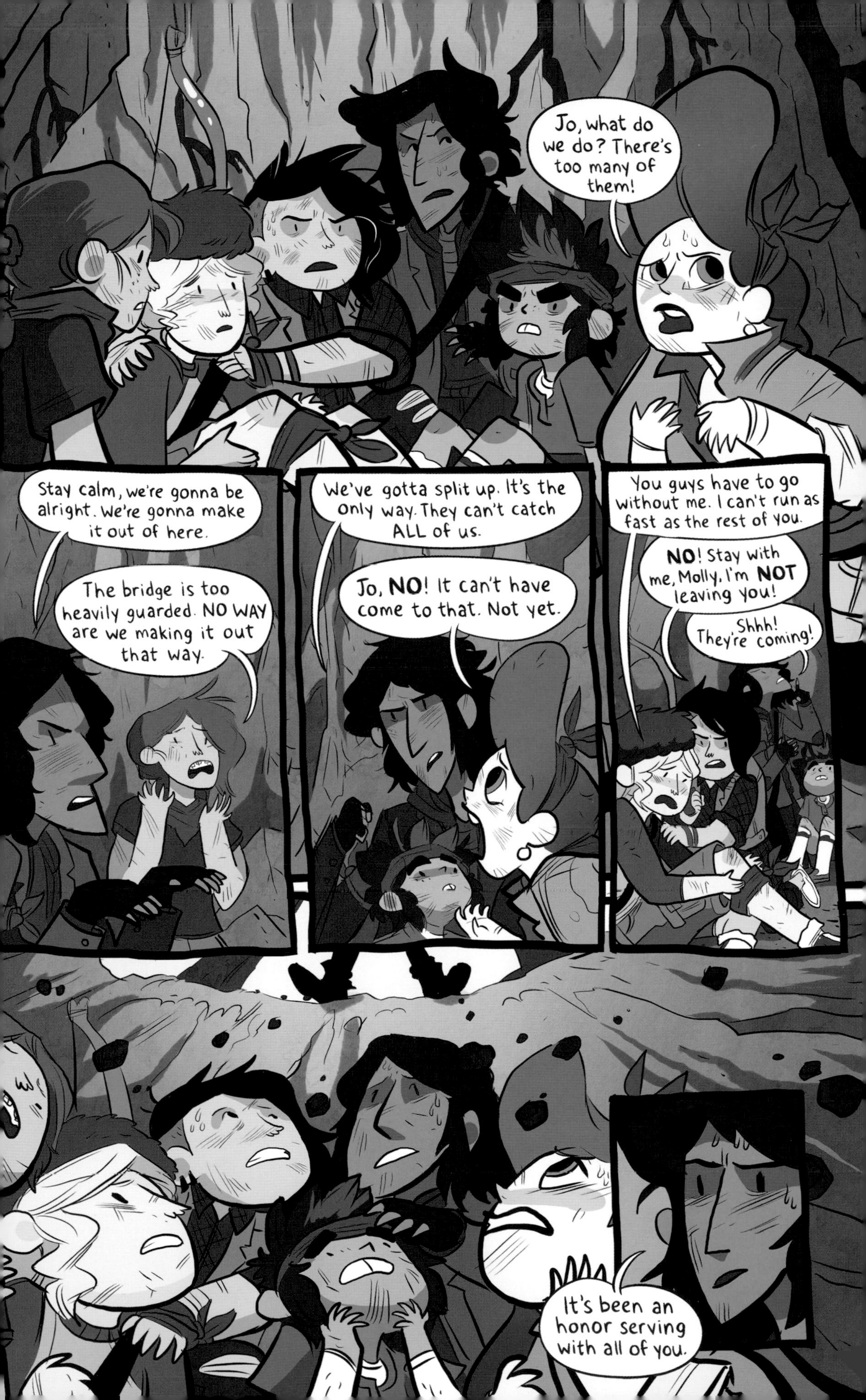
Jo, what do we do? There's too many of them!
Stay calm, we're gonna be alright. We're gonna make it out of here.
The bridge is too heavily guarded. NO WAY are we making it out that way.
We've gotta split up. It's the only way. They can't catch ALL of us.
Jo, NO! It can't have come to that. Not yet.
You guys have to go without me. I can't run as fast as the rest of you.
NO! Stay with me, Molly, I'm NOT leaving you!
Shhh! They're coming!
It's been an honor serving with all of you.

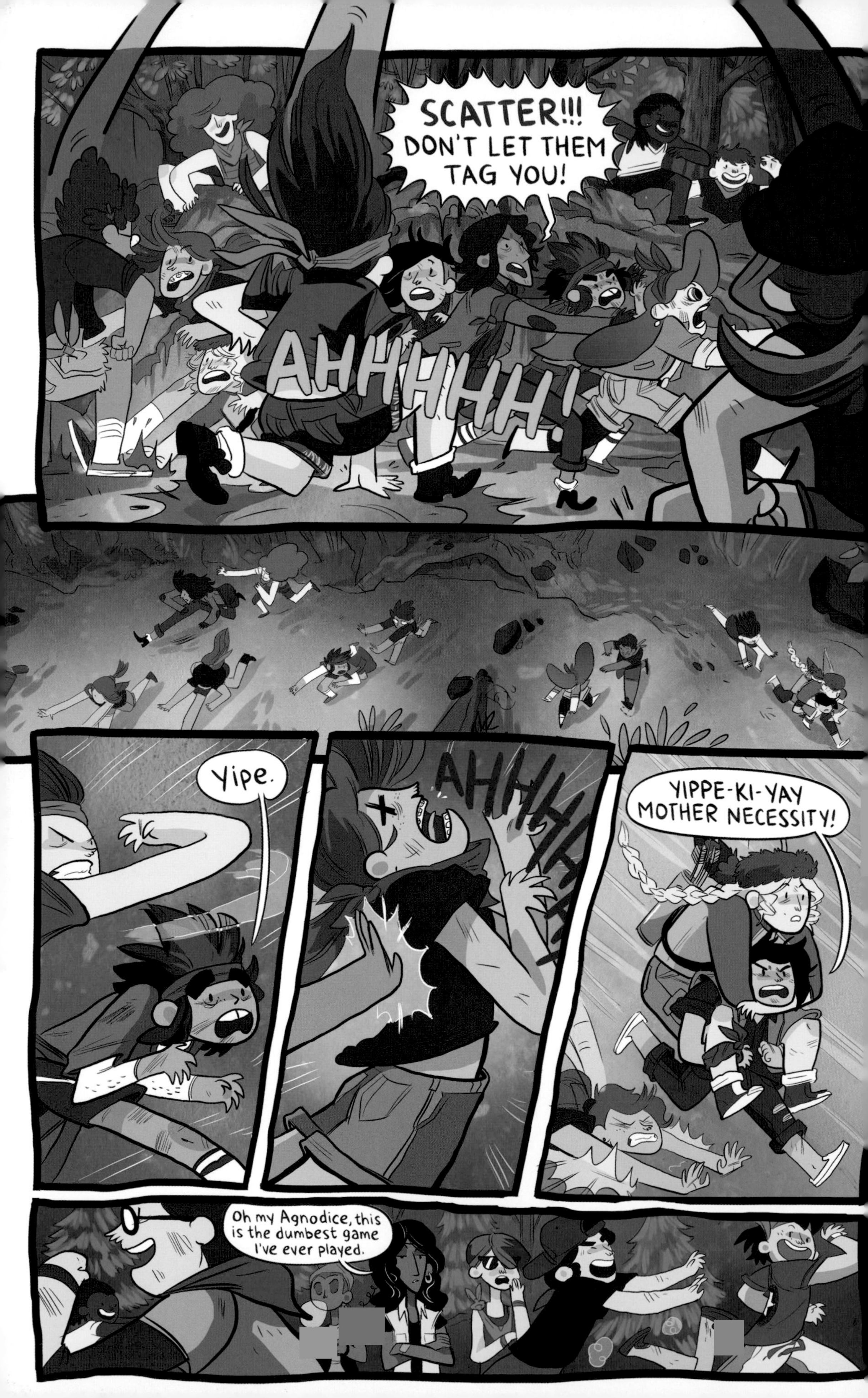
SCATTER!!!
DON'T LET THEM TAG YOU!
AHHHHHH!
Yipe.
AHHHHH
YIPPE-KI-YAY MOTHER NECESSITY!
Oh my Agnodice, this is the dumbest game I've ever played.

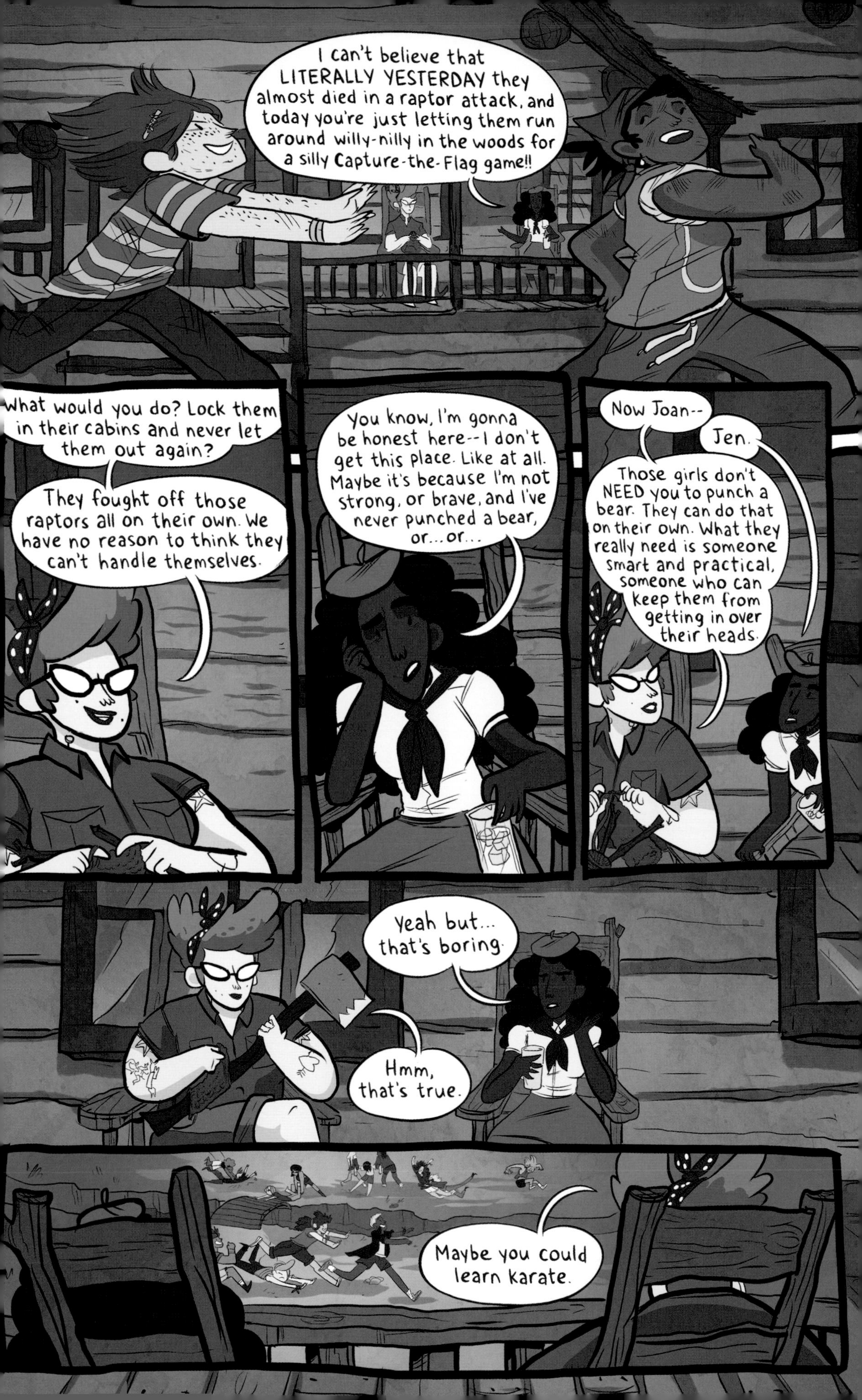
I can't believe that LITERALLY YESTERDAY they almost died in a raptor attack, and today you're just letting them run around willy-nilly in the woods for a silly Capture-the-Flag game!!
What would you do? Lock them in their cabins and never let them out again?
They fought off those raptors all on their own. We have no reason to think they can't handle themselves.
You know, I'm gonna be honest here--I don't get this place. Like at all. Maybe it's because I'm not strong, or brave, and I've never punched a bear, or... or...
Now Joan--
Jen.
Those girls don't NEED you to punch a bear. They can do that on their own. What they really need is someone smart and practical, someone who can keep them from getting in over their heads.
Yeah but... that's boring.
Hmm, that's true.
Maybe you could learn karate.

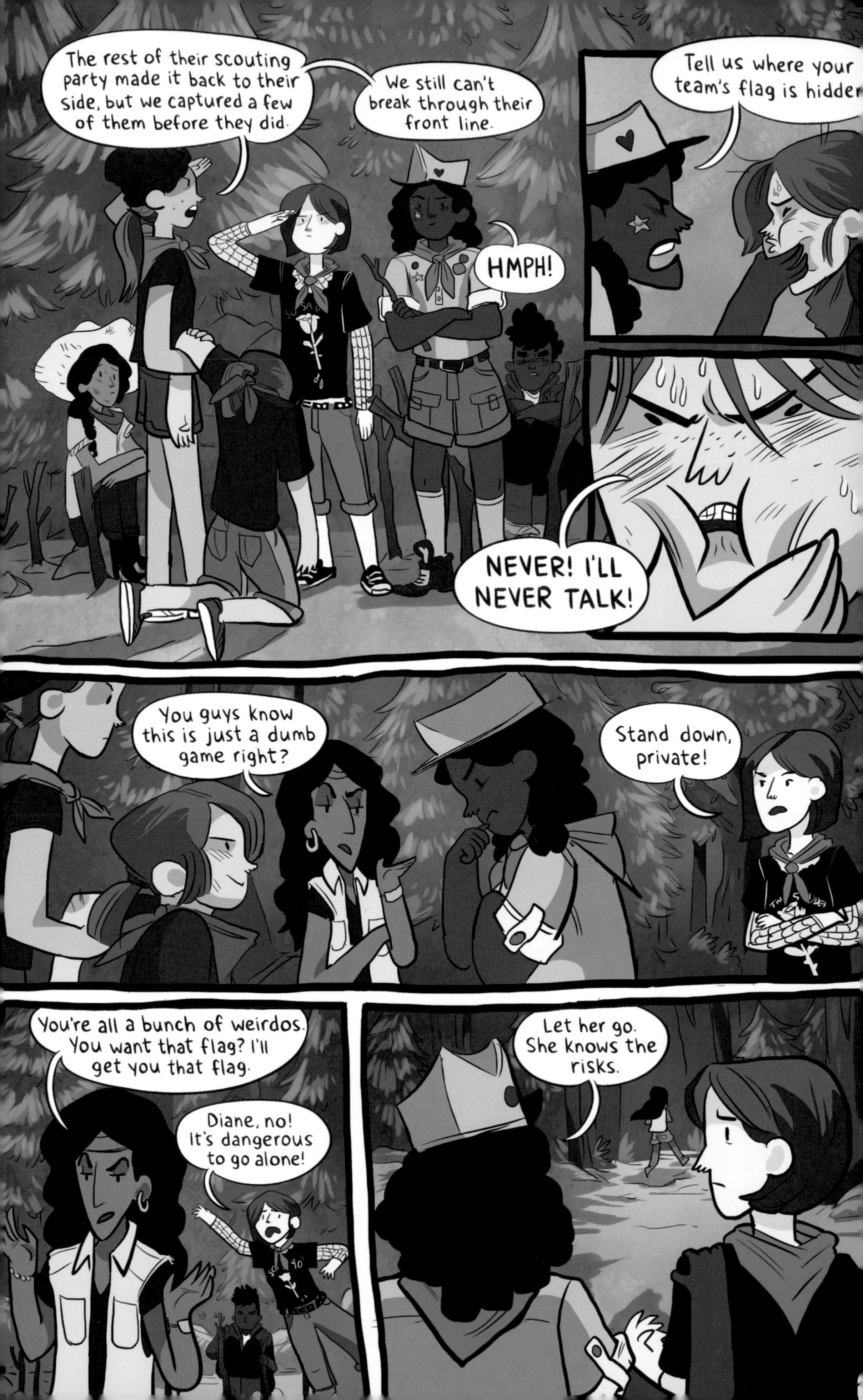

The rest of their scouting party made it back to their side, but we captured a few of them before they did.
We still can't break through their front line.
HMPH!
Tell us where your team's flag is hidden
NEVER! I'LL NEVER TALK!
You guys know this is just a dumb game right?
Stand down, private!
You're all a bunch of weirdos. You want that flag? I'll get you that flag.
Diane, no! It's dangerous to go alone!
Let her go. She knows the risks.

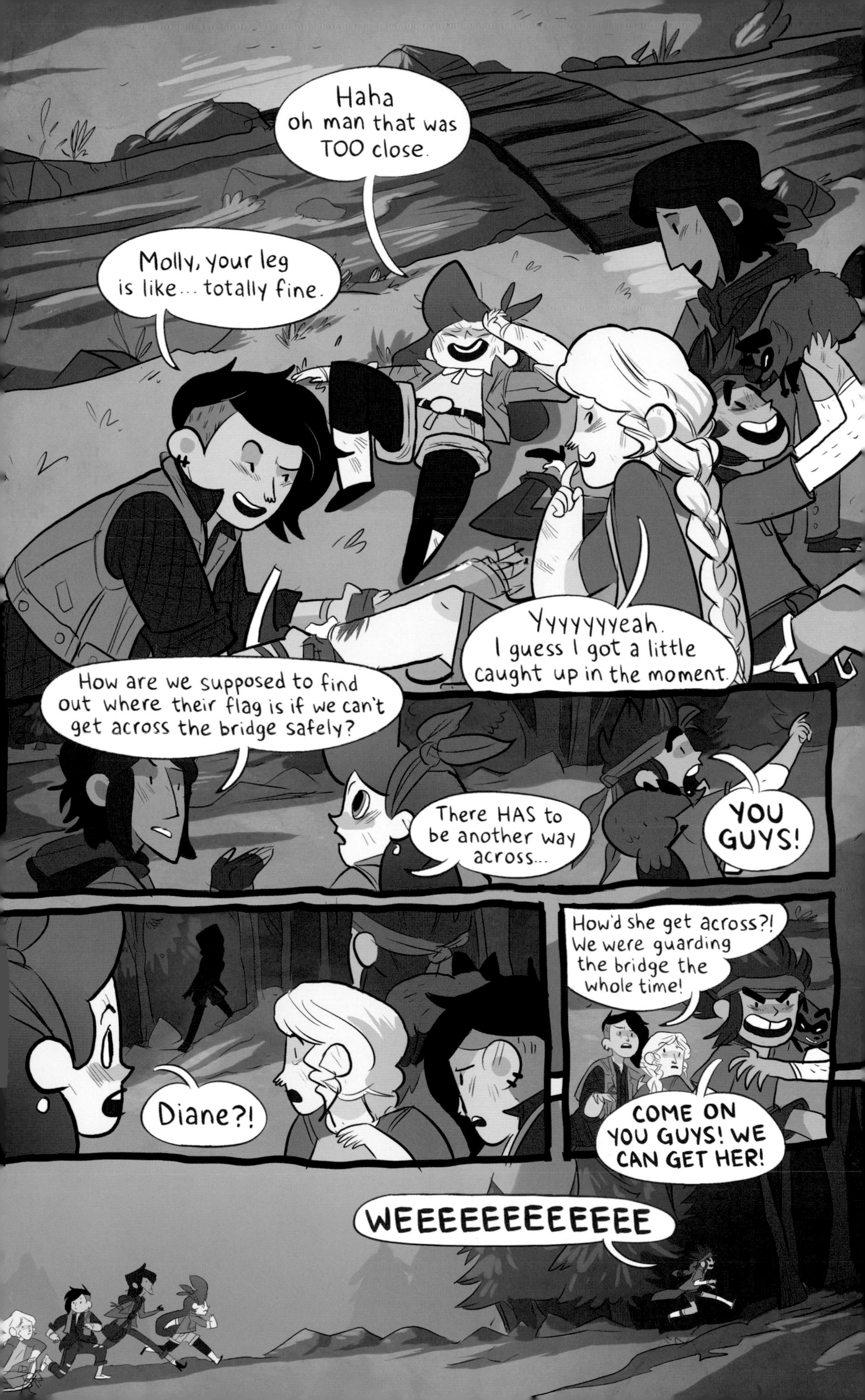
Haha oh man that was TOO close.
Molly, your leg is like... totally fine.
Yyyyyyyeah. I guess I got a little caught up in the moment.
How are we supposed to find out where their flag is if we can't get across the bridge safely?
There HAS to be another way across...
YOU GUYS!
Diane?!
How'd she get across?! We were guarding the bridge the whole time!
COME ON YOU GUYS! WE CAN GET HER!
WEEEEEEEEEEEE

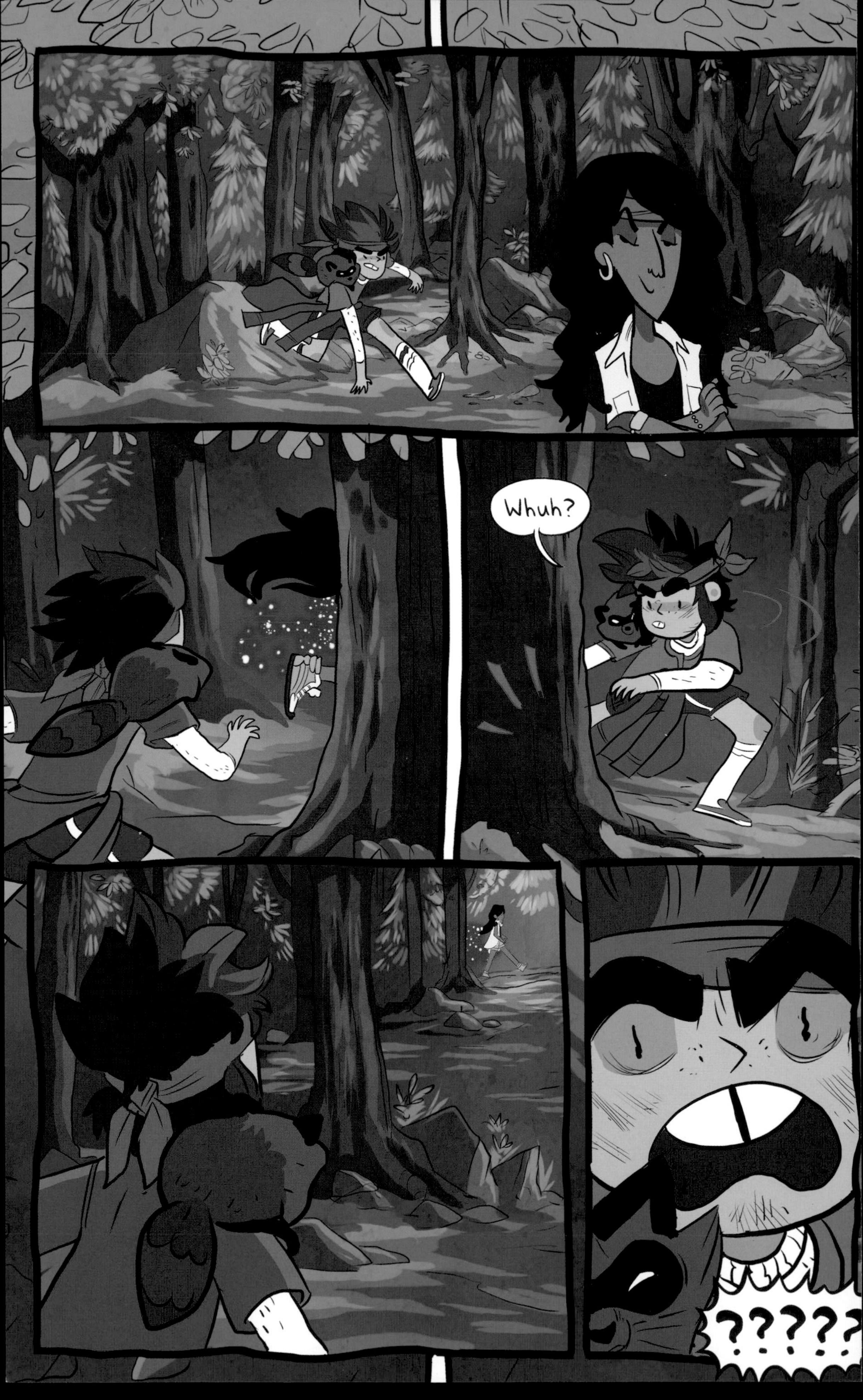
Whuh?
?????

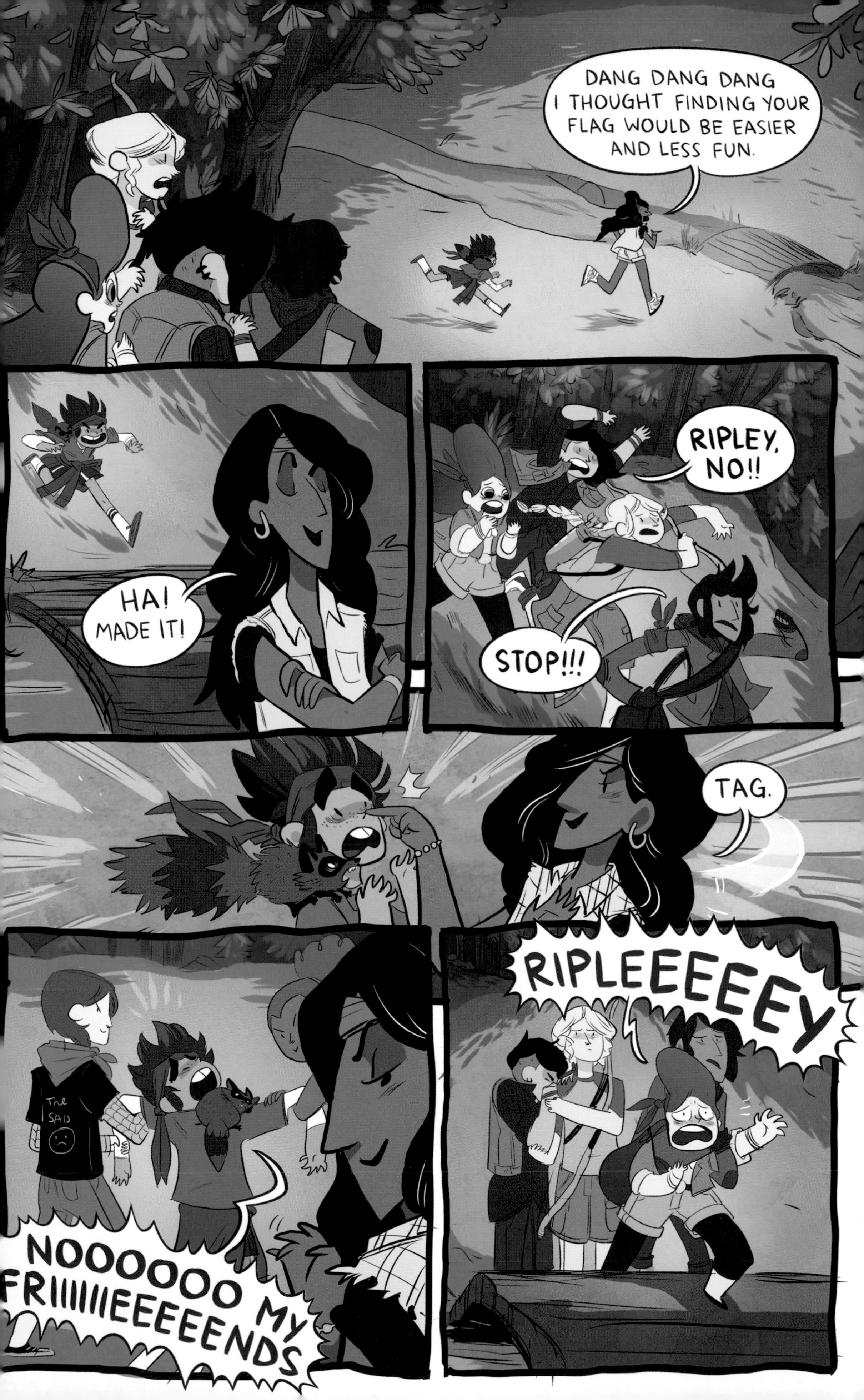
DANG DANG DANG I THOUGHT FINDING YOUR FLAG WOULD BE EASIER AND LESS FUN.
HA! MADE IT!
RIPLEY, NO!!
STOP!!!
TAG.
NOOOOOO MY FRIIIIIIEEEEEENDS
RIPLEEEEEEY
THE SAD

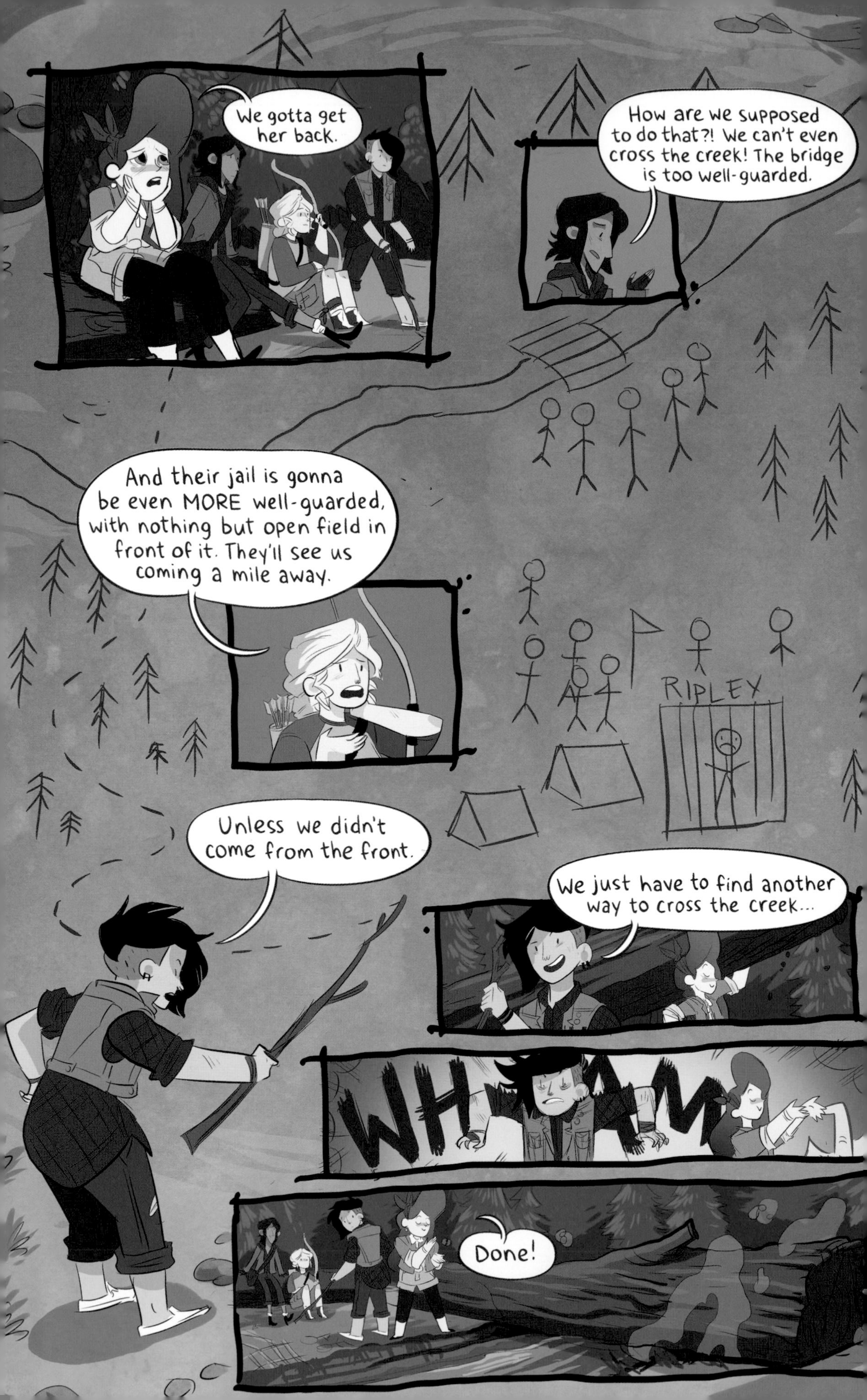
We gotta get her back.
How are we supposed to do that?! We can't even cross the creek! The bridge is too well-guarded.
And their jail is gonna be even MORE well-guarded, with nothing but open field in front of it. They'll see us coming a mile away.
RIPLEY
Unless we didn't come from the front.
We just have to find another way to cross the creek...
WHAM
Done!

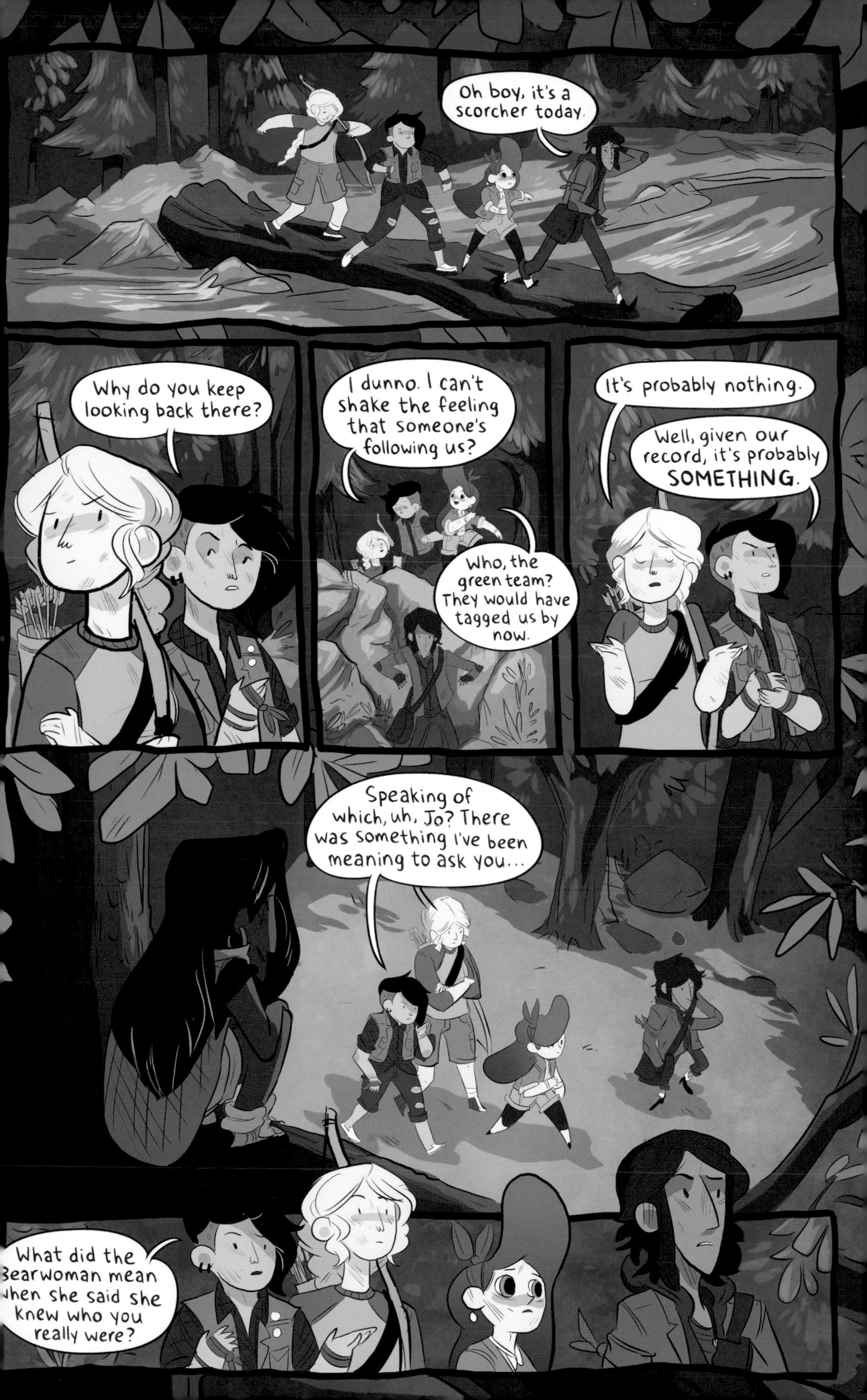
Oh boy, it's a scorcher today.
Why do you keep looking back there?
I dunno. I can't shake the feeling that someone's following us?
Who, the green team? They would have tagged us by now.
It's probably nothing.
Well, given our record, it's probably SOMETHING.
Speaking of which, uh, Jo? There was something I've been meaning to ask you...
What did the Bearwoman mean when she said she knew who you really were?

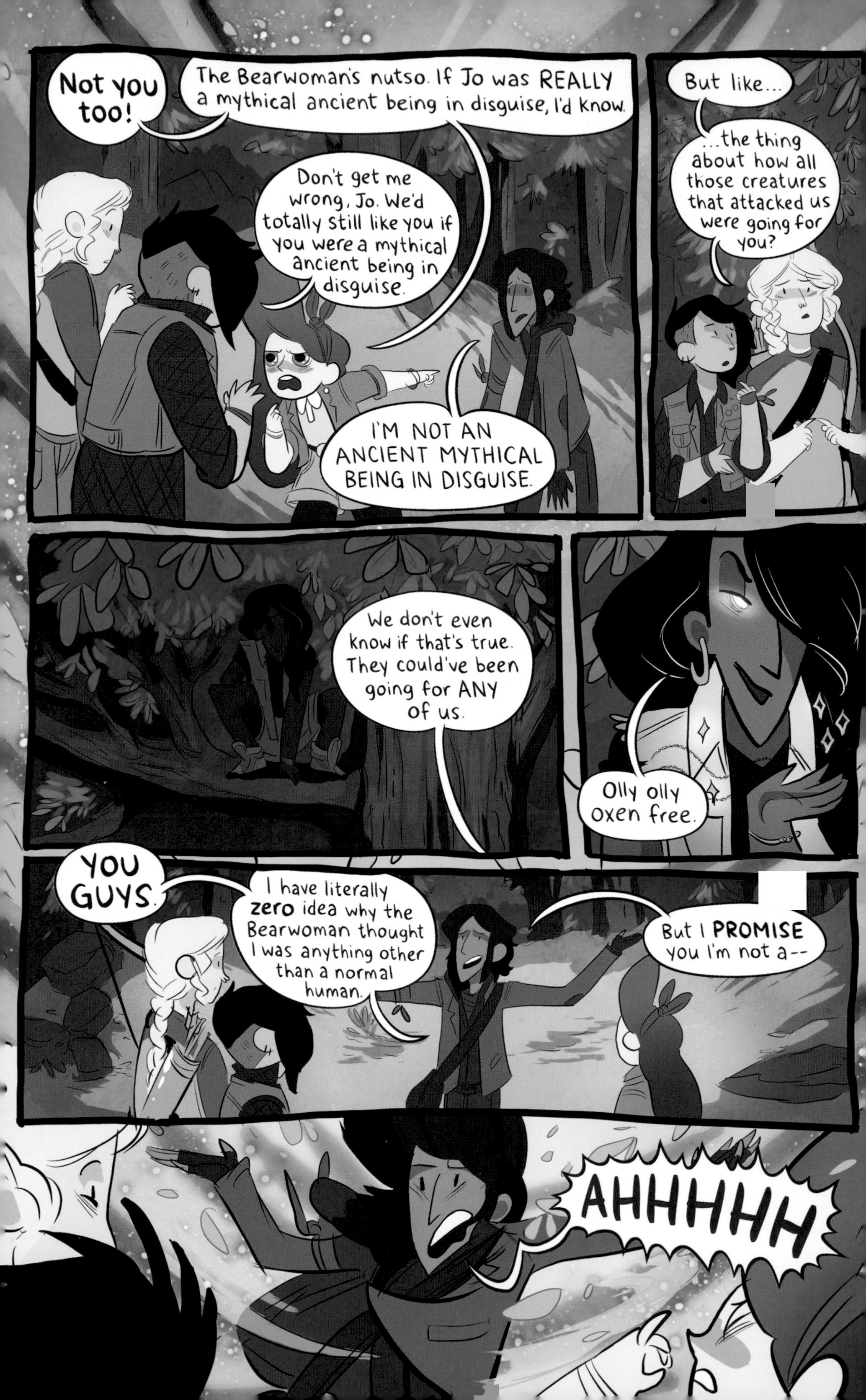
Not you too!
The Bearwoman's nutso. If Jo was REALLY a mythical ancient being in disguise, I'd know.
Don't get me wrong, Jo. We'd totally still like you if you were a mythical ancient being in disguise.
I'M NOT AN ANCIENT MYTHICAL BEING IN DISGUISE.
But like...
...the thing about how all those creatures that attacked us were going for you?
We don't even know if that's true. They could've been going for ANY of us.
Olly olly oxen free.
YOU GUYS.
I have literally zero idea why the Bearwoman thought I was anything other than a normal human.
But I PROMISE you I'm not a--
AHHHHH

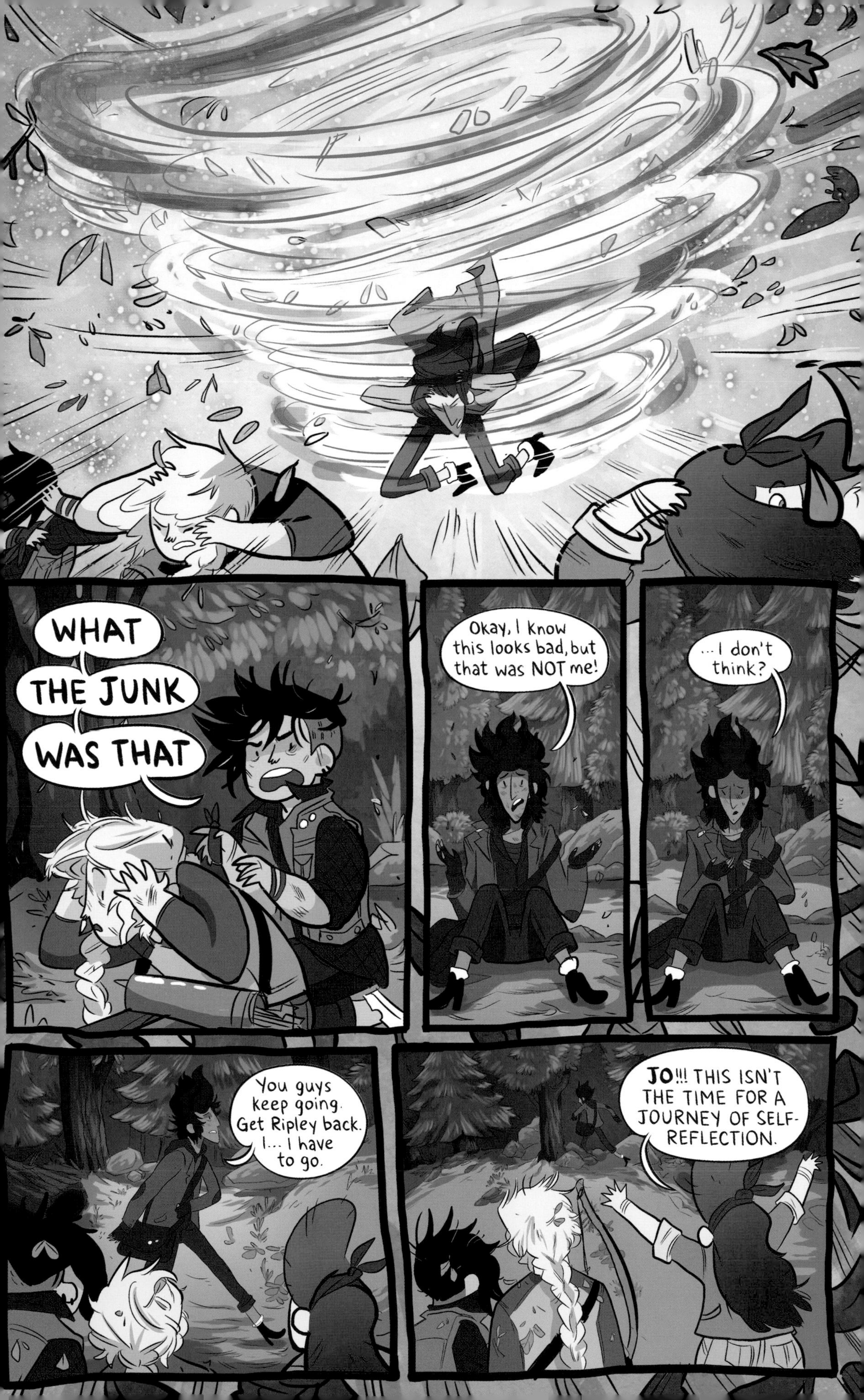
WHAT
THE JUNK
WAS THAT
Okay, I know this looks bad, but that was NOT me!
...I don't think?
You guys keep going. Get Ripley back. I... I have to go.
JO!!! THIS ISN'T THE TIME FOR A JOURNEY OF SELF-REFLECTION.

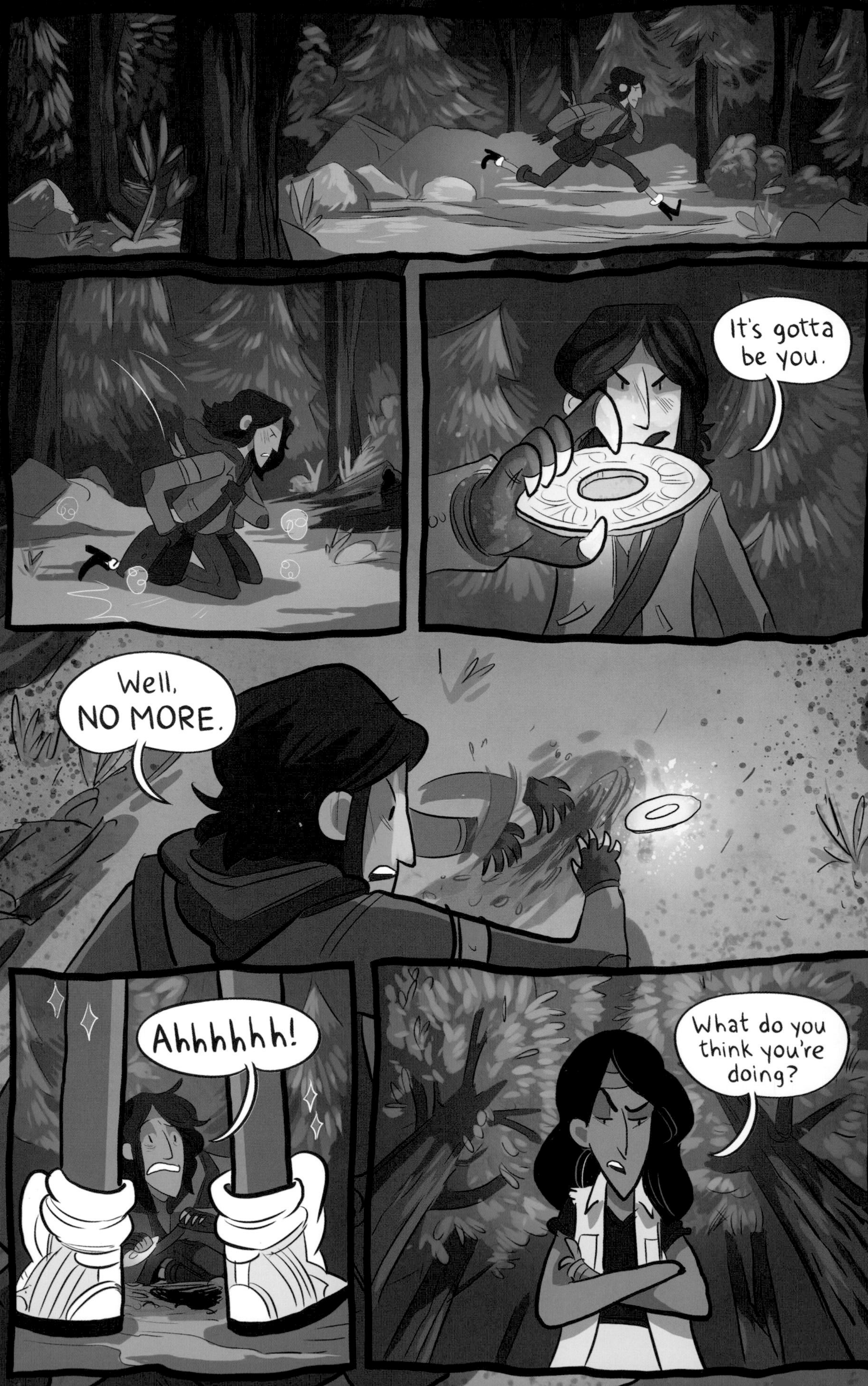
It's gotta be you.
Well, NO MORE.
Ahhhhhh!
What do you think you're doing?

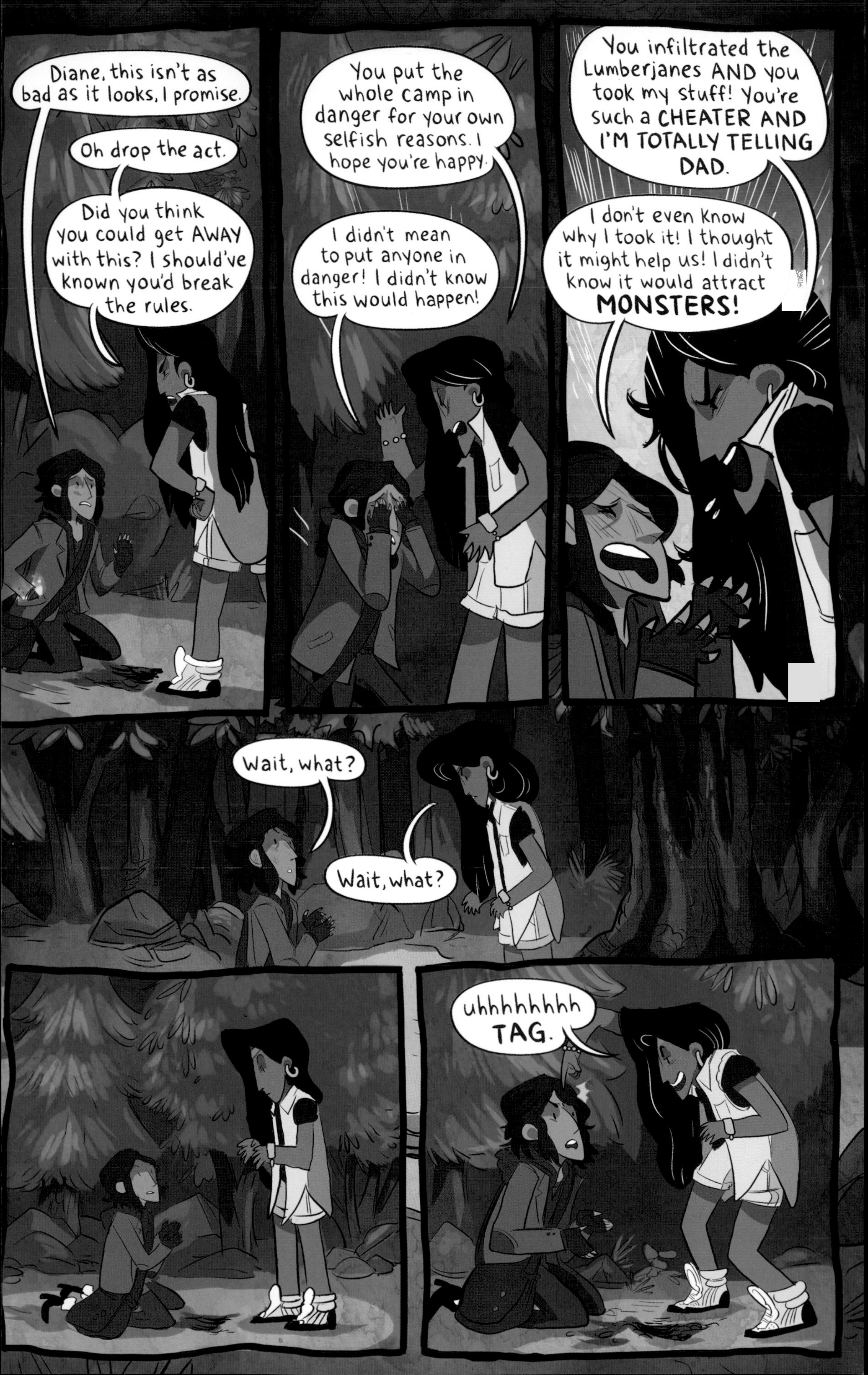
Diane, this isn't as bad as it looks, I promise.
Oh drop the act.
Did you think you could get AWAY with this? I should've known you'd break the rules.
You put the whole camp in danger for your own selfish reasons. I hope you're happy.
I didn't mean to put anyone in danger! I didn't know this would happen!
You infiltrated the Lumberjanes AND you took my stuff! You're such a CHEATER AND I'M TOTALLY TELLING DAD.
I don't even know why I took it! I thought it might help us! I didn't know it would attract MONSTERS!
Wait, what?
Wait, what?
uhhhhhhhh TAG.

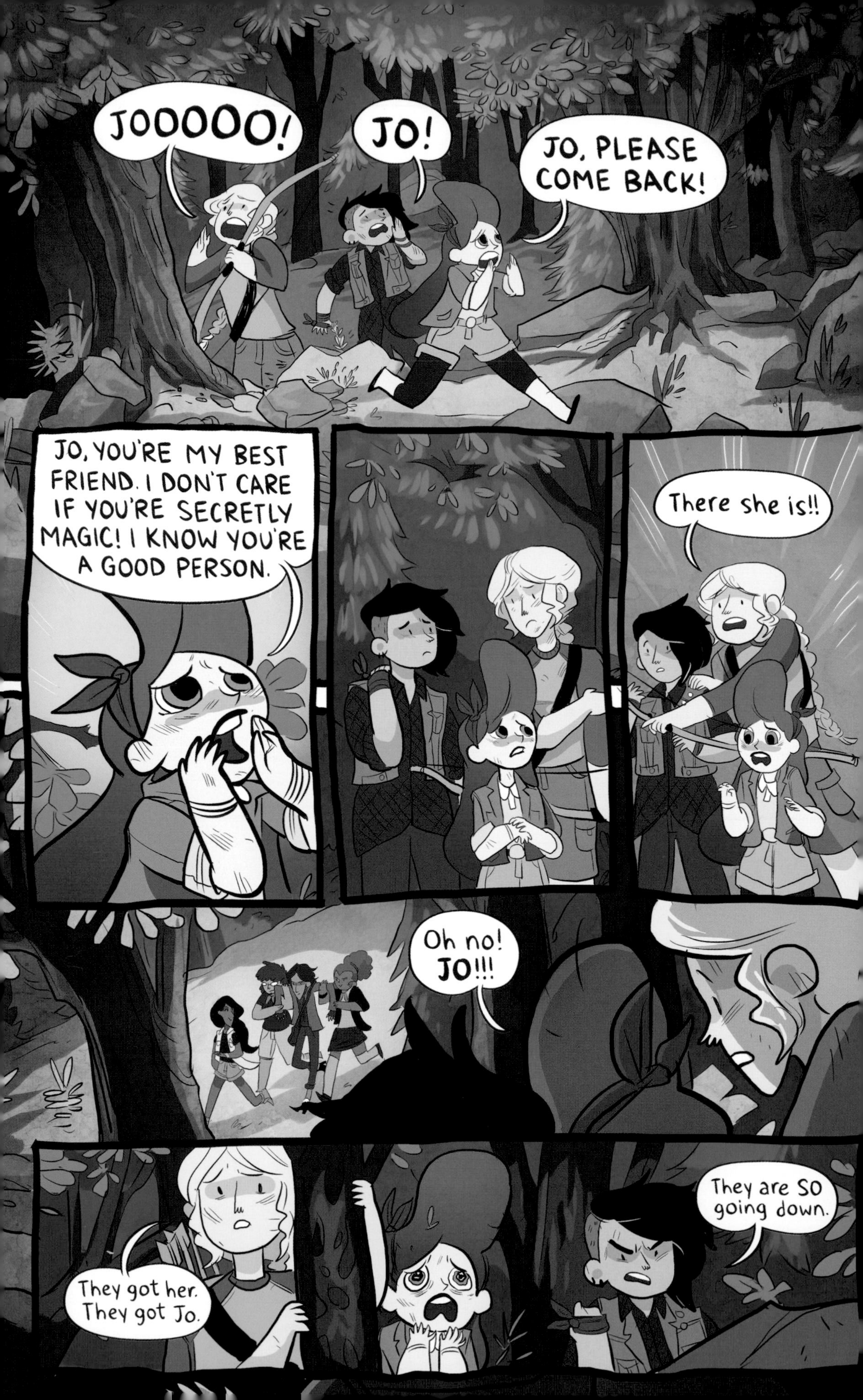
JOOOOO!
JO!
JO, PLEASE COME BACK!
JO, YOU'RE MY BEST FRIEND. I DON'T CARE IF YOU'RE SECRETLY MAGIC! I KNOW YOU'RE A GOOD PERSON.
There she is!!
Oh no! JO!!!
They got her. They got Jo.
They are SO going down.

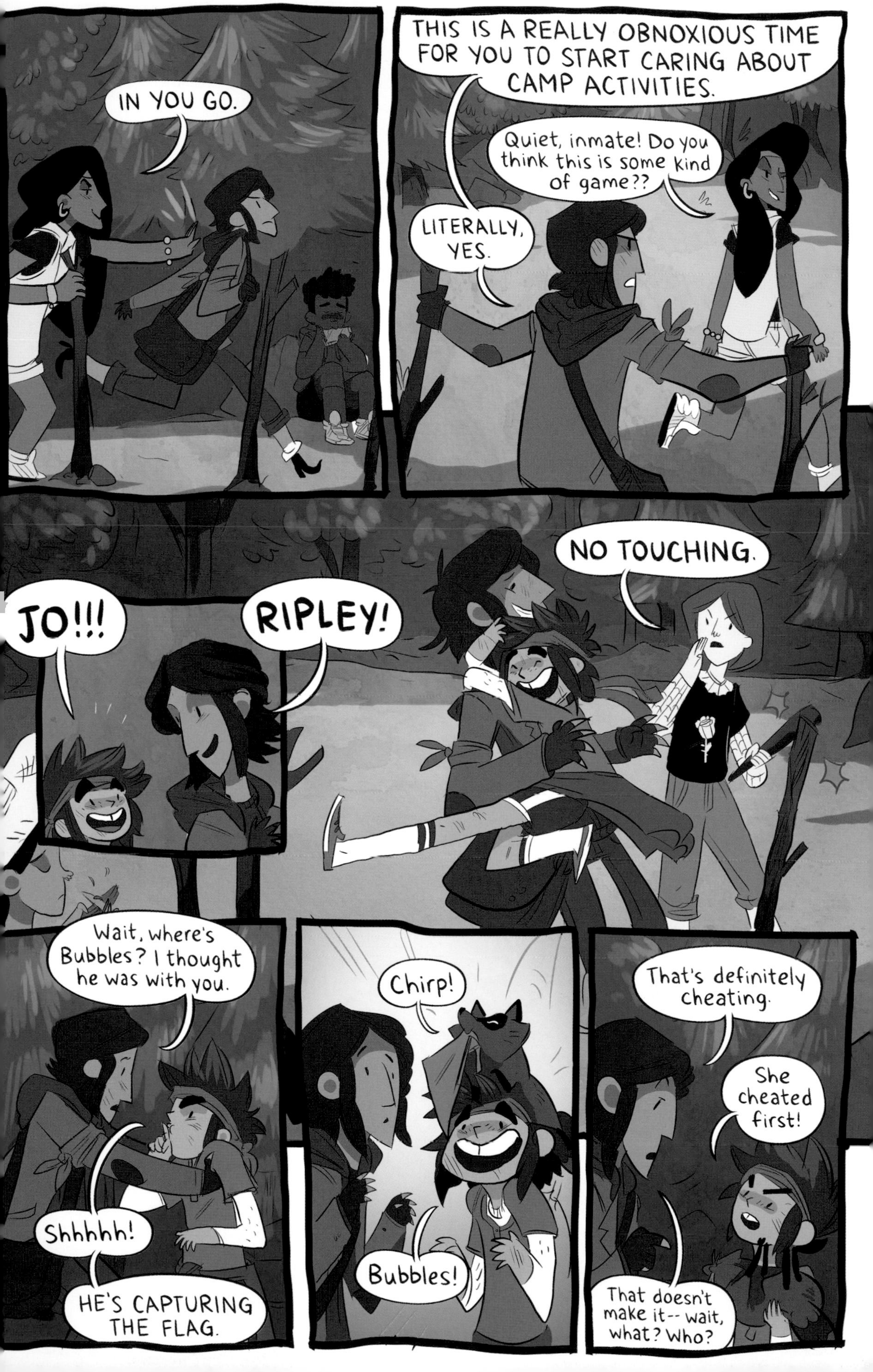
IN YOU GO.
THIS IS A REALLY OBNOXIOUS TIME FOR YOU TO START CARING ABOUT CAMP ACTIVITIES.
Quiet, inmate! Do you think this is some kind of game??
LITERALLY, YES.
JO!!!
RIPLEY!
NO TOUCHING.
Wait, where's Bubbles? I thought he was with you.
Shhhhh!
HE'S CAPTURING THE FLAG.
Chirp!
Bubbles!
That's definitely cheating.
She cheated first!
That doesn't make it-- wait, what? Who?

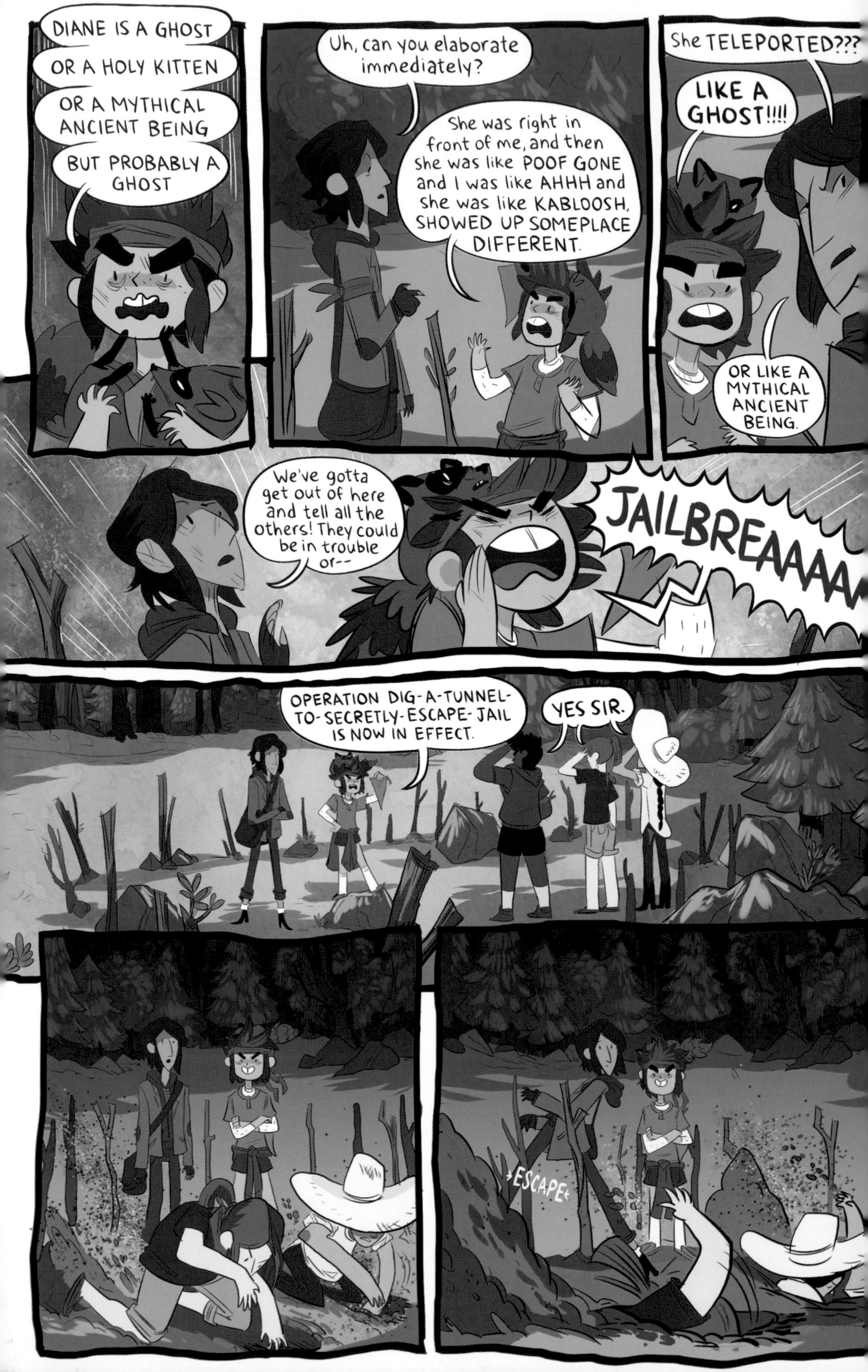
DIANE IS A GHOST
OR A HOLY KITTEN
OR A MYTHICAL ANCIENT BEING
BUT PROBABLY A GHOST
Uh, can you elaborate immediately?
She was right in front of me, and then she was like POOF GONE and I was like AHHH and she was like KABLOOSH, SHOWED UP SOMEPLACE DIFFERENT.
She TELEPORTED???
LIKE A GHOST!!!!
OR LIKE A MYTHICAL ANCIENT BEING.
We've gotta get out of here and tell all the others! They could be in trouble or--
JAILBREAAAAA
OPERATION DIG-A-TUNNEL-TO-SECRETLY-ESCAPE-JAIL IS NOW IN EFFECT.
YES SIR.
ESCAPE

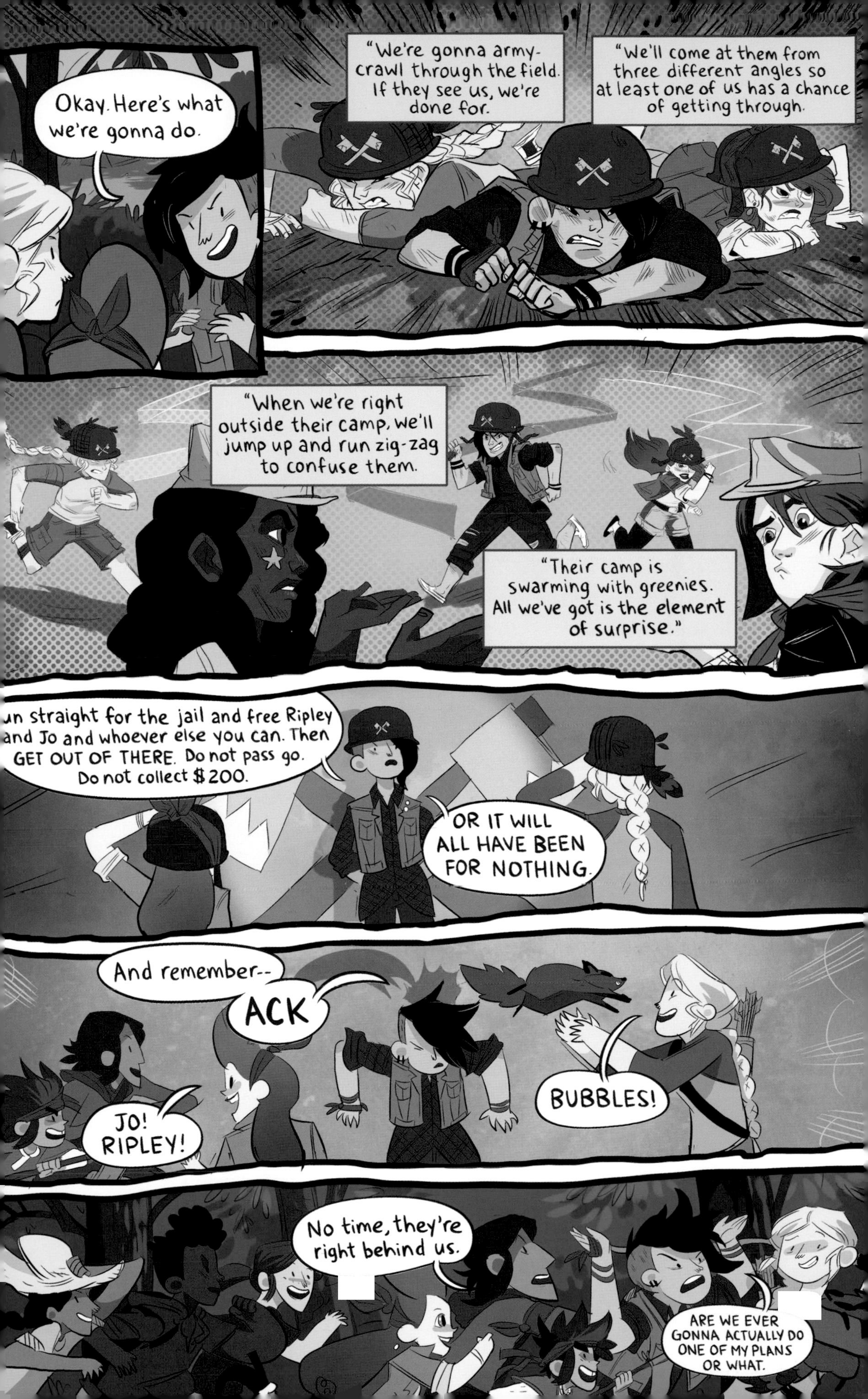
Okay. Here's what we're gonna do.
"We're gonna army-crawl through the field. If they see us, we're done for.
"We'll come at them from three different angles so at least one of us has a chance of getting through.
"When we're right outside their camp, we'll jump up and run zig-zag to confuse them.
"Their camp is swarming with greenies. All we've got is the element of surprise."
un straight for the jail and free Ripley and Jo and whoever else you can. Then GET OUT OF THERE. Do not pass go. Do not collect $200.
OR IT WILL ALL HAVE BEEN FOR NOTHING.
And remember--
ACK
JO! RIPLEY!
BUBBLES!
No time, they're right behind us.
ARE WE EVER GONNA ACTUALLY DO ONE OF MY PLANS OR WHAT.

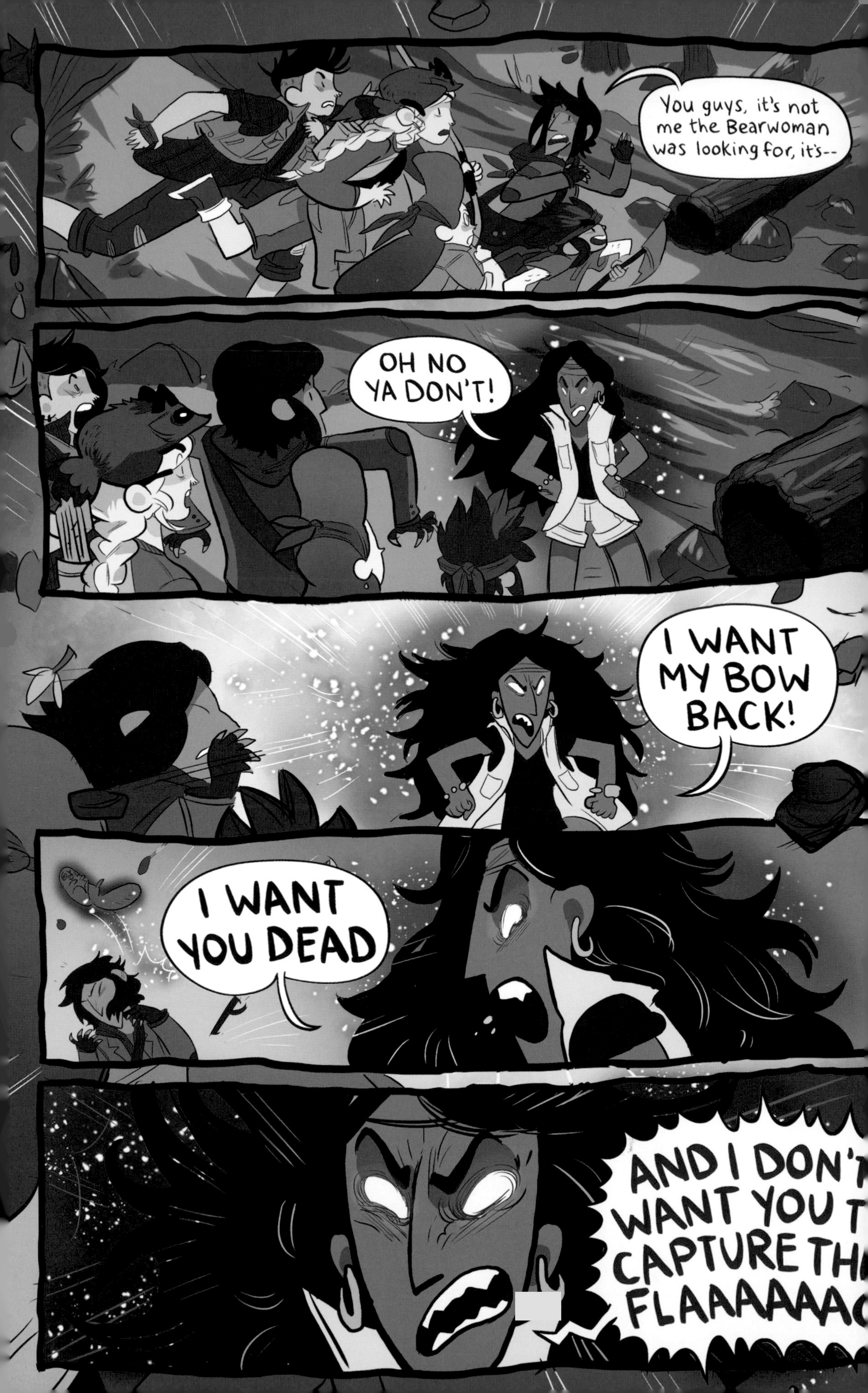
You guys, it's not me the Bearwoman was looking for, it's--
OH NO YA DON'T!
I WANT MY BOW BACK!
I WANT YOU DEAD
AND I DON' WANT YOU T CAPTURE TH FLAAAAAA

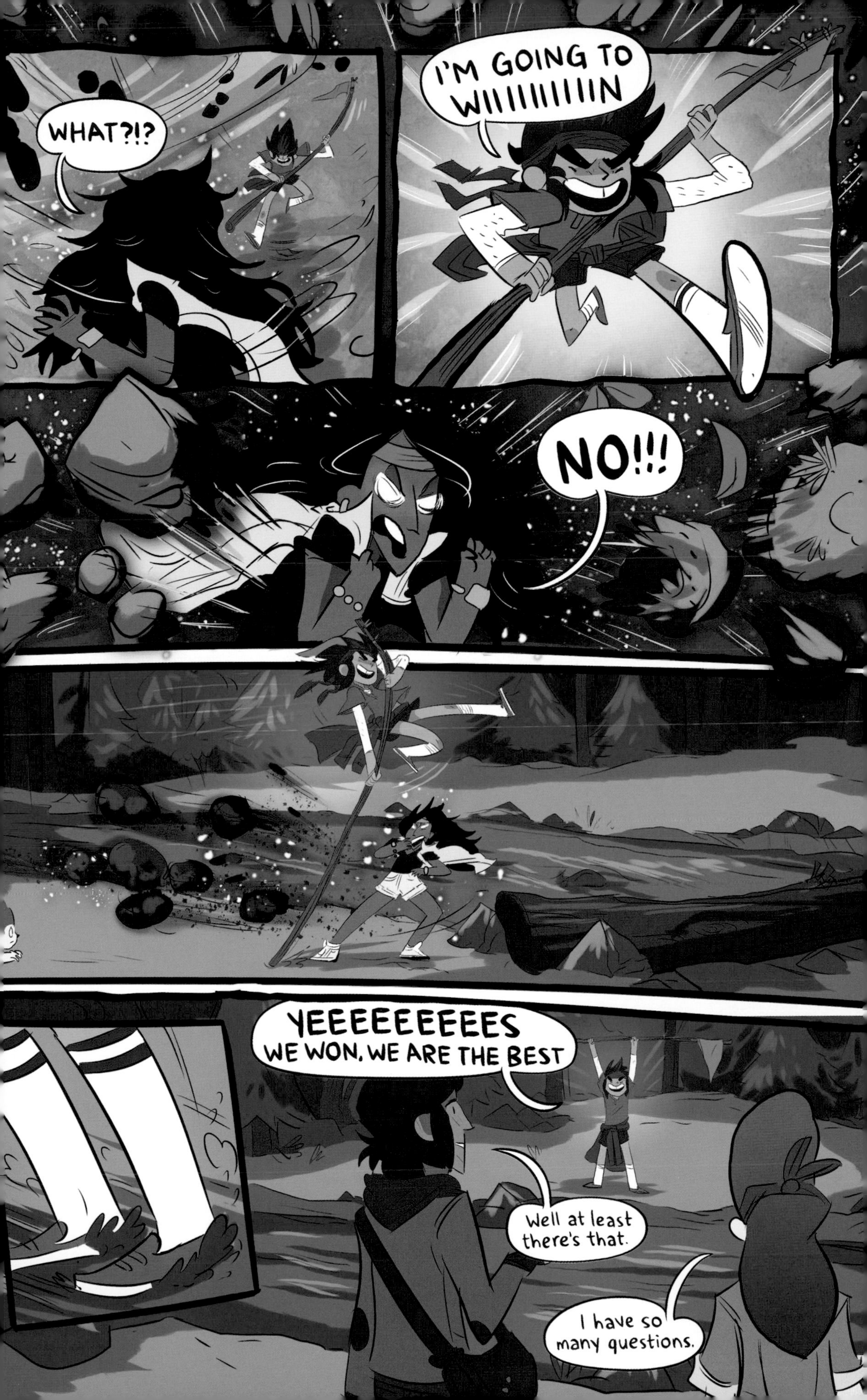
WHAT?!?
I'M GOING TO WIIIIIIIIIN
NO!!!
YEEEEEEEEES
WE WON. WE ARE THE BEST
Well at least there's that.
I have so many questions.

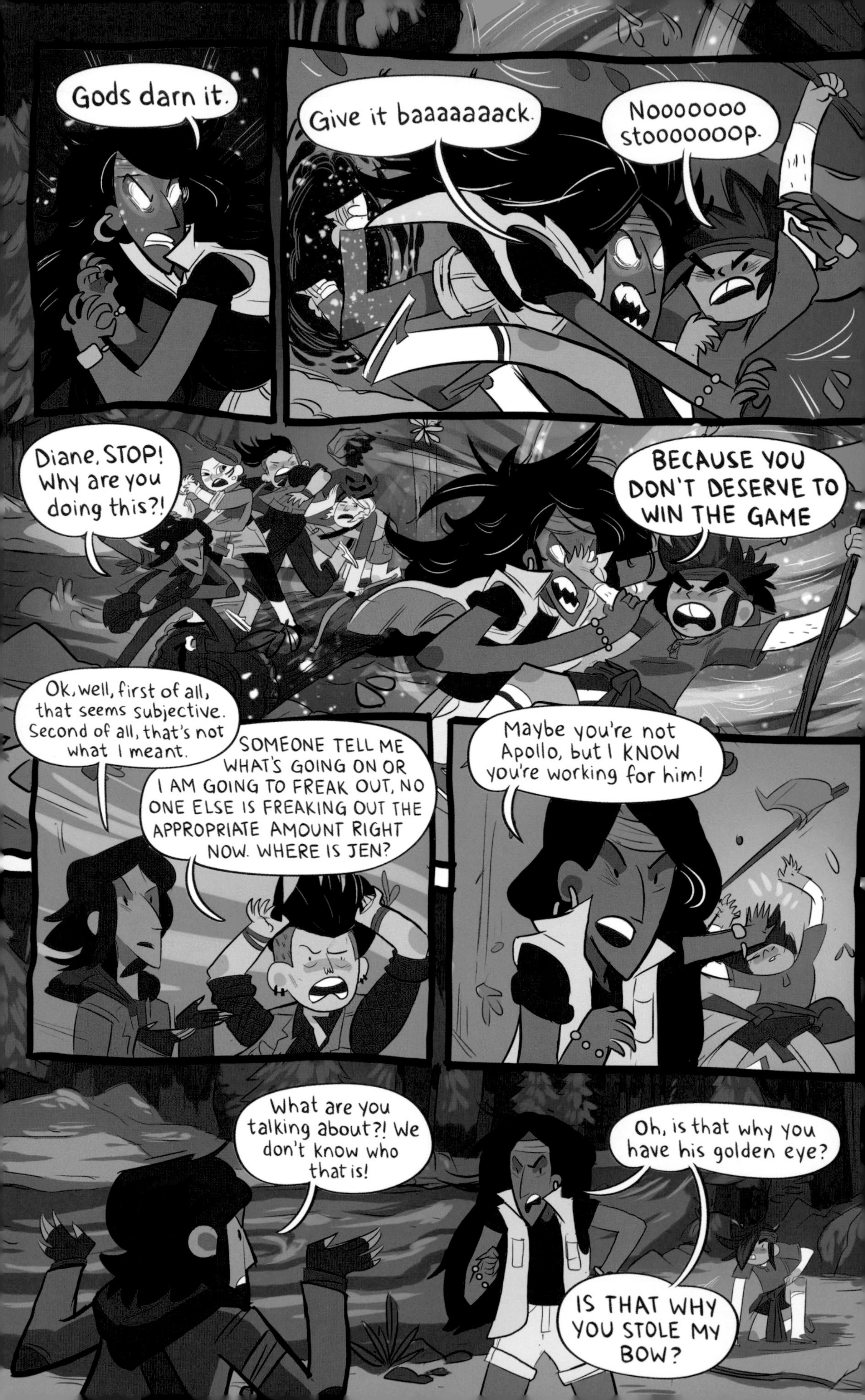
Gods darn it.
Give it baaaaaaack.
Nooooooo stoooooooop.
Diane, STOP! Why are you doing this?!
BECAUSE YOU DON'T DESERVE TO WIN THE GAME
Ok, well, first of all, that seems subjective. Second of all, that's not what I meant.
SOMEONE TELL ME WHAT'S GOING ON OR I AM GOING TO FREAK OUT, NO ONE ELSE IS FREAKING OUT THE APPROPRIATE AMOUNT RIGHT NOW. WHERE IS JEN?
Maybe you're not Apollo, but I KNOW you're working for him!
What are you talking about?! We don't know who that is!
Oh, is that why you have his golden eye?
IS THAT WHY YOU STOLE MY BOW?

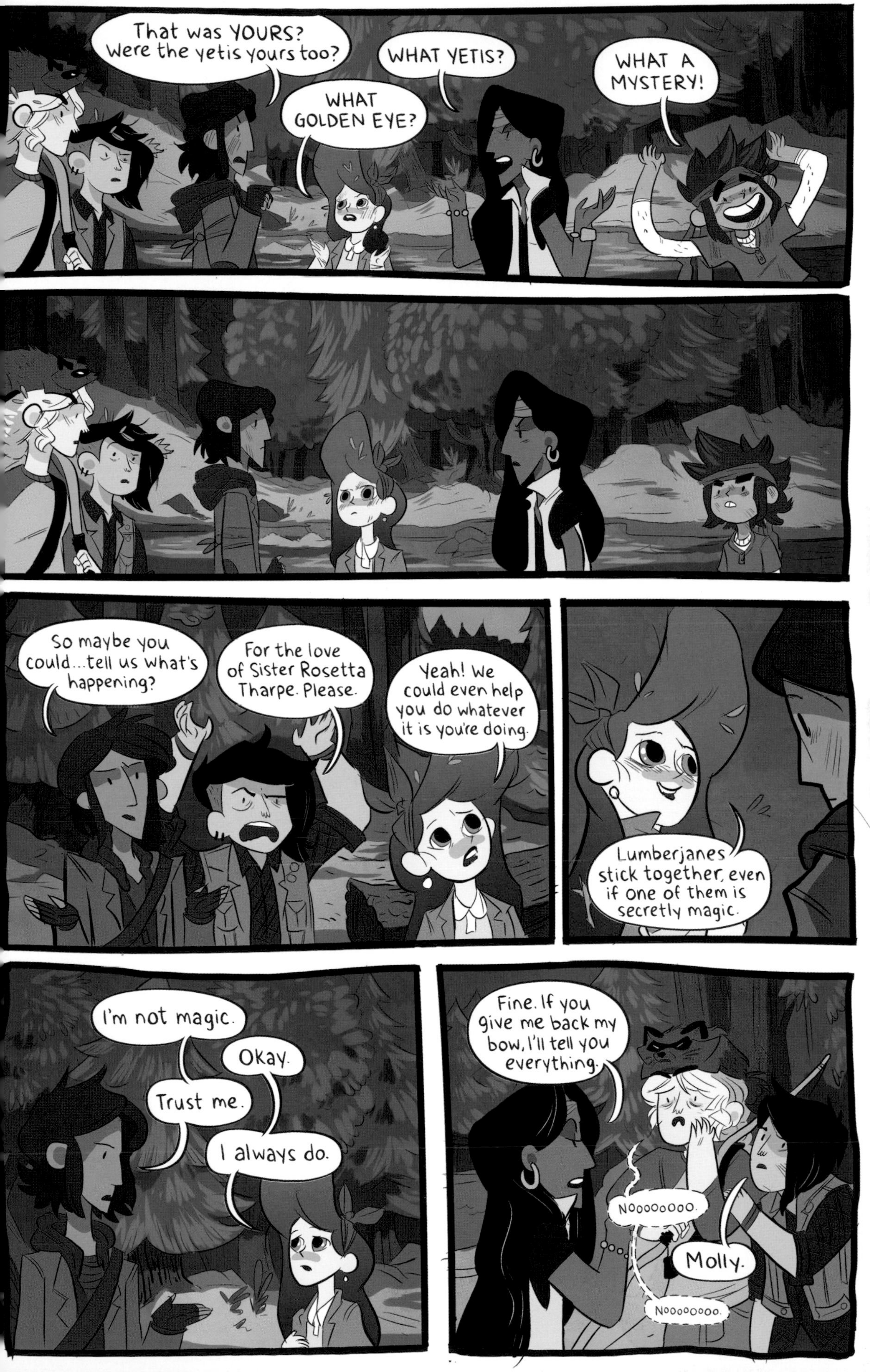

That was YOURS? Were the yetis yours too?
WHAT GOLDEN EYE?
WHAT YETIS?
WHAT A MYSTERY!
So maybe you could...tell us what's happening?
For the love of Sister Rosetta Tharpe. Please.
Yeah! We could even help you do whatever it is you're doing.
Lumberjanes stick together, even if one of them is secretly magic.
I'm not magic.
Okay.
Trust me.
I always do.
Fine. If you give me back my bow, I'll tell you everything.
Nooooooo.
Molly.
Nooooooo.

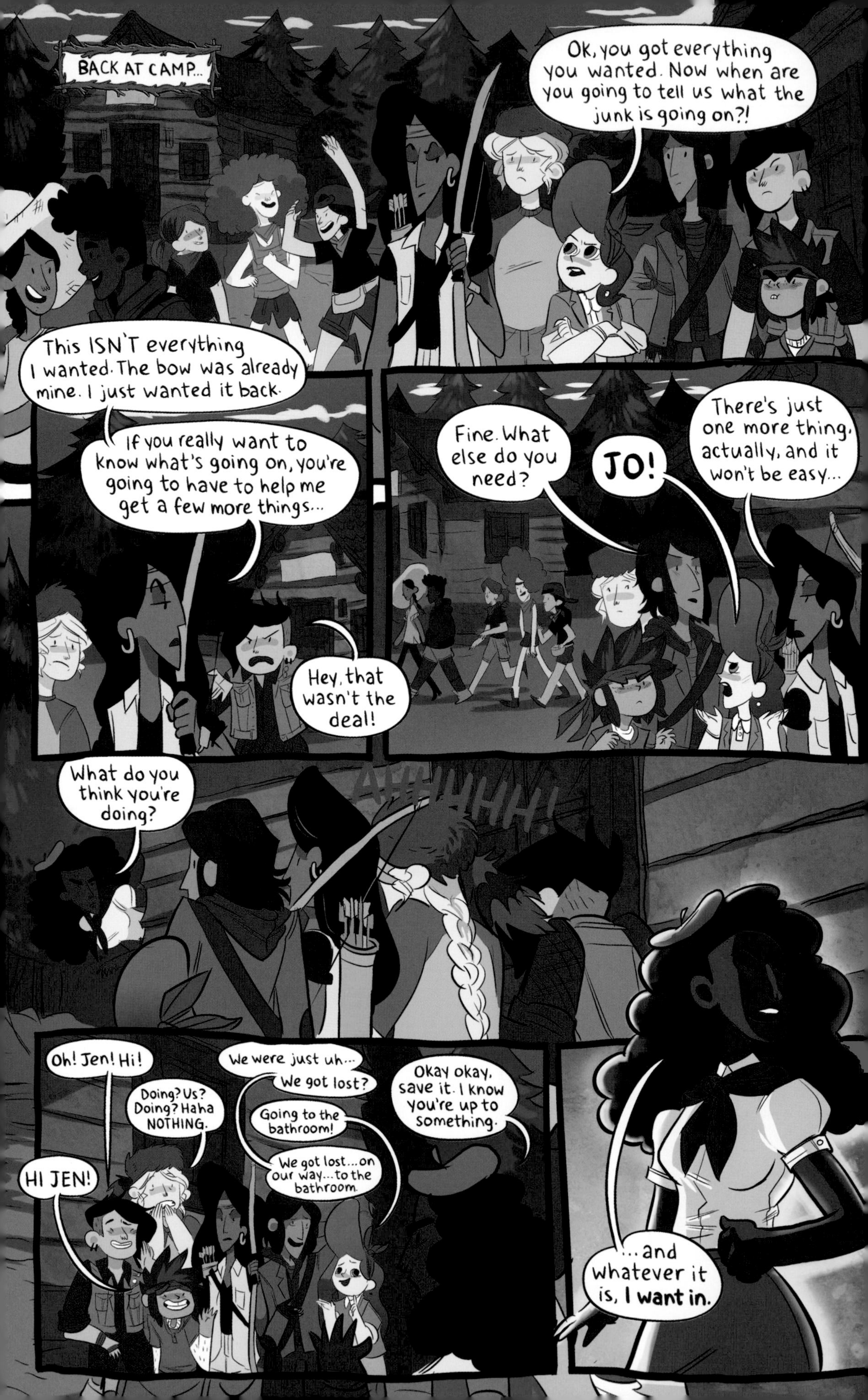

BACK AT CAMP...
Ok, you got everything you wanted. Now when are you going to tell us what the junk is going on?!
This ISN'T everything I wanted. The bow was already mine. I just wanted it back.
If you really want to know what's going on, you're going to have to help me get a few more things...
Hey, that wasn't the deal!
Fine. What else do you need?
JO!
There's just one more thing, actually, and it won't be easy...
What do you think you're doing?
Oh! Jen! Hi!
Doing? Us? Doing? Haha NOTHING.
HI JEN!
We were just uh...
We got lost?
Going to the bathroom!
We got lost... on our way... to the bathroom.
Okay okay, save it. I know you're up to something.
...and whatever it is, I want in.

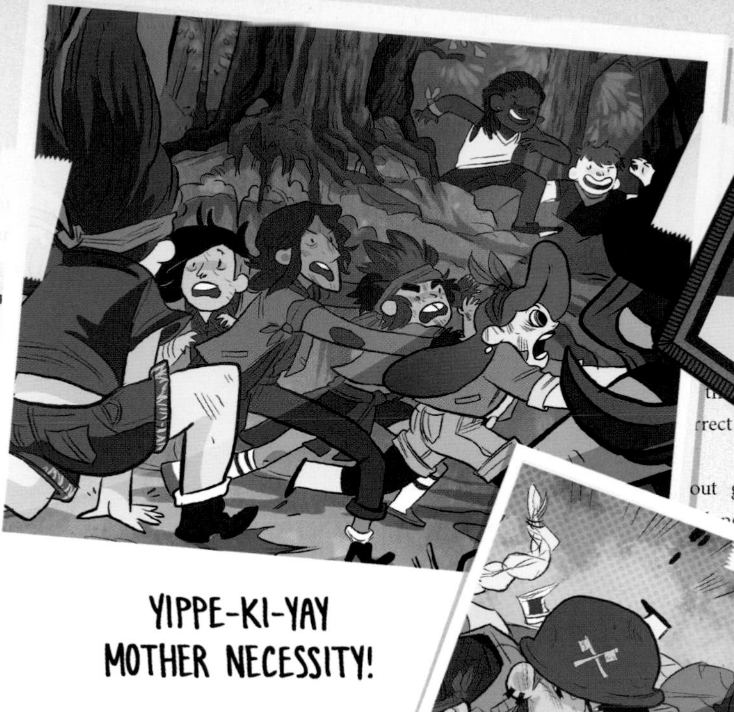
YIPPE-KI-YAY
MOTHER NECESSITY!

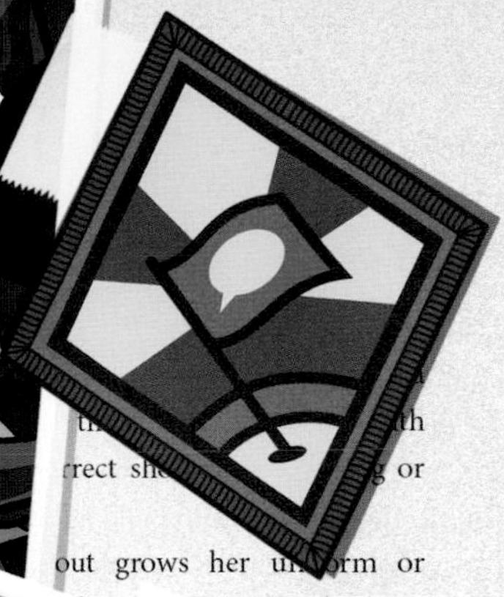

will co

The u
It help
appeara
dress f
Further
Lumbe
to have
part in
Thiskv
Hardc
have
them

th
rrect sh g or
out grows her un rm or
ter Lumberjane.
a she has
her
her

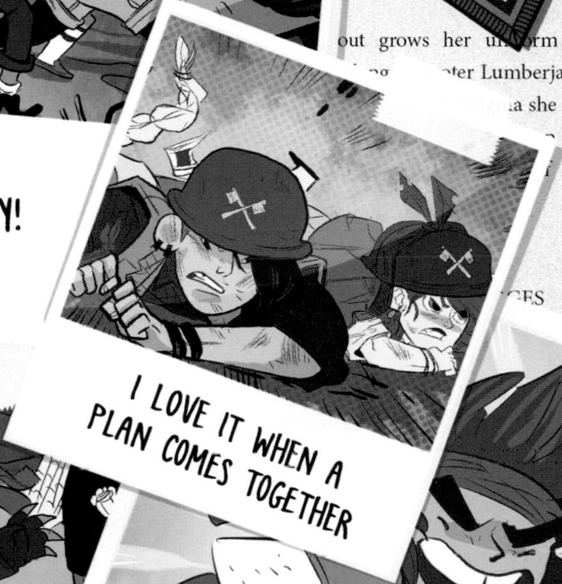
I LOVE IT WHEN A
PLAN COMES TOGETHER

The
yellow, short
emb
the w
choose
slacks,
made o
out-of-dc
green bere
the colla
Shoes ma
heels, rou ... ngs or
socks shou ... ith the shoes or wi
the uniform. Ne ... es, bracelets, or other jewelry do
belong with a Lumberjane uniform.

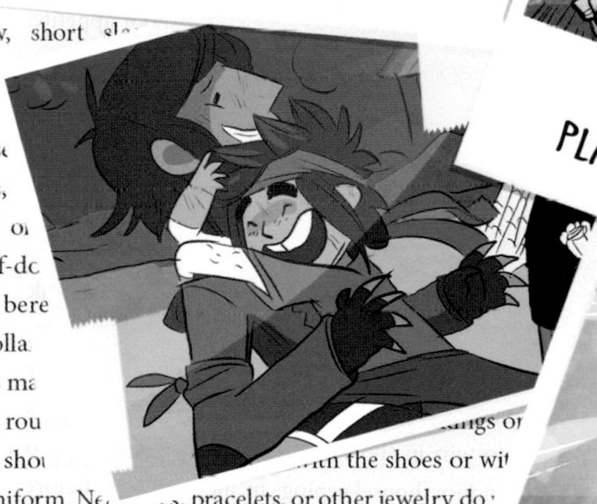

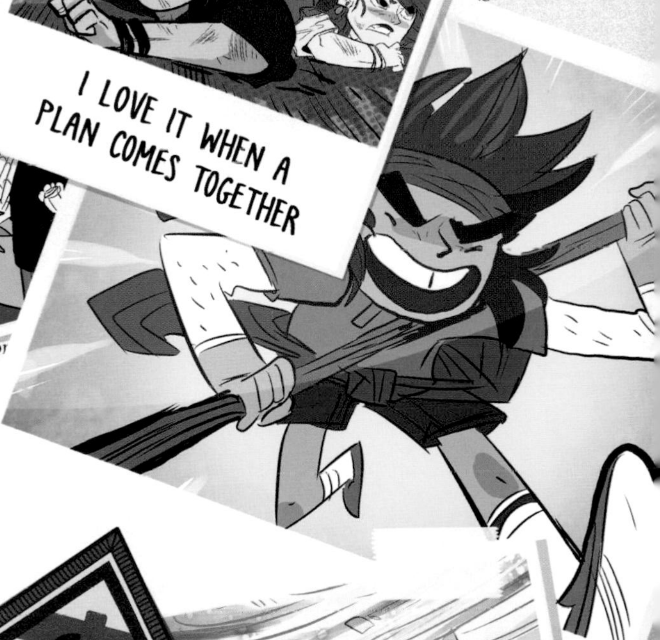

HOW TO WEAR THE UNIFORM

To look well in a uniform demans first of
uniform be kept in good condition—clean
pressed. See that the skirt is the right length
height and build, that the belt is adjusted to
that your shoes and stockings are in keeping
uniform, that you watch your posture and carry
with dignity and grace. If the beret is removed in
be sure that your hair is neat and kept in place wi
insonspicuous clip or ribbon. When you wear
Lumberjane uniform you are identified as a member
this organization and you should be doubly careful to conduct yourself in a way that will show everyone that courtesy and thoughtfullness are part of being a Lumberjane. People are likely to judge a whole nation by the selfishness of a few individuals, to criticize a whole family because of the misconduct of one member, and to feel unkindly toward and organization because of the

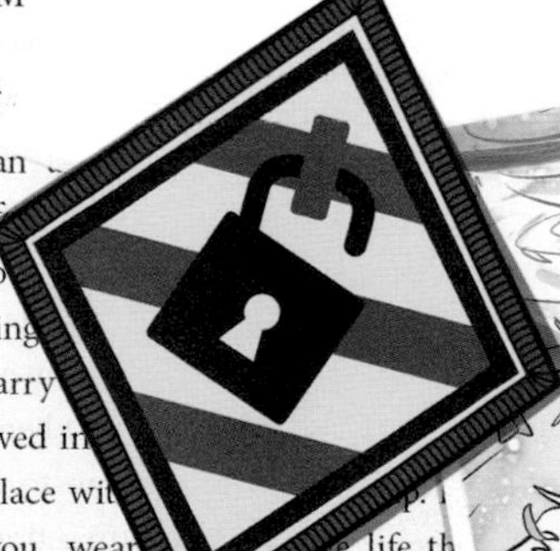

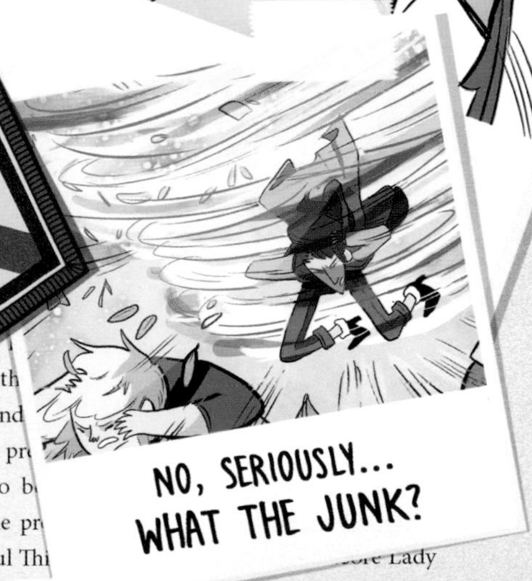
NO, SERIOUSLY...
WHAT THE JUNK?

e life th
another bond
future, and pr
in order to b
Lumberjane pr
Penniquiqul Th ... ore Lady
Types, but m ... s will wish to have one. They
can either bu ... uniform, or make it themselves from
materials available at the trading post.

LUMBERJANES FIELD MANUAL

# CHAPTER SEVEN

*Lumberjanes "Community" Program Field*

## FRIENDSHIP TO THE MAX

*"Together forever."*

There are many things that a Lumberjane will learn while at camp, she will learn how to care for the wildlife available to her and how to use it to better her life and those around her. She will learn the importance of social customs and manners, while at the same time enjoying the chance to break the boundaries that society might place upon her. A Lumberjane will learn how to start a fire, she will learn how to survive in the harsh climates, and learn basic healing necessities to ensure good health for herself and her companions. Above all else, a Lumberjane will learn what it means to be a friend.

The *Friendship to the Max* badge is not just another step for a Lumberjane on her personal journey in camp but something much more. 'Friendship to the Max!' is the camp slogan and it has stood the test of time as the most valuable lesson a Lumberjane will ever learn in her time here. She will be taught everything she needs

to know on how to survive on her own in nature, she will be taught how to stand on her own two feet when she returns home. No matter what she might face there will always be friendship and friendship is something a Lumberjane will teach herself.

To obtain the *Friendship to the Max* badge, a Lumberjane must be able to prove that she not only values the faith and friendship that others have given her but that she truly understands what it means to be a friend. She will put her friends before her without neglecting herself, she will not take advantage of her friends and will be able to show her loyalty and dedication to them not only through her words but her actions. Her fellow Lumberjanes will understand what it means to be a true friend by following her example. The lesson from this badge is something a Lumberjane will take with her for the rest of her life as she learns to understand the

SCRATCH SCRATCH
Mama Bear is in the den. I repeat, Mama Bear is in the den.
Roger that, Yellowtail. Get in position.
Oh gosh this is such a bad idea we are so going to get caught oh gosh oh gosh.
RINGWALD HIGH PHYSICS CLUB

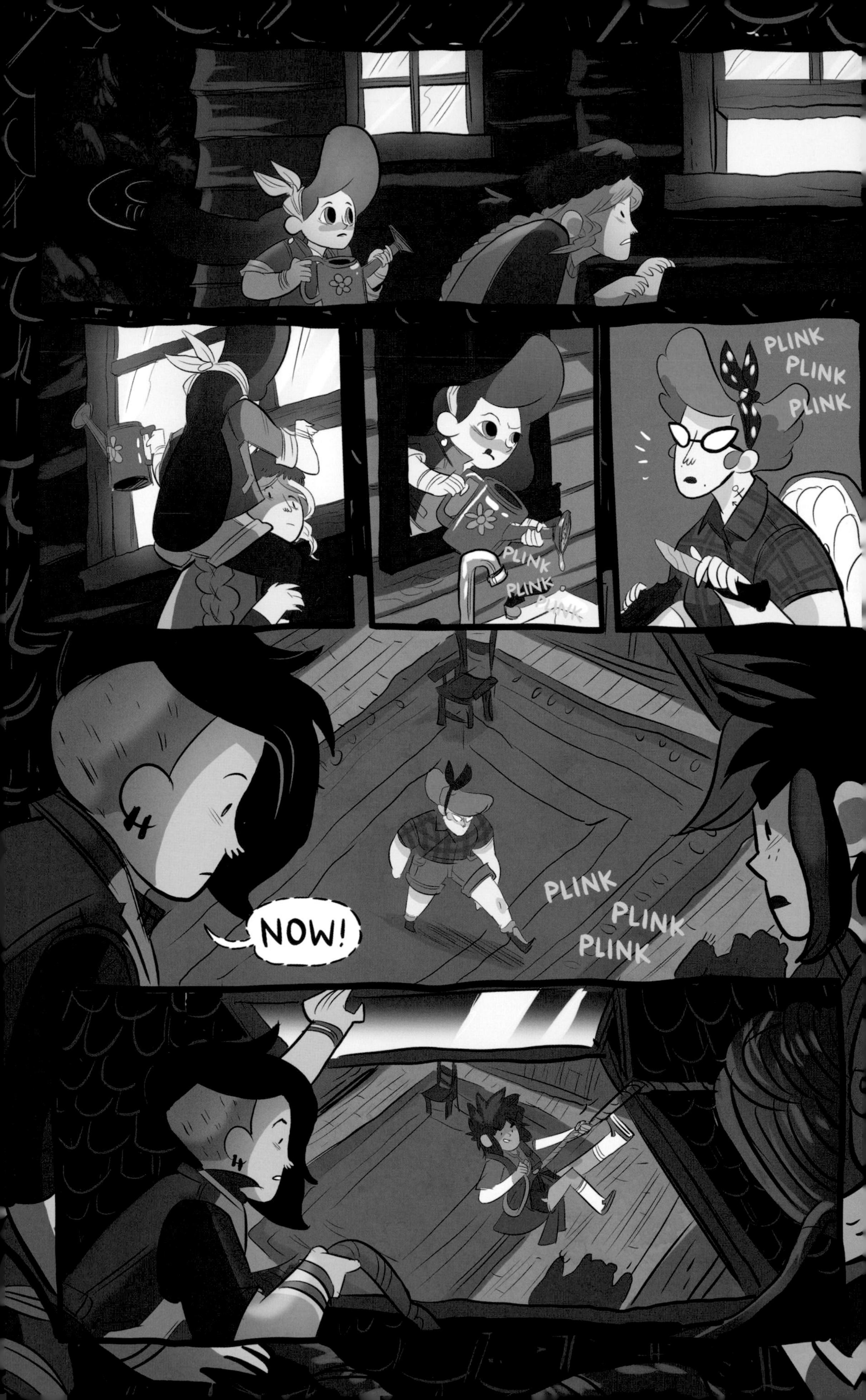
PLINK
PLINK
PLINK
PLINK
PLINK
PLINK
NOW!
PLINK
PLINK
PLINK

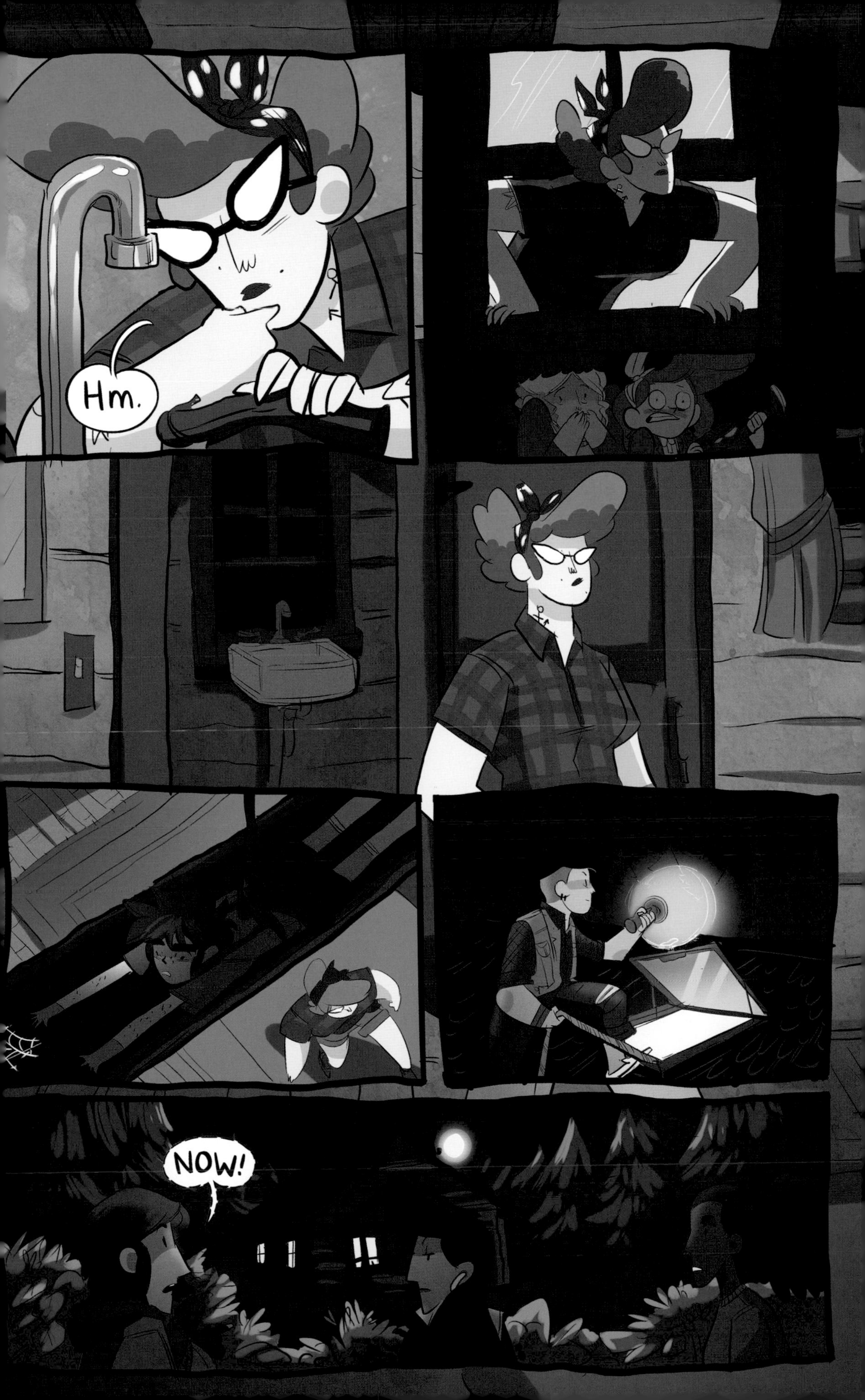
Hm.
NOW!

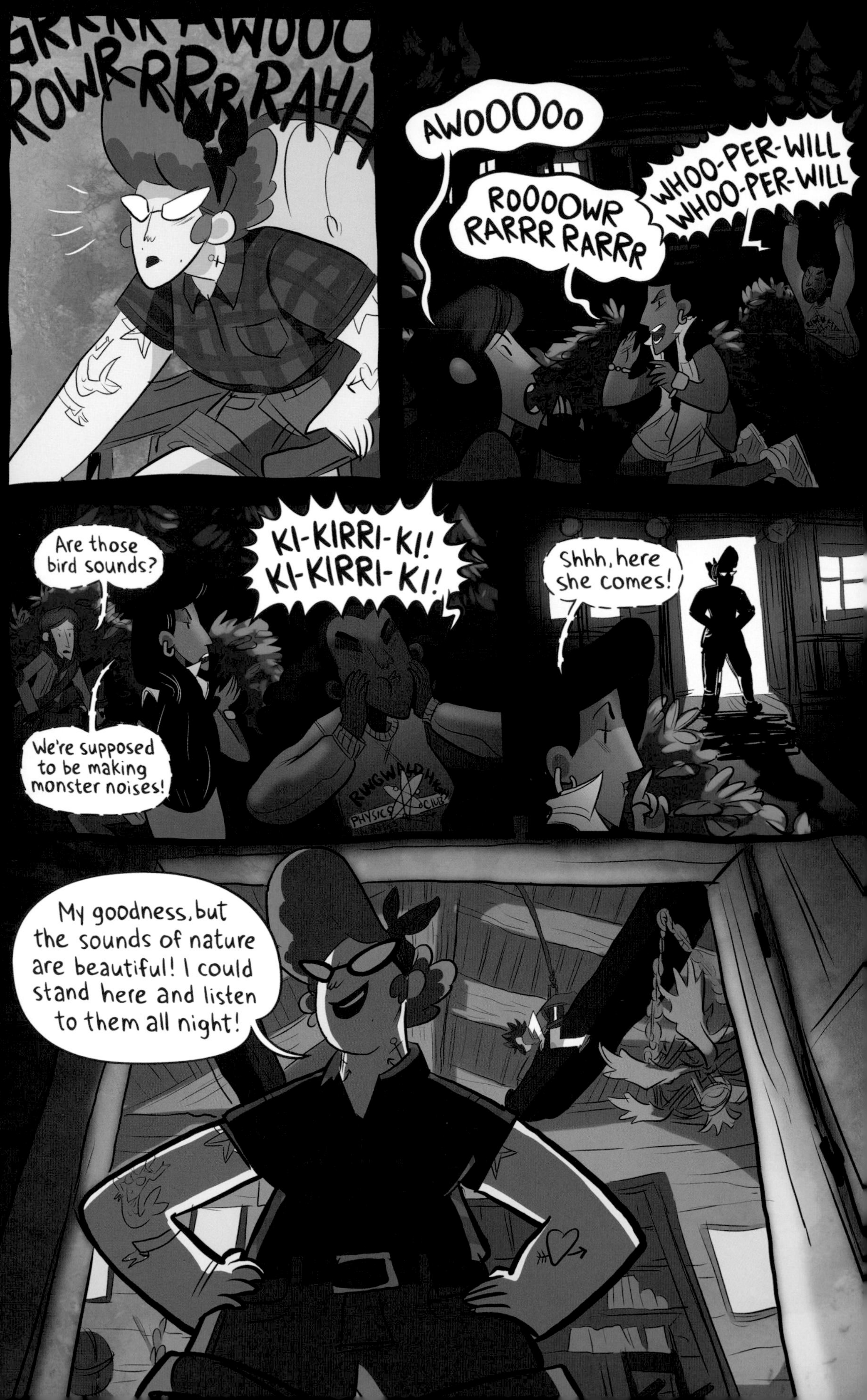
GRRRR AWOOO
ROWR RRRR RAHH
AWOOOOo
ROOOOWR RARRR RARRR
WHOO-PER-WILL WHOO-PER-WILL
Are those bird sounds?
KI-KIRRI-KI! KI-KIRRI-KI!
We're supposed to be making monster noises!
RINGWALD HIGH PHYSICS CLUB
Shhh, here she comes!
My goodness, but the sounds of nature are beautiful! I could stand here and listen to them all night!

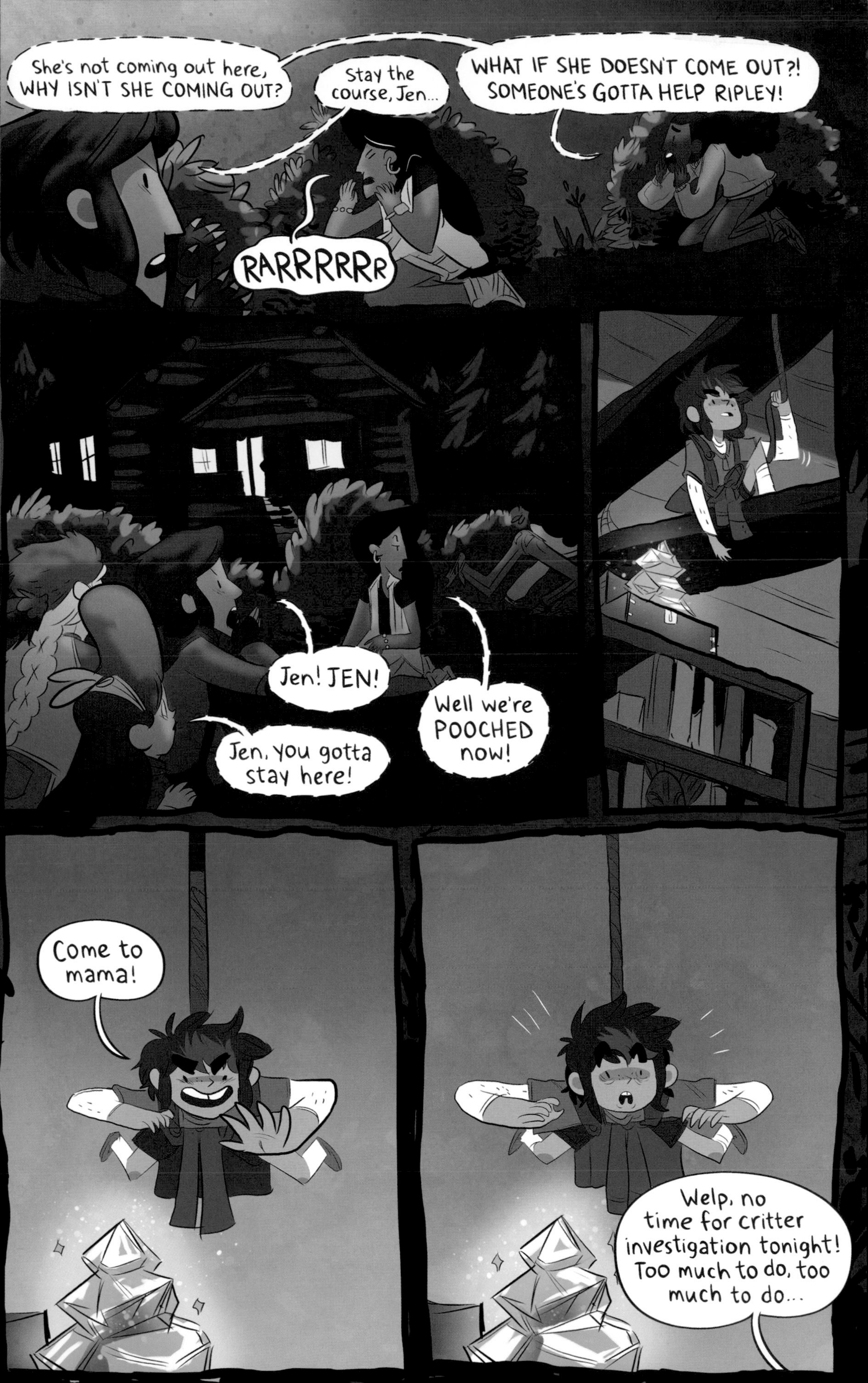
She's not coming out here, WHY ISN'T SHE COMING OUT?
Stay the course, Jen...
WHAT IF SHE DOESN'T COME OUT?! SOMEONE'S GOTTA HELP RIPLEY!
RARRRRRR
Jen! JEN!
Jen, you gotta stay here!
Well we're POOCHED now!
Come to mama!
Welp, no time for critter investigation tonight! Too much to do, too much to do...

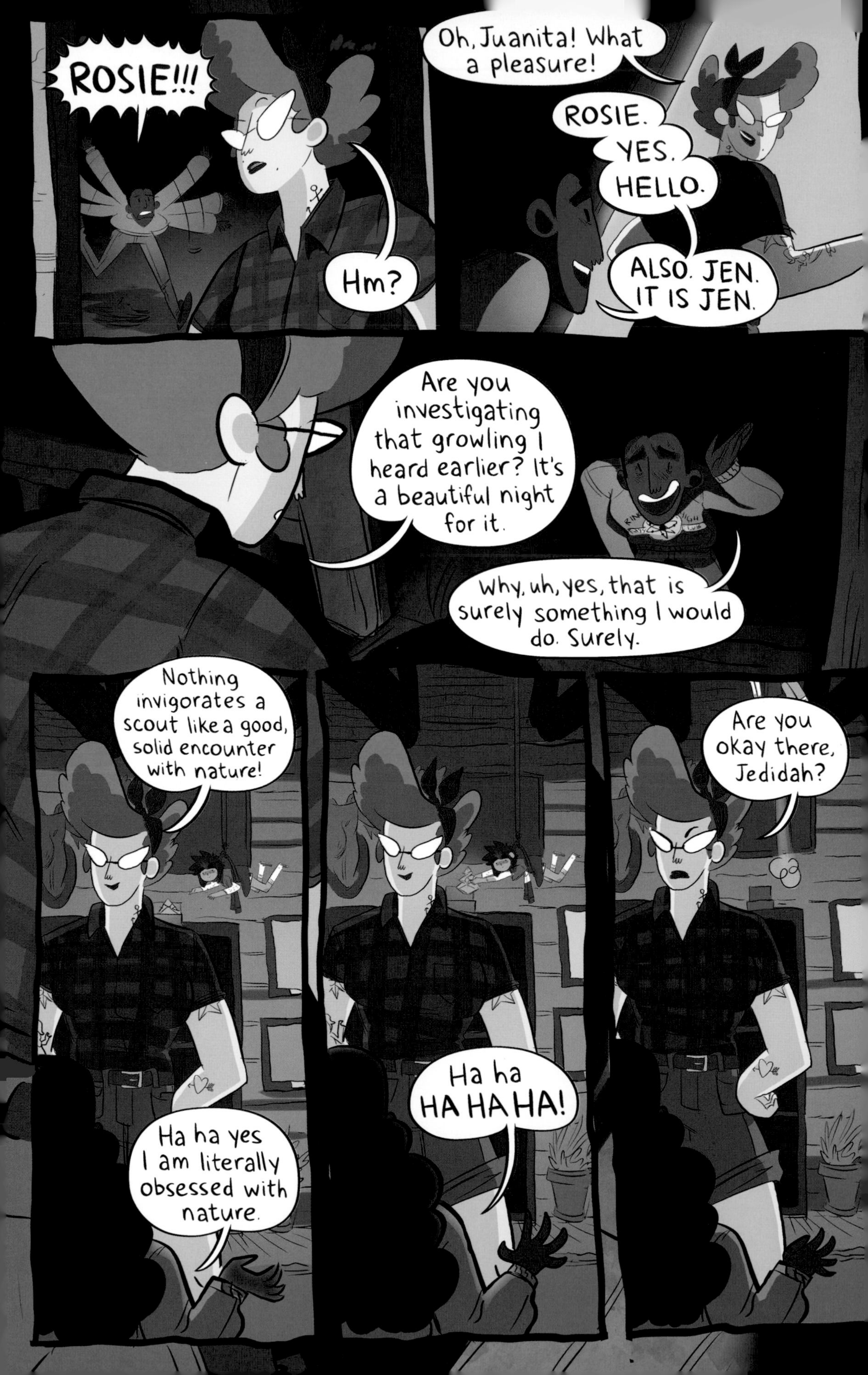
ROSIE!!!
Hm?
Oh, Juanita! What a pleasure!
ROSIE.
YES.
HELLO.
ALSO. JEN. IT IS JEN.
Are you investigating that growling I heard earlier? It's a beautiful night for it.
Why, uh, yes, that is surely something I would do. Surely.
Nothing invigorates a scout like a good, solid encounter with nature!
Ha ha yes I am literally obsessed with nature.
Ha ha HA HA HA!
Are you okay there, Jedidah?

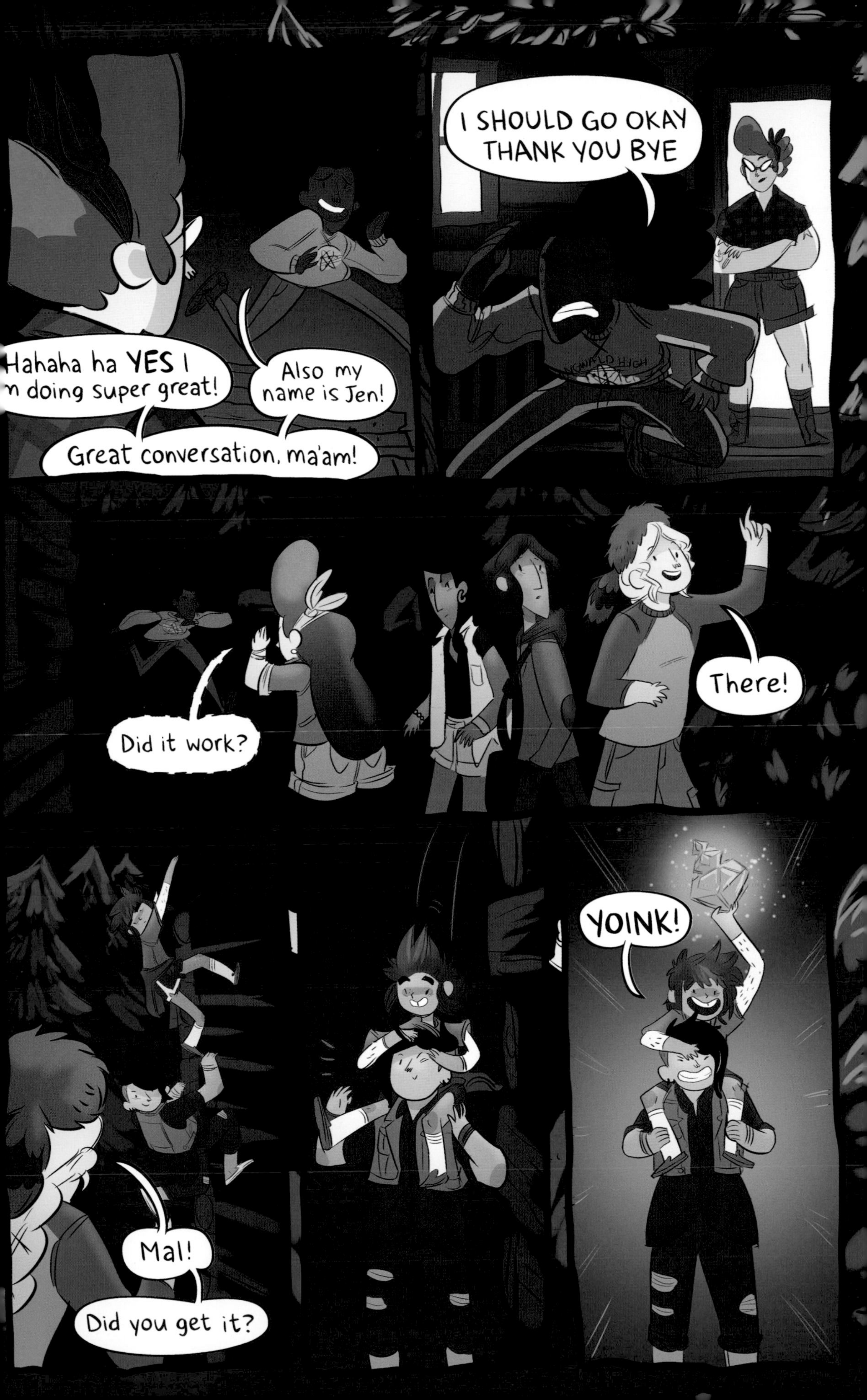
Hahaha ha YES I
m doing super great!
Also my name is Jen!
Great conversation, ma'am!
I SHOULD GO OKAY THANK YOU BYE
Did it work?
There!
Mal!
Did you get it?
YOINK!

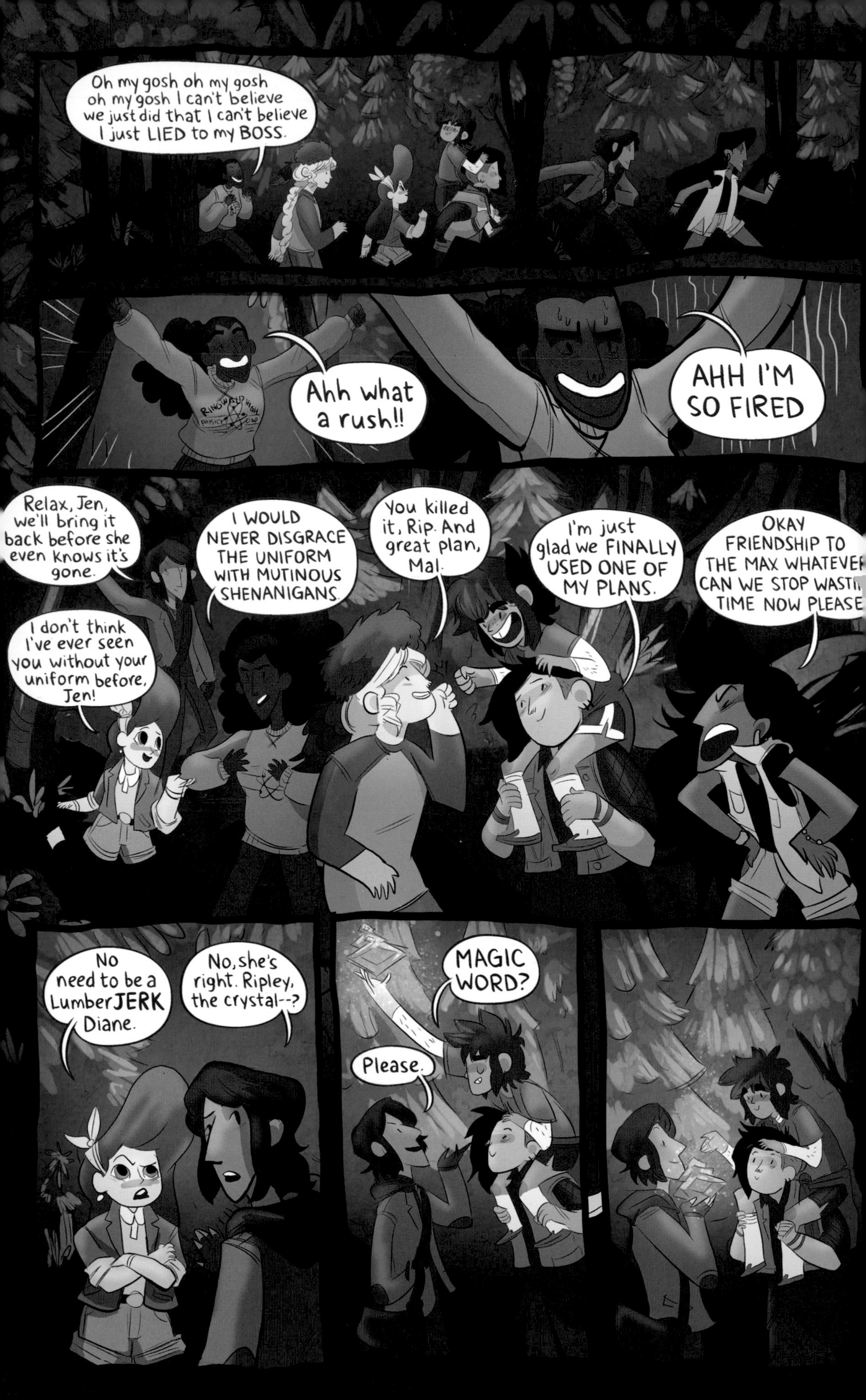

Oh my gosh oh my gosh oh my gosh I can't believe we just did that I can't believe I just LIED to my BOSS.
Ahh what a rush!!
AHH I'M SO FIRED
Relax, Jen, we'll bring it back before she even knows it's gone.
I WOULD NEVER DISGRACE THE UNIFORM WITH MUTINOUS SHENANIGANS.
I don't think I've ever seen you without your uniform before, Jen!
You killed it, Rip. And great plan, Mal.
I'm just glad we FINALLY USED ONE OF MY PLANS.
OKAY FRIENDSHIP TO THE MAX WHATEVER CAN WE STOP WASTING TIME NOW PLEASE
No need to be a LumberJERK Diane.
No, she's right. Ripley, the crystal--?
MAGIC WORD?
Please.

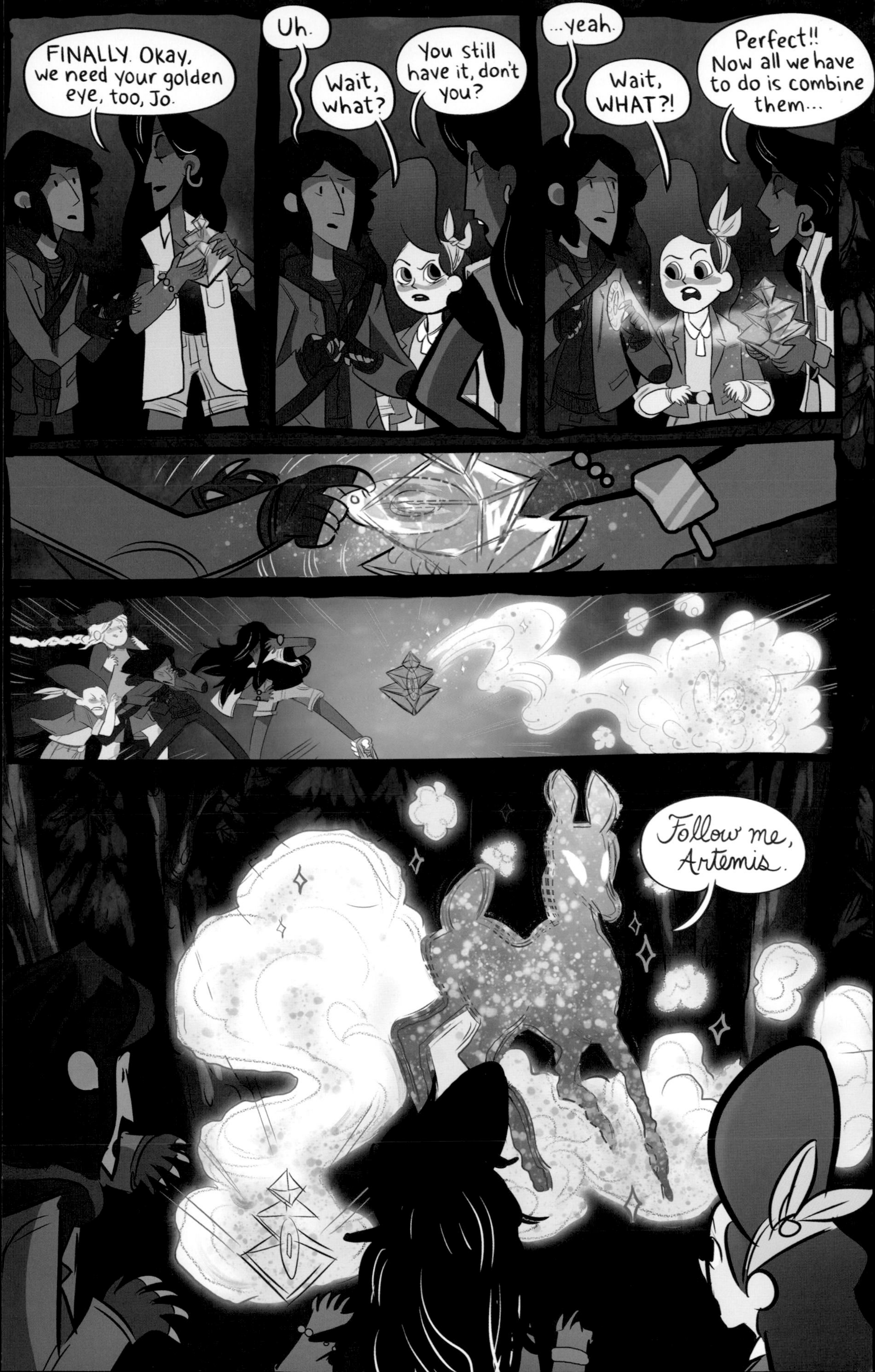
FINALLY. Okay, we need your golden eye, too, Jo.
Uh.
Wait, what?
You still have it, don't you?
...yeah.
Wait, WHAT?!
Perfect!! Now all we have to do is combine them...
Follow me, Artemis.

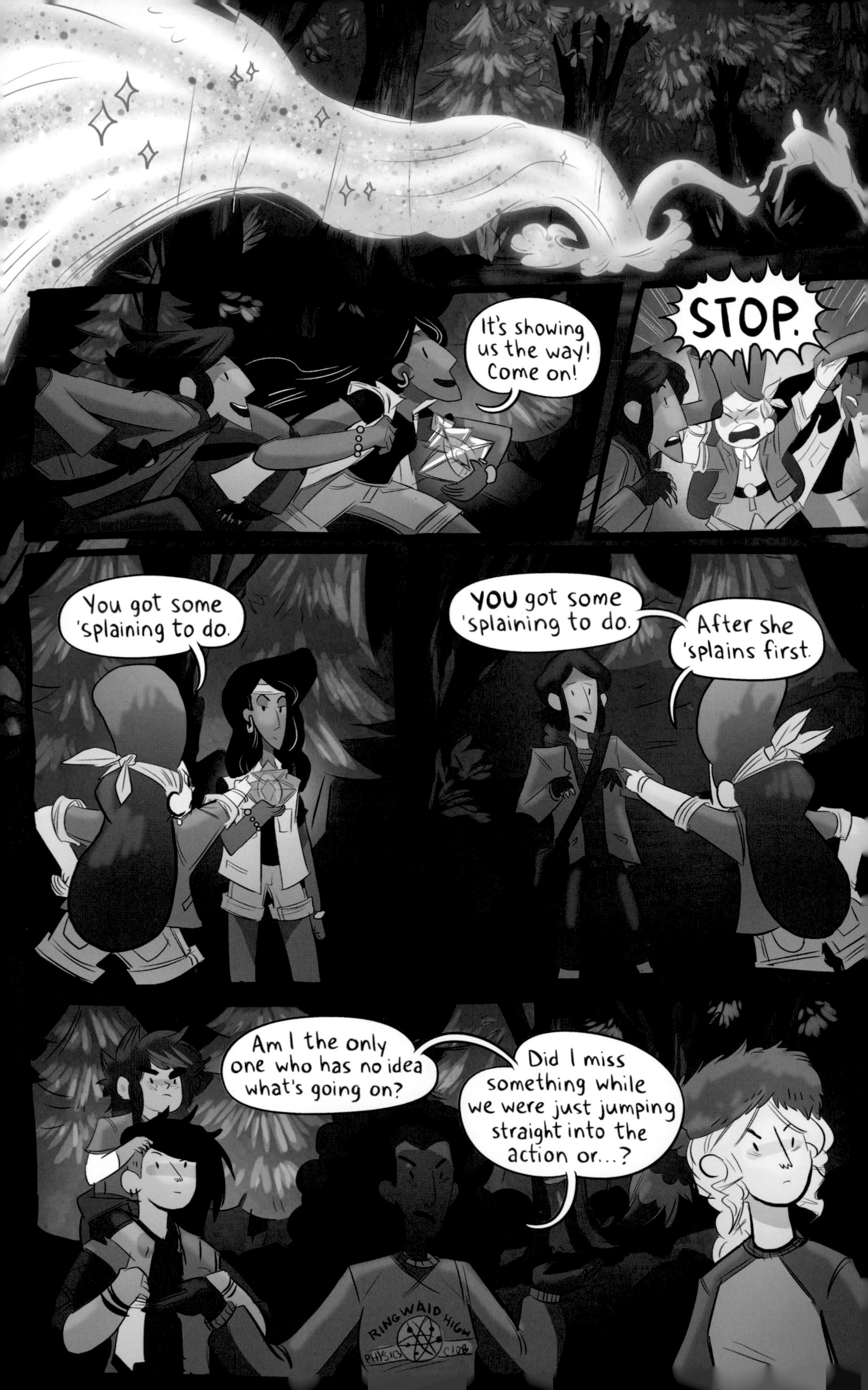

It's showing us the way! Come on!
STOP.
You got some 'splaining to do.
YOU got some 'splaining to do.
After she 'splains first.
Am I the only one who has no idea what's going on?
Did I miss something while we were just jumping straight into the action or...?
RINGWAID HIGH PHYSICS CLUB

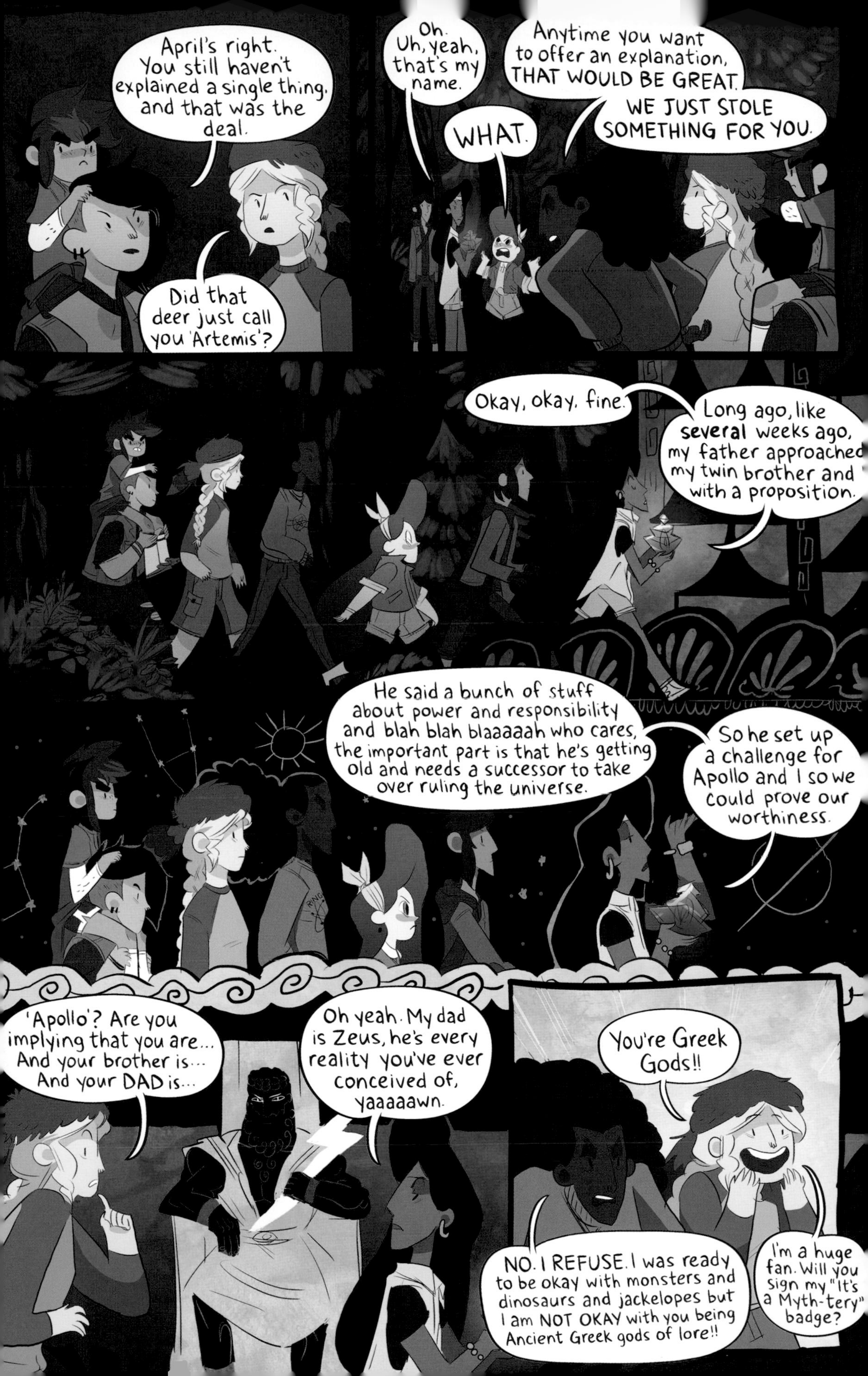
April's right. You still haven't explained a single thing, and that was the deal.
Did that deer just call you 'Artemis'?
Oh. Uh, yeah, that's my name.
WHAT.
Anytime you want to offer an explanation, THAT WOULD BE GREAT.
WE JUST STOLE SOMETHING FOR YOU.
Okay, okay, fine.
Long ago, like **several** weeks ago, my father approached my twin brother and with a proposition.
He said a bunch of stuff about power and responsibility and blah blah blaaaaah who cares, the important part is that he's getting old and needs a successor to take over ruling the universe.
So he set up a challenge for Apollo and I so we could prove our worthiness.
'Apollo'? Are you implying that you are... And your brother is... And your DAD is...
Oh yeah. My dad is Zeus, he's every reality you've ever conceived of, yaaaaawn.
You're Greek Gods!!
NO. I REFUSE. I was ready to be okay with monsters and dinosaurs and jackelopes but I am NOT OKAY with you being Ancient Greek gods of lore!!
I'm a huge fan. Will you sign my "It's a Myth-tery" badge?

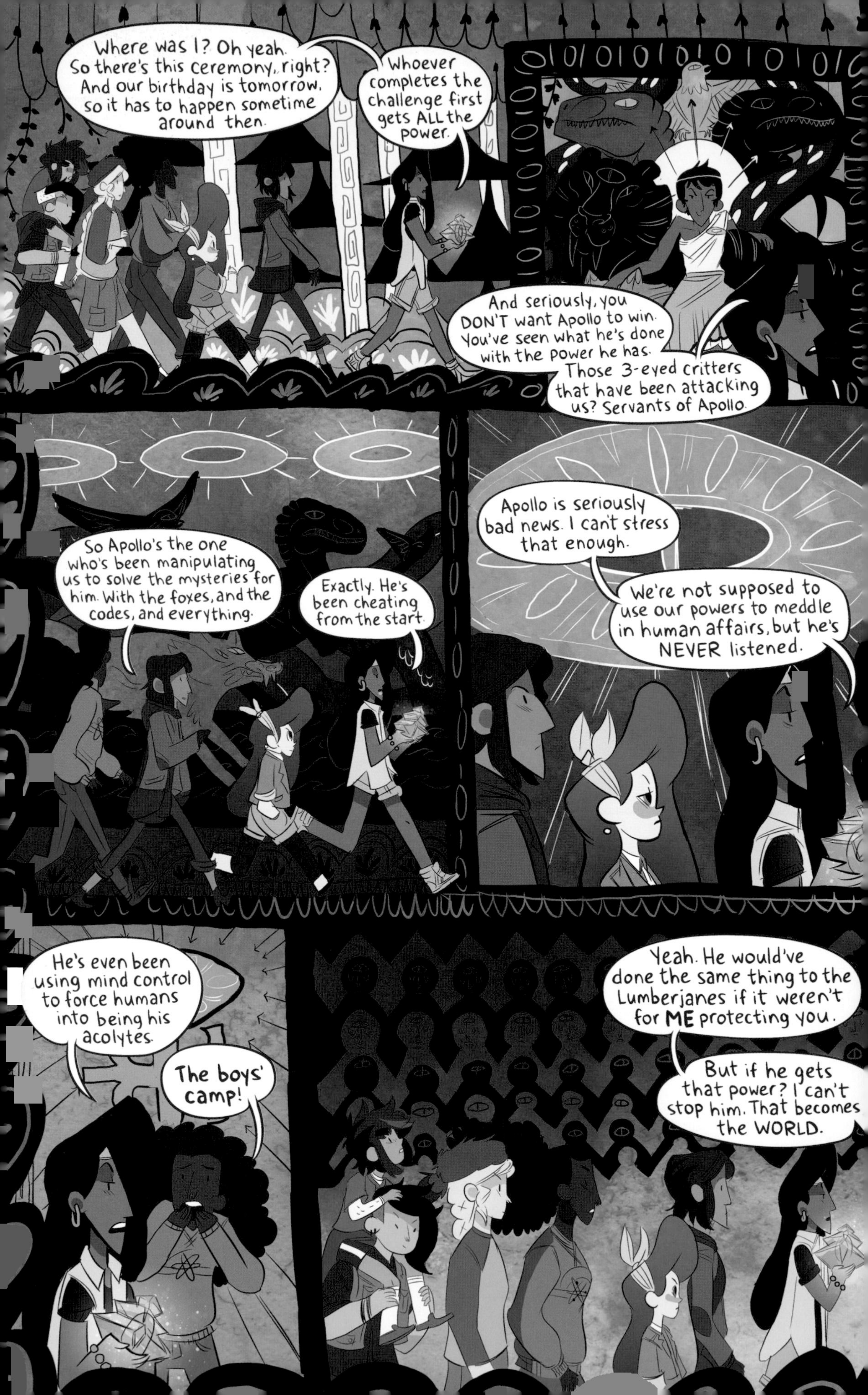
Where was I? Oh yeah. So there's this ceremony, right? And our birthday is tomorrow, so it has to happen sometime around then.
Whoever completes the challenge first gets ALL the power.
And seriously, you DON'T want Apollo to win. You've seen what he's done with the power he has.
Those 3-eyed critters that have been attacking us? Servants of Apollo.
So Apollo's the one who's been manipulating us to solve the mysteries for him. With the foxes, and the codes, and everything.
Exactly. He's been cheating from the start.
Apollo is seriously bad news. I can't stress that enough.
We're not supposed to use our powers to meddle in human affairs, but he's NEVER listened.
He's even been using mind control to force humans into being his acolytes.
The boys' camp!
Yeah. He would've done the same thing to the Lumberjanes if it weren't for ME protecting you.
But if he gets that power? I can't stop him. That becomes the WORLD.

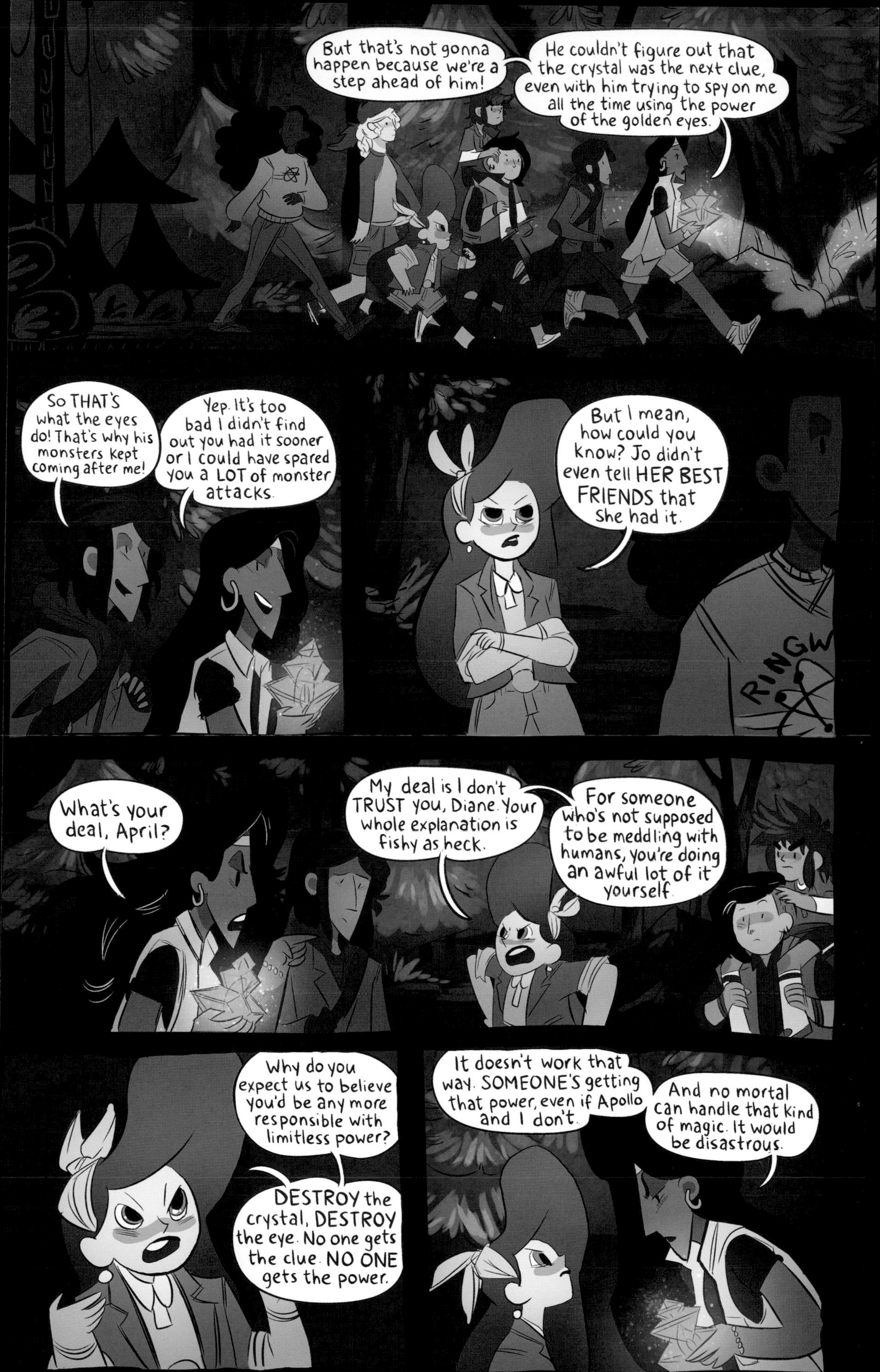
But that's not gonna happen because we're a step ahead of him!
He couldn't figure out that the crystal was the next clue, even with him trying to spy on me all the time using the power of the golden eyes.
So THAT'S what the eyes do! That's why his monsters kept coming after me!
Yep. It's too bad I didn't find out you had it sooner or I could have spared you a LOT of monster attacks.
But I mean, how could you know? Jo didn't even tell HER BEST FRIENDS that she had it.
RINGW
What's your deal, April?
My deal is I don't TRUST you, Diane. Your whole explanation is fishy as heck.
For someone who's not supposed to be meddling with humans, you're doing an awful lot of it yourself.
Why do you expect us to believe you'd be any more responsible with limitless power?
DESTROY the crystal, DESTROY the eye. No one gets the clue. NO ONE gets the power.
It doesn't work that way. SOMEONE'S getting that power, even if Apollo and I don't.
And no mortal can handle that kind of magic. It would be disastrous.

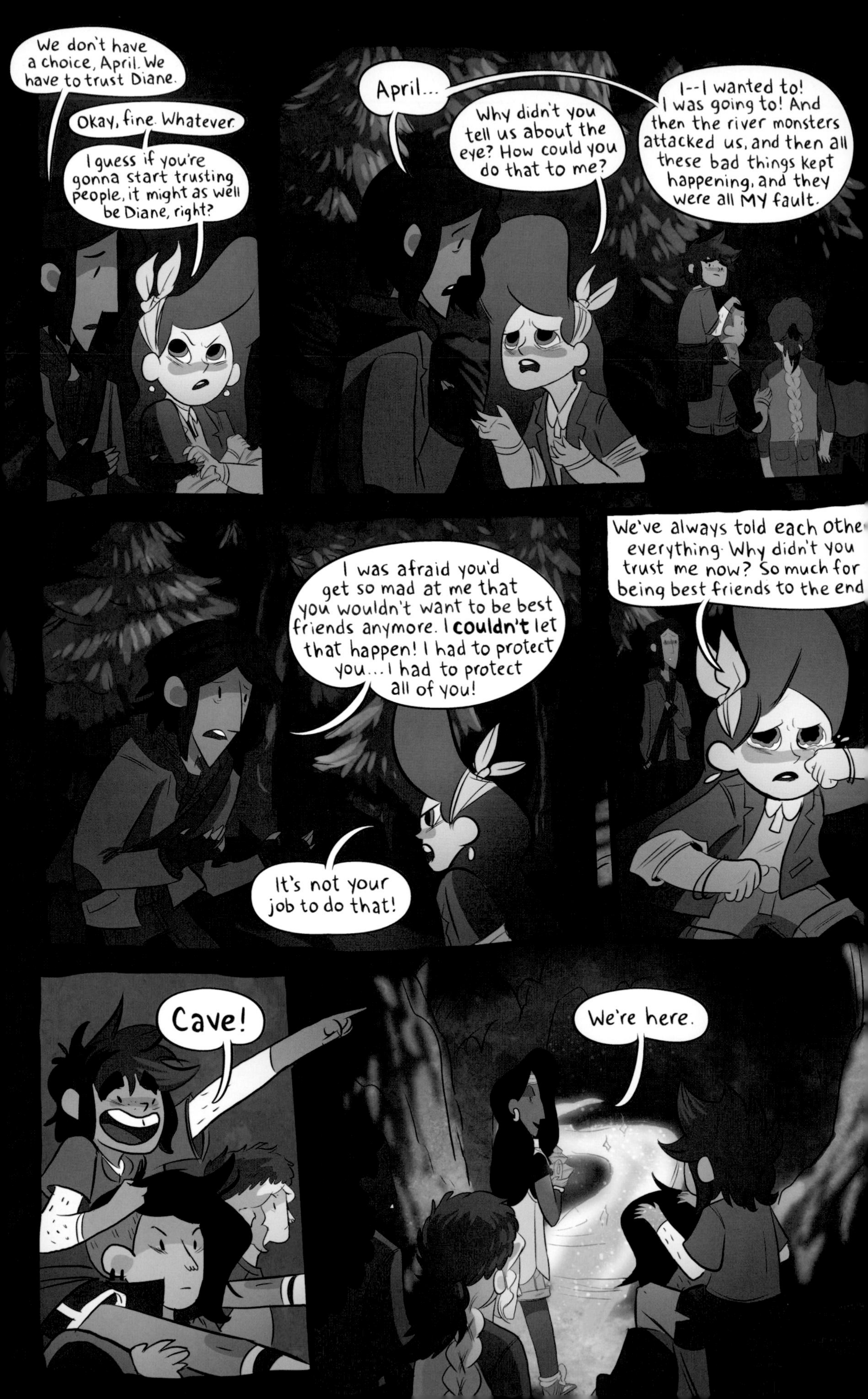

We don't have a choice, April. We have to trust Diane.
Okay, fine. Whatever.
I guess if you're gonna start trusting people, it might as well be Diane, right?
April...
Why didn't you tell us about the eye? How could you do that to me?
I--I wanted to! I was going to! And then the river monsters attacked us, and then all these bad things kept happening, and they were all MY fault.
I was afraid you'd get so mad at me that you wouldn't want to be best friends anymore. I **couldn't** let that happen! I had to protect you... I had to protect all of you!
It's not your job to do that!
We've always told each othe everything. Why didn't you trust me now? So much for being best friends to the end
Cave!
We're here.

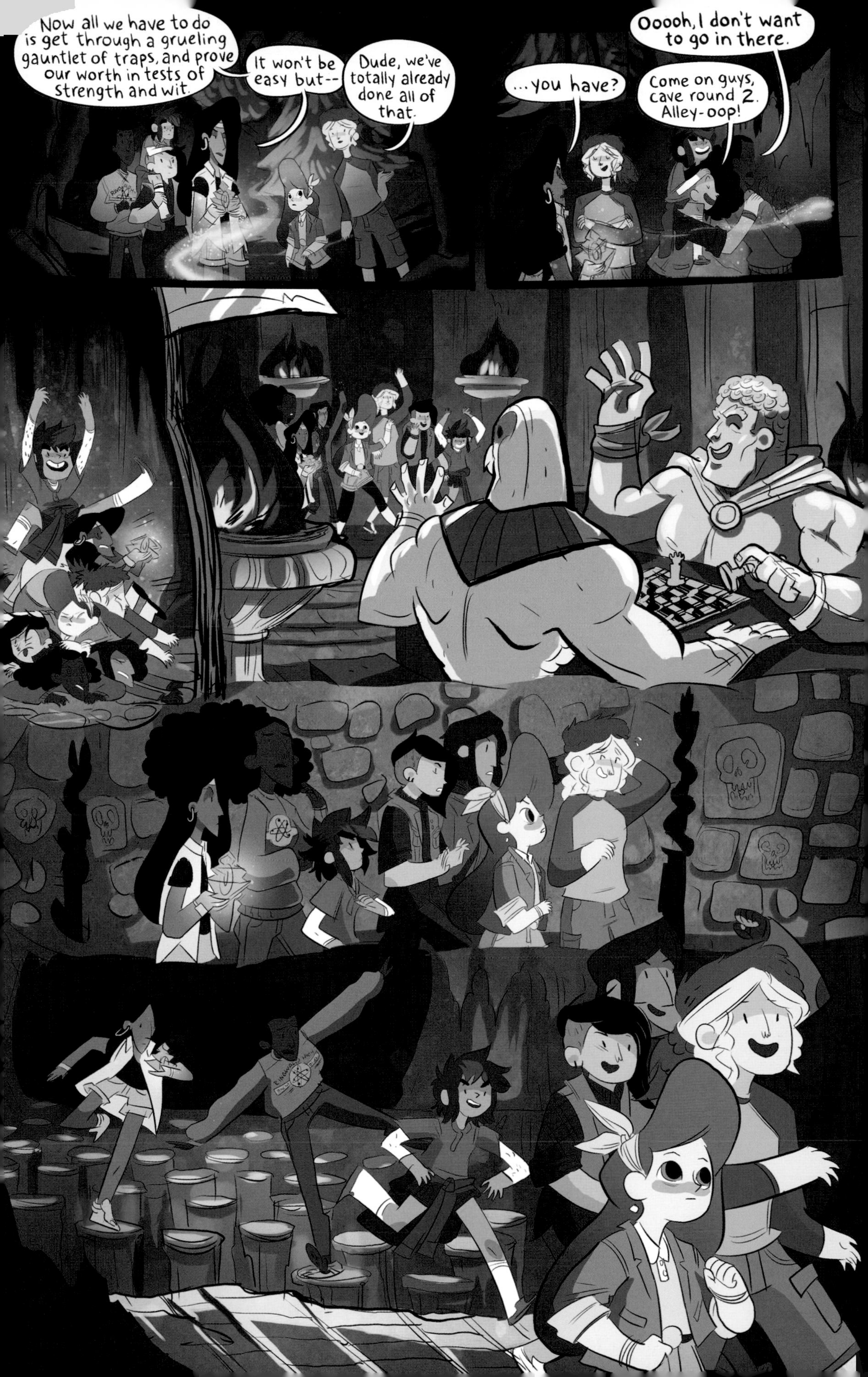
Now all we have to do is get through a grueling gauntlet of traps, and prove our worth in tests of strength and wit.
It won't be easy but--
Dude, we've totally already done all of that.
...you have?
Come on guys, cave round 2. Alley-oop!
Ooooh, I don't want to go in there.

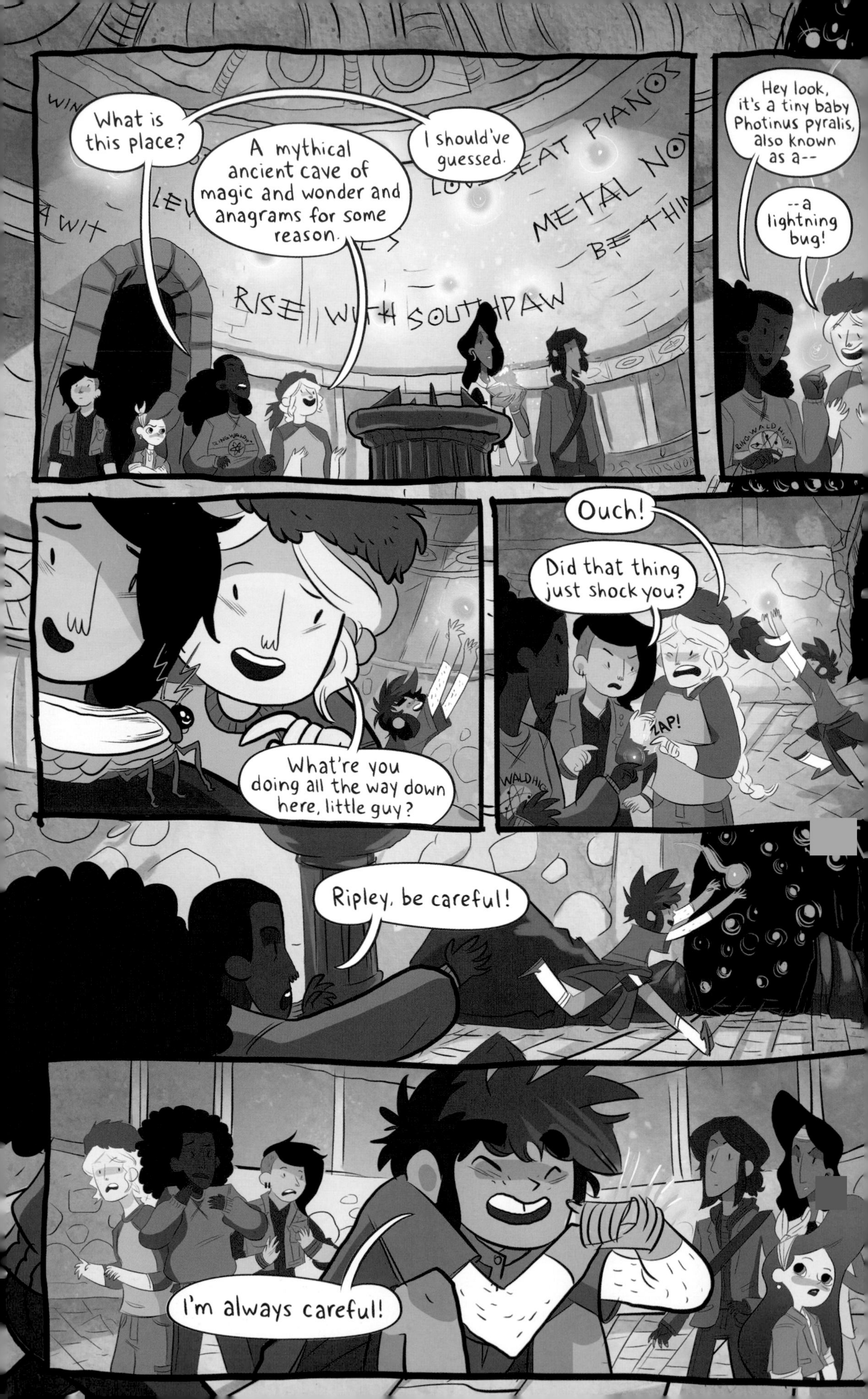
What is this place?
A mythical ancient cave of magic and wonder and anagrams for some reason.
I should've guessed.
RISE WITH SOUTHPAW
METAL NO
Hey look, it's a tiny baby Photinus pyralis, also known as a--
--a lightning bug!
What're you doing all the way down here, little guy?
Ouch!
Did that thing just shock you?
ZAP!
Ripley, be careful!
I'm always careful!

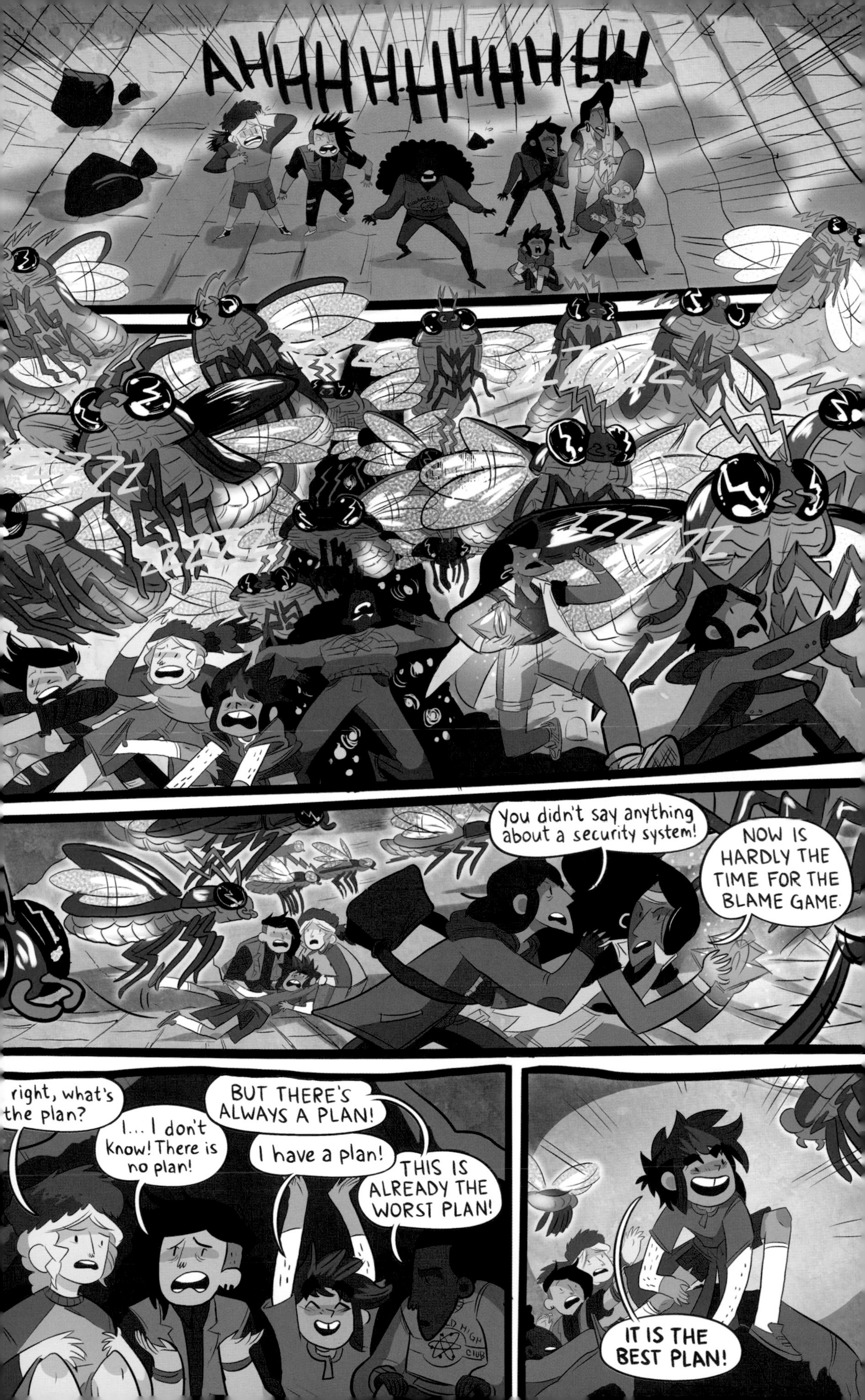
AHHHHHHHHHH
You didn't say anything about a security system!
NOW IS HARDLY THE TIME FOR THE BLAME GAME.
right, what's the plan?
I... I don't Know! There is no plan!
BUT THERE'S ALWAYS A PLAN!
I have a plan!
THIS IS ALREADY THE WORST PLAN!
IT IS THE BEST PLAN!

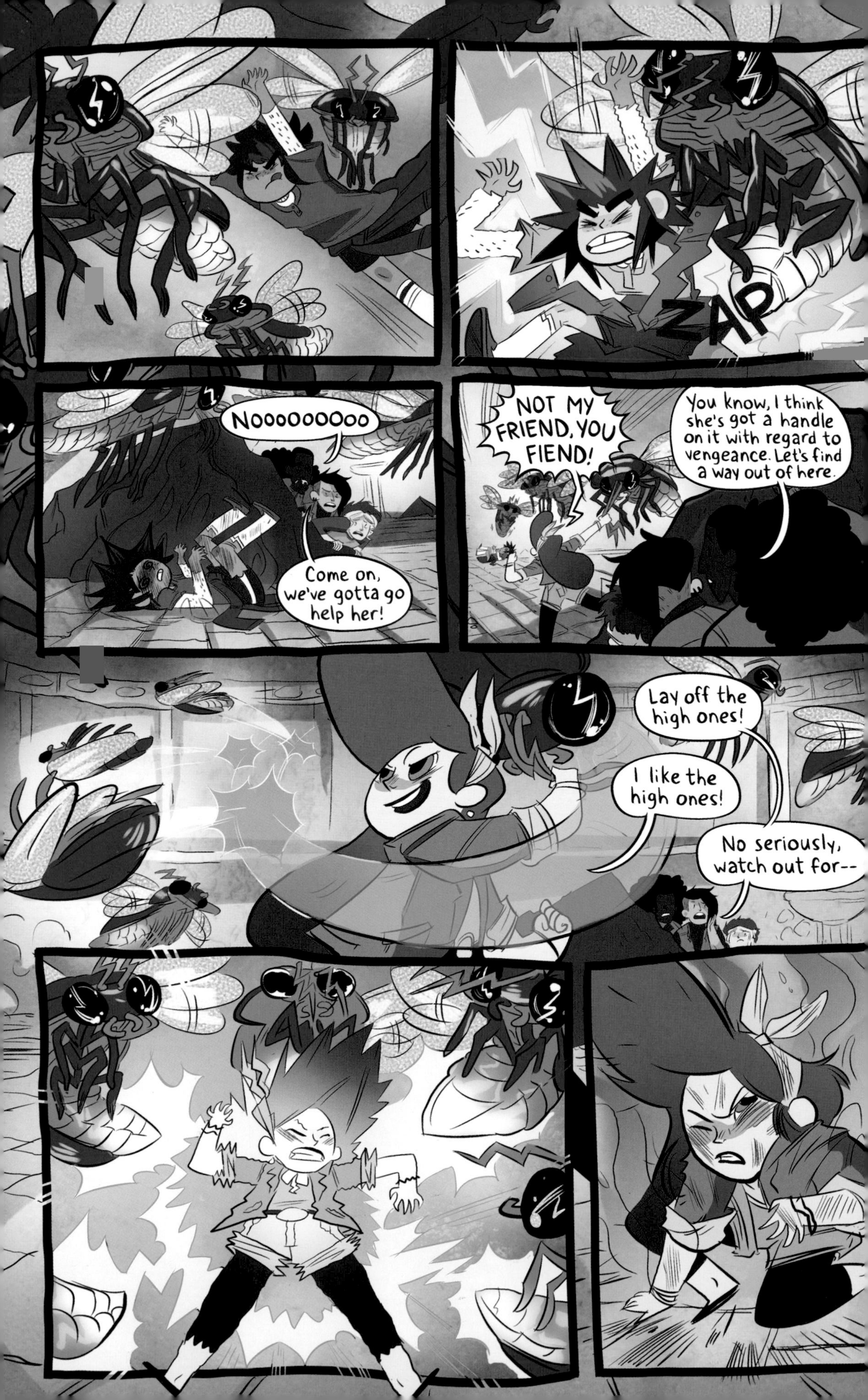

ZAP
Nooooooooo
Come on, we've gotta go help her!
NOT MY FRIEND, YOU FIEND!
You know, I think she's got a handle on it with regard to vengeance. Let's find a way out of here.
Lay off the high ones!
I like the high ones!
No seriously, watch out for--

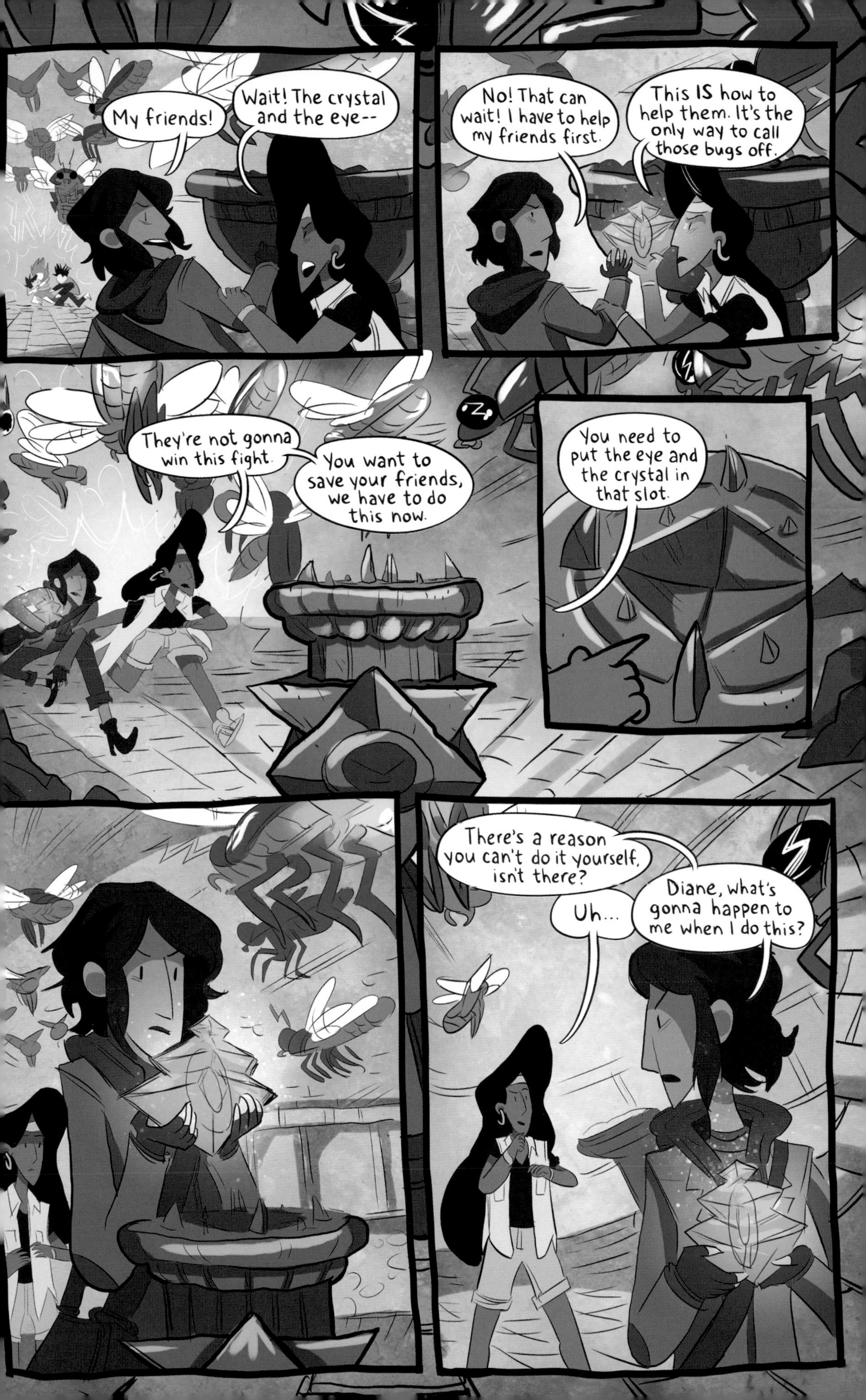
My friends!
Wait! The crystal and the eye--
No! That can wait! I have to help my friends first.
This IS how to help them. It's the only way to call those bugs off.
They're not gonna win this fight.
You want to save your friends, we have to do this now.
You need to put the eye and the crystal in that slot.
There's a reason you can't do it yourself, isn't there?
Uh...
Diane, what's gonna happen to me when I do this?

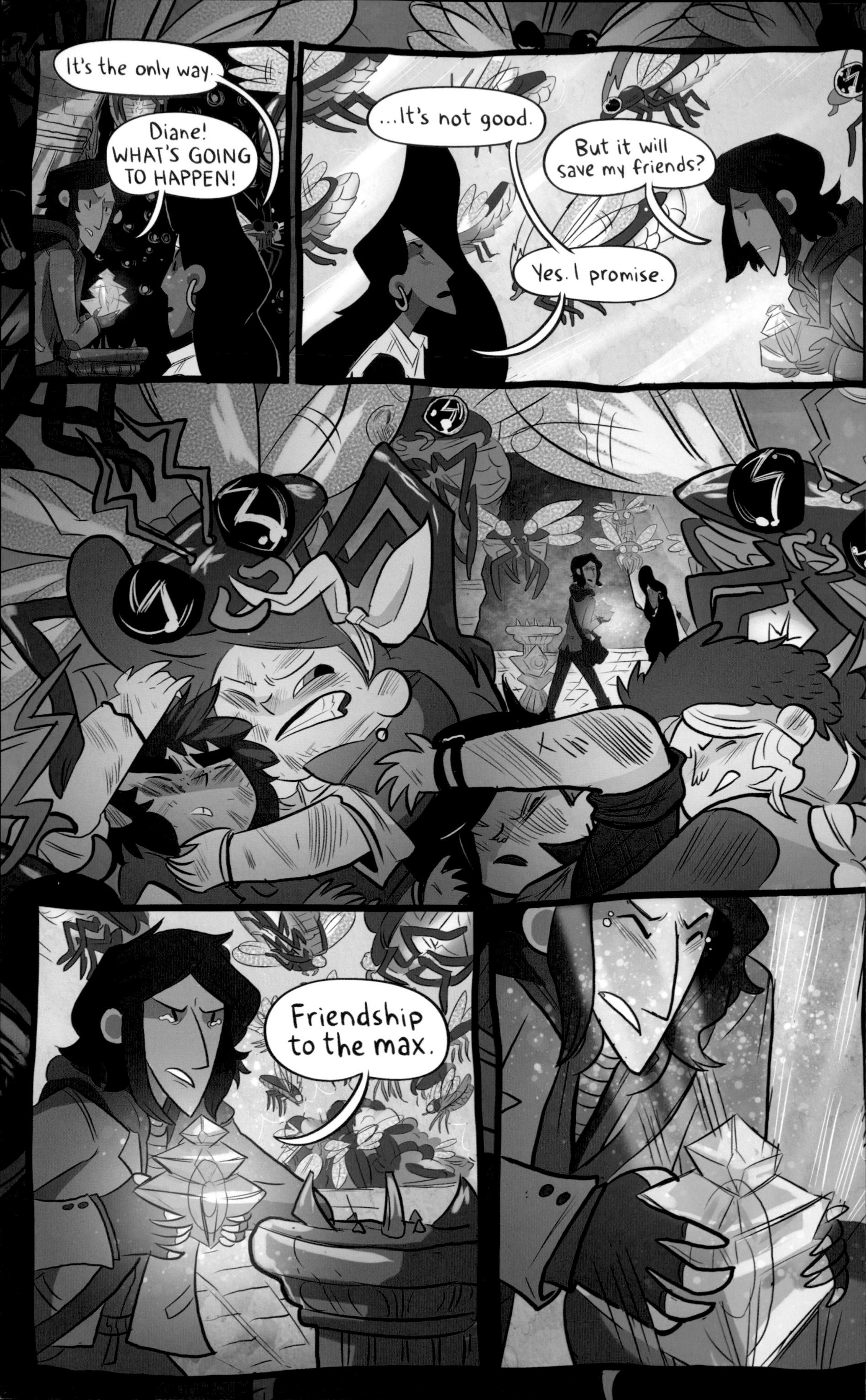

It's the only way.
Diane! WHAT'S GOING TO HAPPEN!
...It's not good.
But it will save my friends?
Yes. I promise.
Friendship to the max.

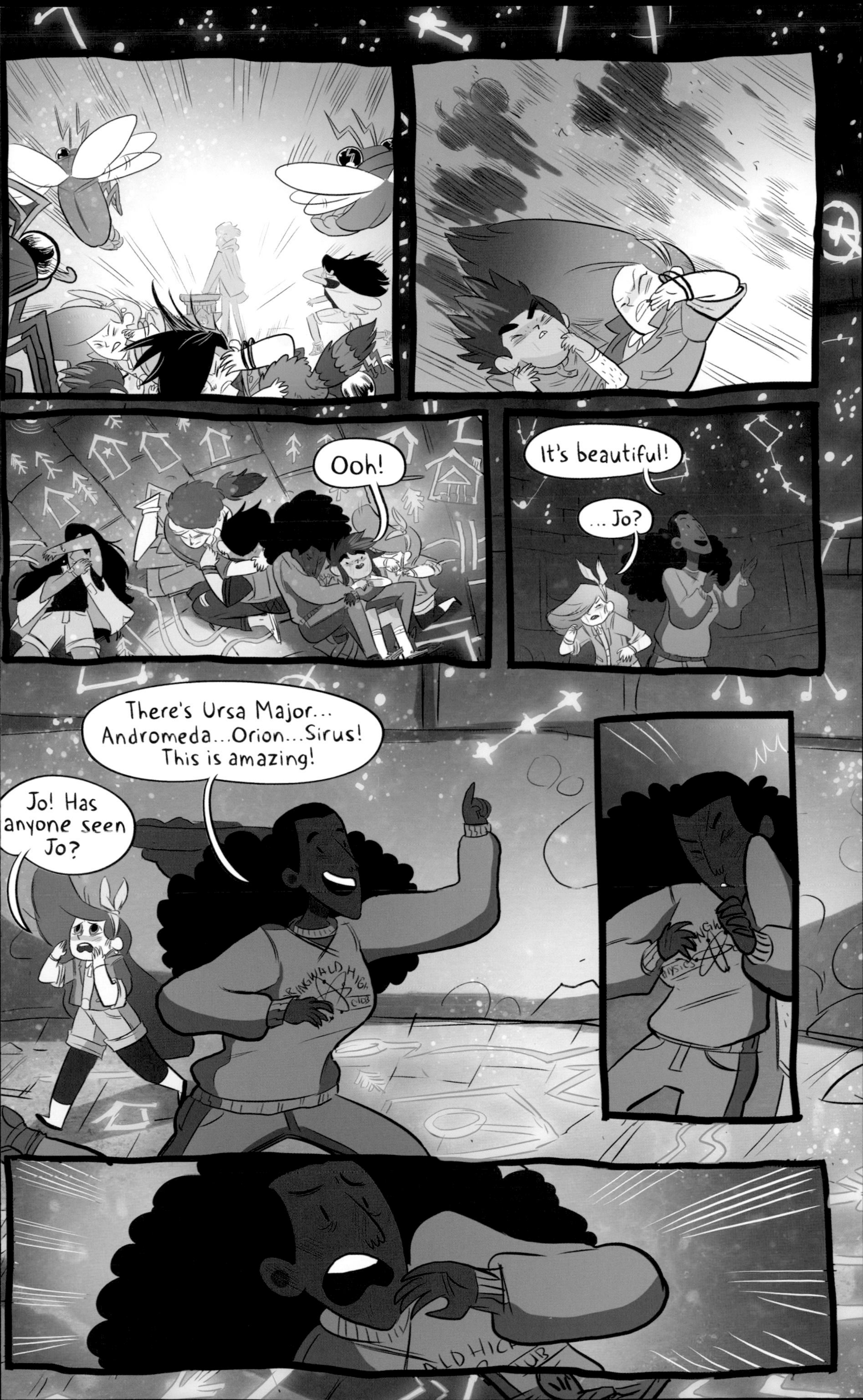
Ooh!
It's beautiful!
...Jo?
There's Ursa Major... Andromeda...Orion...Sirus! This is amazing!
Jo! Has anyone seen Jo?

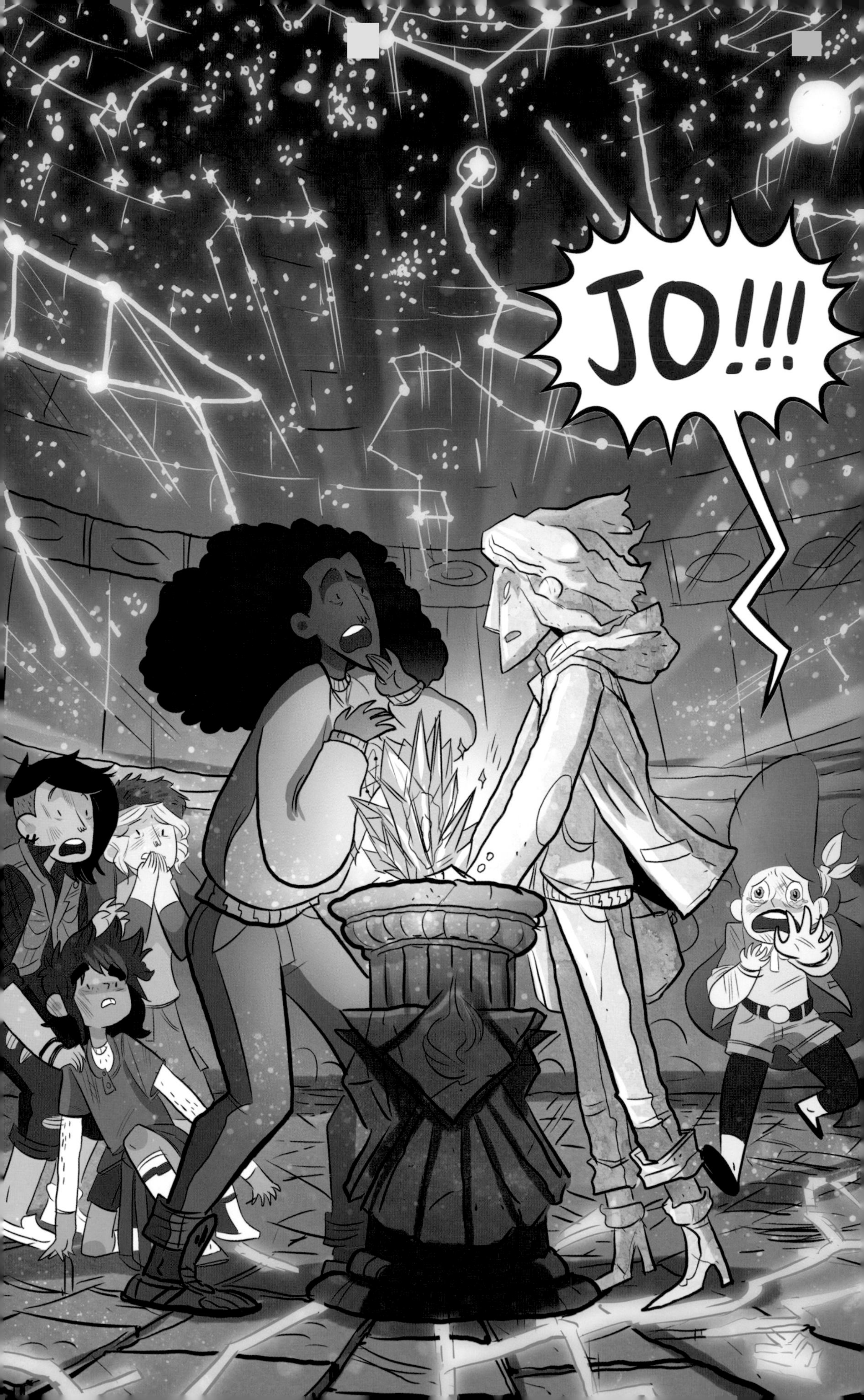
JO!!!

will co

Th

It he

appeara

dress f

Further

Lumbe

to have

part in

Thiskv

Hardc

have

them

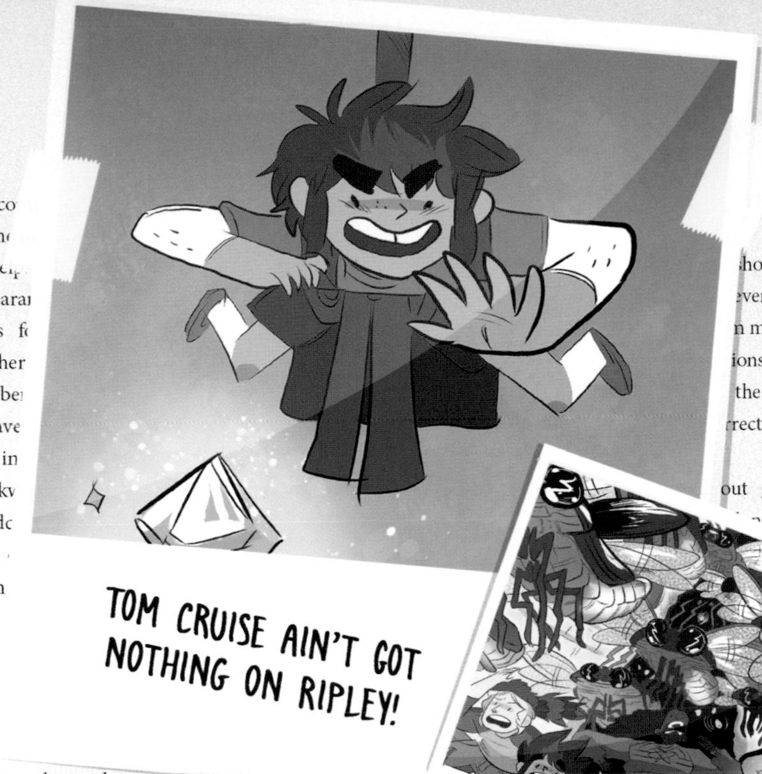

TOM CRUISE AIN'T GOT NOTHING ON RIPLEY!

E UNIFORM

hould be worn at camp

vents when Lumberjanes

n may also be worn at other

ions. It should be worn as a

the uniform dress with

rect shoes, and stocking or

out grows her uniform or

ter Lumberjane.

a she has

her

her

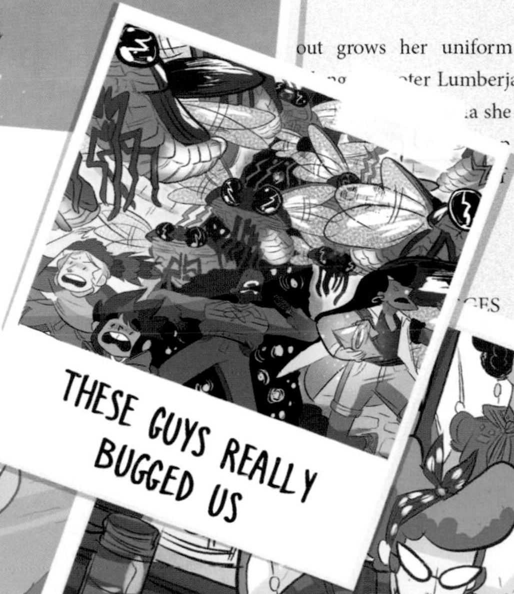

THESE GUYS REALLY BUGGED US

The

yellow, short sl

emb

the w

choose

slacks,

made o

out-of-dc

green bere

the colla

Shoes ma

heels, rou

socks shou ... hoes or wi

the uniform. Ne ... es, bracelets, o ... do

belong with a Lumberjane unifo

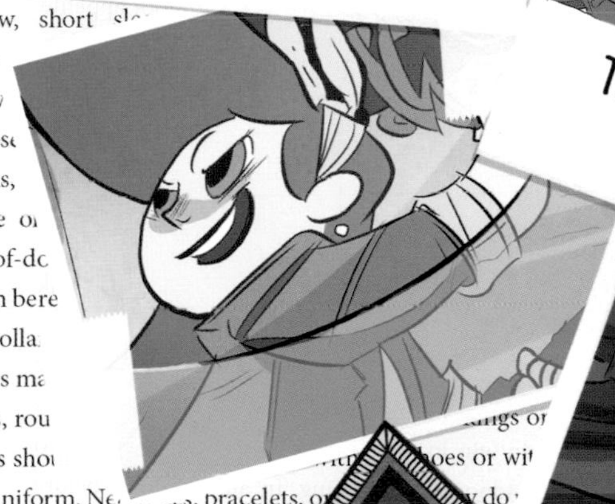

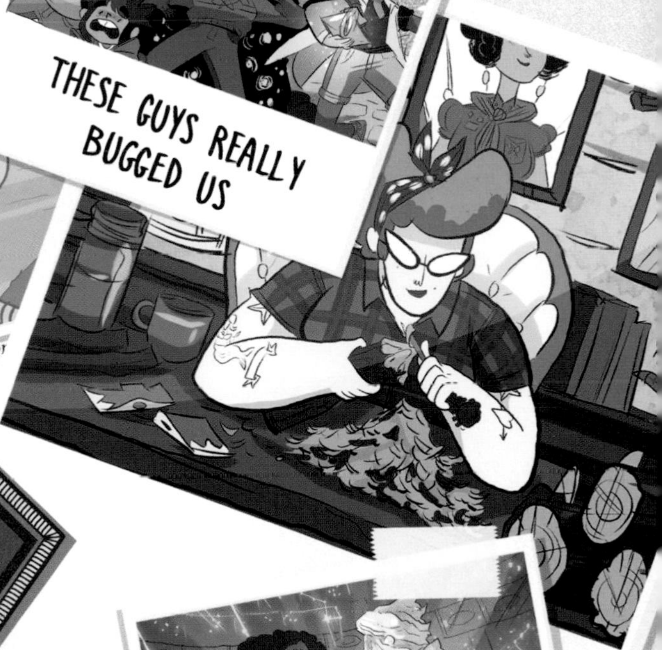

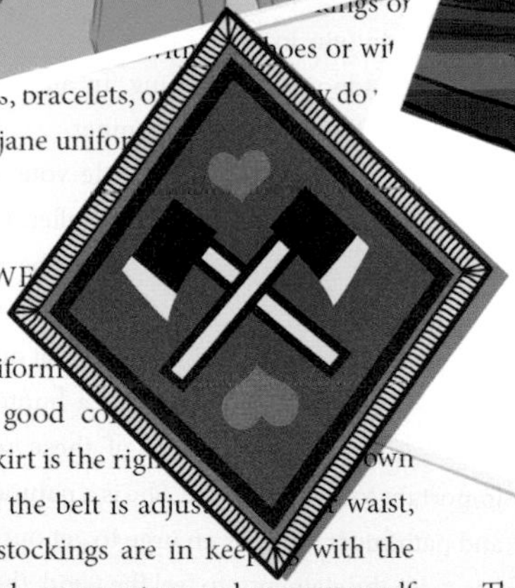

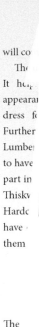

HOW TO WE

To look well in a uniform

uniform be kept in good co

pressed. See that the skirt is the righ ... own

height and build, that the belt is adjus ... waist,

that your shoes and stockings are in kee ... with the

uniform, that you watch your posture and carry yourself with dignity and grace. If the beret is removed indoors, be sure that your hair is neat and kept in place with an insonspicuous clip or ribbon. When you wear a Lumberjane uniform you are identified as a member of this organization and you should be doubly careful to conduct yourself in a way that will show everyone that courtesy and thoughtfullness are part of being a Lumberjane. People are likely to judge a whole nation by the selfishness of a few individuals, to criticize a whole family because of the misconduct of one member, and to feel unkindly toward and organization because of the

The unifor

helps to cre

in a group.

active life th

another bond

future, and pr

in order to b

Lumberjane pr

Penniquiqul Thi ... re Lady

Types, but m ... will wish to have one. They

can either bu ... , or make it themselves from

materials available at the trading post.

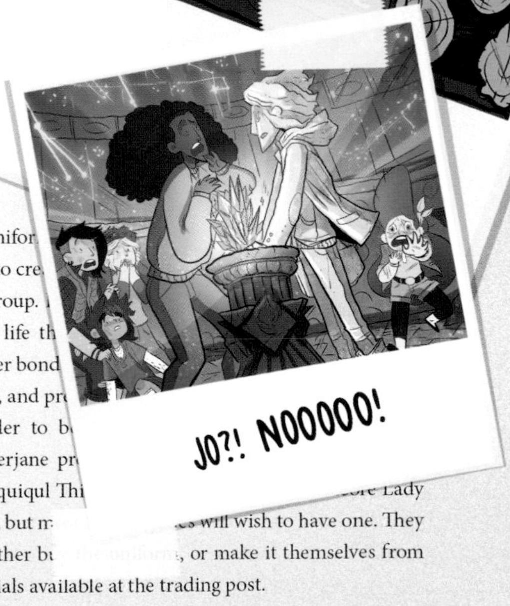

JO?! NOOOOO!

LUMBERJANES FIELD MANUAL

# CHAPTER EIGHT

*Lumberjanes "Out-of-Doors" Program Field*

## SPACE JAMBORIE

*"This jam breaks the laws of physics."*

Like any well rounded young woman, a Lumberjane will understand the importance of music and will do her best to remain educated enough in all music venues to ensure the ability of polite conversation. Being a Lumberjane is more than learning skills for the great outdoors but also coming to terms on how to be a well rounded individual. She will explore the keys and notes that come with a variety of music, will be able to have a basic understanding of how to read a music sheet, and will at the very least be able to understand the importance of a steady beat even if she is not as musically inclined as her fellow scouts.

Music brings joy to everyone in life, from the earth as we understand it to beyond the stars that are impossible to know. The importance of the *Space Jamborie* badge is that it teaches poise under pressure as well as creative thinking. This badge is not earned by a well written

sonnet that hits every note that a text book would recommend but it is earned by the creative thinking that the scout puts into her work. The piece that she writes is meant to be something personal yet able to share, it will be judged by her cabin leader who will know if the scout is pushing herself.

To obtain the *Space Jamborie* badge a Lumberjane must compose and perform her own original piece. In this performance they will be able to judged on their understanding of music and on their stage presence. They are not required to perform on their own as to be a Lumberjane means to be constantly surrounded by friends, but only the main performer can earn badge at a time. While music can be considered subjective by society this badge is not judged by the standard of others but instead it is judged by the standard that a Lumberjane holds herself to. Her music will be honest

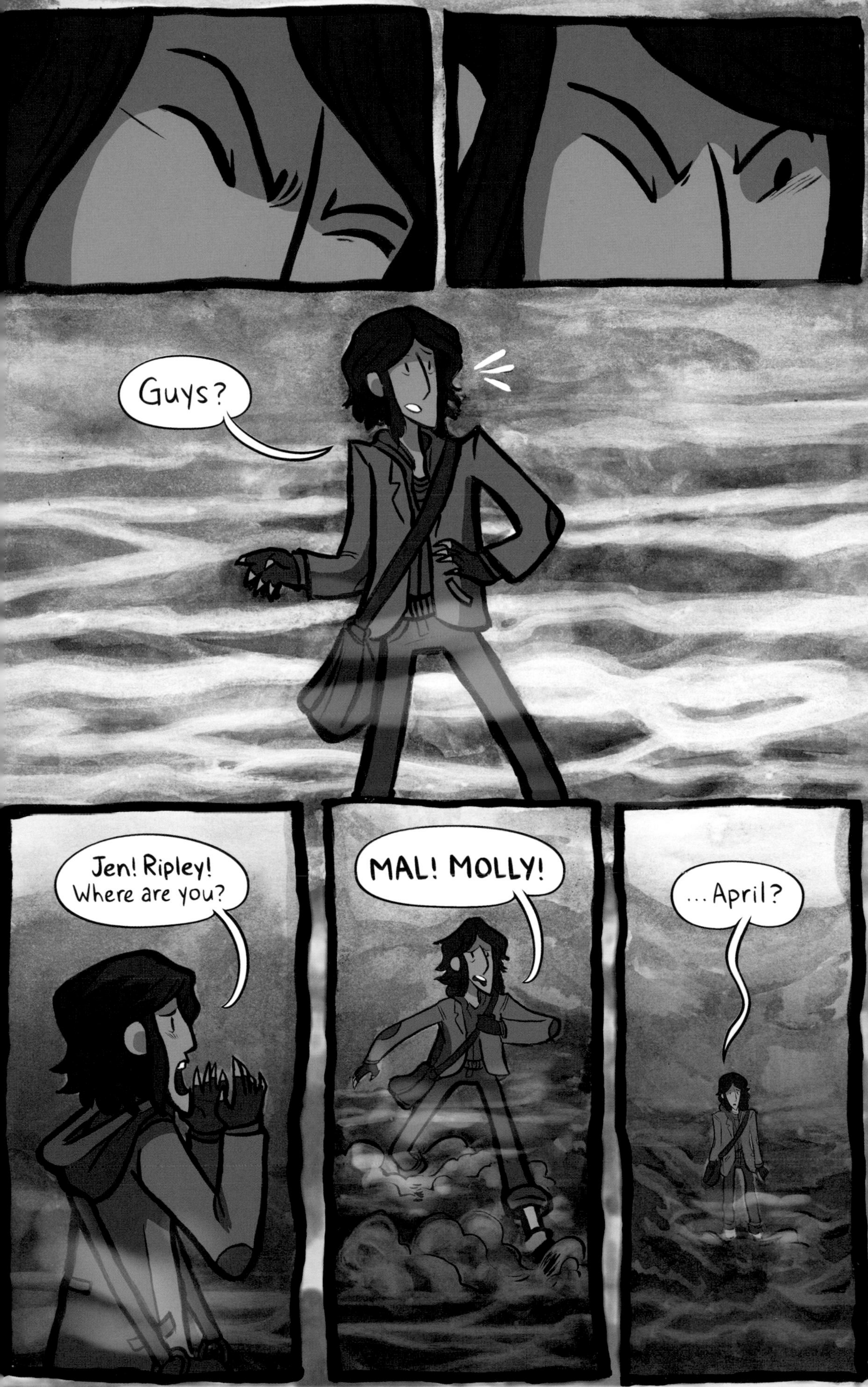
Guys?
Jen! Ripley!
Where are you?
MAL! MOLLY!
...April?

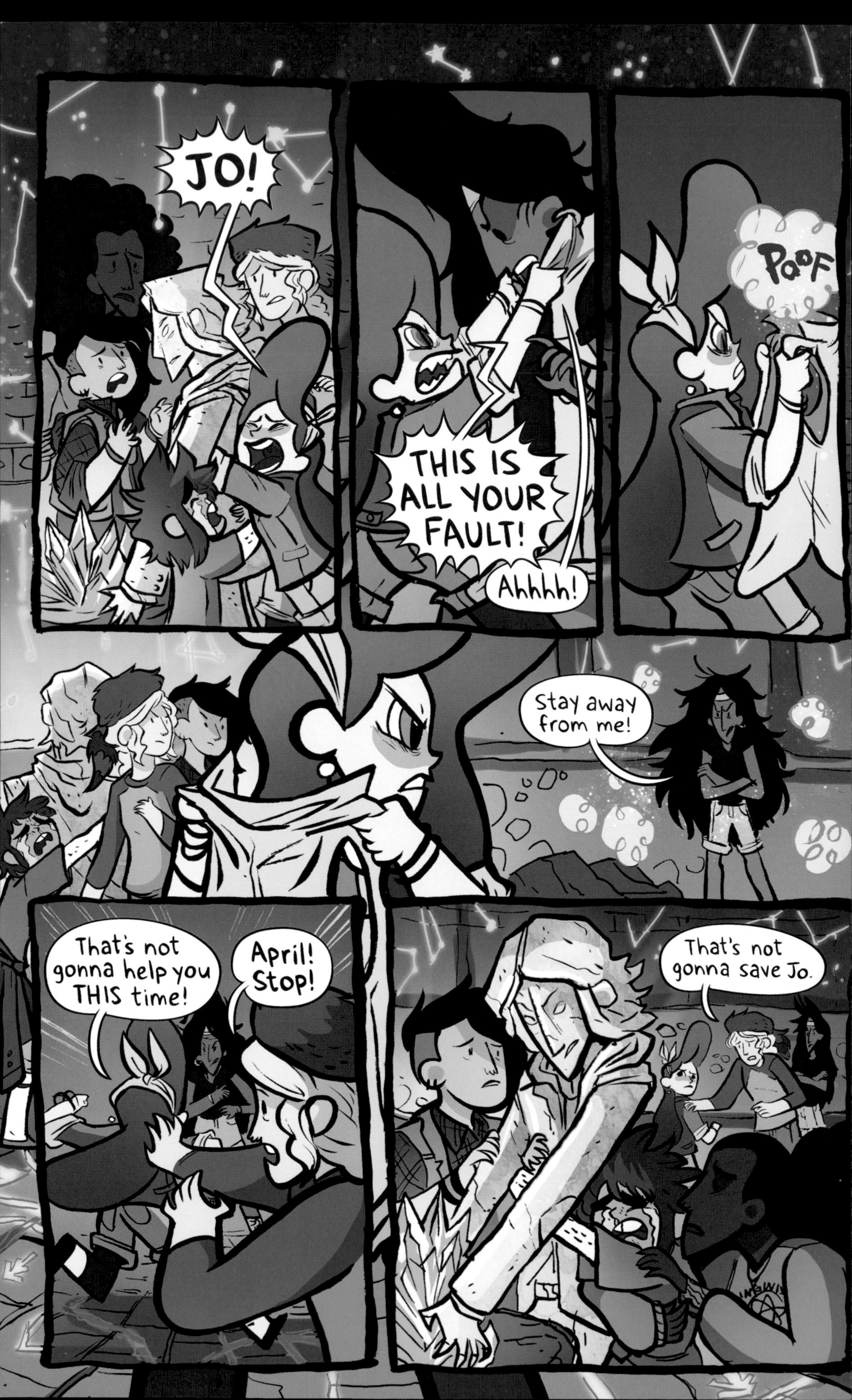
JO!
THIS IS ALL YOUR FAULT!
Ahhhh!
POOF
Stay away from me!
That's not gonna help you THIS time!
April! Stop!
That's not gonna save Jo.

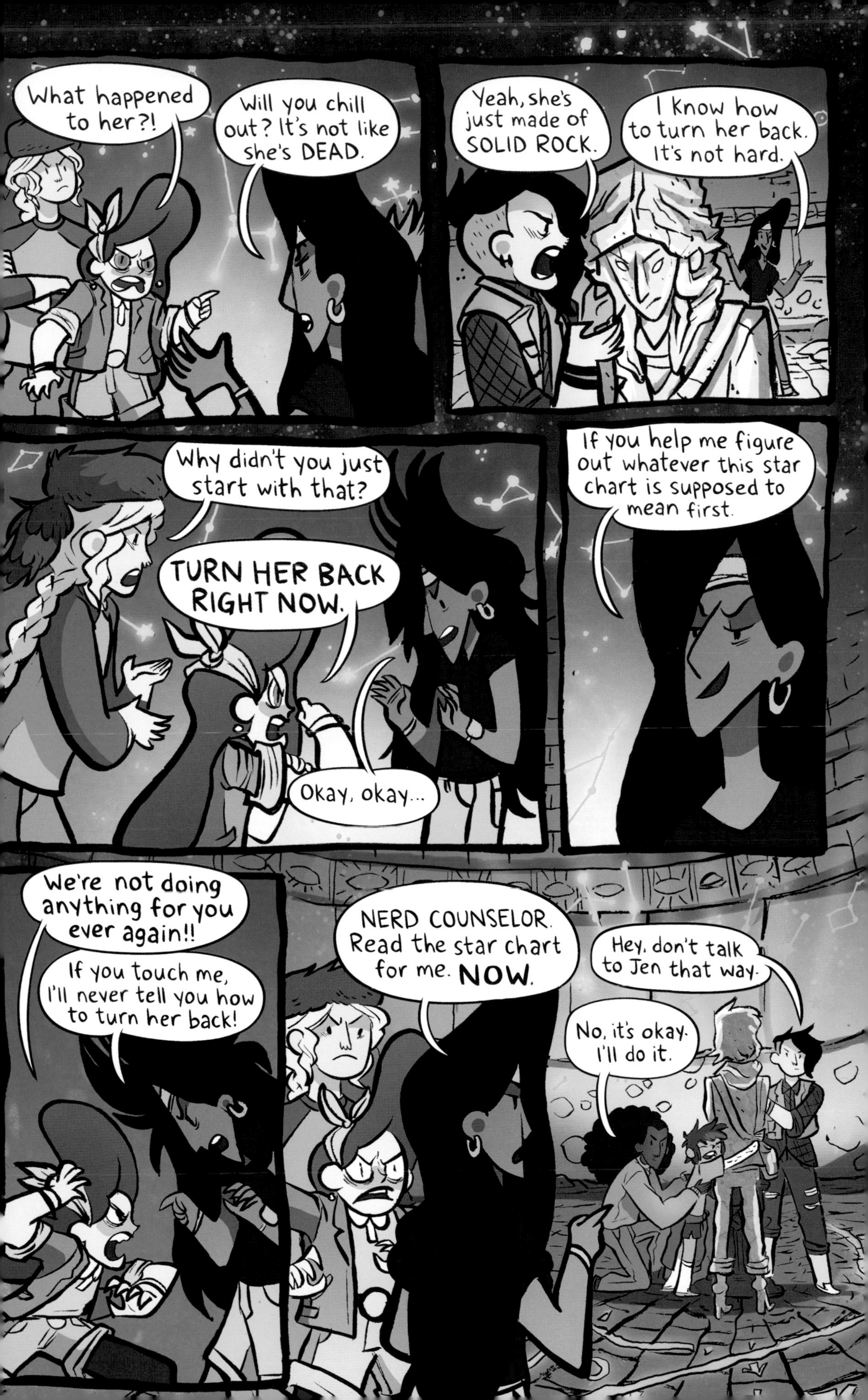
What happened to her?!
Will you chill out? It's not like she's DEAD.
Yeah, she's just made of SOLID ROCK.
I know how to turn her back. It's not hard.
Why didn't you just start with that?
TURN HER BACK RIGHT NOW.
Okay, okay...
If you help me figure out whatever this star chart is supposed to mean first.
We're not doing anything for you ever again!!
If you touch me, I'll never tell you how to turn her back!
NERD COUNSELOR. Read the star chart for me. NOW.
Hey, don't talk to Jen that way.
No, it's okay. I'll do it.

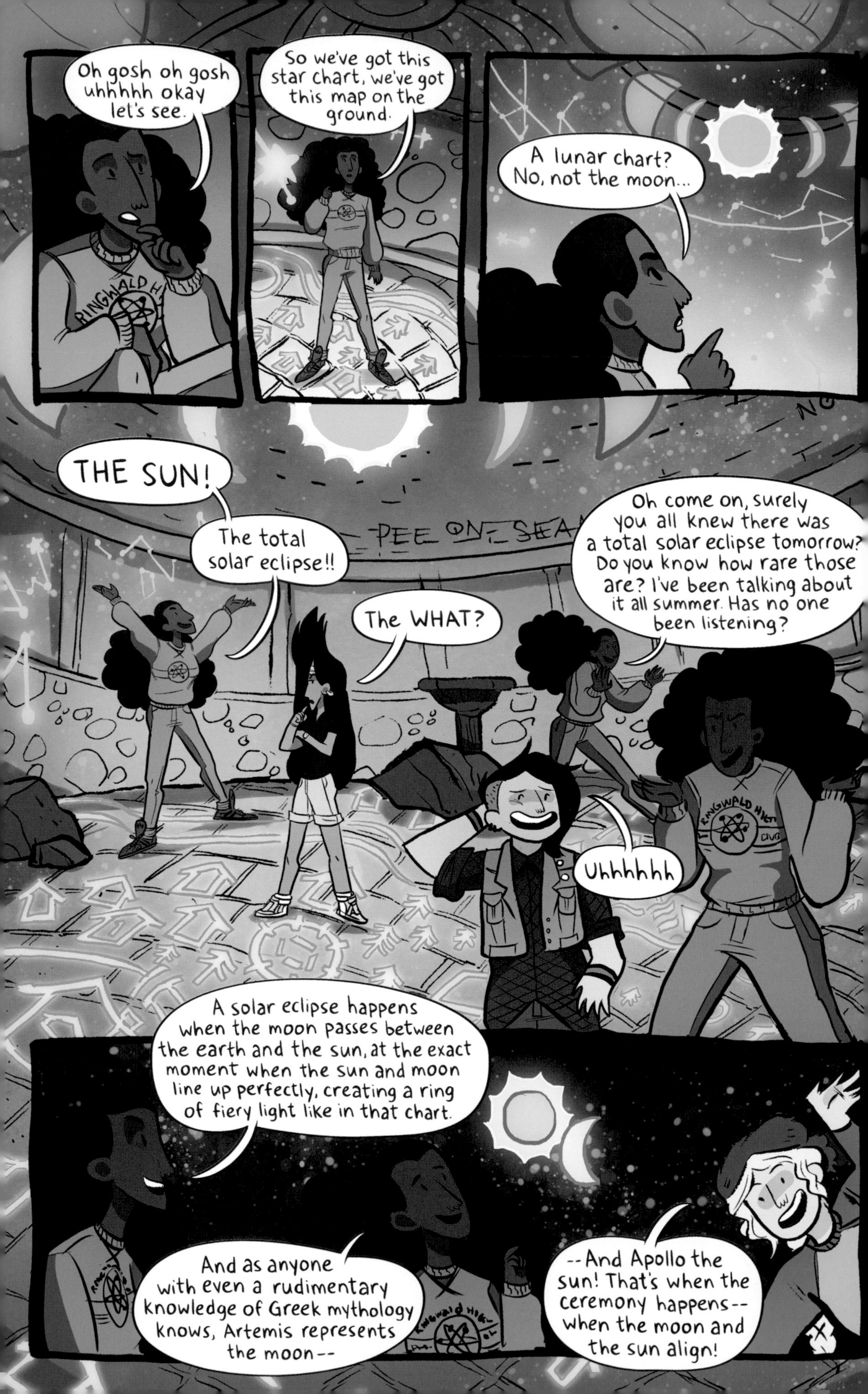
Oh gosh oh gosh uhhhhh okay let's see.
So we've got this star chart, we've got this map on the ground.
A lunar chart? No, not the moon...
THE SUN!
The total solar eclipse!!
The WHAT?
Oh come on, surely you all knew there was a total solar eclipse tomorrow? Do you know how rare those are? I've been talking about it all summer. Has no one been listening?
Uhhhhhh
A solar eclipse happens when the moon passes between the earth and the sun, at the exact moment when the sun and moon line up perfectly, creating a ring of fiery light like in that chart.
And as anyone with even a rudimentary knowledge of Greek mythology knows, Artemis represents the moon--
--And Apollo the sun! That's when the ceremony happens--when the moon and the sun align!

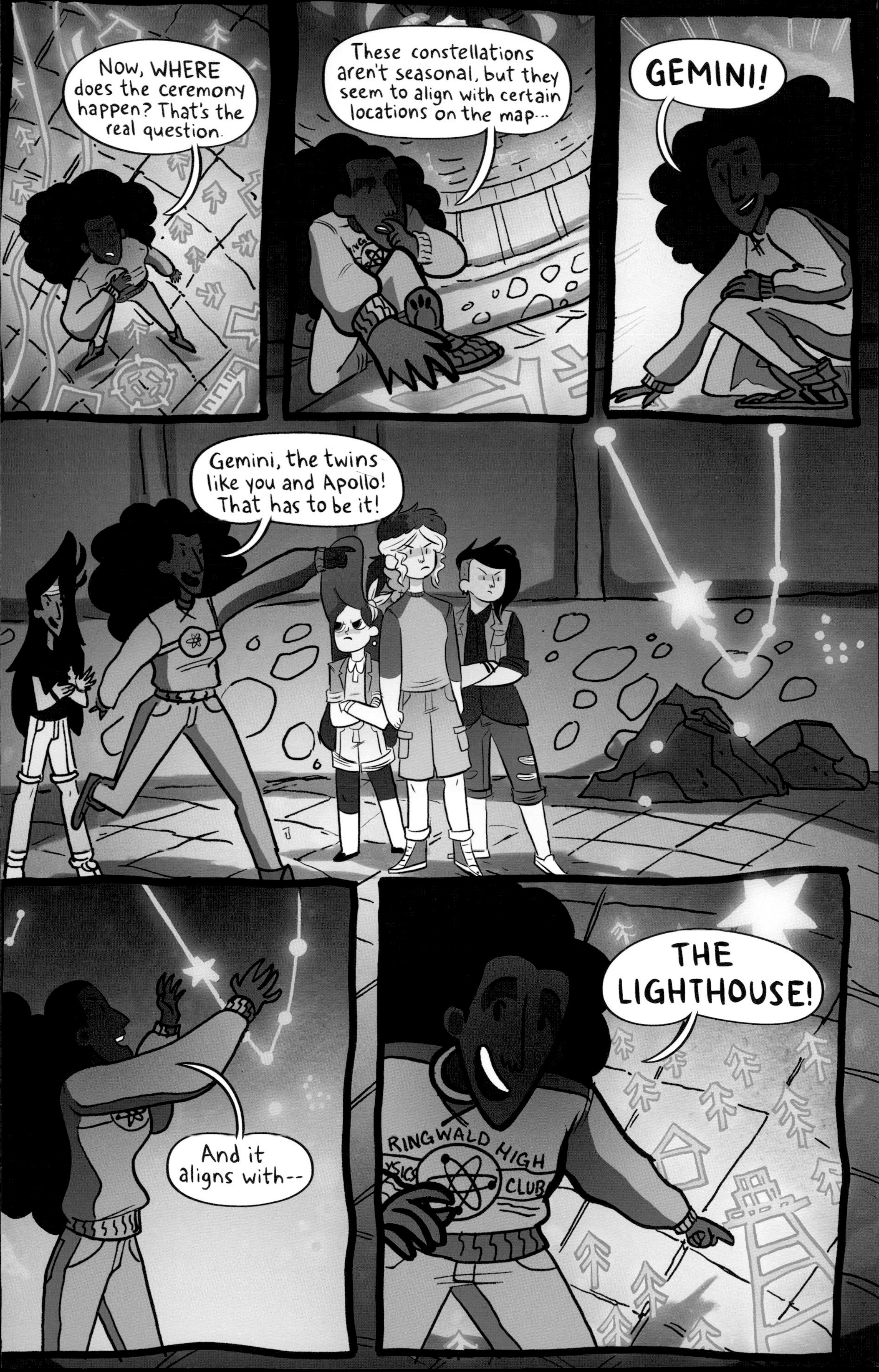
Now, WHERE does the ceremony happen? That's the real question.
These constellations aren't seasonal, but they seem to align with certain locations on the map...
GEMINI!
Gemini, the twins like you and Apollo! That has to be it!
And it aligns with--
THE LIGHTHOUSE!
RINGWALD HIGH
CLUB

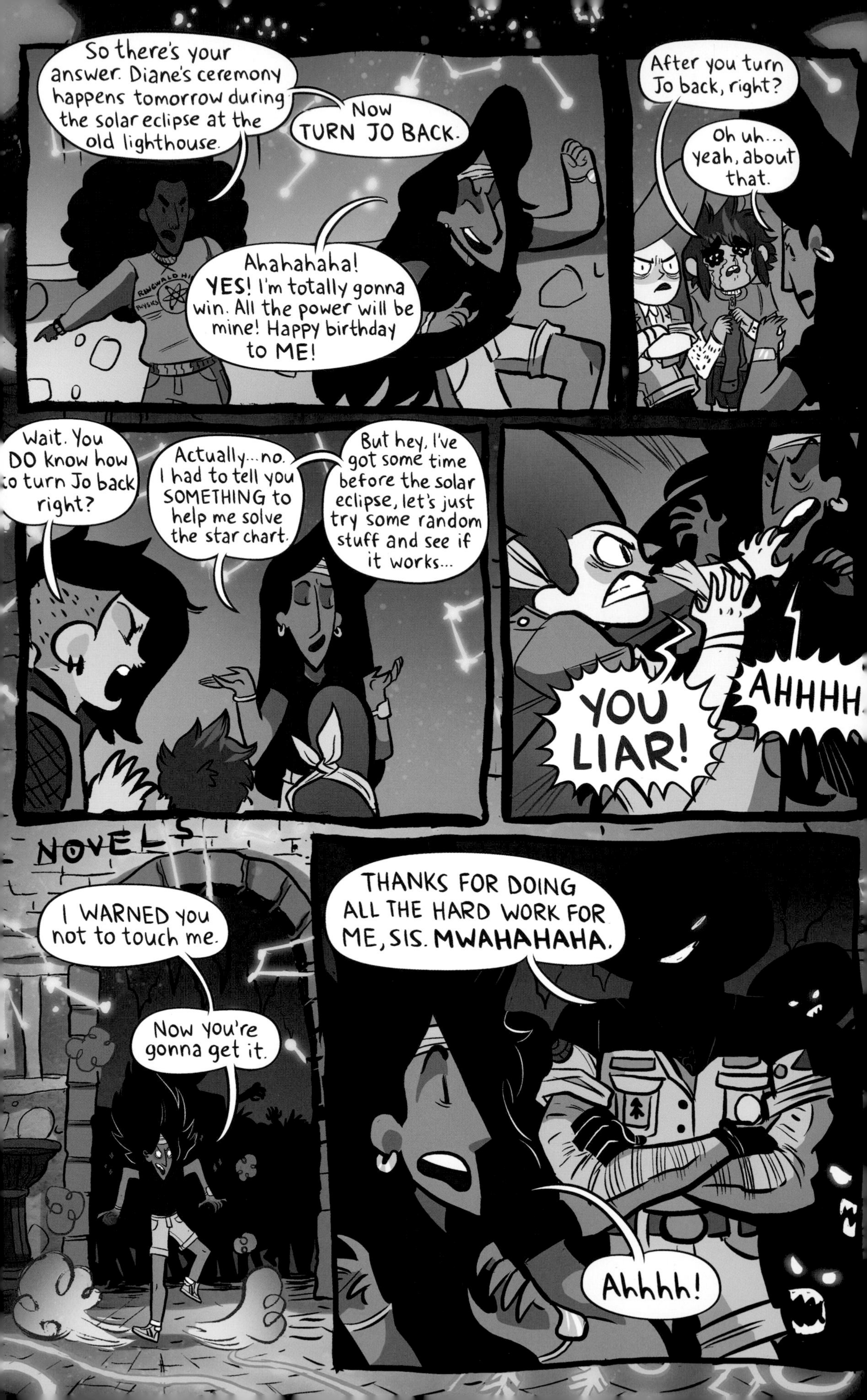
So there's your answer. Diane's ceremony happens tomorrow during the solar eclipse at the old lighthouse.
Now TURN JO BACK.
Ahahahaha! YES! I'm totally gonna win. All the power will be mine! Happy birthday to ME!
RINGWALD HI PHYSICS
After you turn Jo back, right?
Oh uh... yeah, about that.
Wait. You DO know how to turn Jo back right?
Actually... no. I had to tell you SOMETHING to help me solve the star chart.
But hey, I've got some time before the solar eclipse, let's just try some random stuff and see if it works...
YOU LIAR!
AHHHH
NOVELS
I WARNED you not to touch me.
Now you're gonna get it.
THANKS FOR DOING ALL THE HARD WORK FOR ME, SIS. MWAHAHAHA.
Ahhhh!

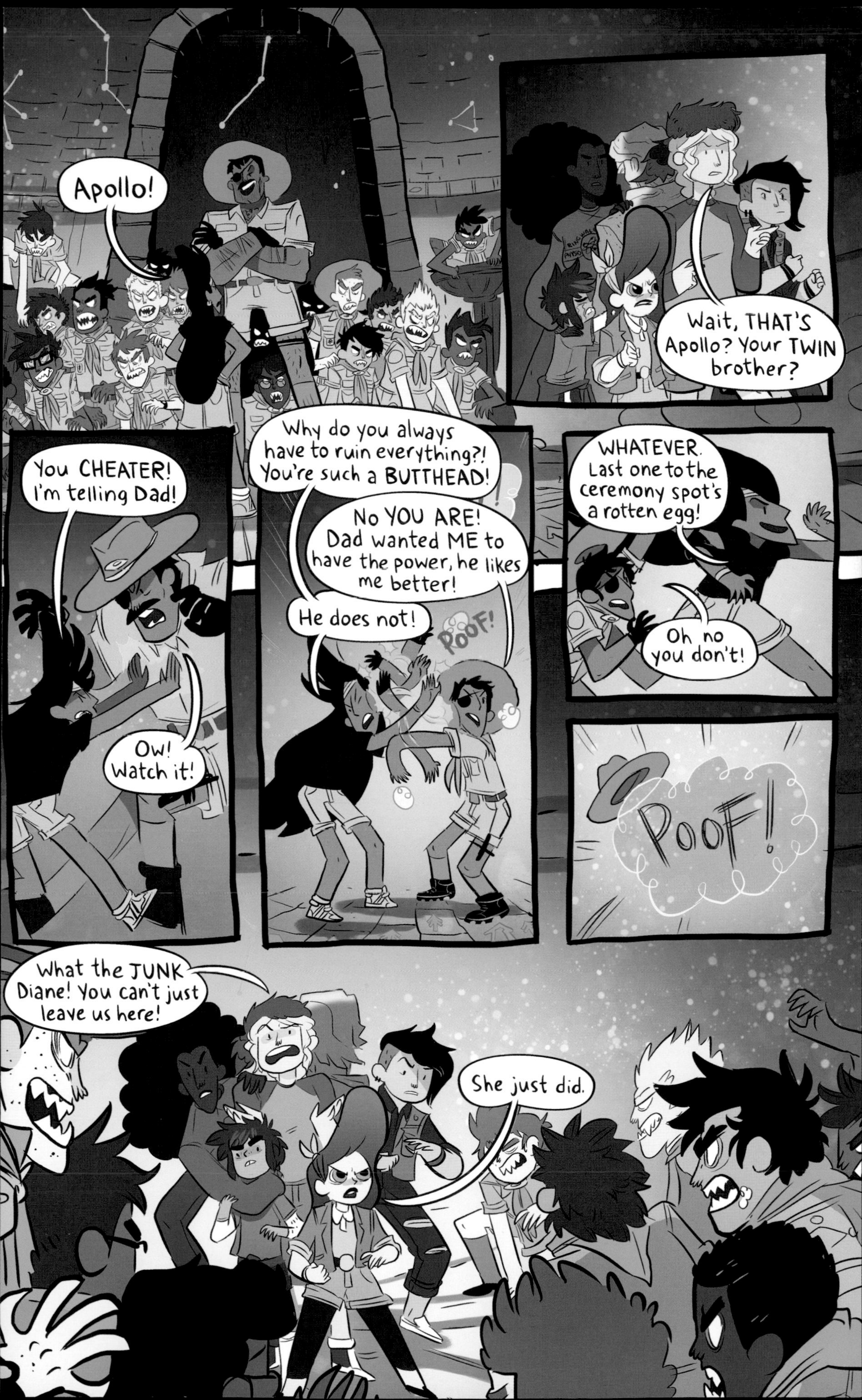

Apollo!
Wait, THAT'S Apollo? Your TWIN brother?
You CHEATER! I'm telling Dad!
Ow! Watch it!
Why do you always have to ruin everything?! You're such a BUTTHEAD!
No YOU ARE! Dad wanted ME to have the power, he likes me better!
He does not!
POOF!
WHATEVER. Last one to the ceremony spot's a rotten egg!
Oh no you don't!
POOF!
What the JUNK Diane! You can't just leave us here!
She just did.

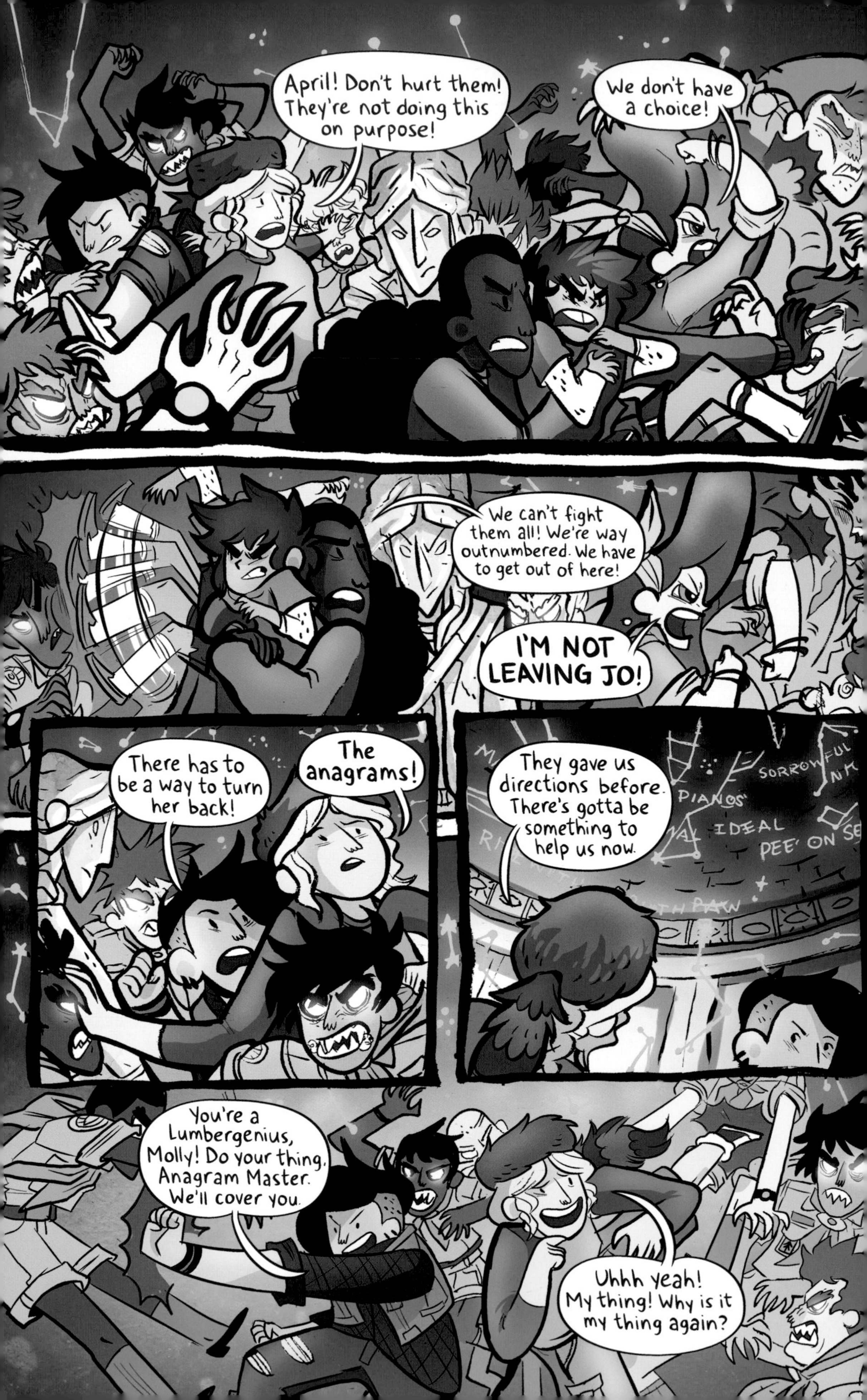
April! Don't hurt them! They're not doing this on purpose!
We don't have a choice!
We can't fight them all! We're way outnumbered. We have to get out of here!
I'M NOT LEAVING JO!
There has to be a way to turn her back!
The anagrams!
They gave us directions before. There's gotta be something to help us now.
PIANOS
IDEAL
You're a Lumbergenius, Molly! Do your thing, Anagram Master. We'll cover you.
Uhhh yeah! My thing! Why is it my thing again?

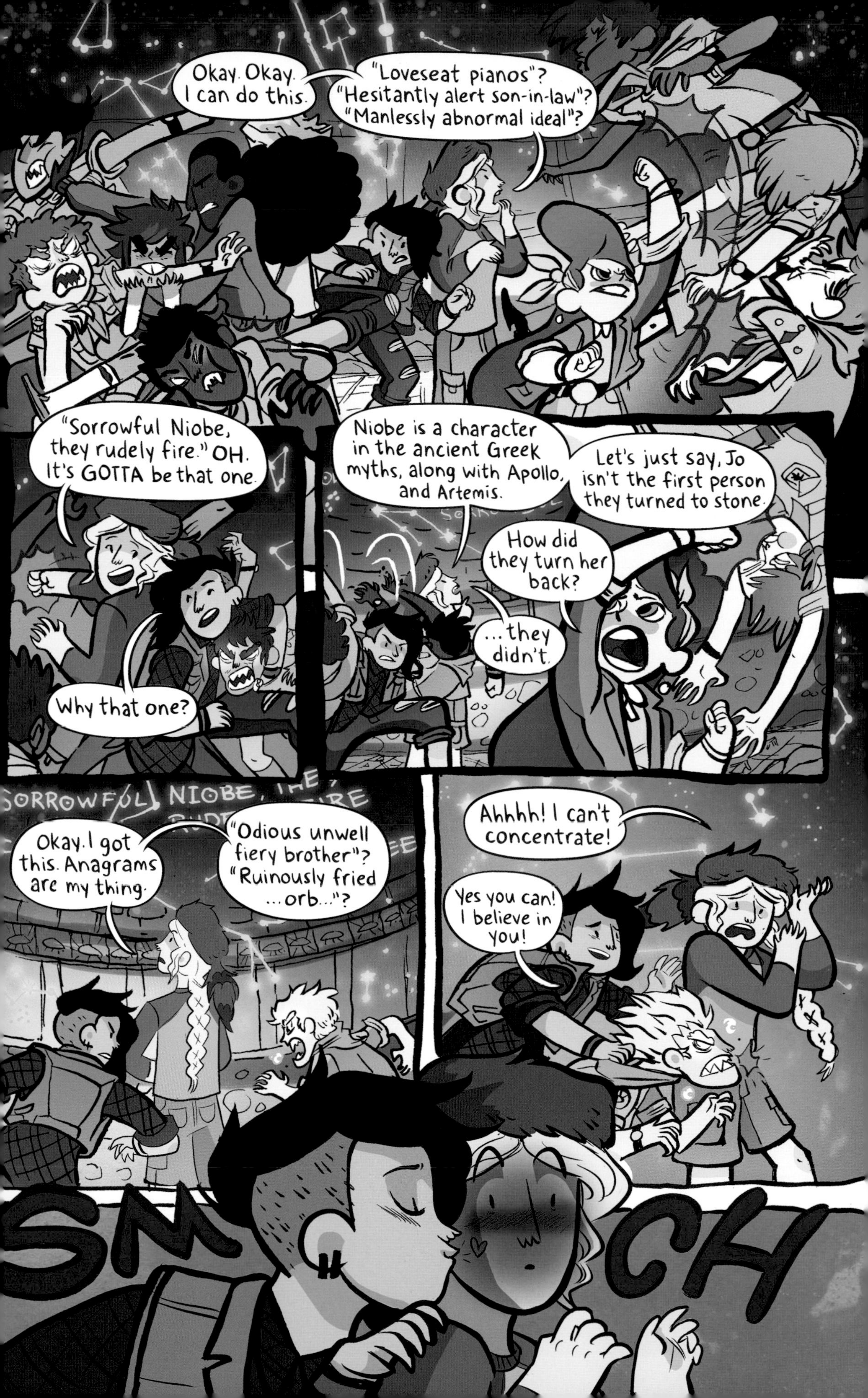
Okay. Okay. I can do this.
"Loveseat pianos"? "Hesitantly alert son-in-law"? "Manlessly abnormal ideal"?
"Sorrowful Niobe, they rudely fire." OH. It's GOTTA be that one.
Why that one?
Niobe is a character in the ancient Greek myths, along with Apollo, and Artemis.
Let's just say, Jo isn't the first person they turned to stone.
How did they turn her back?
...they didn't.
SORROWFUL NIOBE,
Okay. I got this. Anagrams are my thing.
"Odious unwell fiery brother"? "Ruinously fried ...orb..."?
Ahhhh! I can't concentrate!
Yes you can! I believe in you!
SM
CH

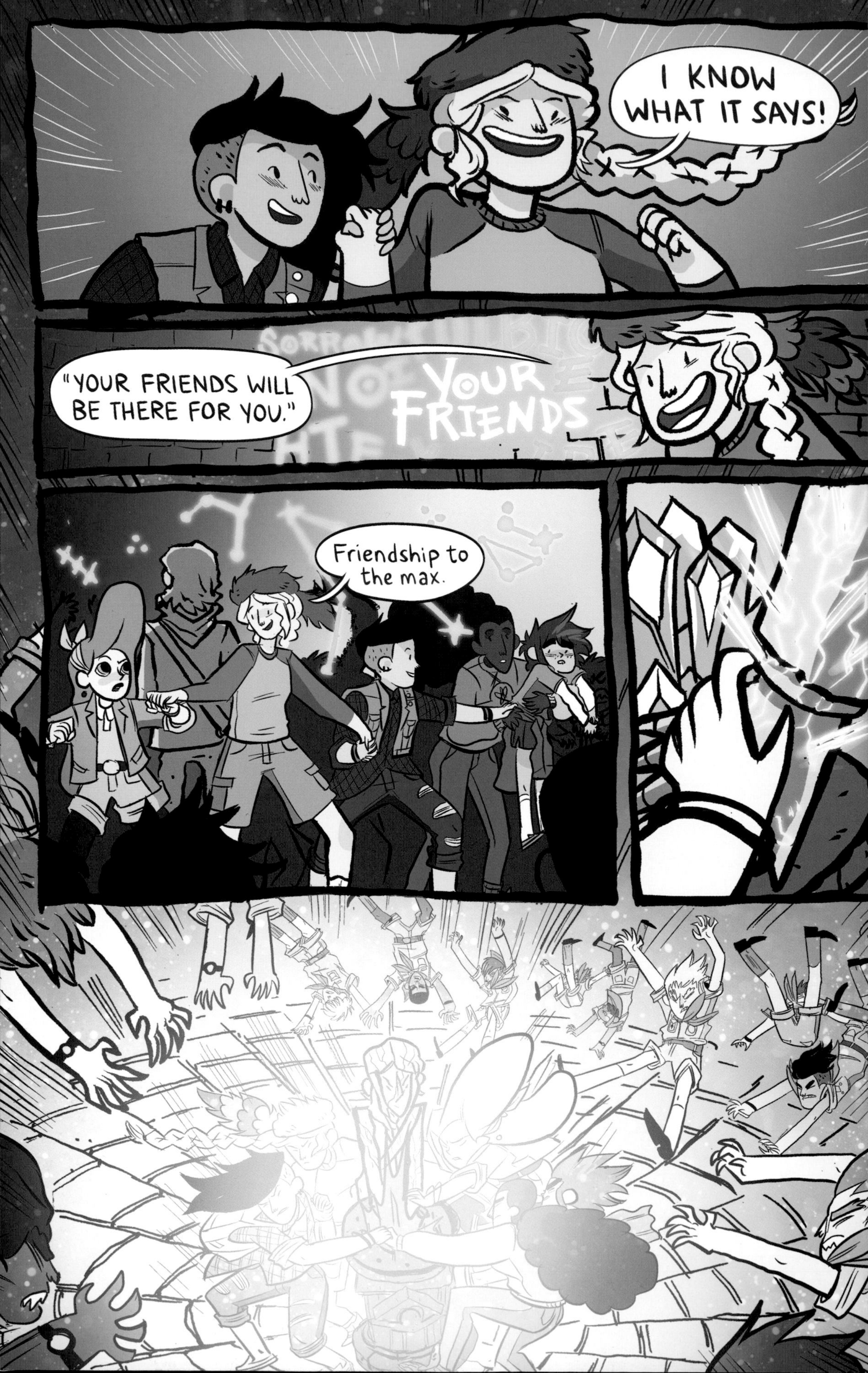
I KNOW WHAT IT SAYS!
"YOUR FRIENDS WILL BE THERE FOR YOU."
YOUR FRIENDS
Friendship to the max.

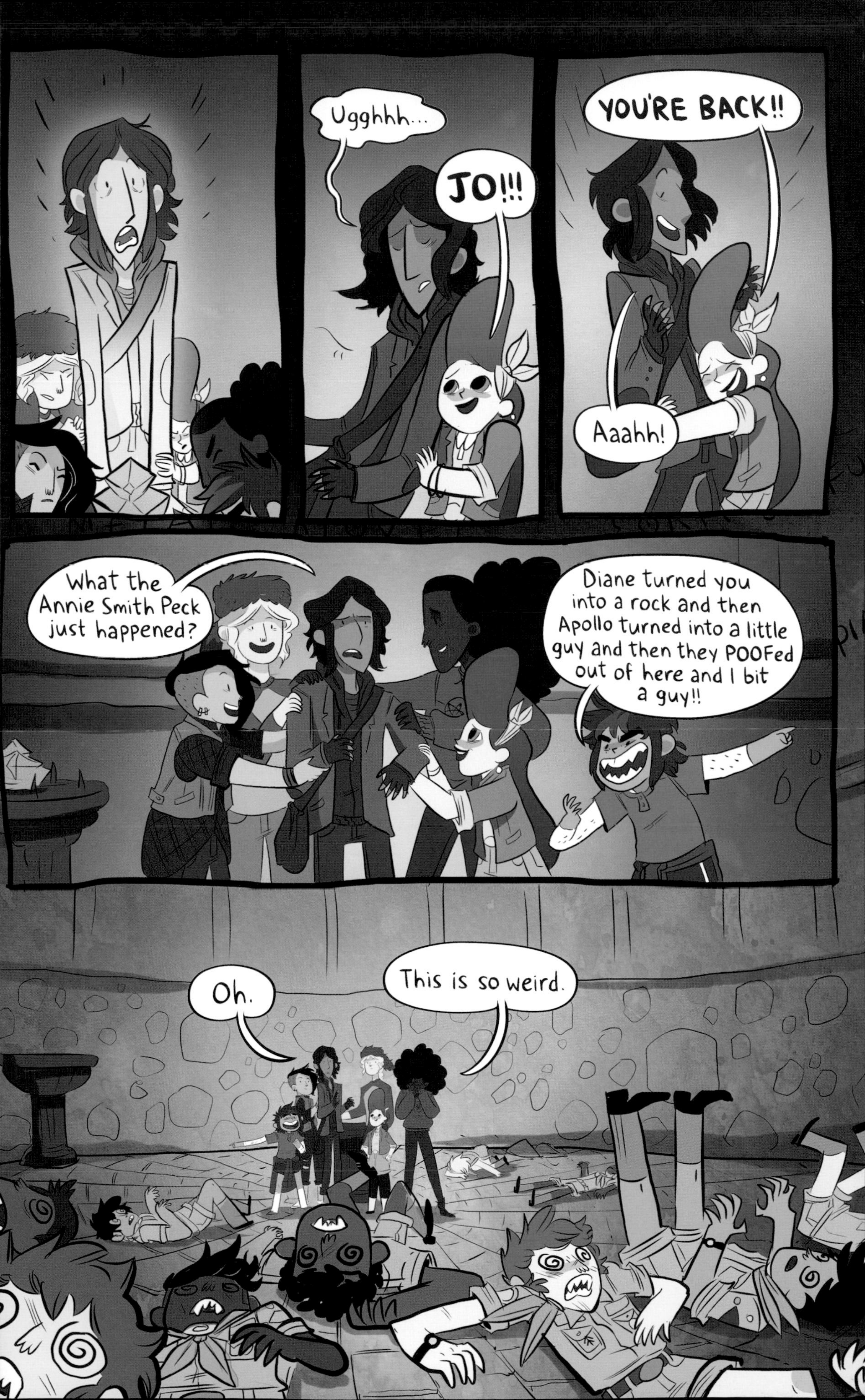
Ugghhh...
JO!!!
YOU'RE BACK!!
Aaahh!
What the Annie Smith Peck just happened?
Diane turned you into a rock and then Apollo turned into a little guy and then they POOFed out of here and I bit a guy!!
Oh.
This is so weird.

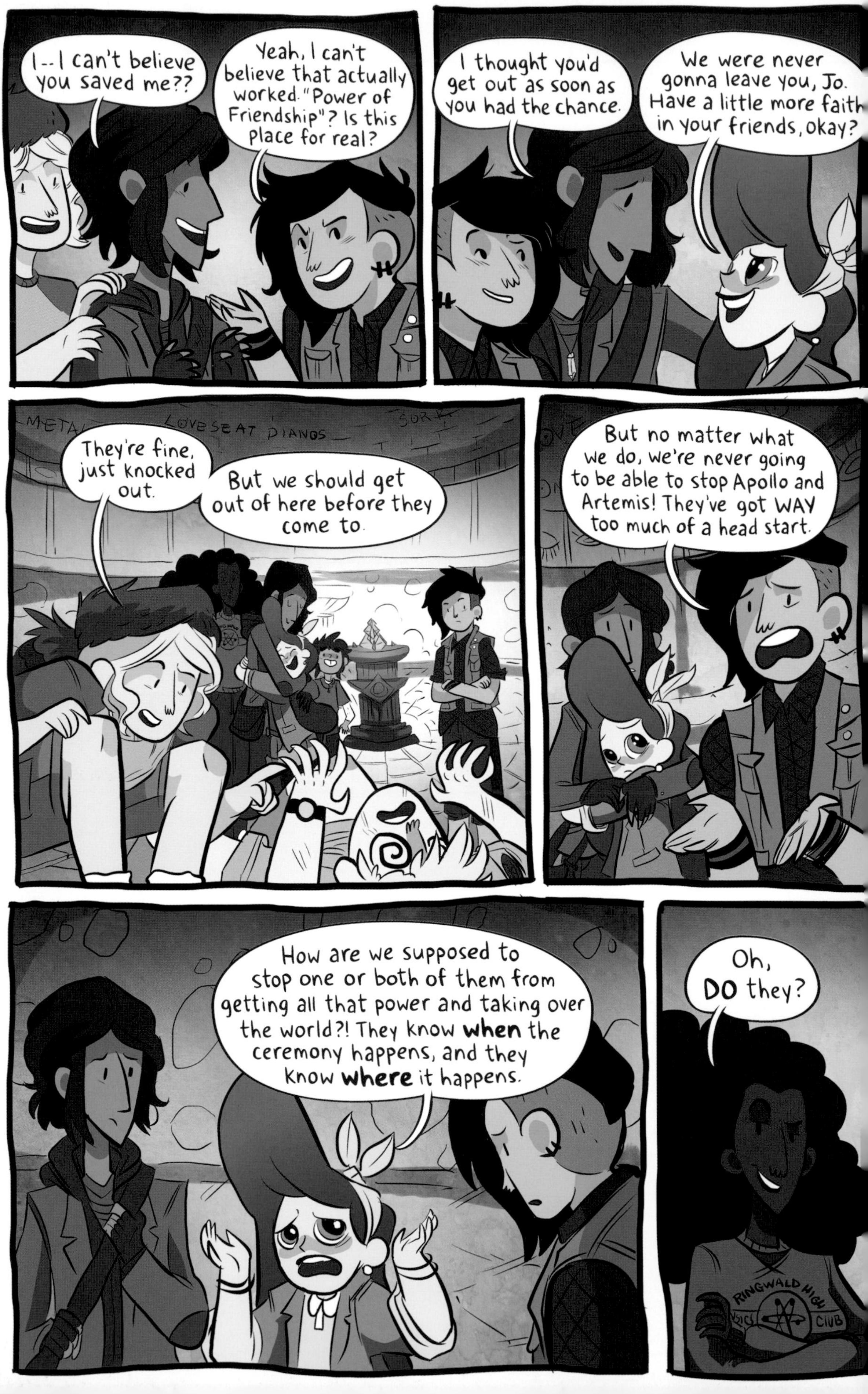
I--I can't believe you saved me??
Yeah, I can't believe that actually worked. "Power of Friendship"? Is this place for real?
I thought you'd get out as soon as you had the chance.
We were never gonna leave you, Jo. Have a little more faith in your friends, okay?
LOVESEAT PIANOS
They're fine, just knocked out.
But we should get out of here before they come to.
But no matter what we do, we're never going to be able to stop Apollo and Artemis! They've got WAY too much of a head start.
How are we supposed to stop one or both of them from getting all that power and taking over the world?! They know **when** the ceremony happens, and they know **where** it happens.
Oh, **DO** they?
RINGWALD HIGH
CLUB

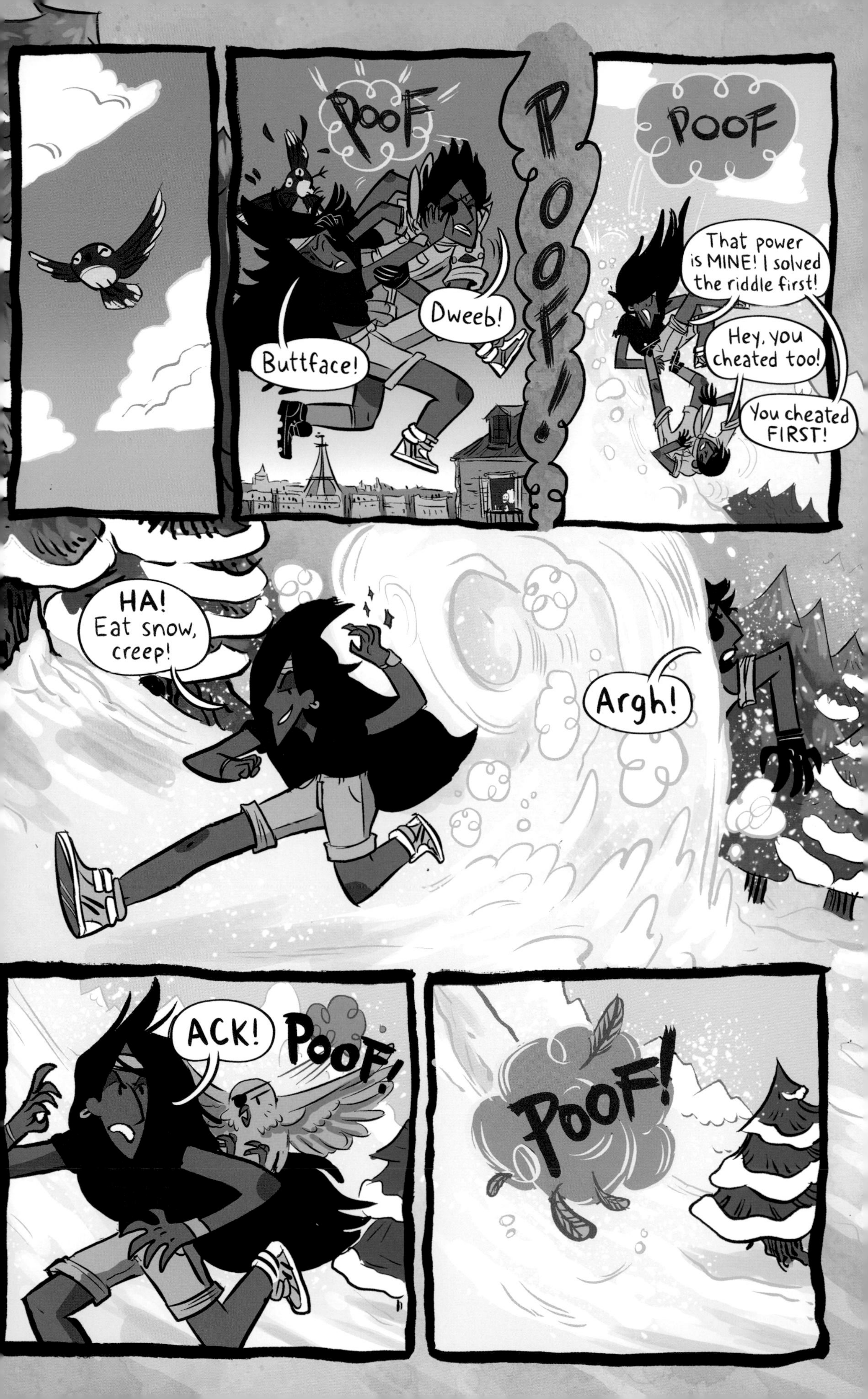
POOF
Dweeb!
Buttface!
POOOF!
POOF
That power is MINE! I solved the riddle first!
Hey, you cheated too!
You cheated FIRST!
HA! Eat snow, creep!
Argh!
ACK!
POOF!
POOF!

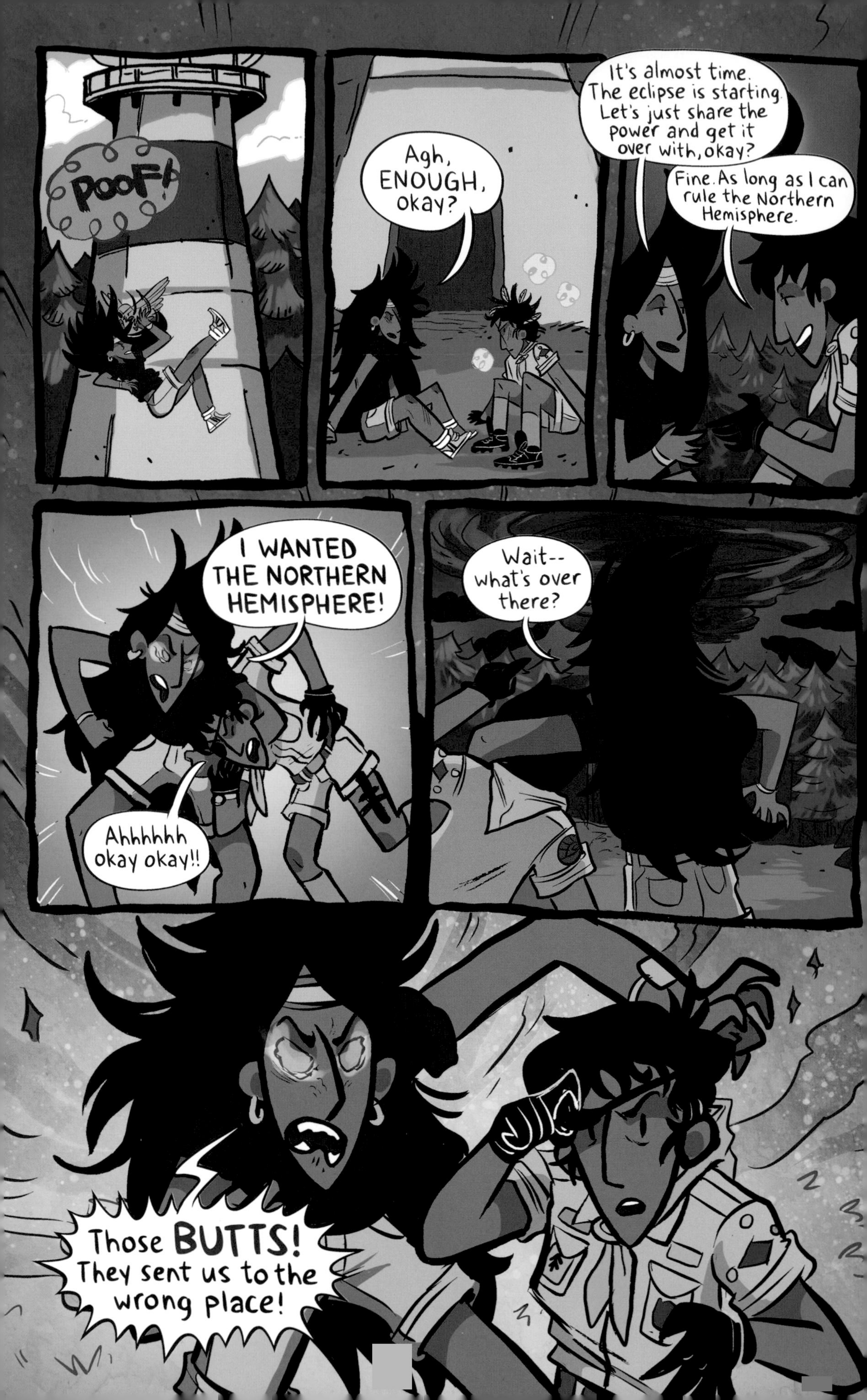
POOF!
Agh, ENOUGH, okay?
It's almost time. The eclipse is starting. Let's just share the power and get it over with, okay?
Fine. As long as I can rule the Northern Hemisphere.
I WANTED THE NORTHERN HEMISPHERE!
Ahhhhhh okay okay!!
Wait-- what's over there?
Those BUTTS! They sent us to the wrong place!

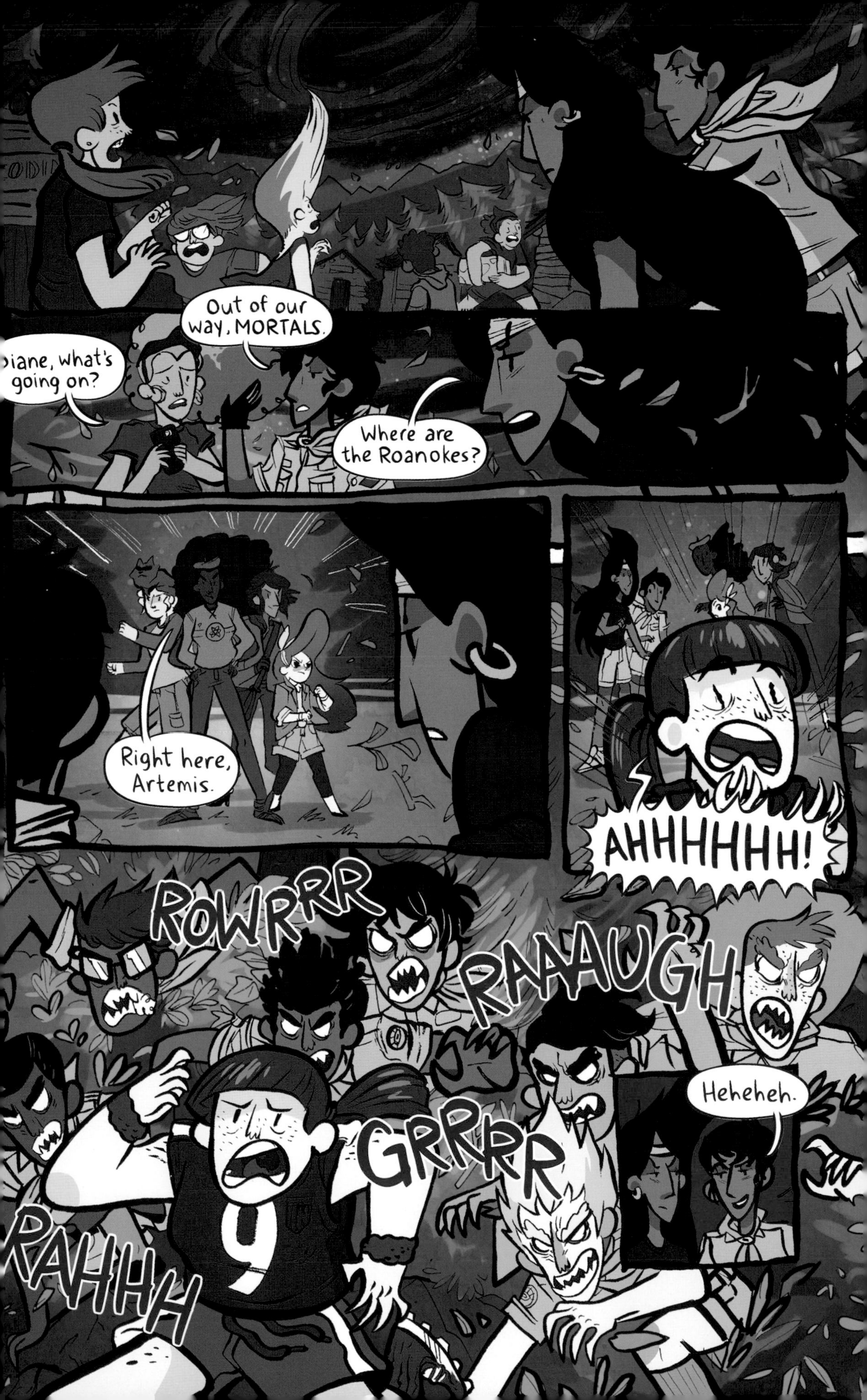

Out of our way, MORTALS.
iane, what's going on?
Where are the Roanokes?
Right here, Artemis.
AHHHHHH!
ROWRRR
RAAAUGH
Heheheh.
GRRRR
RAHHH

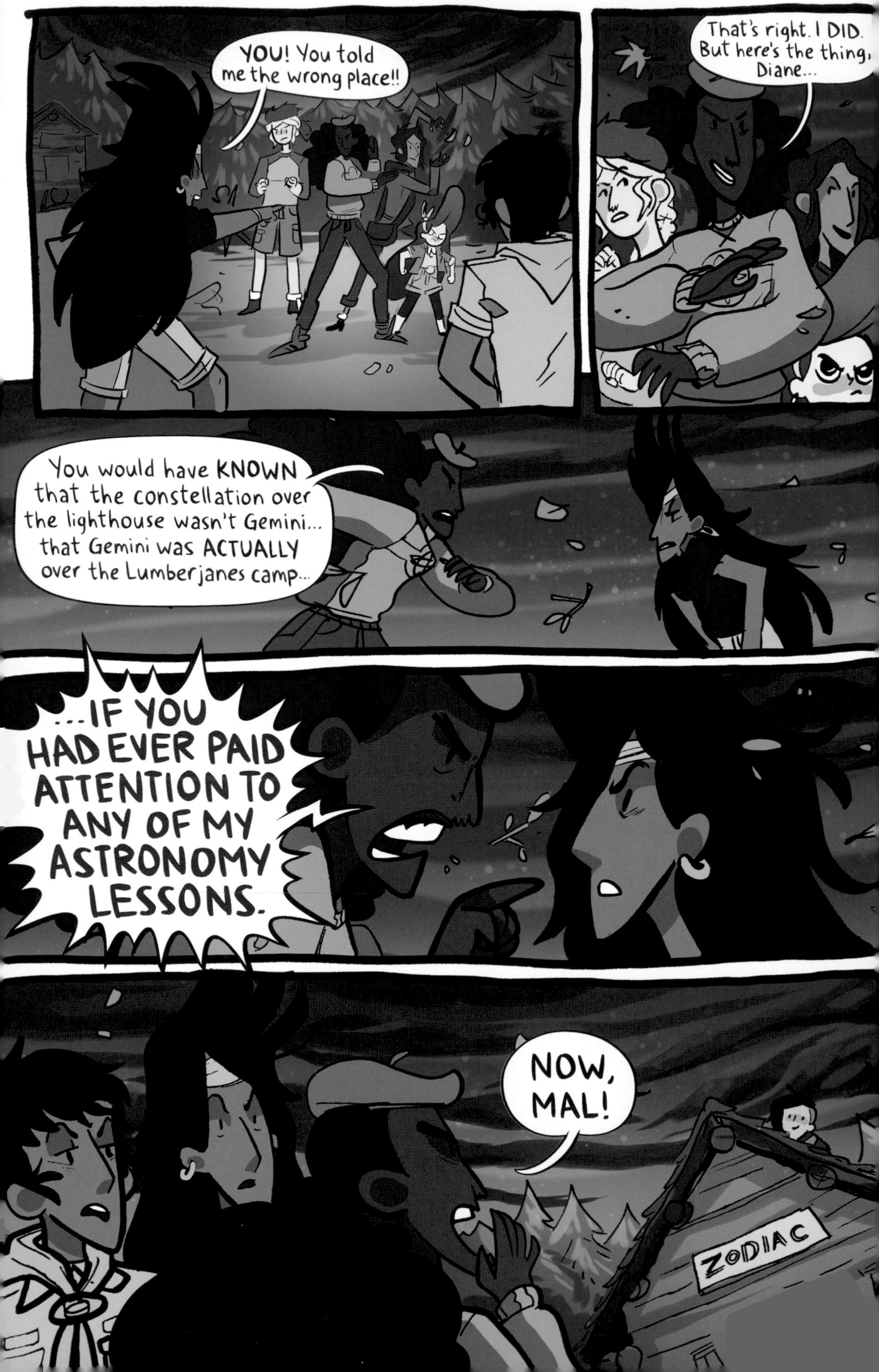
YOU! You told me the wrong place!!
That's right. I DID. But here's the thing, Diane...
You would have KNOWN that the constellation over the lighthouse wasn't Gemini... that Gemini was ACTUALLY over the Lumberjanes camp...
...IF YOU HAD EVER PAID ATTENTION TO ANY OF MY ASTRONOMY LESSONS.
NOW, MAL!
ZODIAC

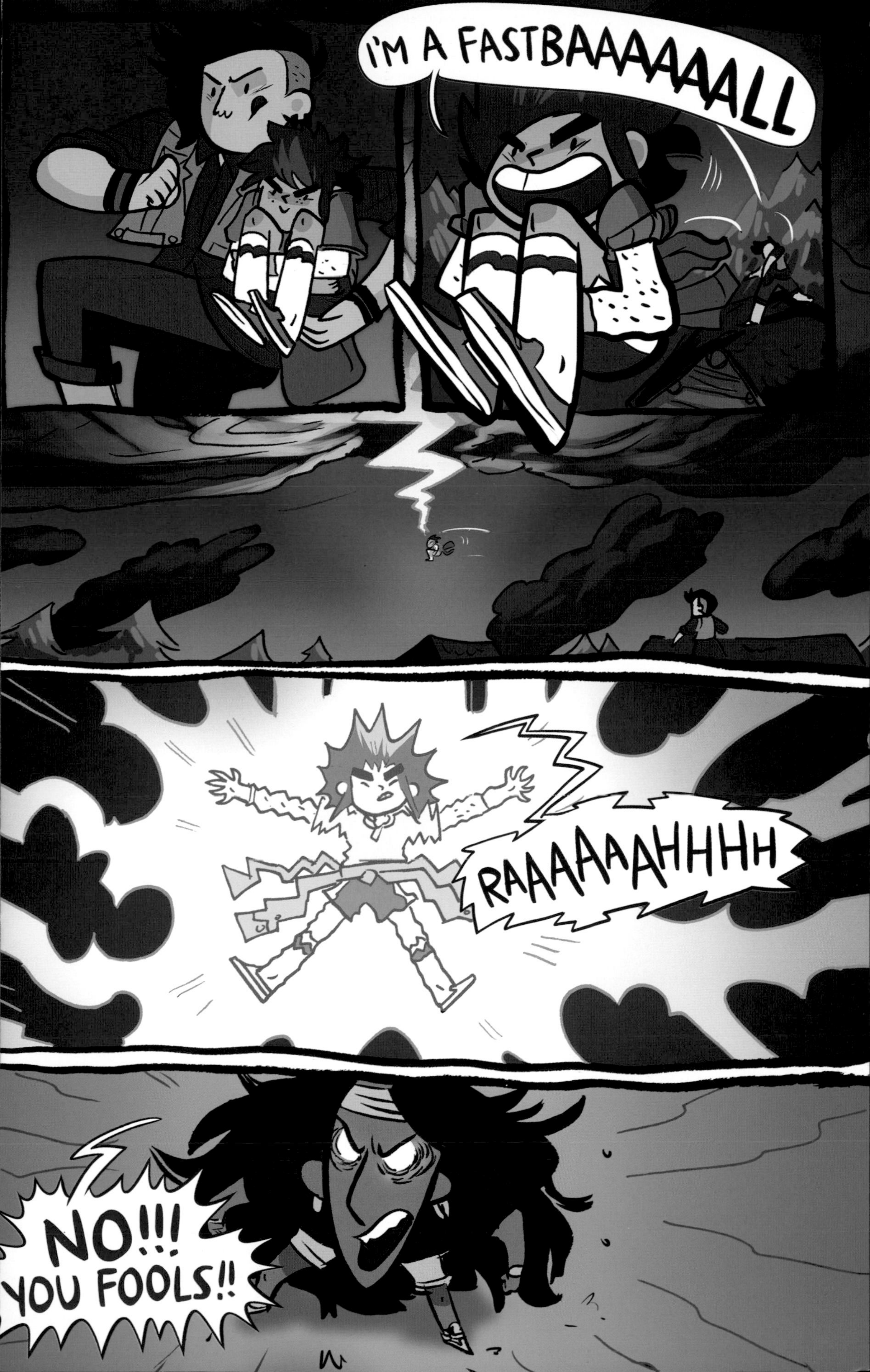
I'M A FASTBAAAAAAALL
RAAAAAAHHHH
NO!!!
YOU FOOLS!!

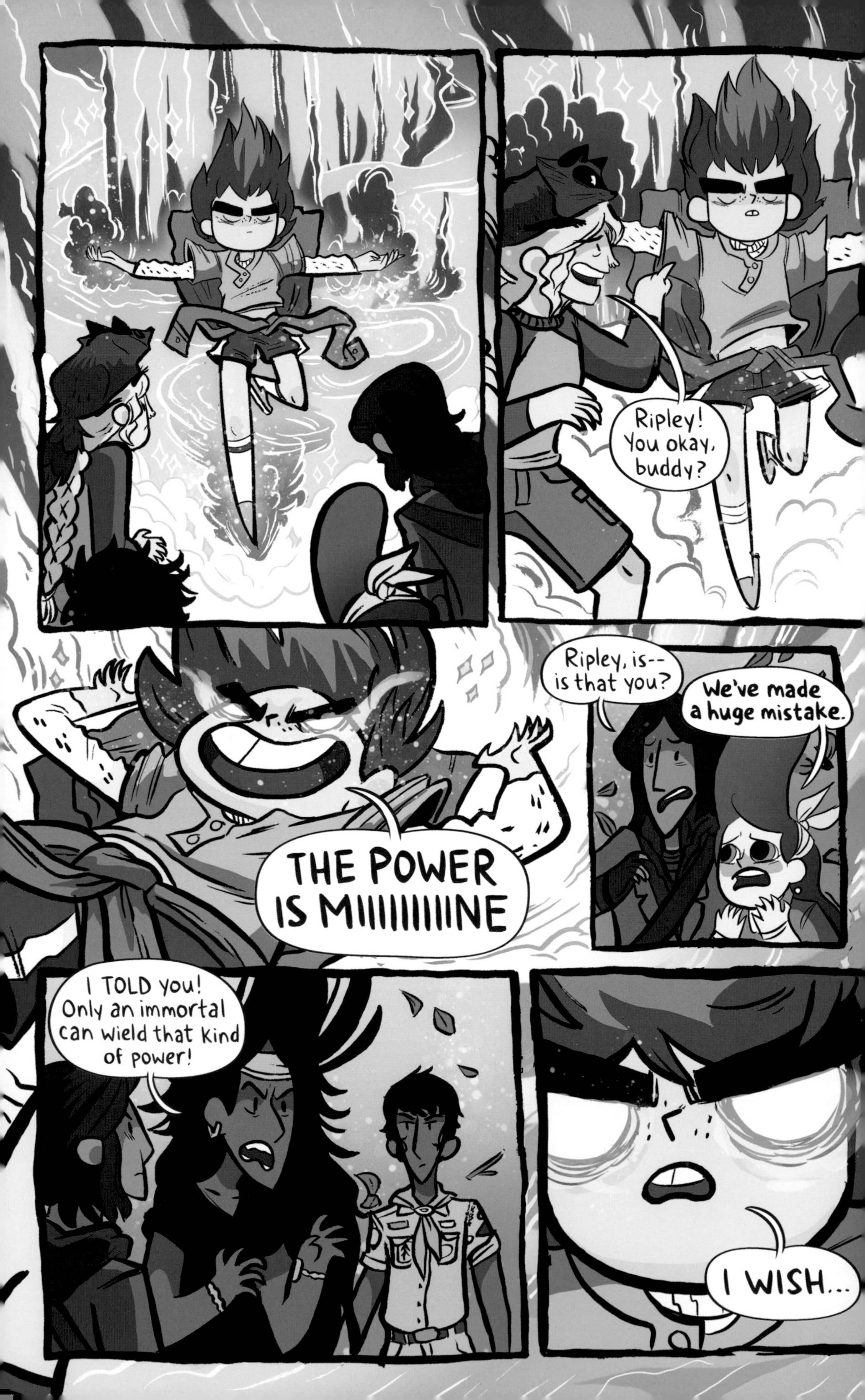

Ripley! You okay, buddy?
THE POWER IS MIIIIIIIIINE
Ripley, is-- is that you?
We've made a huge mistake.
I TOLD you! Only an immortal can wield that kind of power!
I WISH...

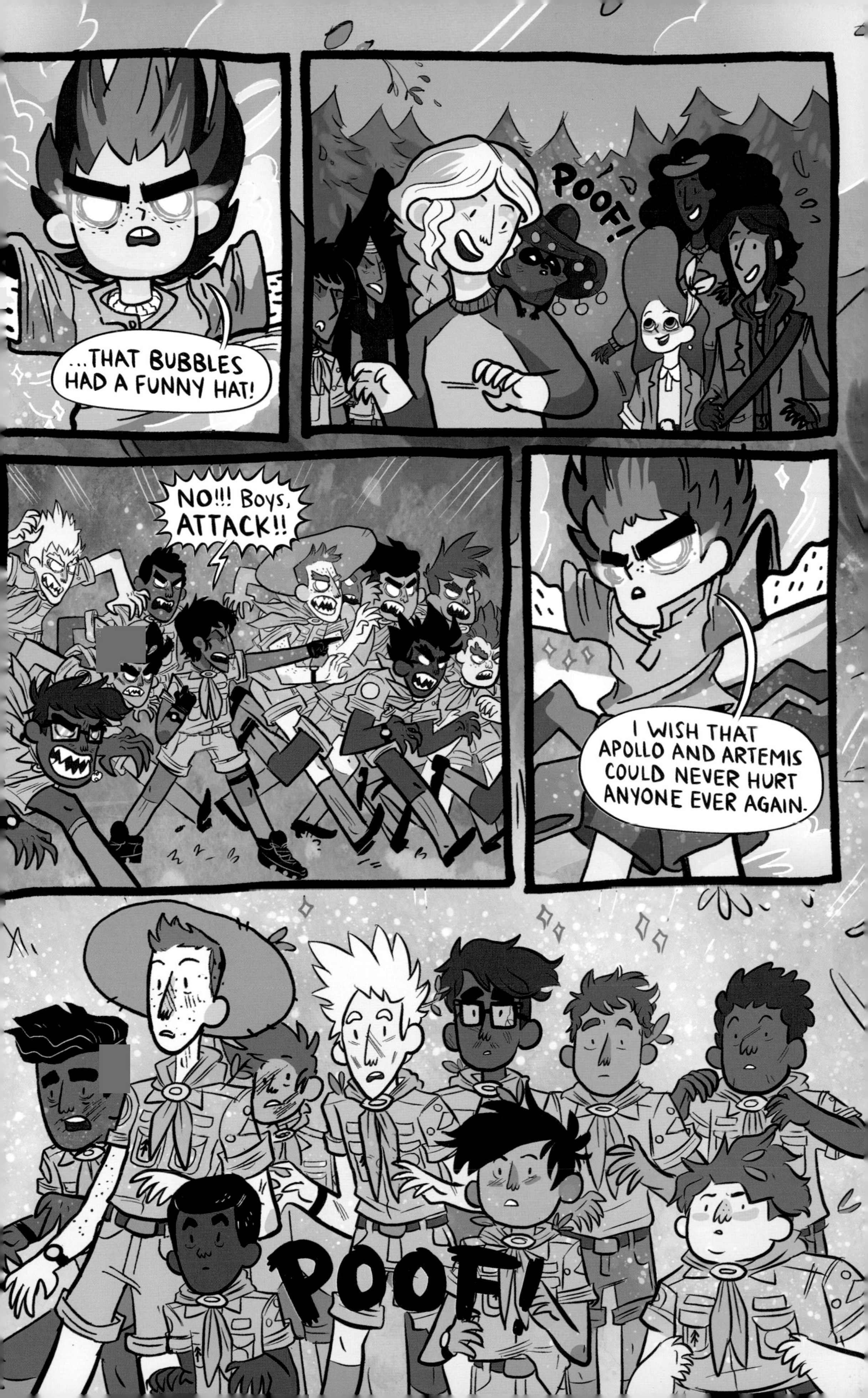
...THAT BUBBLES HAD A FUNNY HAT!
POOF!
NO!!! Boys, ATTACK!!
I WISH THAT APOLLO AND ARTEMIS COULD NEVER HURT ANYONE EVER AGAIN.
POOF!

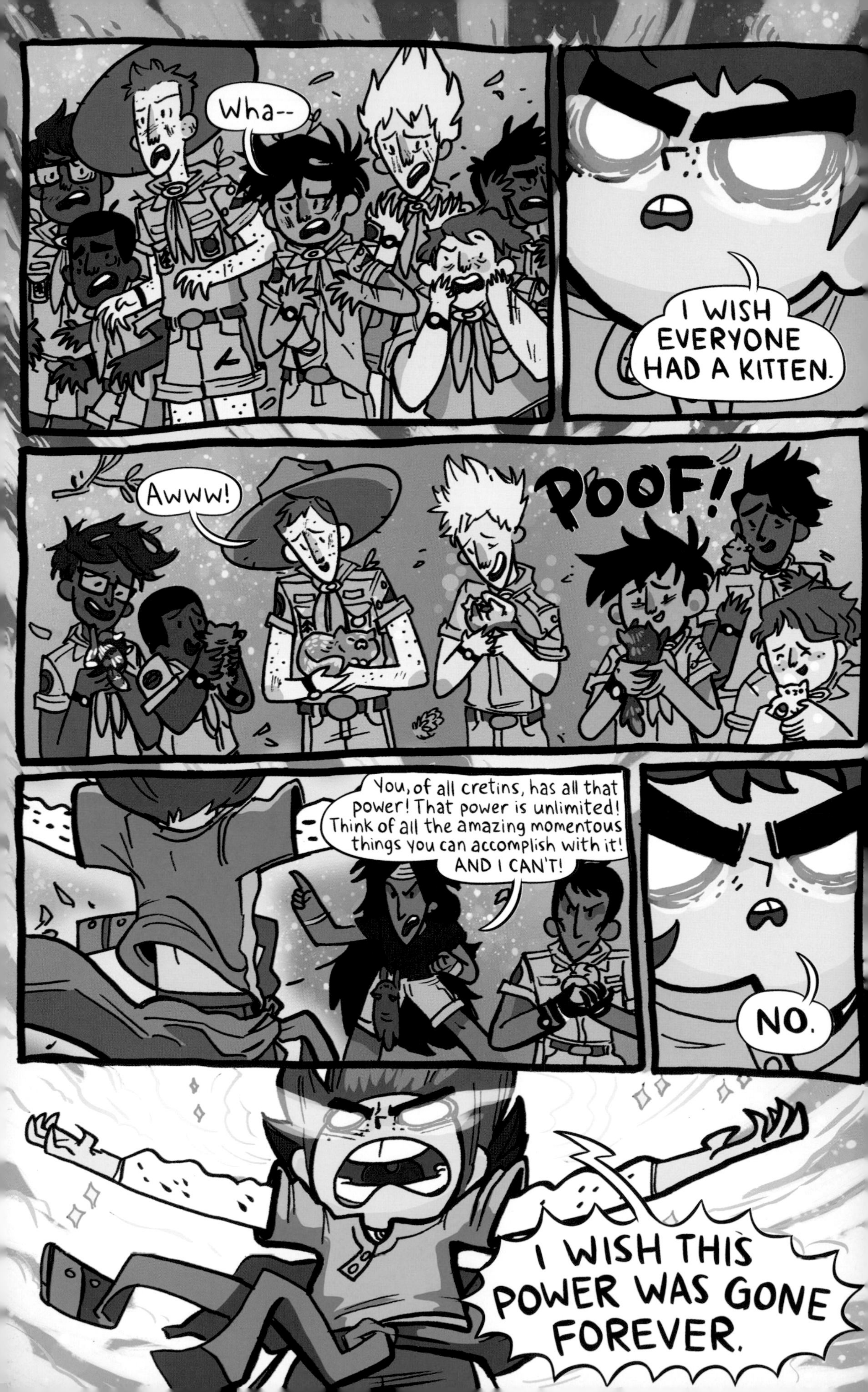
Wha--
I WISH EVERYONE HAD A KITTEN.
Awww!
POOF!
You, of all cretins, has all that power! That power is unlimited! Think of all the amazing momentous things you can accomplish with it! AND I CAN'T!
NO.
I WISH THIS POWER WAS GONE FOREVER.

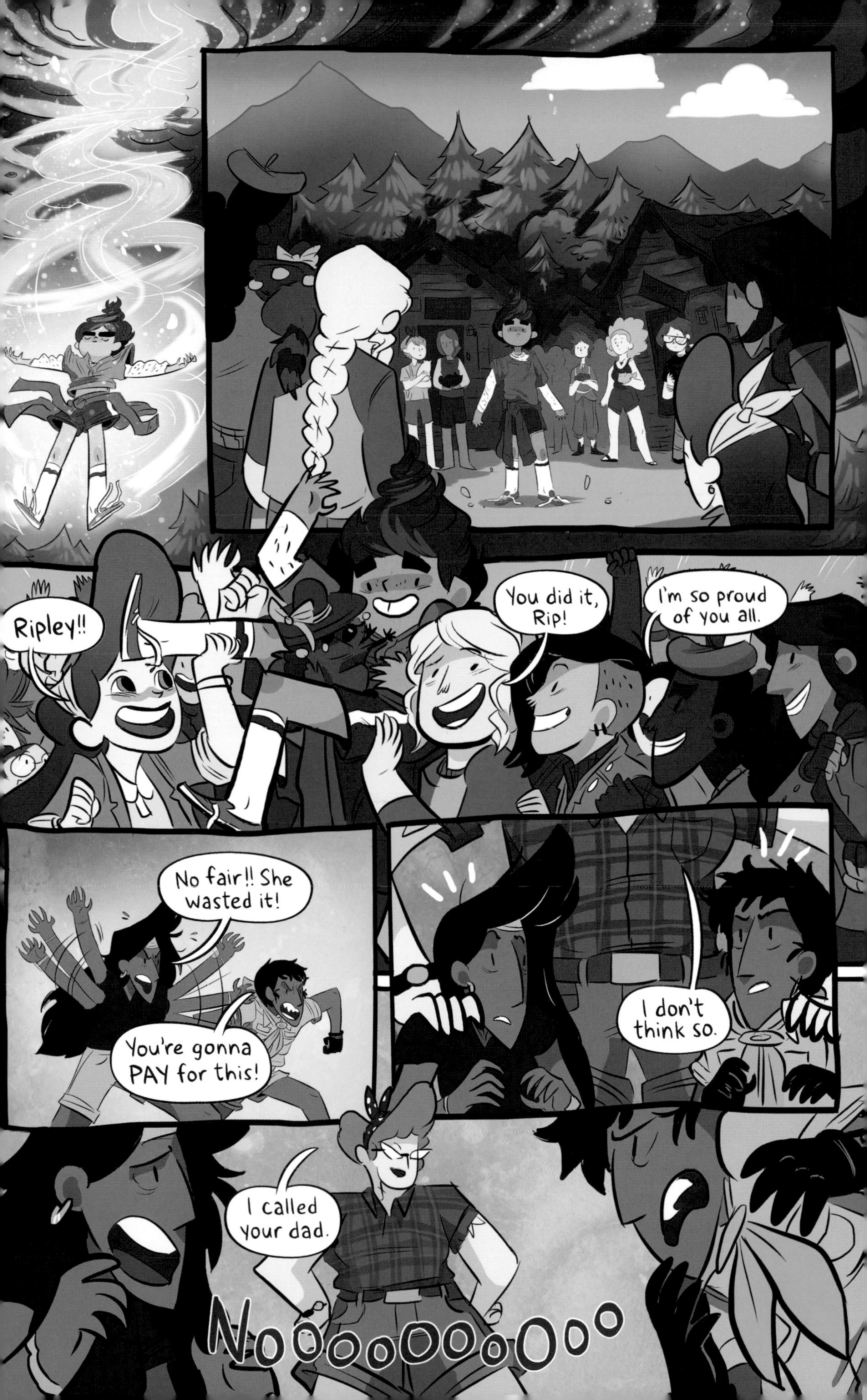
Ripley!!
You did it, Rip!
I'm so proud of you all.
No fair!! She wasted it!
You're gonna PAY for this!
I don't think so.
I called your dad.
NoooooOooooOoo

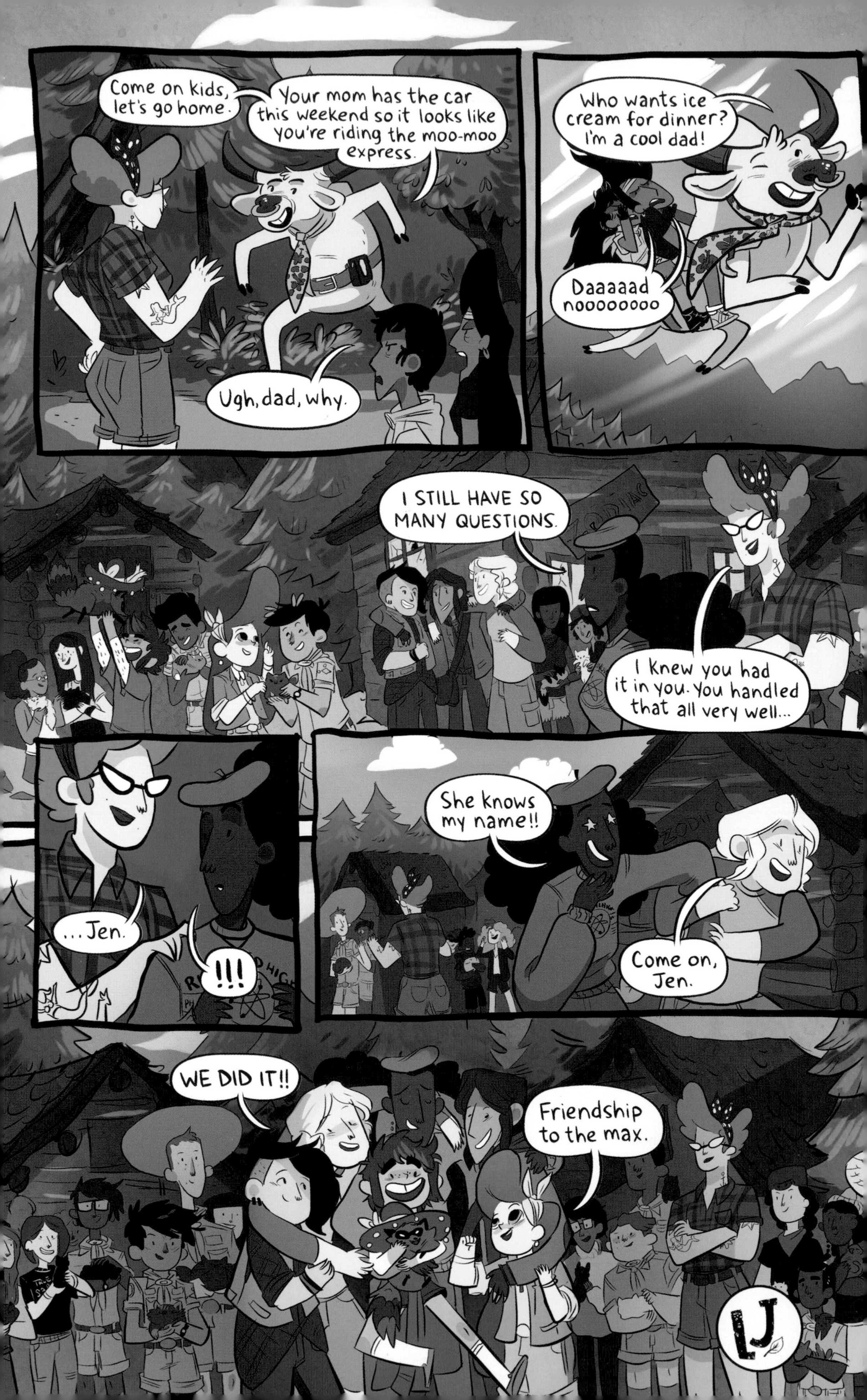
Come on kids, let's go home.
Your mom has the car this weekend so it looks like you're riding the moo-moo express.
Ugh, dad, why.
Who wants ice cream for dinner? I'm a cool dad!
Daaaaad noooooooo
I STILL HAVE SO MANY QUESTIONS.
I knew you had it in you. You handled that all very well...
...Jen.
!!!
She knows my name!!
Come on, Jen.
WE DID IT!!
Friendship to the max.

will co

The
It help
appearan
dress f
Further
Lumber
to have
part in
Thiskv
Hardo
have
them

**RUMBLE, YOUNG LADY, RUMBLE**

The
yellow, short sl
emb
the w
choose
slacks,
made o
out-of-do
green bere
the colla
Shoes ma
heels, rou
socks sho
the uniform. Ne
belong with a Lumberjane uniform.

**YOU KNOW WHAT I'M SUPER-SAYIN'?**

HOW TO WEAR

To look well in a unifo
uniform be kept in g
pressed. See that the ski
height and build, that the
that your shoes and stock
uniform, that you watch your
with dignity and grace. If the beret
be sure that your hair is neat and kept in place with an
insconspicuous clip or ribbon. When you wear a
Lumberjane uniform you are identified as a member of
this organization and you should be doubly careful to
conduct yourself in a way that will show everyone that
courtesy and thoughtfullness are part of being a
Lumberjane. People are likely to judge a whole nation by
the selfishness of a few individuals, to criticize a whole
family because of the misconduct of one member, and to
feel unkindly toward and organization because of the

E UNIFORM

should be worn at camp
events when Lumberjanes
may also be worn at other
ions. It should be worn as a
the uniform dress with
rect shoes, and stocking or

out grows her uniform or
ter Lumberjane.
a she has
her
her

The unifor
helps to cre
in a group.
active life th
another bond
future, and pr
in order to b
Lumberjane pr
Penniquiqul Thi
Types, but m
can either bu
materials available at the trading post.

**SUPES ADORBS**

# COVER GALLERY

*Lumberjanes "Literature" Program Field*

## CON-QUEST

*"Divide and conquer, it actually works."*

A Lumberjane will face many trials during her time at camp. It is through these trials that she grows and learns what kind of Lumberjane she truly is, but not all trials are meant for just one person. At camp there will be many obstacles and challenges that the Lumberjanes will face as a team. The teams could be divided by cabins or they may be divided by the counselor in charge of the group. In these groups the Lumberjane scout will learn what it means to work in a team, what it means to take charge and what it means to step back to let the best equipped person lead them to success. It is their grace under pressure that will get the Lumberjane scout through any of these trials.

These competitions will challenge Lumberjanes against their peers. In the practice for the *Con-Quest* badge, a Lumberjane will understand what it means to win and lose. She will learn from her mistakes and gain experience to better ensure her team's success. She will bring out the best of everyone she works with. She will be cordial and work with grace as she continues this challenge. If she wins then she will not belittle the efforts of the other team, she will understand that keeping a level head after success can be more challenging than keeping it during the competition.

To obtain the *Con-Quest* badge, the Lumberjanes must display their knowledge in the art of war. They must be able to look at their challenge and understand what it takes to win. They must be able to understand what they are capable of and the capabilities of their fellow scouts. The team that earns the *Con-Quest* is not necessarily the winner of the challenge but the team that was able to utilize its members and the tools at their disposal ot the best of their abilities.

During the first summer that the Lumberjane attends

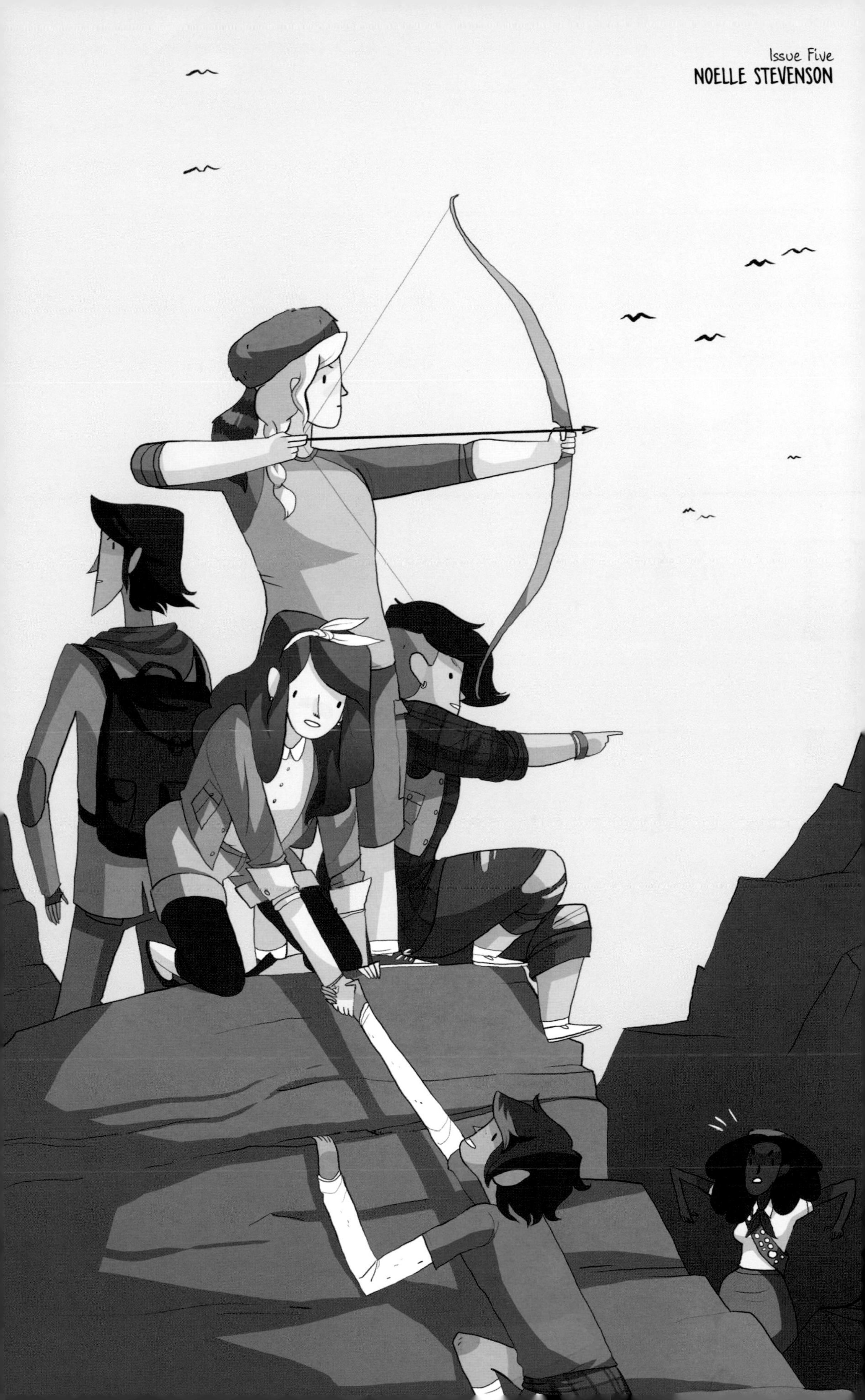
Issue Five
NOELLE STEVENSON

Issue Five Variant
**PERRY MAPLE**

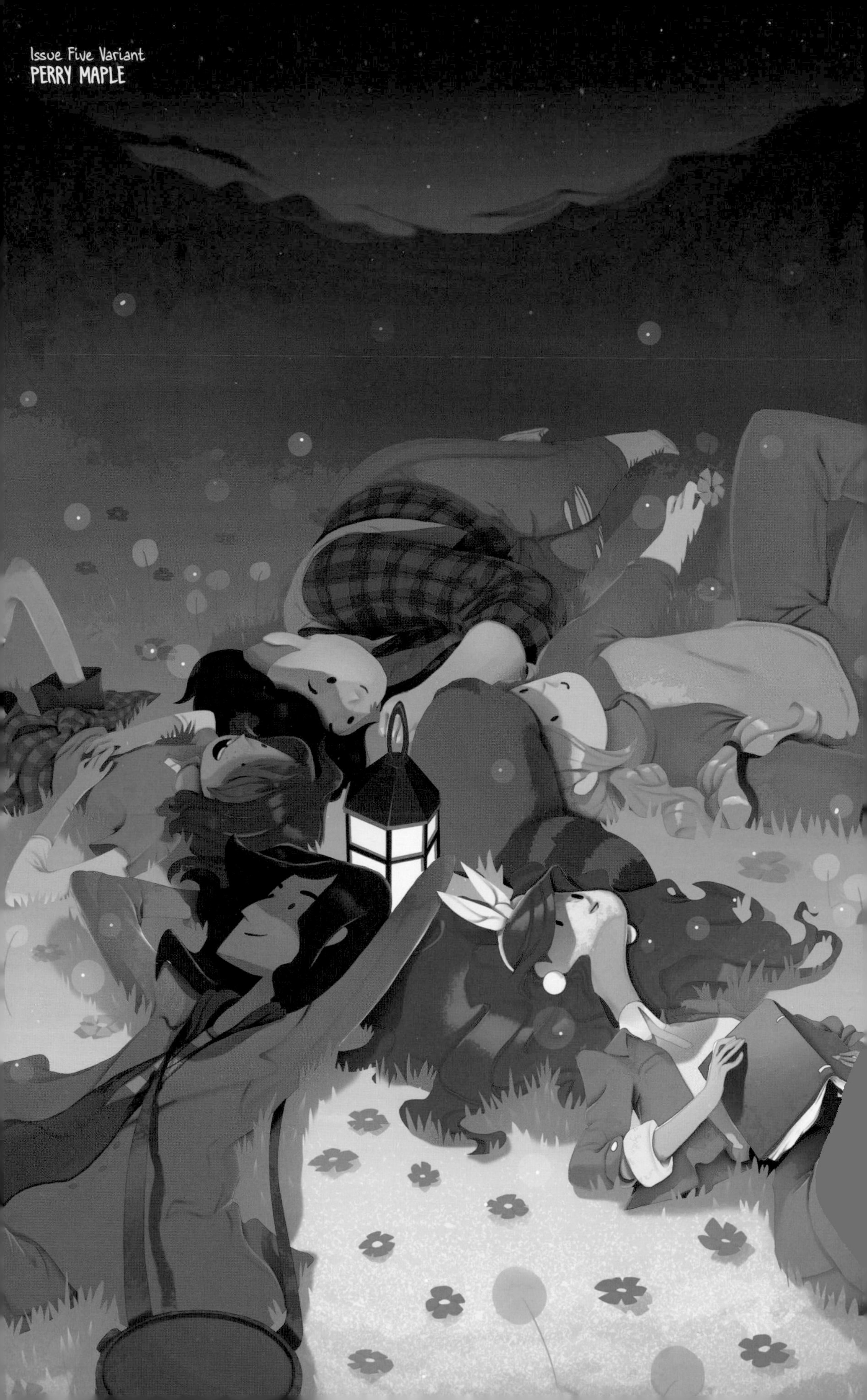

Issue Six
NOELLE STEVENSON

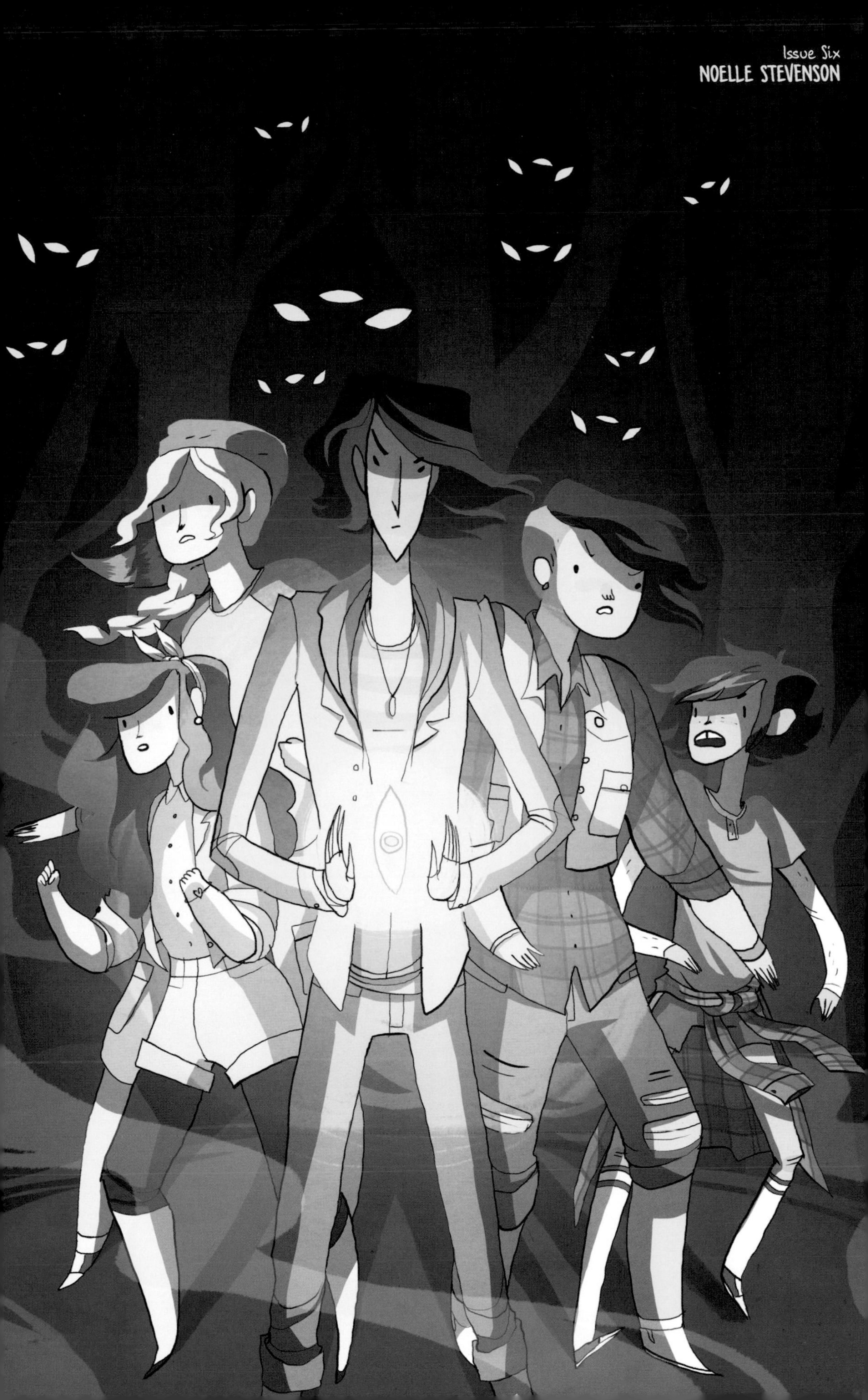

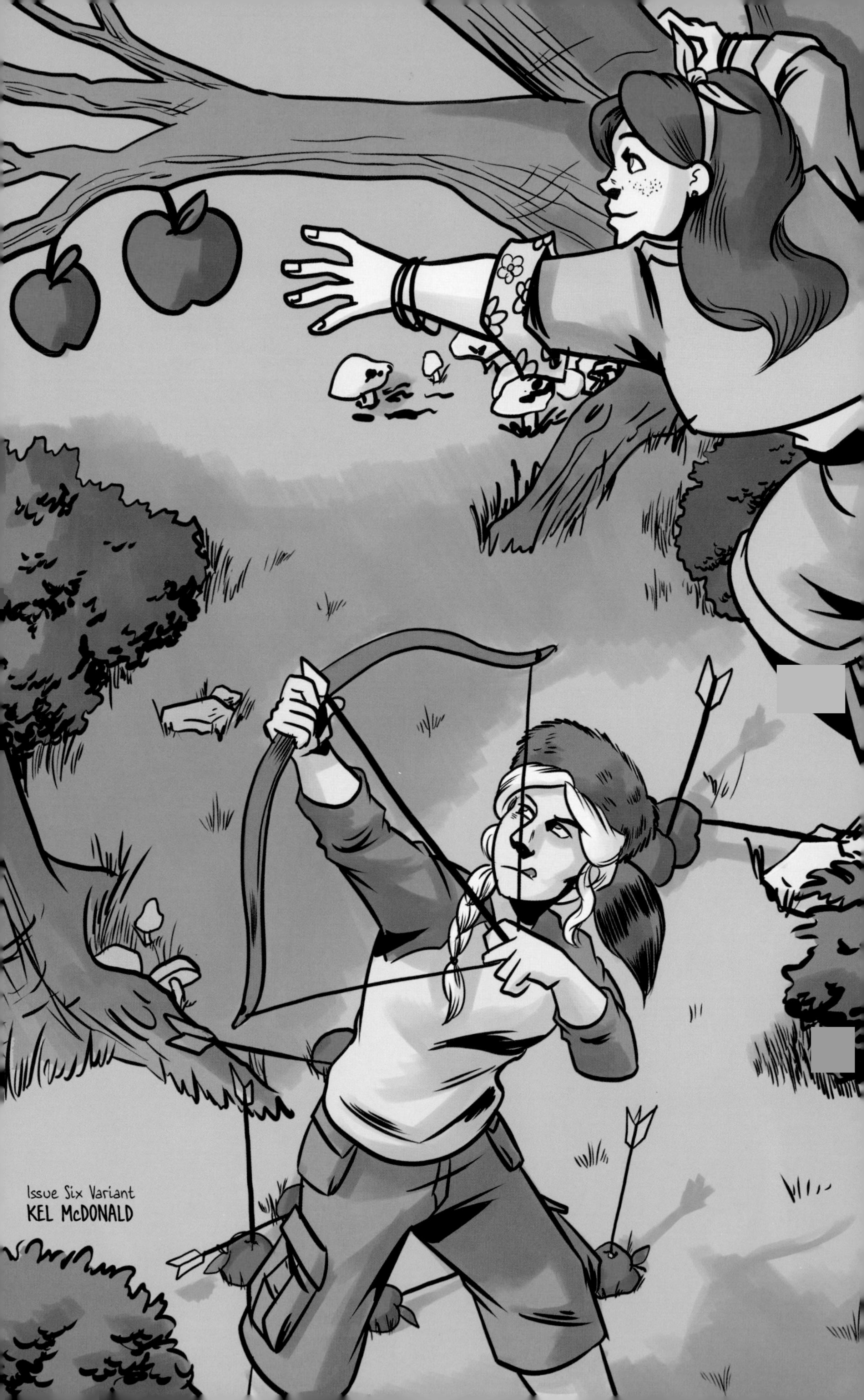
Issue Six Variant
KEL McDONALD

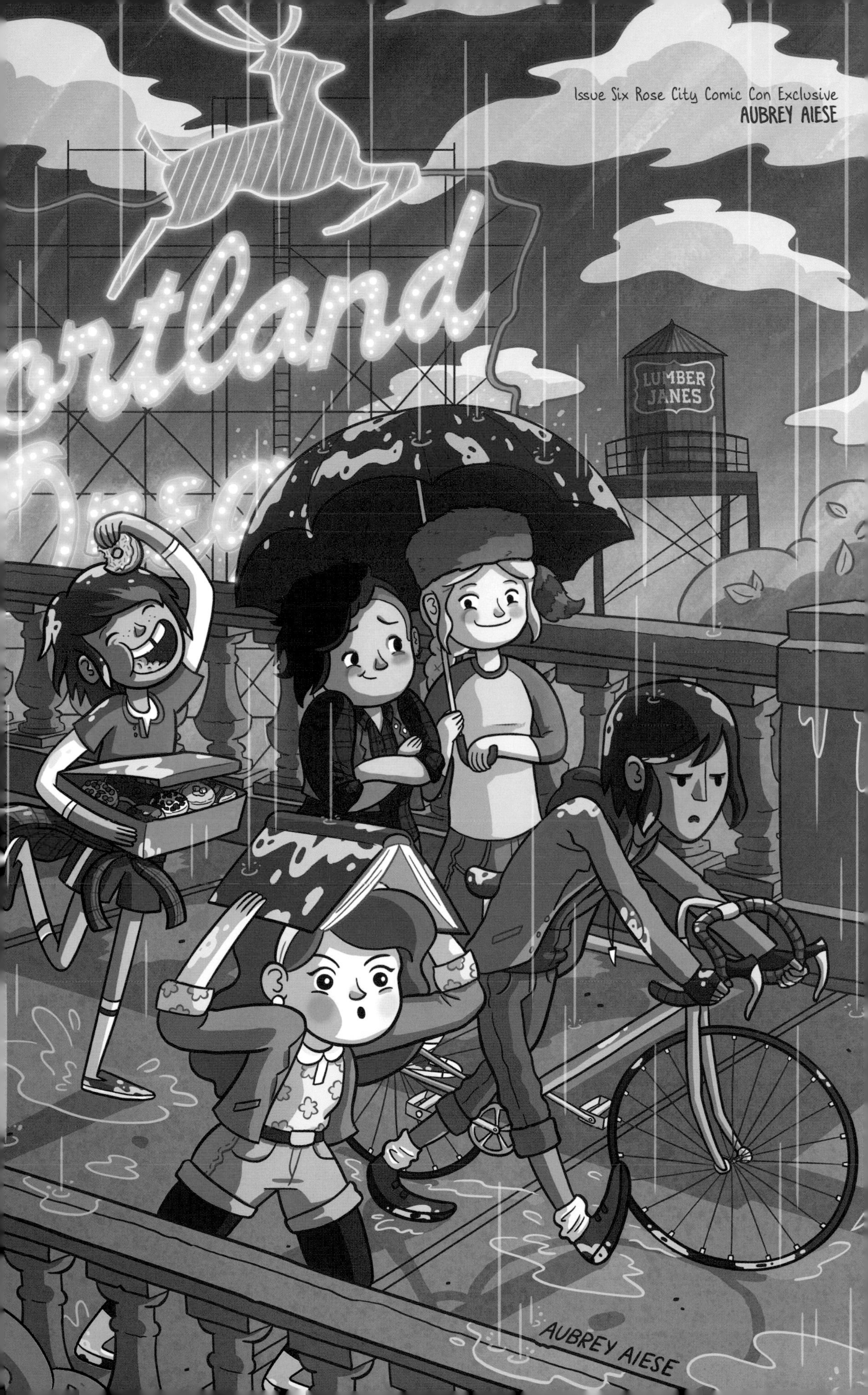
Issue Six Rose City Comic Con Exclusive
AUBREY AIESE
ortland
LUMBER JANES
AUBREY AIESE

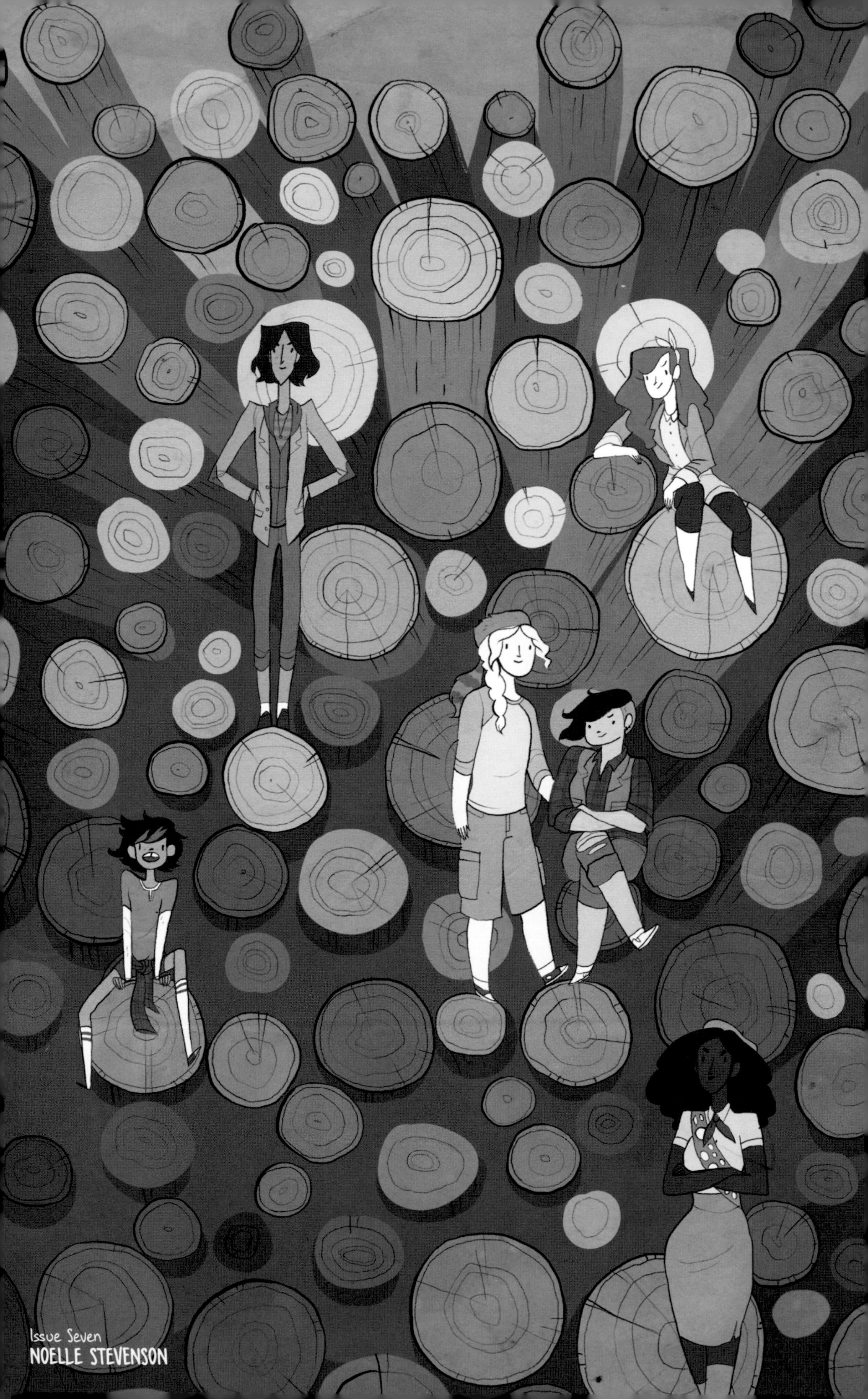
Issue Seven
NOELLE STEVENSON

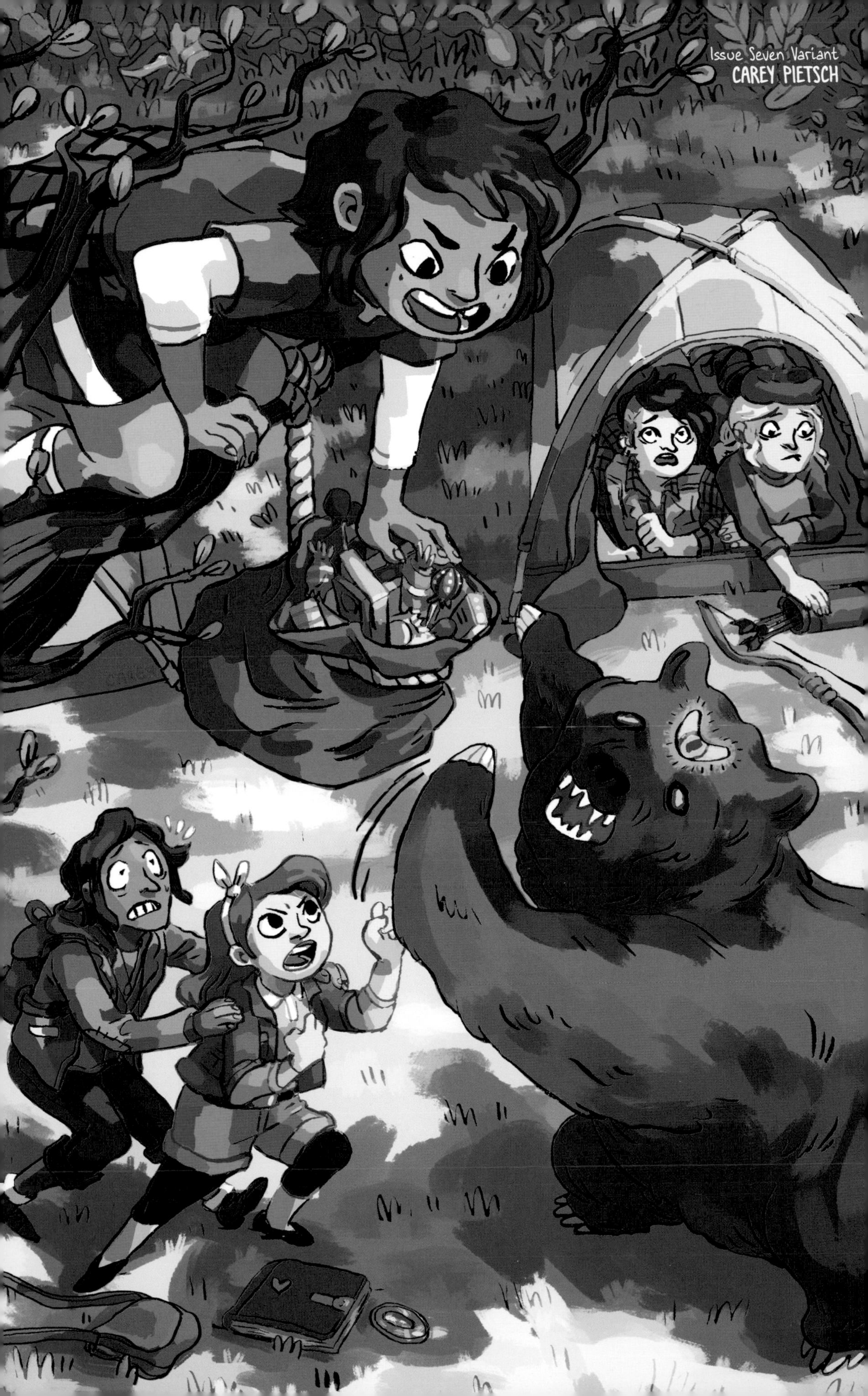
Issue Seven Variant
CAREY PIETSCH

Issue Eight
NOELLE STEVENSON

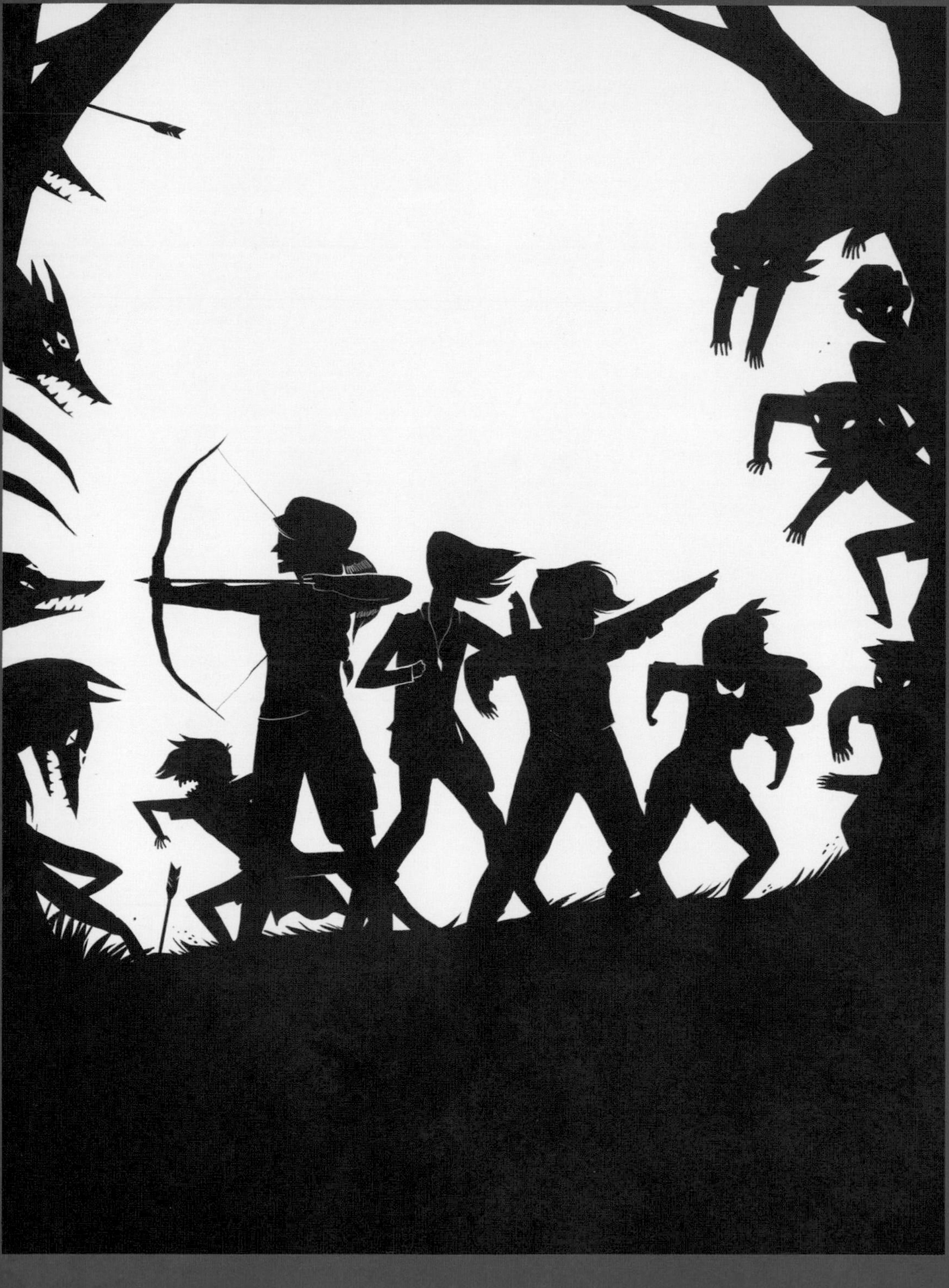

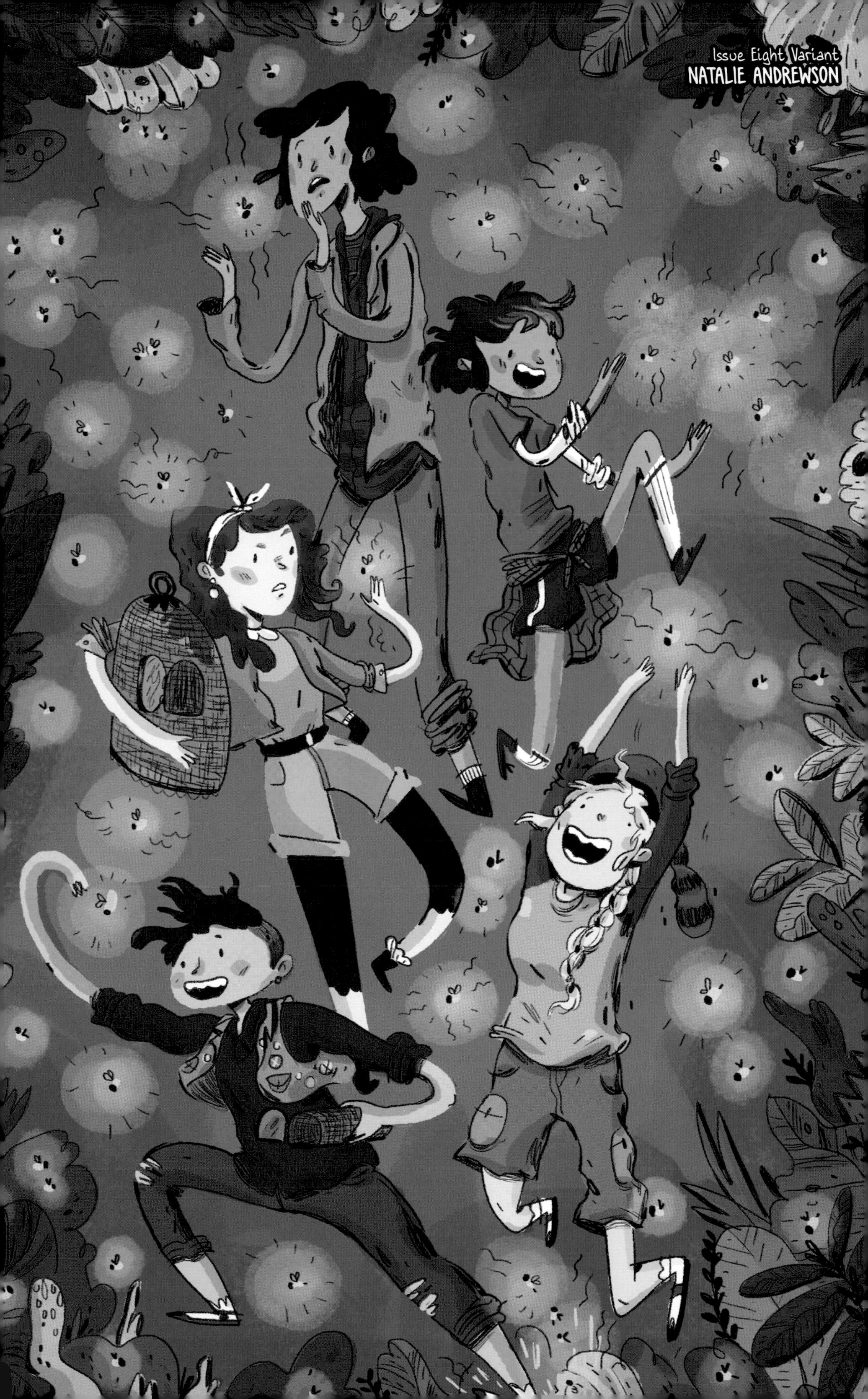
Issue Eight Variant
NATALIE ANDREWSON

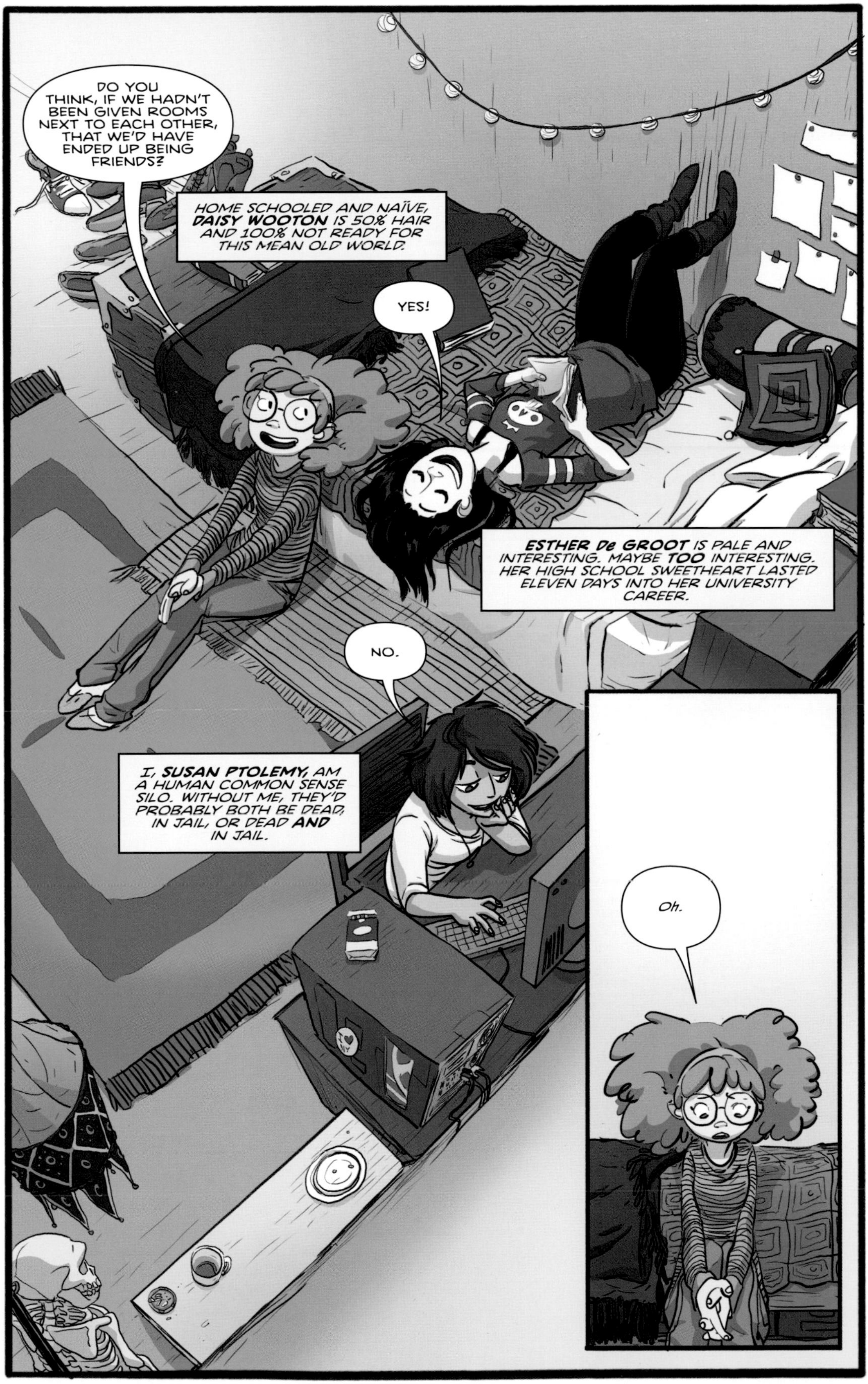
DO YOU THINK, IF WE HADN'T BEEN GIVEN ROOMS NEXT TO EACH OTHER, THAT WE'D HAVE ENDED UP BEING FRIENDS?
HOME SCHOOLED AND NAÏVE, DAISY WOOTON IS 50% HAIR AND 100% NOT READY FOR THIS MEAN OLD WORLD.
YES!
ESTHER De GROOT IS PALE AND INTERESTING. MAYBE TOO INTERESTING. HER HIGH SCHOOL SWEETHEART LASTED ELEVEN DAYS INTO HER UNIVERSITY CAREER.
NO.
I, SUSAN PTOLEMY, AM A HUMAN COMMON SENSE SILO. WITHOUT ME, THEY'D PROBABLY BOTH BE DEAD, IN JAIL, OR DEAD AND IN JAIL.
Oh.

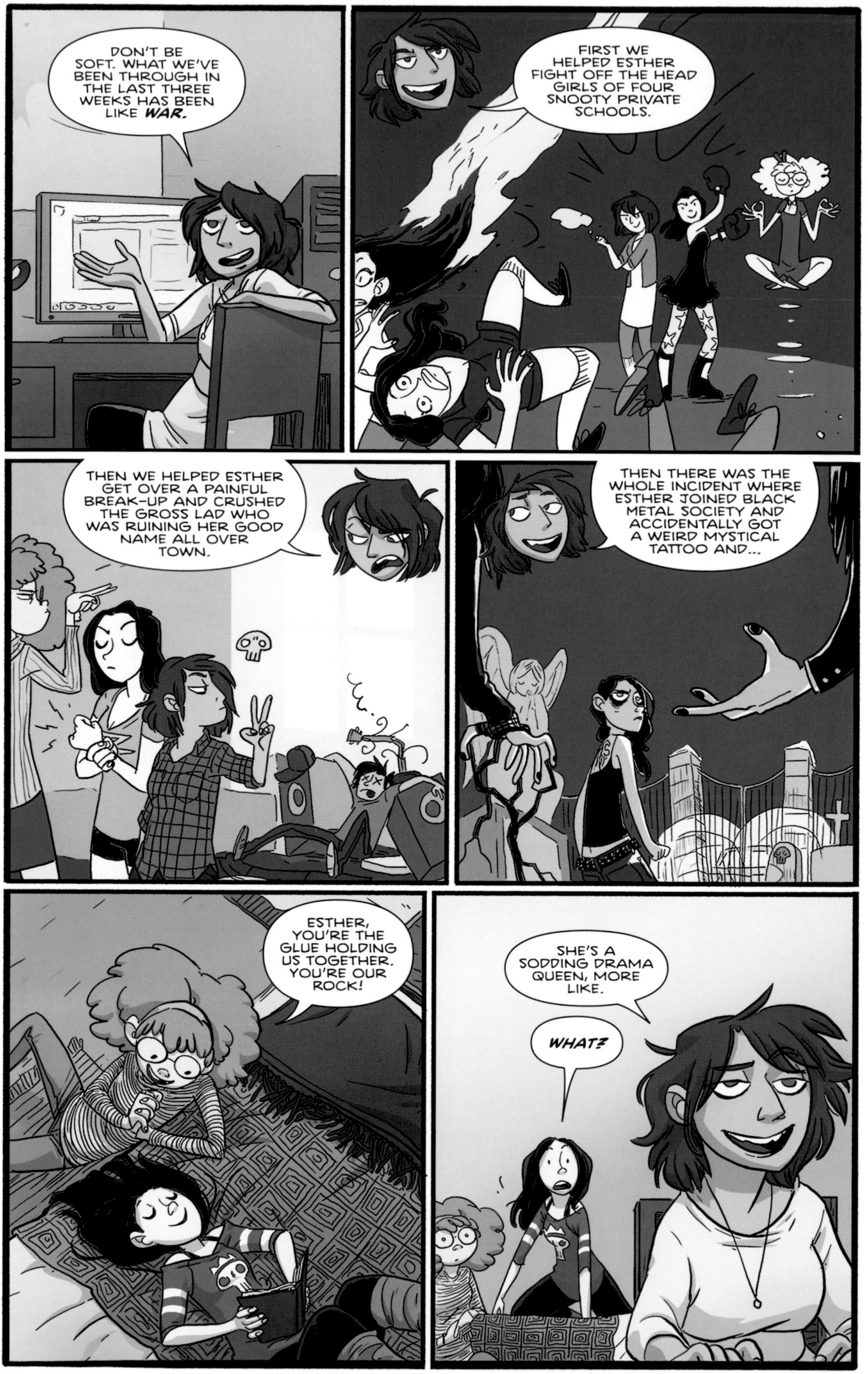

DON'T BE SOFT. WHAT WE'VE BEEN THROUGH IN THE LAST THREE WEEKS HAS BEEN LIKE WAR.
FIRST WE HELPED ESTHER FIGHT OFF THE HEAD GIRLS OF FOUR SNOOTY PRIVATE SCHOOLS.
THEN WE HELPED ESTHER GET OVER A PAINFUL BREAK-UP AND CRUSHED THE GROSS LAD WHO WAS RUINING HER GOOD NAME ALL OVER TOWN.
THEN THERE WAS THE WHOLE INCIDENT WHERE ESTHER JOINED BLACK METAL SOCIETY AND ACCIDENTALLY GOT A WEIRD MYSTICAL TATTOO AND...
ESTHER, YOU'RE THE GLUE HOLDING US TOGETHER. YOU'RE OUR ROCK!
SHE'S A SODDING DRAMA QUEEN, MORE LIKE.
WHAT?

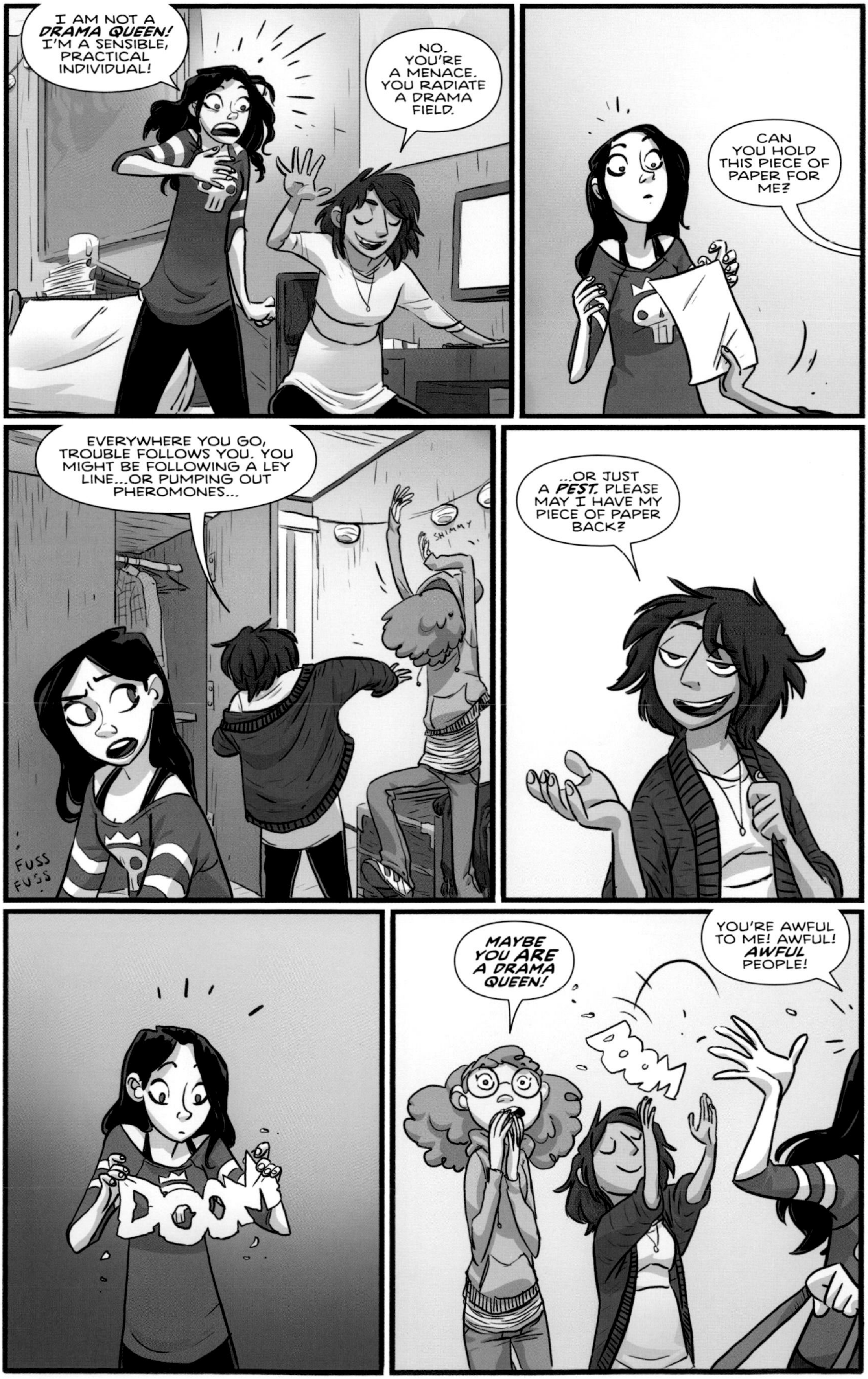
I AM NOT A *DRAMA QUEEN!* I'M A SENSIBLE, PRACTICAL INDIVIDUAL!
NO. YOU'RE A MENACE. YOU RADIATE A DRAMA FIELD.
CAN YOU HOLD THIS PIECE OF PAPER FOR ME?
EVERYWHERE YOU GO, TROUBLE FOLLOWS YOU. YOU MIGHT BE FOLLOWING A LEY LINE...OR PUMPING OUT PHEROMONES...
SHIMMY
FUSS FUSS
...OR JUST A *PEST.* PLEASE MAY I HAVE MY PIECE OF PAPER BACK?
DOOM
*MAYBE YOU ARE A DRAMA QUEEN!*
YOU'RE AWFUL TO ME! AWFUL! *AWFUL* PEOPLE!
BOOM

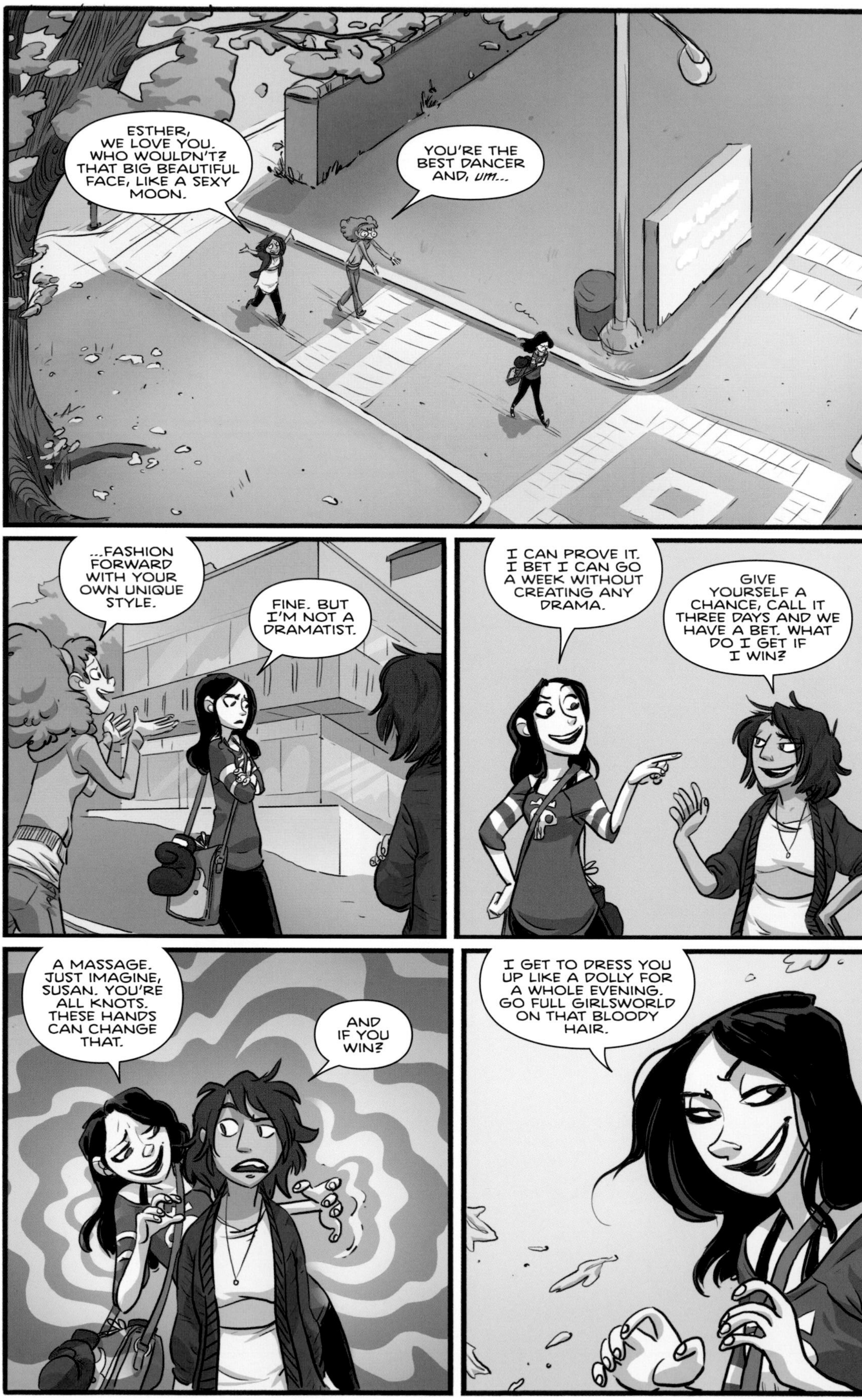
ESTHER, WE LOVE YOU. WHO WOULDN'T? THAT BIG BEAUTIFUL FACE, LIKE A SEXY MOON.
YOU'RE THE BEST DANCER AND, *UM*...
...FASHION FORWARD WITH YOUR OWN UNIQUE STYLE.
FINE. BUT I'M NOT A DRAMATIST.
I CAN PROVE IT. I BET I CAN GO A WEEK WITHOUT CREATING ANY DRAMA.
GIVE YOURSELF A CHANCE, CALL IT THREE DAYS AND WE HAVE A BET. WHAT DO I GET IF I WIN?
A MASSAGE. JUST IMAGINE, SUSAN. YOU'RE ALL KNOTS. THESE HANDS CAN CHANGE THAT.
AND IF YOU WIN?
I GET TO DRESS YOU UP LIKE A DOLLY FOR A WHOLE EVENING. GO FULL GIRLSWORLD ON THAT BLOODY HAIR.

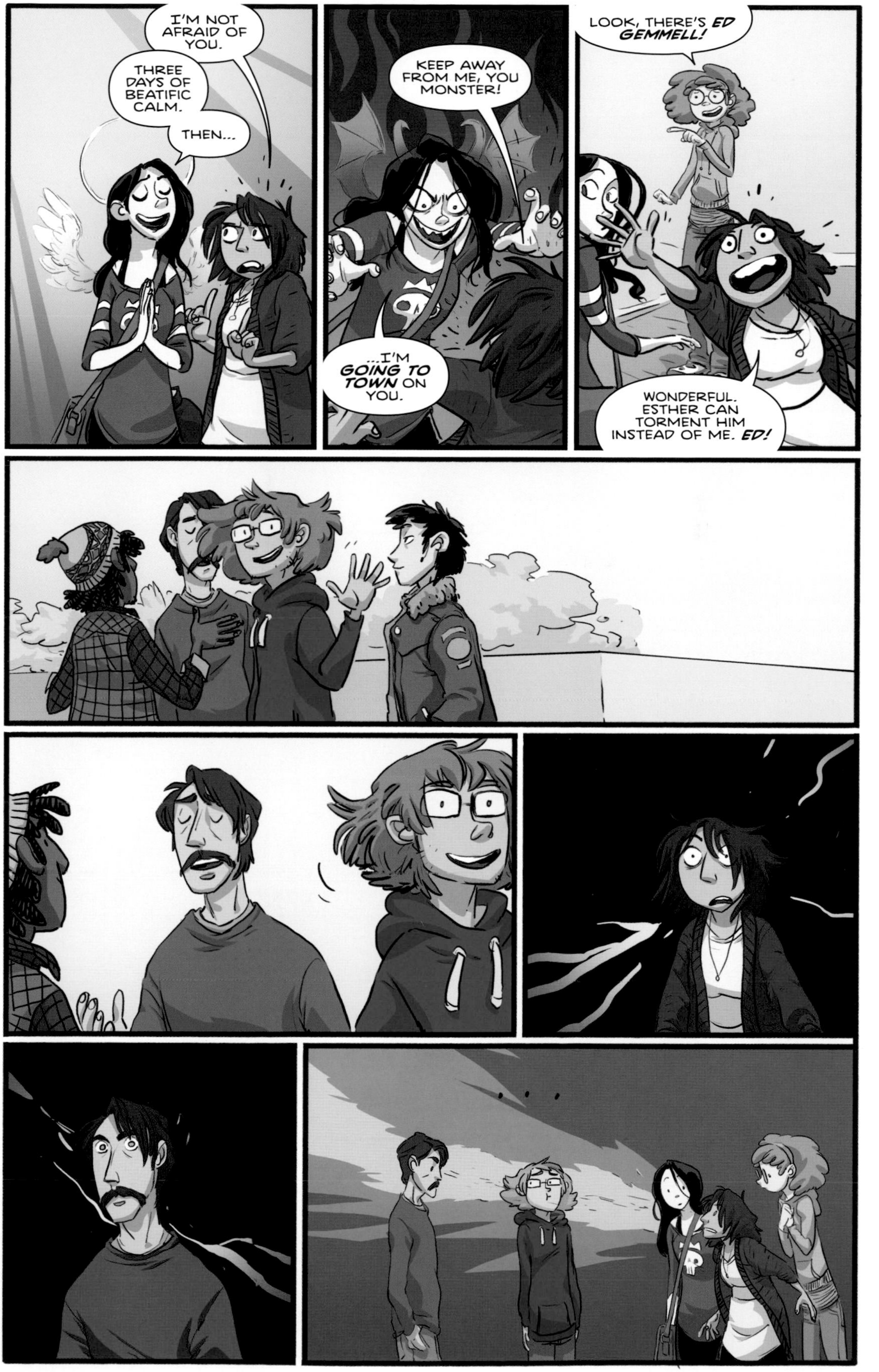
I'M NOT AFRAID OF YOU.
THREE DAYS OF BEATIFIC CALM.
THEN...
KEEP AWAY FROM ME, YOU MONSTER!
...I'M GOING TO TOWN ON YOU.
LOOK, THERE'S ED GEMMELL!
WONDERFUL. ESTHER CAN TORMENT HIM INSTEAD OF ME. ED!
. . .

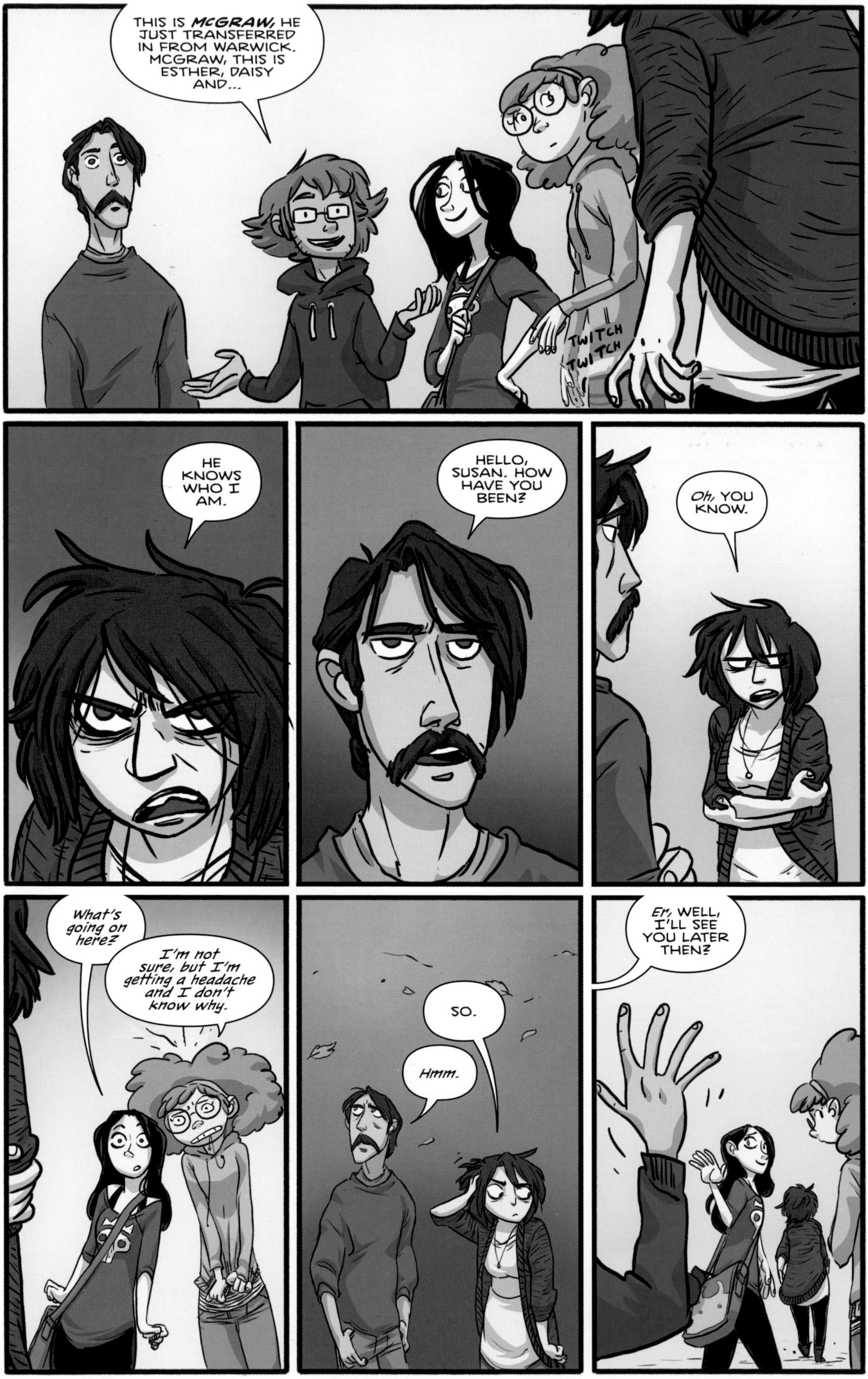
THIS IS McGRAW, HE JUST TRANSFERRED IN FROM WARWICK. McGRAW, THIS IS ESTHER, DAISY AND...
TWITCH TWITCH
HE KNOWS WHO I AM.
HELLO, SUSAN. HOW HAVE YOU BEEN?
Oh, YOU KNOW.
What's going on here?
I'm not sure, but I'm getting a headache and I don't know why.
SO.
Hmm.
Er, WELL, I'LL SEE YOU LATER THEN?

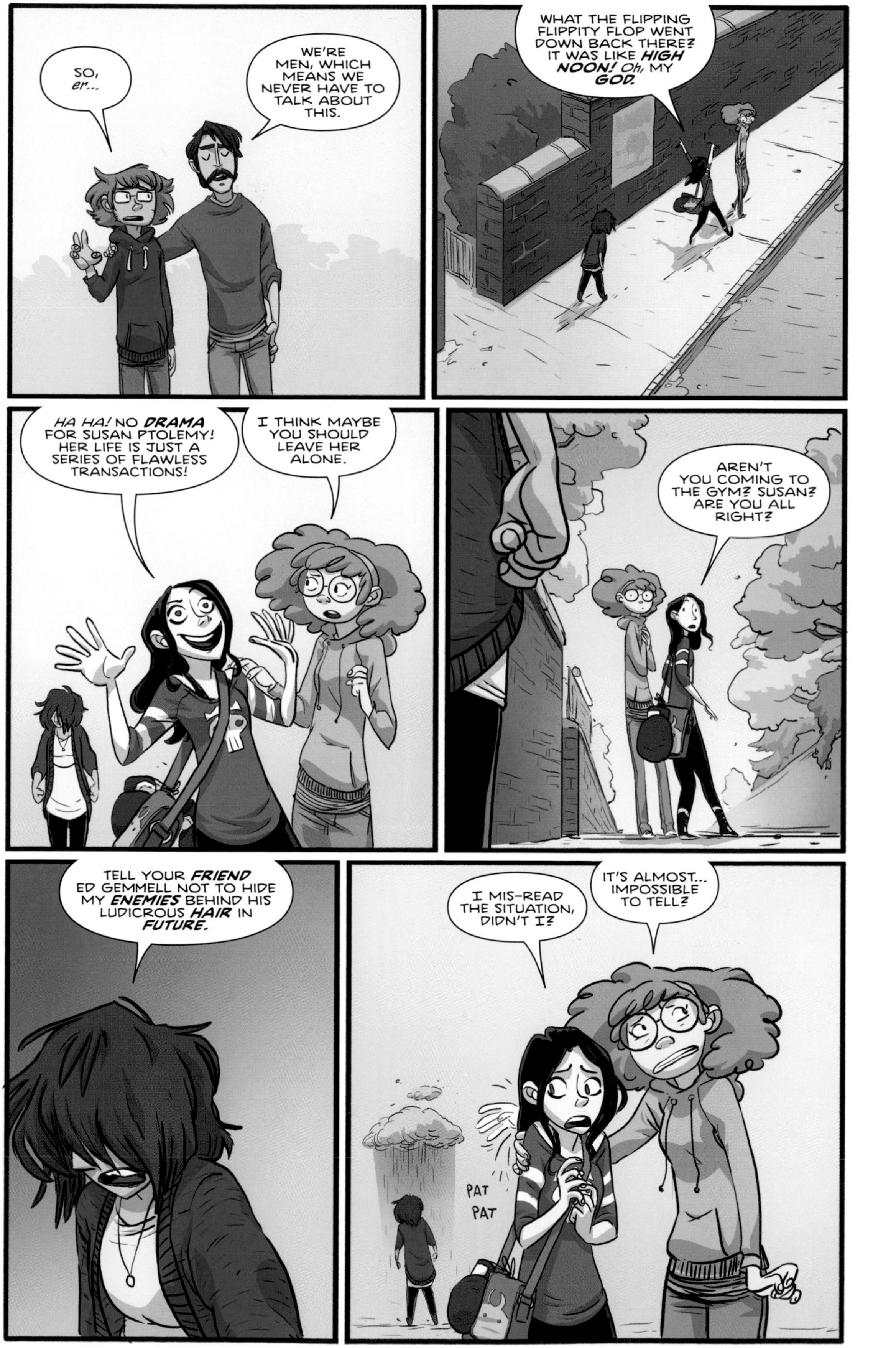
SO, *er...*
WE'RE MEN, WHICH MEANS WE NEVER HAVE TO TALK ABOUT THIS.
WHAT THE FLIPPING FLIPPITY FLOP WENT DOWN BACK THERE? IT WAS LIKE ***HIGH NOON!*** *Oh,* MY ***GOD.***
*HA HA!* NO ***DRAMA*** FOR SUSAN PTOLEMY! HER LIFE IS JUST A SERIES OF FLAWLESS TRANSACTIONS!
I THINK MAYBE YOU SHOULD LEAVE HER ALONE.
AREN'T YOU COMING TO THE GYM? SUSAN? ARE YOU ALL RIGHT?
TELL YOUR ***FRIEND*** ED GEMMELL NOT TO HIDE MY ***ENEMIES*** BEHIND HIS LUDICROUS ***HAIR*** IN ***FUTURE.***
I MIS-READ THE SITUATION, DIDN'T I?
IT'S ALMOST... IMPOSSIBLE TO TELL?
PAT
PAT

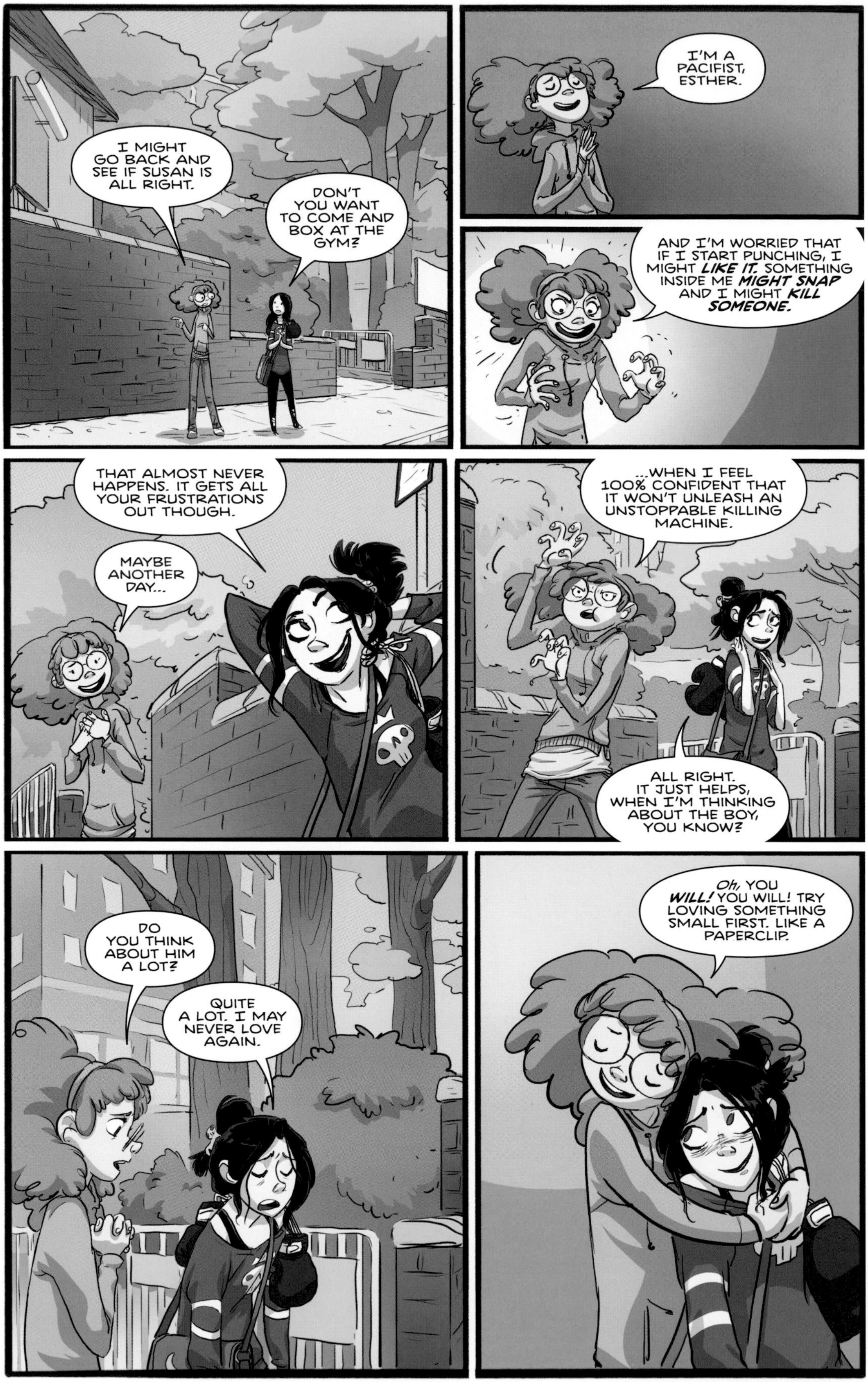
I MIGHT GO BACK AND SEE IF SUSAN IS ALL RIGHT.
DON'T YOU WANT TO COME AND BOX AT THE GYM?
I'M A PACIFIST, ESTHER.
AND I'M WORRIED THAT IF I START PUNCHING, I MIGHT **LIKE IT.** SOMETHING INSIDE ME **MIGHT SNAP** AND I MIGHT **KILL SOMEONE.**
THAT ALMOST NEVER HAPPENS. IT GETS ALL YOUR FRUSTRATIONS OUT THOUGH.
MAYBE ANOTHER DAY...
...WHEN I FEEL 100% CONFIDENT THAT IT WON'T UNLEASH AN UNSTOPPABLE KILLING MACHINE.
ALL RIGHT. IT JUST HELPS, WHEN I'M THINKING ABOUT THE BOY, YOU KNOW?
DO YOU THINK ABOUT HIM A LOT?
QUITE A LOT. I MAY NEVER LOVE AGAIN.
*Oh,* YOU **WILL!** YOU WILL! TRY LOVING SOMETHING SMALL FIRST. LIKE A PAPERCLIP.

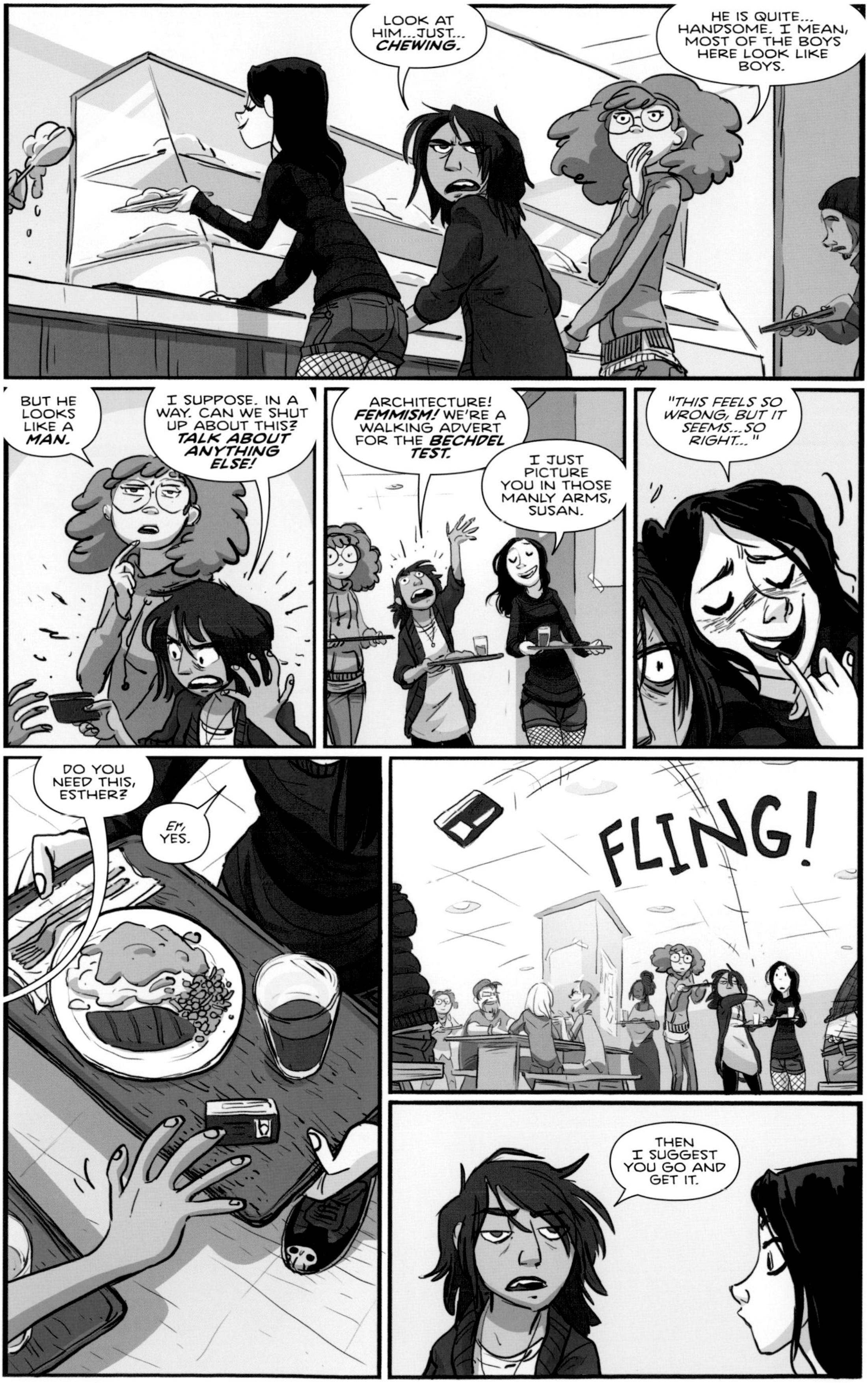
LOOK AT HIM...JUST... CHEWING.
HE IS QUITE... HANDSOME. I MEAN, MOST OF THE BOYS HERE LOOK LIKE BOYS.
BUT HE LOOKS LIKE A MAN.
I SUPPOSE. IN A WAY. CAN WE SHUT UP ABOUT THIS? TALK ABOUT ANYTHING ELSE!
ARCHITECTURE! FEMMISM! WE'RE A WALKING ADVERT FOR THE BECHDEL TEST.
I JUST PICTURE YOU IN THOSE MANLY ARMS, SUSAN.
"THIS FEELS SO WRONG, BUT IT SEEMS...SO RIGHT..."
DO YOU NEED THIS, ESTHER?
EM, YES.
FLING!
THEN I SUGGEST YOU GO AND GET IT.

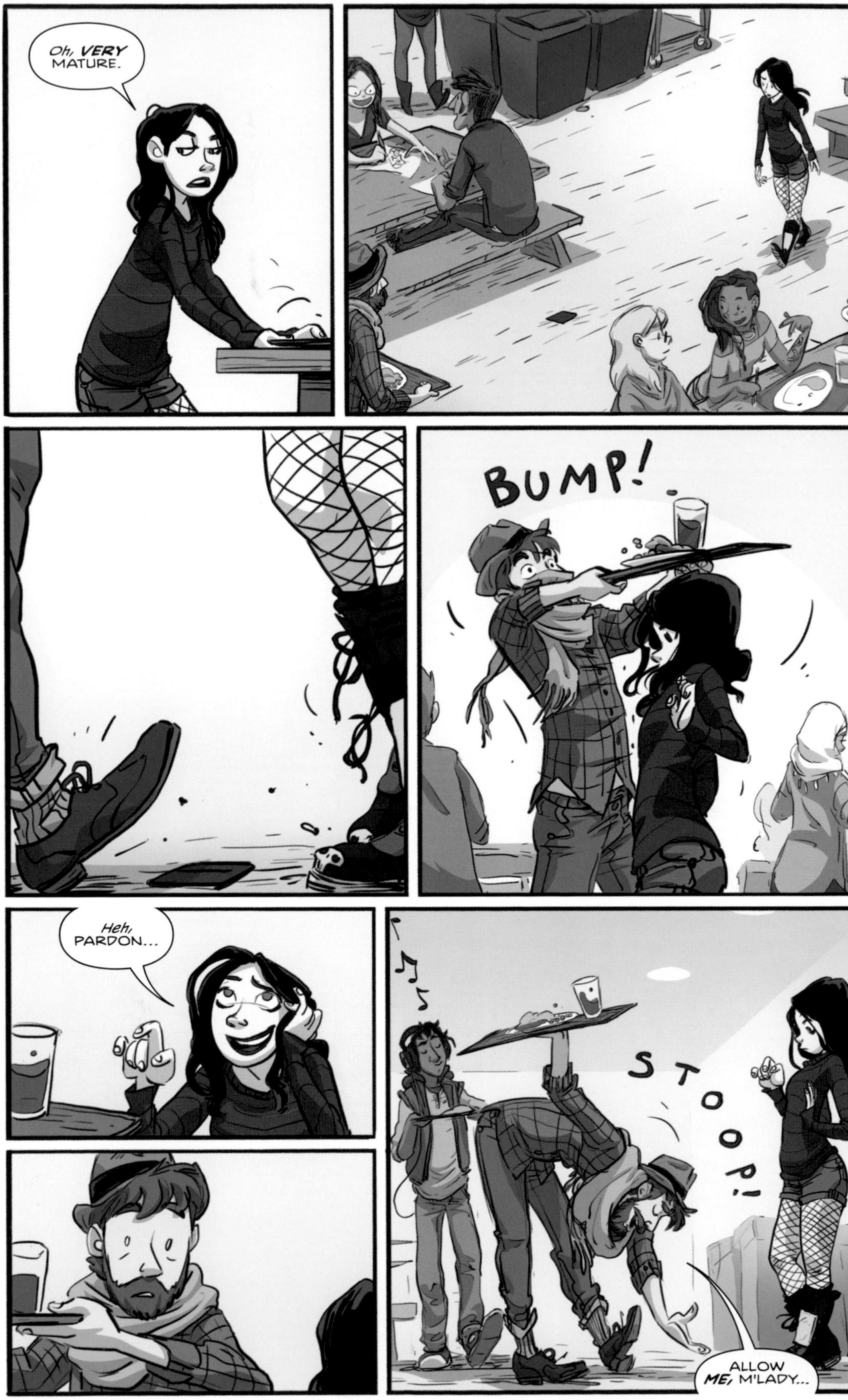
Oh, VERY MATURE.
BUMP!
Heh, PARDON...
STOOP!
ALLOW ME, M'LADY...

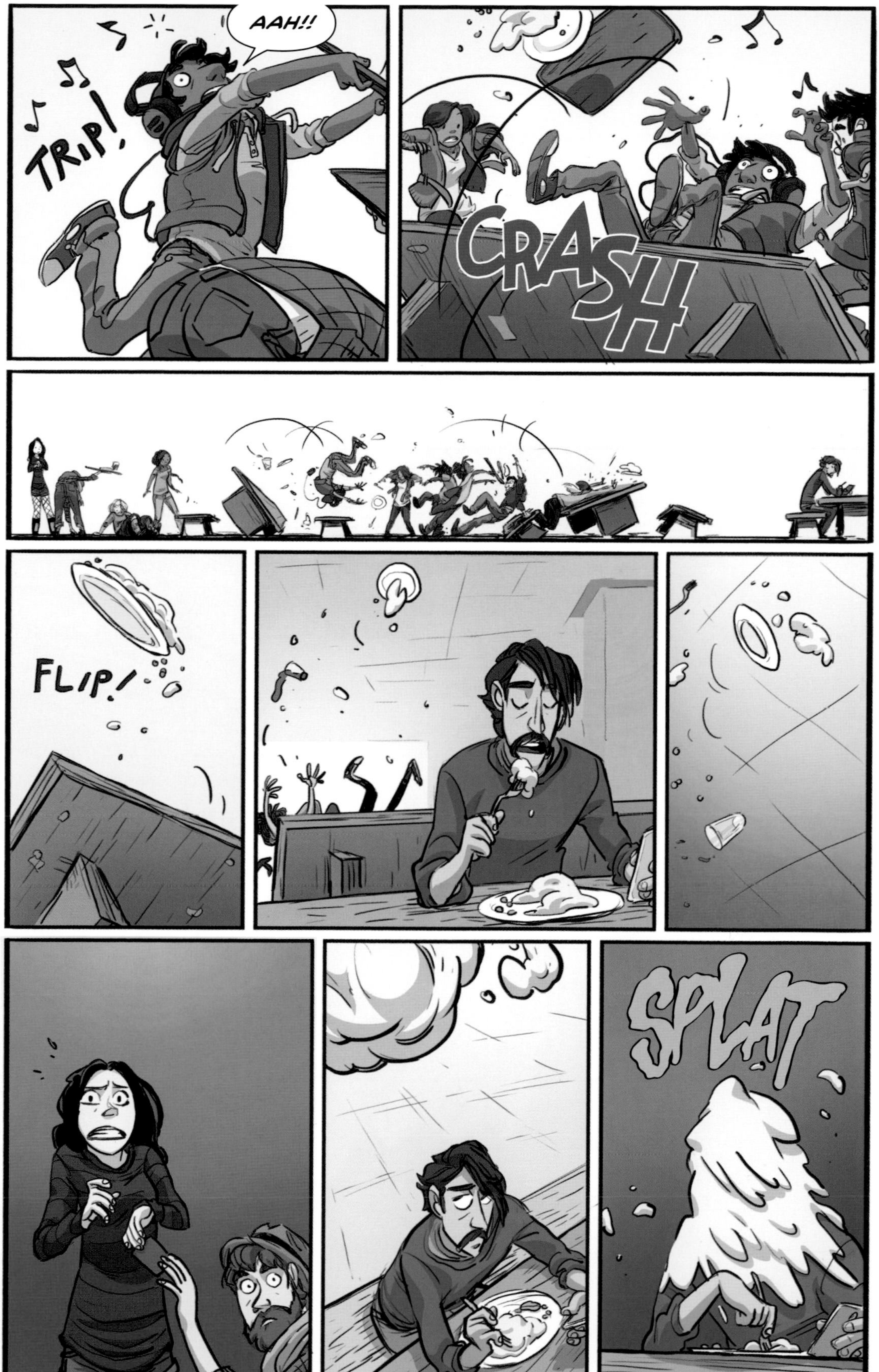
AAH!!
TRIP!
CRASH
FLIP!
SPLAT

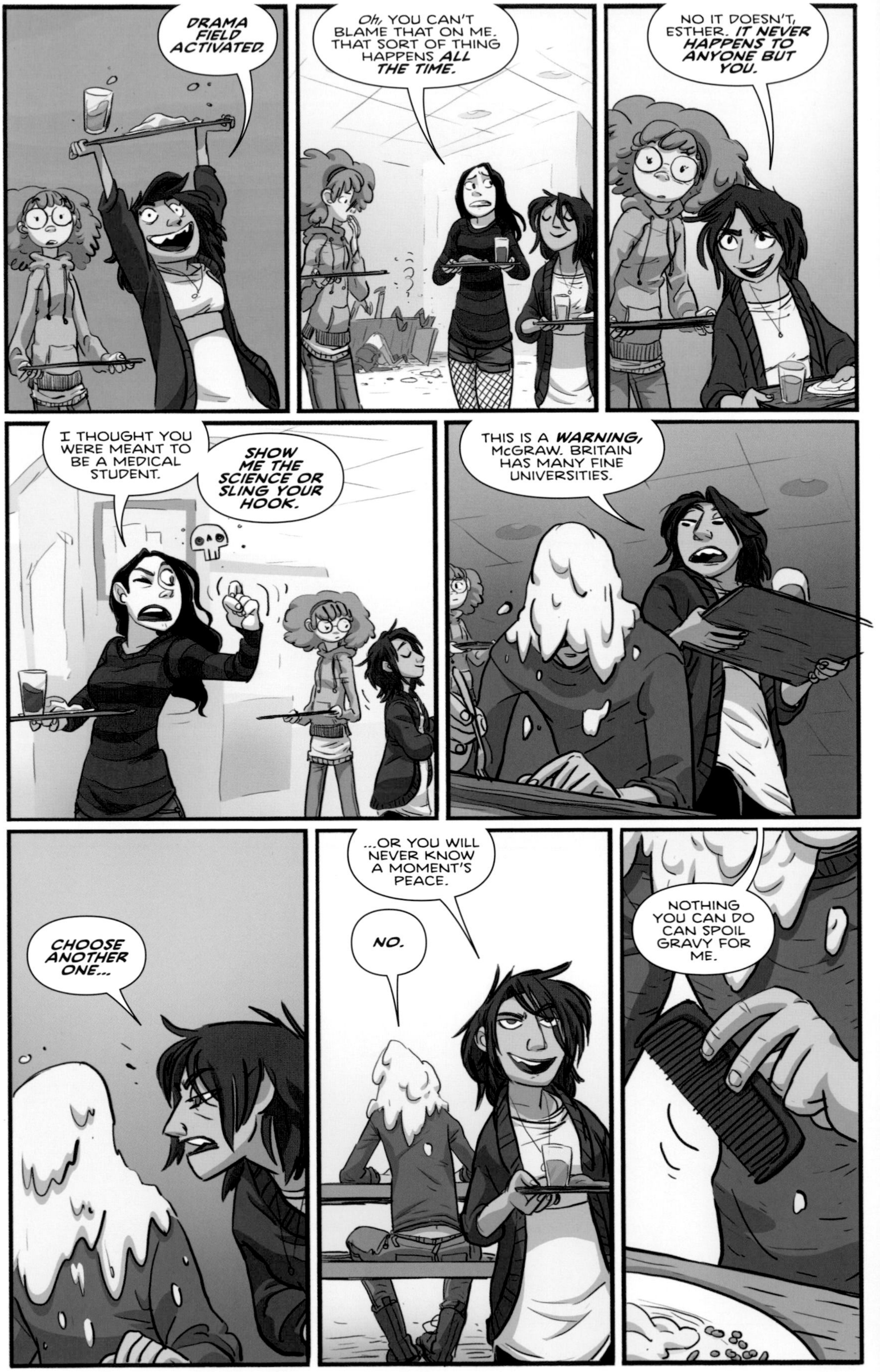
DRAMA FIELD ACTIVATED.
Oh, YOU CAN'T BLAME THAT ON ME. THAT SORT OF THING HAPPENS ALL THE TIME.
NO IT DOESN'T, ESTHER. IT NEVER HAPPENS TO ANYONE BUT YOU.
I THOUGHT YOU WERE MEANT TO BE A MEDICAL STUDENT.
SHOW ME THE SCIENCE OR SLING YOUR HOOK.
THIS IS A WARNING, McGRAW. BRITAIN HAS MANY FINE UNIVERSITIES.
CHOOSE ANOTHER ONE...
...OR YOU WILL NEVER KNOW A MOMENT'S PEACE.
NO.
NOTHING YOU CAN DO CAN SPOIL GRAVY FOR ME.

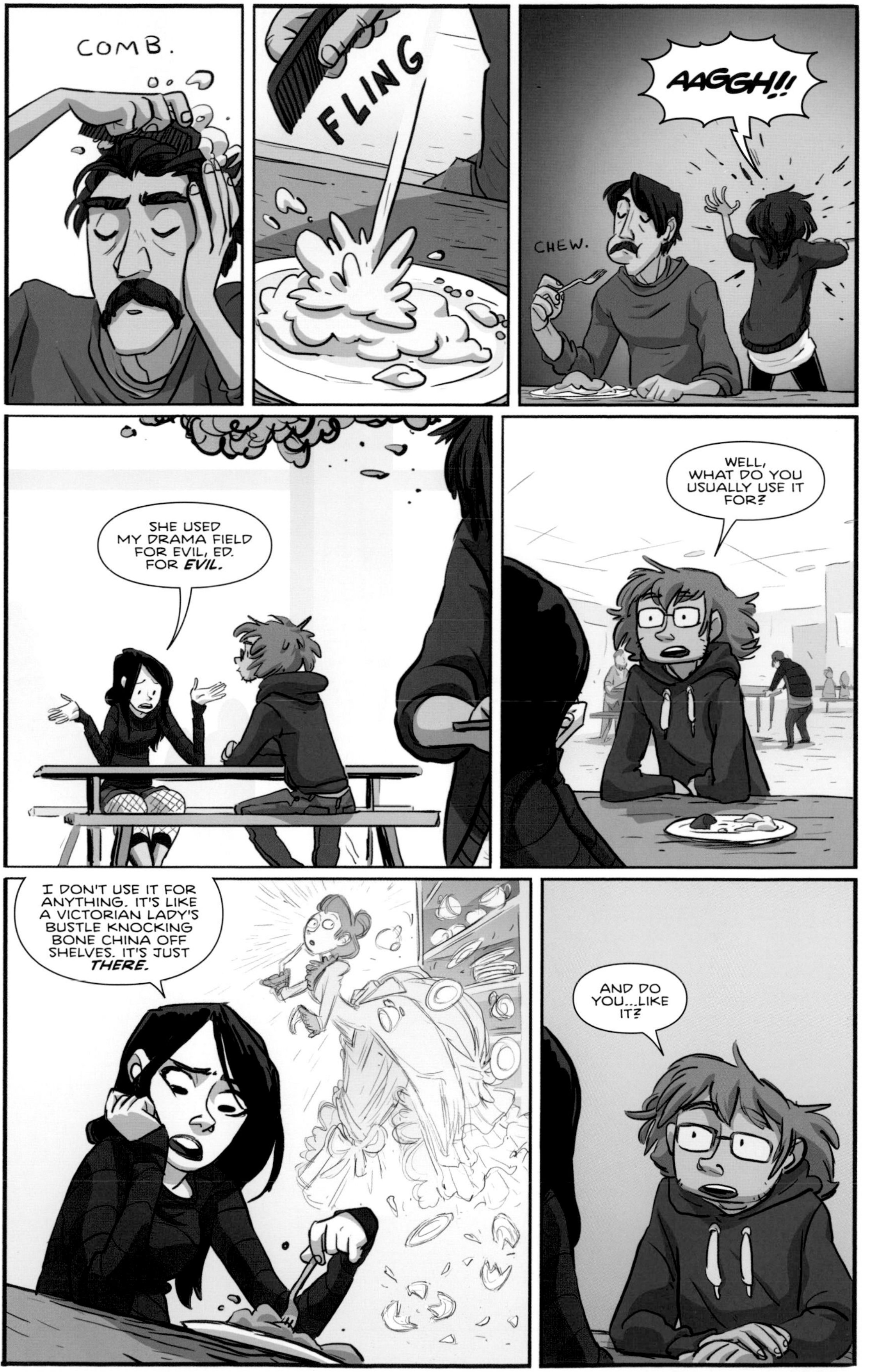
COMB.
FLING
AAGGH!!
CHEW.
SHE USED MY DRAMA FIELD FOR EVIL, ED. FOR EVIL.
WELL, WHAT DO YOU USUALLY USE IT FOR?
I DON'T USE IT FOR ANYTHING. IT'S LIKE A VICTORIAN LADY'S BUSTLE KNOCKING BONE CHINA OFF SHELVES. IT'S JUST THERE.
AND DO YOU...LIKE IT?

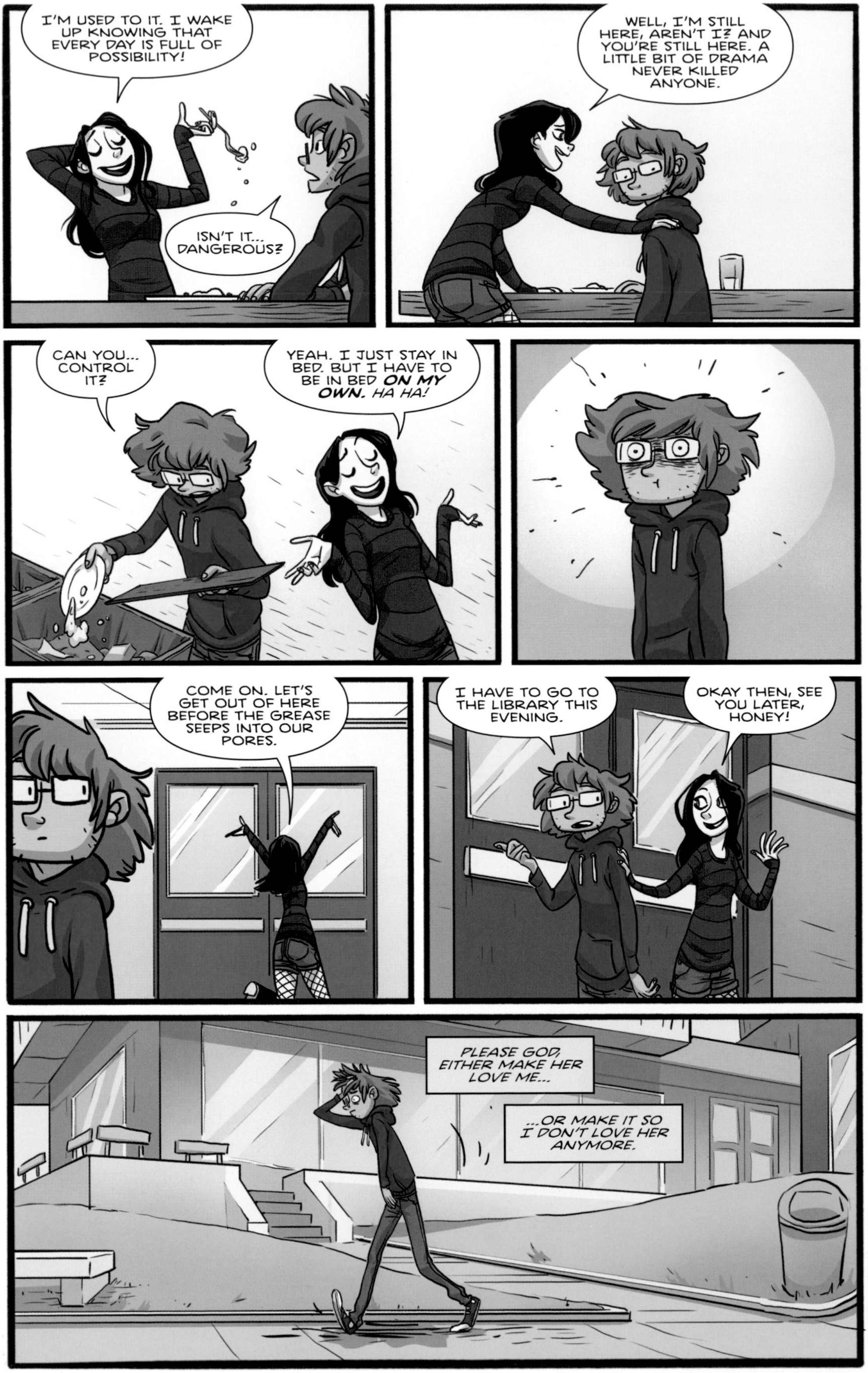
I'M USED TO IT. I WAKE UP KNOWING THAT EVERY DAY IS FULL OF POSSIBILITY!
ISN'T IT... DANGEROUS?
WELL, I'M STILL HERE, AREN'T I? AND YOU'RE STILL HERE. A LITTLE BIT OF DRAMA NEVER KILLED ANYONE.
CAN YOU... CONTROL IT?
YEAH. I JUST STAY IN BED. BUT I HAVE TO BE IN BED ***ON MY OWN.*** *HA HA!*
COME ON. LET'S GET OUT OF HERE BEFORE THE GREASE SEEPS INTO OUR PORES.
I HAVE TO GO TO THE LIBRARY THIS EVENING.
OKAY THEN, SEE YOU LATER, HONEY!
*PLEASE GOD, EITHER MAKE HER LOVE ME...*
*...OR MAKE IT SO I DON'T LOVE HER ANYMORE.*

CONTINUED IN GIANT DAYS VOLUME ONE!

LJ

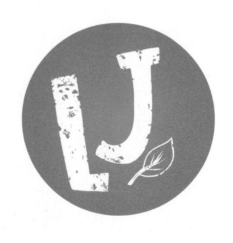